# THE RED-STAINED WINGS

# THE
# RED-STAINED
# WINGS

## ELIZABETH BEAR

**TOR**

A TOM DOHERTY ASSOCIATES BOOK
NEW YORK

This is a work of fiction. All of the characters, organizations, and events portrayed in this novel are either products of the author's imagination or are used fictitiously.

A Tor Book
Published by Tom Doherty Associates
175 Fifth Avenue
New York, NY 10010

www.tor-forge.com

Tor® is a registered trademark of Macmillan Publishing Group, LLC.

The Library of Congress Cataloging-in-Publication Data is available upon request.

ISBN 978-0-7653-8015-9 (hardcover)
ISBN 978-1-4668-7208-0 (ebook)

Our books may be purchased in bulk for promotional, educational, or business use. Please contact your local bookseller or the Macmillan Corporate and Premium Sales Department at 1-800-221-7945, extension 5442, or by email at MacmillanSpecialMarkets@macmillan.com.

First Edition: May 2019

Printed in the United States of America

0  9  8  7  6  5  4  3  2  1

*To Beth*

The uninked pen
Drips
With possibility.

—The poetess
Ümmühan

Dragon Lake

Eighteen
River Crossing

Wretched Mountain

Singing Towers

THE SONG
PRINCIPALITIES

BITTER SEA

Stone Lily

10,000 Mile Tomb
Dragon Roads

Amoy

D O M

Guran

SEA
of
STORMS

Banner Isles

RHYS DAVIES

# The Red-Stained Wings

1

OVER THE GOLD STONE WALLS OF SARATHAI-TIA, THE LONG NIGHT DARK-
ened toward sunrise. The Veil rose across the sky and the light of the
heavenly river dimmed. Phosphorescence crawled along the top of
the battlements, where the Dead Man was careful not to lean.

That glow revealed the presence of shards of dragonglass embedded
edgewise in the mortar: quick as razors, and slow poison to whatever
they might slice.

The Dead Man rested a hand on the butt of one of his twin pistols,
instead. If the gesture was a threat, the threat was not one he consciously
intended. He gazed outward, across the plain and the river that ran silt-
white between its banks beyond. He had lowered his veil, and breathed
the rainy air unfiltered.

That *was* a threat, or a statement, and it was an intentional one.

The Dead Man was waiting for the war to come.

He looked out over a city designed to be defended, which was a small
but solid blessing. The Alchemical Emperor, in his day, had raised his
throne city above the rich mud of the broad and flooding river valley
by summoning the small mountain it stood upon from the very bones
of the earth. Sarathai-tia's outer walls were living rock, the same living
rock as the steep terraced slopes that rose within them. A single road
spiraled from the base of the city to the palace at its peak, joined to

itself at intervals by alleys lined with overhanging shops and houses. The alleys would be easy to block with rubble, forcing an invading force to fight uphill the entire length.

The city was surrounded by the mighty river on three sides, and connected to the mainland only by a broad causeway that would normally be flooded in the rainy season, and all of which was in range of the city's cannon. The villages that surrounded Sarathai-tia were built on stilts or floated on houseboats, and the farms grew rich between them when the annual floods receded.

Sarathai-tia's outer wall was pierced by only two gates: the main gate that faced the causeway, away from the river . . . and the Queen's Gate, the water gate, reached by a stair that ran down from the palace to the Mother River, surrounded by hanging gardens and suspended on pillars. The back side of the mountain was even steeper than the fore, and it would be quick work indeed to knock the stair off its pillars and use the resulting rubble to fill up more alleys and build barricades.

Sad, to destroy an architectural marvel, but sadder things happened in wars.

From his perch on the heights, the Dead Man could see a long way indeed across the flat, white river and the endless bottomlands it meandered through. He could see the villages and the piers lining the Mother River—called Relentless, called Deep-Hearted, called Butter of the Earth—on both sides. He could see the long, rich fields and the river so wide and slow and clotted with rafts of roots and lotus that it had become a slowly moving garden as the summer wore on.

The vanguard of the enemy reached the river's far shore as those of Mrithuri's people who had not yet evacuated to the fortress city were still setting flame to huts and bridges and whatever boats they could get to, under a hail of enemy arrows. They were leaving as little behind for the enemy's forces to use as they could.

"Burn them," the Dead Man had said. So now, as was his duty, he stood and watched as the livelihood of Mrithuri's people floated away on the breast of the wide white Sarathai, blazing atop the reflections of their own flames. If his cheeks were damp, and it was not with sweat, there was no one present now to question him.

Until there was.

A step scraped the stones behind him. He was not startled; the battlements were well-manned and he had not thought himself entirely alone. He fastened the end of his veil across his face with a practiced gesture before he turned. His right hand did not leave the gun until he saw who came toward him.

A woman, the skin of her muscled arms silk-dark against the white of her sleeveless tunic, hurrying. Her tight, steel-colored curls gave a lie to her unlined face, and bangles on her wrists chimed merrily although her expression was stern. The Aezin Wizard, Ata Akhimah.

She paused to stare over the Dead Man's shoulder—suddenly, as if distracted from whatever it was that she had come so urgently to say. She shook her head. "Who wages war in the rainy season?"

"It does seem an unfathomable choice."

"Maybe cholera will thin their ranks for us." She sounded as if the prospect pleased her.

The Dead Man couldn't fault the sentiment. He cleared his throat. "Were you seeking me?"

The Wizard gestured toward the distance. "Was that what you were looking at?"

He knew without turning what she meant, but he turned anyway rather than stand with his back to it. The gates in the city's outer walls, a catapult's throw and a bit more away from the walls of the palace, still stood open. Farmers and fishers and tradespeople from the surrounding countryside poured into Sarathai-tia—those who had not chosen to take to their boats, or take their chances on the open road rather than in the squalor and starvation of a besieged city.

Beyond the bustle of boats and wagons, beyond the rivers of humanity and the river of pale water, beyond the flames consuming one stilt-legged hut after another, beyond the first jeering vanguards of the enemy—the main bulk of the advancing army had not yet come into view over the horizon. What *was* plainly visible was a long, black smudge against the sky, in the wrong direction to be the edge of the Veil sliding across the brilliant night.

It looked like smoke, but smoke never moved with such volition. Such sinister coordination: the flocking of many minds into a single consensus. Tendrils sought out from the dark mass, seethed and lifted, collapsed back. The body roiled and dappled, showing glimpses of sky beyond.

Carrion birds tracked the advancing forces, heralding the army as thunder heralds the storm.

At that moment, a shrill sound rent the air. A woman's scream, meant to carry. Not in the city, or beyond the walls, as might be expected—but in the extensive, rain-soaked palace garden below and behind Ata Akhimah.

The Dead Man eyeballed the Wizard.

The Wizard sighed. "I guess we had better go see what's fucked up this time."

THEY RAN. SIDE BY SIDE, WET SOLES SLAPPING. OTHER DEFENDERS OF THE palace might be closer, it was true. But other defenders of the palace might not be as equipped to deal with the sorts of oddities that seemed to be making a more and more frequent appearance at Mrithuri Rajni's court in these strange days.

There came no second cry.

Their pelting steps carried them into the garden grounds, out of breath and slipping in the mud. The Dead Man's veil sucked annoyingly against his mouth with each gasp for breath, the fabric slack and moist in the humid atmosphere. As he had expected, they were not the only searchers in the garden. Men and women carrying torches and lanterns fanned out along the gravel trails. Ata Akhimah glanced about at the bobbing pools of light, sighed, and outstretched one hand, pale palm upright.

A column of yellow-white light flared upward, hissing and shedding sparks, too bright to look at directly. It rose to the treetops and flowered, spreading brilliant chrysanthemum petals in every direction. It wasn't a witchlamp such as the Dead Man had seen Rasan Wizards hang, but more like a captive lightning bolt, and it sounded angry as a trapped cat.

Conveniently, at that moment, the cry came again.

This time, the Dead Man recognized the voice. "Chaeri," he said tiredly, and turned toward the sound.

Ata Akhimah was a step ahead of him. She darted into the strange, stippled shadows that fell hard-edged and jet-black where flowering branches, not yet fully leafed, broke the actinic light of her pillar. The Dead Man followed her, pistol in his hand.

They came to the garden wall and followed it along—just a few steps, into an open patch among flowering shrubs. Akhimah stepped to the side so that the Dead Man could come up with her—or possibly to clear his line of sight, and field of fire if necessary.

Chaeri, the queen's handmaiden, stood with her back to them. Her dark hair spiraled down her back in artfully casual locks. She wore a tunic and trousers that were wet with rainwater, and mud spattered her bare ankles among the jingling bracelets.

She faced down two men—a large and muscular one, mustached, sword-wearing, in what the Dead Man took to be some kind of local uniform, and a small and round one in the seamed and petal-skirted black coat of a Rasan Wizard. They seemed quite familiar. The Dead Man's chest itched as he realized that he had seen them only a few hours before. They had accompanied the assassin disguised as the poetess Ümmühan when she—he?—attempted to murder the young queen, Mrithuri.

The Dead Man had taken a pistol ball to the chest that had been intended for Mrithuri, and only the twinned lucks that that ball had first passed through her general, and that a Godmade priest had been near enough to work a miracle, had saved him.

These men he now looked at—or their likenesses—had vanished away when the assassin they accompanied was killed.

Studying them more closely, the Dead Man could see that the likenesses were not perfect. *This* captain and Wizard were considerably more haggard-looking and road-stained than the previous set. And the Wizard held a child-sized bundle of cloth to his chest, with light showing in the creases as if he shrouded a heatless, living coal.

Chaeri was drawing in her breath for one more good scream when the man with the mustache said, "Call her off. We surrender."

His Sarathai was accented, but comprehensible.

"They're spies!" Chaeri said. "Assassins!" She ducked back between Akhimah and the Dead Man. "I caught them coming over the wall again! Shoot them!"

"What's in the bundle?" Akhimah asked. It made the Dead Man feel kindly toward her, as he too was inclined to investigate the mysteries of the situation rather than acting precipitately.

"They came over the *wall*," Chaeri interjected. "If you let them talk, they'll Wizard you into believing their lies, like that other one."

"I believe I can withstand their blandishments," Akhimah said kindly. The light of her spitting tower of cold fire limned the strong bones of her face. "A persuasive tongue is one of the gifts of my order, rather than that of Dr.—"

"Tsering," the Rasan Wizard said. He stepped forward, still clutching his bundle. The Dead Man thought it moved.

The Rasan cleared his throat. "Tsering-la. This is Captain Vidhya. We are emissaries from Sayeh Rajni."

"Where's the poetess?" the Dead Man said.

Vidhya rocked back. "How do you know—?"

"One question at a time," Ata Akhimah said gently. And, indeed, everyone fell silent, including the slowly growing crowd of garden searchers. She nodded to Tsering-la, who fumbled with the luminescent cloth-wrapped object tucked under his arm. He pulled back a fold, and a bedraggled crimson-and-gold head emerged, hesitantly. A broken crest of feathers fluffed.

"Pretty bird?" the phoenix said faintly.

"Guang Bao," Tsering-la said. "He is Sayeh Rajni's familiar. She sent him with us to prove we were her men." He smiled. "Now it's your turn."

"Someone sent an apparition of the two of you, along with an assassin disguised by illusion to look like the poetess, to murder Her Abundance Mrithuri Rajni," Akhimah said.

A guard cleared his throat, or maybe it was one of the acrobats who were sheltering in the palace.

"Speak," Ata Akhimah said.

"Are these who they seem to be?" It was an acrobat, the Dead Man noticed. Amruth, the matriarch Ritu's son.

"I only engage in *royal* prophecy," Akhimah replied dryly.

"No Ümmühan this time," the Dead Man noted.

Ata Akhimah reached into her pocket and produced a silver clip that seemed empty in the difficult light. She held it up, and the Dead Man surmised it must contain the single strand of silver hair that had been sewn into her jacket by unknown hands. "No, she must be captive. That's why she was the focus of the illusion."

"Yes," Vidhya said. "The poetess, our rajni, her heir, and Tsering's apprentice Nazia are all captive of Himadra." He turned his head and spat into wet moss. "Our kingdom lies in ruins—if there are even ruins there. We came to beg you for aid. Instead, we come flying before an army."

"A great volcano beneath the Bitter Sea has shaken the city down," Tsering-la said. "And then boiled it in a cloud of steam and poison."

The Dead Man spoke to Chaeri over his shoulder, in the politest tone he could muster. "Just out of curiosity, what *were* you doing in the bushes?"

"Feeding the songbirds," she said primly, as if recollecting herself. Perhaps his tone had not been polite enough. He heard her dusting off her hands.

There were, indeed, rather a lot of seeds scattered on the earth nearby, and trampled into the mud. No birds were in evidence, but then there was a lot of fuss going on.

"Is that Himadra's army in pursuit of you?" the Dead Man asked, returning his attention to Vidhya.

Sayeh's guard captain glanced up at him from beneath furrowed brows. "You mean you don't know already?"

"Only there are a number of armies wandering about the country-side lately, and this one rather came out of nowhere," the Dead Man snapped.

"Yes they did." Vidhya leaned against the stone wall as if nothing else kept him upright. "They've got an illusionist, I think."

"Yes," Akhimah said. "We found out."

"Anuraja. It's Anuraja's men."

"From the *north?*" said Akhimah.

The round little Rasan Wizard in his torn once-black coat shrugged hard enough to split the shoulder seam further. The phoenix made an indignant mumble.

Ata Akhimah sighed tiredly. "I think we'd better go inside and have a word with Her Abundance."

Tsering-la's answering sigh was one of relief. "Thank you."

Ata Akhimah slapped dust off her sleeve and let the tower of light die. "Don't thank me. You've arrived in a city that is about to be under siege. We can use all the Wizards we can get."

CLARITY BURNED THROUGH THE YOUNG RAJNI'S VEINS WITH THE LUCID potency of venom. It made her restless. It made her ruthless. It made her fierce.

She sat among cushions and regarded her advisors, chafing her arms with her palms. Trying to drive the prickling heat through them. Syama, her bear-dog, lay against her hip—eyes sleepy, but brindled body quivering with the tension Mrithuri was communicating.

At least the venom gave Mrithuri concentration. Everything else was terrible.

She could not recall the last time she had really slept. She could not even imagine, any longer, what being rested might feel like except in absences. She vaguely remembered joints and eyes and thoughts that did not grit sluggishly and ache inside her.

The venom helped with that, too. Much more than the tea she now lifted from a low traylike table set among the rugs and cushions, all the while wishing very much that it were wine. Before her were arrayed most of her nearest and most trusted: sharp little Hnarisha with his delicate bones and rounded features; Yavashuri, the maid of the bedchamber who knew (probably literally) where the bodies were buried; Druja, the agent who traveled to foreign lands; her general, Pranaj; and her newly acquired dependent, the unexpectedly clever and wicked Lady Golbahar.

Oh, and that asshole Mi Ren, the Song princeling who thought Mrithuri ought to marry him, and who nobody could quite figure out how to get rid of without offending his powerful family, from whom he had requested troops and money on behalf of the rajni he supposed must inevitably become his ticket to true regal power.

Missing only were her body servant Chaeri, whom she had not seen since before this meeting when Chaeri brought her her Eremite serpents; her Wizard, Ata Akhimah; and the Dead Man, sent to her rescue by the foreign Wizard who had trained Ata Akhimah.

All of them—the ones who were present—were very upset about a siege that could not succeed. Mrithuri had explained that it could not succeed, because Sarathai-tia was raised above a floodplain, and the Mother River would inevitably rise and sweep any besiegers away. Her illustrious ancestor, the Alchemical Emperor, had designed his capital city that way.

Mrithuri's people did not dare raise their voices to her. But that did not in the least stop them from raising their voices at one another, despite mostly being in agreement. The exception was Mi Ren. The foreign half-prince, or near-prince, or whatever he was—Mrithuri could never keep the endless and varied intricacies of ranks in the endless and varied Song principalities organized in her head, which was one of the many reasons she had Hnarisha—was cheerfully yelling at everyone, despite apparently having no idea what was going on and no idea that he had no idea. One of Mi Ren's lackeys stood beside him, looking impassively embarrassed and holding his coat.

No one else really dared to yell back at him, which was a pity. Although Mrithuri was not sure that her nerves and head could have stood the rise in volume. She could not even hear the plainchant of the cloistered nuns who lived within her palace but separate from it, which under normal circumstances would have echoed through the filigree panels piercing the walls between the two separate and interlocking realms. She had very little idea what any of them were saying. There was too much competition. Perhaps she would wait until they exhausted themselves, and then make them take turns.

She reached out and fondled Syama's ears, trying to soothe both of them. The bear-dog grumbled too low in her throat for anyone to hear, though Mrithuri felt it vibrating through her guardian's deep barrel. Mrithuri smoothed her palms over Syama's ears, knowing how sensitive she was to noise. Syama sighed and leaned her head on Mrithuri's knee.

*It will be fine*, Mrithuri told herself, hoping she was not lying. It had to be fine: she had so many responsibilities.

Still, she sighed—and Syama's head came up sharply—when the door to the room slid aside and everyone momentarily stopped shouting at each other to turn and face whoever might be coming in. Mrithuri breathed relief to see Chaeri, and Ata Akhimah with a bundle in her arms, and behind them the Dead Man, and two—

She startled to her feet. Syama surged up also, hackles raised, growling to be heard now. "What are *they* doing here? Why have you brought them into my presence?"

She knew these men. They—or rather their shadows—had entered her court before, in the company of the illusion-draped assassin who had worn the shade of a famous poetess, and who had tried to murder Mrithuri. Syama had dealt with the agent—sadly in such a manner as to leave him unavailable for questioning—but not before he had killed her former general and wounded her . . . friend, the Dead Man, while those two were rushing to defend Mrithuri.

"Hold your wrath, my rajni," said Ata Akhimah. "These are the true men, come from your cousin Sayeh with a message, and not shades such as the illusionist used to disguise the attempt upon your life. They come with a surety."

With a flourish, she unwrapped one coil of the bundle she held in her arms, revealing the draggled, miserable head of—

"Is that a phoenix?"

Despite herself, Mrithuri took a step forward. Syama escorted her uncertainly.

"Guang Bao, Your Abundance," said the narrow-waisted, mustached man in the unkempt military uniform. From their previous, albeit fraudulent, introduction, Mrithuri recognized him as her cousin's captain of the guard, one Vidhya. He confirmed that name, and introduced the little round Wizardy fellow beside him as Tsering-la. "My rajni sent Guang Bao with us to prove our authenticity as messengers, just before she was captured—"

Mrithuri raised a hand, and both Captain Vidhya and the rising murmurs of her courtiers fell silent. She should have thought of that an hour ago. "Captured."

Hnarisha stepped forward. He wasn't much bigger than Tsering-la, though lighter of bone. Mrithuri knew better than to underestimate either one of them.

"By your cousin Anuraja," the captain said. "He is holding her hostage, with two of her ladies. We sent men back to scout, and so learned who had taken her. His ally Himadra has kidnapped the prince Drupada, her son."

Mrithuri's world whirled. She put a hand out and touched Syama for steadiness, a warm and solid object in a world she abruptly did not understand. "That is . . . quite an insult," she said.

"Yes, Your Abundance."

Theological, as well as personal.

She was overwrought. She *knew* she was overwrought. And she knew that if she showed it, she would be destroying her people's confidence and morale. She kept her voice flat, perhaps a little venomous, and said, "That is an insult not just to our cousin's royal person, but to the royal persons of everyone else in our family. Sayeh and Drupada's inviolacy is *sacred*. Anuraja and Himadra dare to *kidnap* a ruling rajni and her son?"

The captain looked at the Wizard. "Yes, Your Abundance," the Wizard said.

Mrithuri pressed her lips together. She swallowed until her throat lost the tightness that presaged a rising scream.

If one could kidnap a queen or a prince, could one not also execute one?

Mi Ren stepped forward—around Lady Golbahar, who glared after him but really couldn't do much more, given the difference in ranks. He bowed before Mrithuri with a flourish of glittering rings. "Your Abundance," he said, as if he were saying *my love*. "I have sent doves to Song with messages for my father. I have informed him that you have agreed to be my bride—"

*Not exactly.*

"—and that his men must come to your relief if I am to rule by your side."

*Definitely not what I said.* Mrithuri smiled, and laid the back of her hand against his sleeve. "It is a long way to Song, my lord Mi Ren."

His face fell, but with true self-absorption he rallied and simpered. "They will come. I am my father's favorite son."

*Mother, how bad are the rest of them?*

"Then we will look for them at the enemy's back." She stepped back, swallowing both fury and laughter. "Go now," she told them, when she could make her voice low and throaty and confident again. "All of you. Except for Chaeri. There will be court in the Great Hall in an hour. You must prepare for it. Find our friends some fresh clothes, and get that poor bird to the austringers."

"Rajni," the Dead Man said, his eyes pleading above his veil. He leaned forward, silently begging for her word to stay.

She dismissed him with a gesture.

If he stayed, she would collapse against him. And she could not bear that he see her so. He must think her strong, powerful. He must think her a worthy rajni, or he would not want her—he who had seen caliphs and Wizard-Princes, and so much of the world.

When the door had closed behind everyone except Chaeri, Syama, and Mrithuri, Mrithuri turned to Chaeri as Chaeri held out her arms. Mrithuri went into the embrace and rested her forehead on Chaeri's shoulder. Tears burned the edges of her eyes as Chaeri comforted and coaxed her.

"I am here for you now, my rajni. You do not have to be strong anymore. Rest a moment. You know I can make it right."

Mrithuri let loose a trembling sigh and felt some of the grief and panic leave her. "Did I shame myself?"

"No one noticed anything," Chaeri assured her.

"You are the only one who knows me, Chaeri."

"There is nothing so bad you cannot tell me," Chaeri said, stroking Mrithuri's hair. Chaeri was only a few years older than Mrithuri, but for the moment the rajni felt very young, and very much like she needed the mother she had lost so long ago. "There is nothing you can tell me that is so bad I will not love you still."

"I have nothing bad *to* tell you," Mrithuri said. "Except that I did not realize until just now that I am afraid."

Chaeri stroked her hair again. "Let me fetch your pets, my rajni."

"It's not wise," Mrithuri said. "It is too soon."

Chaeri bent to kiss her brow. "My rajni. This is war."

Sayeh Rajni looked up at the towering, seamless walls of Sarathaitia and felt . . . a little faint, quite honestly. She had raged, in her heart. But she raged quite coldly, quite inwardly, keeping her pretty face smooth as years of artifice could make it.

Now the rage was frozen in a wash of even colder fear, for she did not know how she had been brought so quickly by her enemy from her own lands to those of her cousin Mrithuri. And she had not known what a citadel she would be forced to face when she got here.

But here she was, helpless in her enemy's keeping. And not even the enemy she had meant to surrender herself to.

Her broken leg was splinted and stretched out before her in the horse litter on which she reclined. It jolted with every rough step the pair of

grays she was suspended between took, and the view of the rump of
the horse before her never changed. The pain was not precisely bearable, but since she had no *choice* but to bear it, she gritted her teeth and
managed.

Ümmühan rode beside her on a docile old mare; Nazia, who was
still not very much of a rider, chose to walk beside the litter mostly.
They had ridden through the bright night, and with the darkening of
day—there was the golden city of Sarathai-tia rising across the river,
that should have been weeks of travel from Ansh-Sahal.

Sayeh did not wish to speak. There were enemy soldiers on the horses
behind and before her, tasked with controlling the animals who carried their raja's most honored hostage. Those would be trusted and
seasoned men, Sayeh knew, and not rough recruits who would not understand the seriousness of the work assigned to them. Whatever she said,
they would notice and report, and she did not care to give away the
advantage of allowing her enemy to know she felt fear, or anxiety, or
confusion.

She had wept when first captured, wept and screamed, it was true. She
had engaged in what was surely the finest display of hysterics the lands
under the Mother River had seen in her lifetime. That had been occa-
sioned by the discovery that she had given herself into the wrong hands,
the hands of her cousin Anuraja, and not those of Himadra—also a
cousin, it was true, but the cousin who held her young son as hostage.
If she had to be captive, she would rather be captive where she might be
able to use her wiles, her political sense, even her (admittedly aging)
beauty to influence and protect Drupada, who was her only child, her
heir, and all she had left of her husband now that he was gone.

Ümmühan would not lie, it seemed. Sayeh had come to learn that
lying, in her sect, was not just a sin but a kind of blasphemy. But she
needn't correct misapprehensions in others, and so the guards had been
allowed to think Sayeh's raving was a fever from her broken leg. It was
not a hard notion to sell; she *was* as weak as a nestling, and the pain
whitened her face and dewed it, even now.

So she did not wish to speak, and she did not speak. But she caught
Ümmühan's eye.

And Ümmühan raised an eyebrow over the veil she had abruptly resumed wearing, as if to suggest that she would explain eventually. Or

possibly as if to suggest that she, too, had no idea how they had come this far. Speaking glances were all very well, but they were still not exactly *language*.

A clatter of hooves approaching made Sayeh glance over her shoulder, but she could see nothing but the chest and mane of the trailing gray. From the sudden tension in the back of the soldier riding before her, however, she expected that she would soon have her long-delayed conference with her enemy.

Perhaps she was correct, she thought later. But if so, once again, it had not been the enemy she expected.

A woman rode up beside her litter, beyond Ümmühan. Her tall, arch-nosed red bay mare struggled through the verdant rainy-season growth along the road's shoulder, but the rider did not seem concerned for its footing. The horse's trappings were rich and well-cared-for. Perhaps more well-cared-for than the mare. Her saddle was gilded over ornaments carved into the leather, and her saddle blanket was a tiger skin with the snarling face intact and taxidermied. The edges of the skin were finished with tassels and flashing jewels.

The rider was built on the same model as the mare: tall and muscular, with mahogany skin and black hair piled in intricate braids and glittering with ornaments. Her jerkin was red leather with peaked shoulders, and carved and gilded and jeweled as extravagantly as the mare's harness. She wore it over silks in a peacock color that dazzled the eye with a mauve countersheen, and the cloak thrown over her shoulders was trimmed with the fur and tanned paws of a wolf.

She was rough with the reins, making the red mare struggle with the bit and her balance, and did not seem to care at all. Sayeh did not like the way she treated the mare. But the woman met her eyes, and despite the woman's cruel hands, Sayeh felt drawn to her, bathed in a charismatic warmth.

Nazia, at the shoulder Sayeh was turned away from, made a sharp sound under her breath. Ümmühan suddenly had her hands full as her mare tried to sidle away from the bloody-mouthed bay with its rolling eye and pinned ears. She didn't have room to turn the mare in a circle, because the heedless rider in the wolf-trimmed cloak was crowding them, and Sayeh, helpless in the horse litter, was in the way on the other side.

Ümmühan managed to balance her mount, though, and Sayeh had only a few bad moments. The woman let her bay fight its way forward, kicked it hard across the path of the first litter-bearer, and dropped back to push between Nazia and Sayeh.

Sayeh had a few bad moments more as the woman turned her clear brown eyes on Sayeh and said, "So you're the Sahali rajni."

There was a shimmer of color at the back of her eyes, Sayeh thought, like the shimmer behind a cat's eyes in the dark. She had a catlike face, also, with a snub nose and a slightly undershot jaw. The woman had a cold expression that was no expression at all, as if she had forgotten how to wear a human face.

"This is Her Abundance Sayeh Rajni," Nazia said, when Sayeh couldn't quite organize her thoughts between the ache of her broken leg and the woman's stare. She felt like it went right into her, through her, peeled back the layers of her soul like the petals of a rose and rummaged around in there. It was horrid, and intoxicating, and she wanted to relax and fall into that stare and let all her troubles be forever over.

"Let me know you," the woman said, her voice velvety.

Sayeh's mouth opened to say yes. Ümmühan's hand went out to touch the pole of the horse litter, a silent warning.

Sayeh snapped her jaw shut again. She gritted her teeth and closed her fingers on the bruised and swollen muscles of her splinted thigh, sending a spike of pure, white, unfiltered pain through her body. It blinded her and cleared her head at the same time, and the rush of sensations left her dizzy. She clutched at the poles of the litter and accidentally placed her hand over Ümmühan's.

The poetess's hand was warm and dry, despite the humidity and rising warmth of the morning. Her touch clarified Sayeh's thoughts that much further.

Sayeh got a breath and said, "Who are you?"

The woman grinned wolfishly. Sayeh got the impression that she was . . . amused . . . by the resistance. "Ravani," she said, as if that explained everything. "I am an advisor to the raja."

Sayeh thought of Himadra, and of the black-haired man on a tiger-caparisoned horse who had ridden beside him. She thought of how that man's eyes had glanced off her without acknowledgment but—she thought—not without seeing.

Ravana, he had been called.

Ravana.

A cold sensation rose up inside Sayeh like icy water in a spring. She shivered and managed to make herself look away. "What do you want with me, Ravani?"

She made herself say the name, even when her tongue and teeth and lips, her very flesh, seemed to peel away from it. *Ravani.* A simple word, but it hurt coming out of her.

"I don't know." Ravani directed her eyes ahead. "An alliance, perhaps? An acquaintanceship, for certain."

"To use me."

Ravani laughed. "You're already a hostage. I imagine the raja will wish to speak to you by night's end. Don't you think that *you* could use a few people who have his ear, and might wish to speak for you? And . . . for your son?"

Sayeh was silent. Ravani's words weren't illogical. But the creeping sensation that filled her, that those words presented the only reasonable path for her to take, and that everything else led to destruction— *that* was not rational.

"You do not know what I sacrificed to bring that child into the world."

Ravani reached across and laid a palm against Sayeh's cheek. She stroked its smoothness and Sayeh shivered. "I can extrapolate."

Ümmühan's touch helped to anchor her. The pain helped to anchor her. *This person is my enemy. She offers nothing that does not have a hook in it somewhere.*

Still, she obviously *wanted* something from Sayeh. And Sayeh did need allies in Anuraja's entourage, since apparently she was doomed to be a part of it whether she willed that or not.

"I am grateful for the consideration," she said at last, schooling her voice into its softest and most gracious tones. "I am grateful that you sought me out, Ravani."

Again, the name was bitter in her mouth. She swallowed saliva for having said it. *Is there a curse on her name?*

"What do you want of me?" Sayeh asked, when Ravani let the silence hang. She could feel Ümmühan and Nazia beside her, both breathing shallowly.

"I don't know yet," Ravani said, quite easily.

It was not the courtly fencing gesture Sayeh had expected next, and it disarmed her.

She was still remustering her forces when Ravani continued, "You are a true-born descendant of the Alchemical Emperor. His blood flows bright in your veins. His gifts to his daughters are your gifts. I am certain of this. You speak to animals; you have the hand of the Mother upon you."

"I have a little talent," Sayeh said. "Not what my cousin is said to have inherited. And what about you?"

"I have the raja's ear," Ravani said, low enough that perhaps the soldiers on the litter-bearing horses would not quite hear her. "I am loyal, of course."

"Of course," Sayeh said.

Ravani looked at her speculatively. "Do you happen to play chaturanga?"

"I was once accounted good at it," Sayeh admitted.

"Hmm," Ravani purred. "You will be bored while that leg heals. And I am always bored. Once you are settled, I will bring the board. I think that if we spend some time together, you can come to see how our purpose might benefit you. You might consider a true alliance with Anuraja. Surely that is more pleasant than hostageship. It would certainly offer you a position of more strength."

Nazia made another sound, a little hum low in her throat like a worried dog. Sayeh almost saw Ravani's ears prick, wolflike, to hear it. The corners of her mouth tilted. It wasn't a smile.

"I see your point," admitted Sayeh.

"Excellent," Ravani said. "I'm sure we can be of benefit to one another. Send your girl if you wish to talk to me, and I shall come and see you by and by, when I think I can be of use."

She jerked the horse's reins savagely. It half-reared, settling on its haunches and pawing in distress. Ravani yanked the bay mare's head around and kicked her much harder than needful, sending her careering back down the line of the army at a good clip. Despite her terrible horsewomanship, she could ride. She sat the mare's canter well, Sayeh thought, for the few strides that it was visible.

"Ugh," Nazia breathed, when she was gone.

"Ravani," Sayeh said. "Ravana. Remember him?"

Ümmühan nodded.

"Are they twins?"

Ümmühan frowned after the woman with the tigerskin horse-blanket. "They're something."

"I don't trust her," Nazia said, and seemed as if she might be about to say more. But she wiped the back of her hand across her mouth and shook her head as if she were shaking off the chill of premonition.

"Neither do I," said Sayeh. "But I need allies if I'm going to rescue my child."

HIMADRA HAD LIED ABOUT THE ARMY.

It was far from his first time lying about such things. One did not garner a reputation as a master strategist by telling people all about your plans. Nor, in fact, by telling them anything they did not need to know in order to do their jobs and solve the problems they encountered doing them. Knowing what information each such job required was one of the chief parts of *Himadra*'s duty, and there were certainly people who needed to know things that *he* didn't. The ones he trusted to do so, he also trusted to sort out what he needed to be made aware of.

One also did not gain a reputation as a master strategist by sticking to an old plan when a better opportunity presented itself.

He and Ravana and his small group of men had been on a scouting expedition in his neighbor's territory when the earth tremors that began the destruction of Ansh-Sahal struck. Himadra had realized instantly that he could use those tremors as a ruse, and that if he rode into his cousin Sayeh's damaged city and offered help, other opportunities might present themselves. The help would be real, after all, and the very worst that would come of it was that she would owe him.

Also real would be the opportunity for reconnaissance. The fib about an army at his back would be enough threat, he thought, to keep his widowed cousin from developing bright ideas about taking Himadra himself as an honored guest—which was a polite way of saying "hostage." Sayeh was a gifted politician, and she would think of political solutions before brute-force ones. Also, Himadra was certain that Ravana could spirit him away if necessary, although he preferred to owe the sorcerer as little as possible. Debts to magic-wielders had a way of accruing interest until they began to multiply.

But when Himadra's clever sergeant Navin saw a chance to make off with Sayeh's heir—her miracle child—Himadra had agreed to it. There *was* a hostage worth having. Especially as Sahal-Sarat seemed to be drifting inevitably from a period of cheating to one of fighting, as was the way of government among the squabbling kingdoms that had once been an empire. The move toward war was largely at the instigation of another of Himadra's many cousins, the wealthy Anuraja of Sarathai-lae, whose kingdom controlled the mouth of the Mother River, and therefore trade across the Arid Sea.

Anuraja was the last of the previous generation, older even than Sayeh Rajni, and he had dreams of empire reclaimed and of sitting on the Peacock Throne. A throne he did not hold, for it was in the palace of their very young cousin Mrithuri. Himadra, however, had accepted something that Anuraja had not, despite having buried five wives without living issue.

Himadra had accepted that the fragile body that housed his acute mind would get no heirs of its own. He had two brothers, it was true. Both much younger than he, for there had been children born between Himadra and these surviving siblings who had inherited the same curse Himadra had, and who had not survived their first hours. Neither of the surviving brothers seemed ill, but who could say what would happen to *their* descendants, when they got of age to get some?

Himadra's brothers were both guests fostered at Anuraja's palace, under Anuraja's thumb. Himadra had not seen them in years now. Who knew where their loyalties lay?

He could not say where the curse—or lethal sport, if that was what it was—had entered his father's house, or if it would end before that line died away entirely. But Himadra was a soldier, and soldiers are gambling men by nature.

Sayeh was the daughter of his father's father's brother. And Sayeh's line showed no evidence of being touched by the curse.

Himadra might get no heirs. But now he had stolen one.

Ansh-Sahal wouldn't miss the boy. Judging by the billowing plume of smoke and steam receding to the west behind them, and by the brutal shocks that still jolted the rocky passages of the mountains called the Razorbacks under his mare Velvet's steady feet, Himadra did not think there was much of Ansh-Sahal left to do any missing.

He guided Velvet around a recent rockfall, trying to think clearly despite the fog of pain that rose from his frail bones to cloud his wits. If Sayeh Rajni was alive, Himadra mused, she might thank him for rescuing her child.

Well, probably not. But a man could hope.

Himadra hoped the pretty rajni had herself survived, and managed to get some of her people away. She was like him, he thought. A misfit. Stuck in a body that was not shaped to obey the dictates of a mind that knew very well what *it* had been made for.

In Sayeh's case, to be a queen. In Himadra's, to be a mighty warrior. *Well*, he said to himself. *We both get by.*

And maybe with the leverage of her child and her damaged kingdom—and if Sayeh lived—Sayeh could be induced to marry again. If not Himadra, one of his brothers. There were odder things in politics than a dynastic marriage between a third-sex rajni of four decades and a prince of twelve. And such an alliance would repair *both* of their positions *and* that of the boy.

Himadra thought he could make a convincing argument, with the resources at his disposal. Especially if he had a bargaining chip good enough to get his brothers back.

What would he do, he wondered, if Anuraja took it into his mind to offer to exchange Vivaan and Rayesh for Drupada? Himadra did not think Anuraja would *harm* the boy. But he would want the leverage over Sayeh. The question was, would he want it more than leverage over Himadra?

Himadra would rather have Sayeh as an ally. But he couldn't afford Anuraja—wealthy, well-armed—as an enemy. Perhaps he could convince Sayeh that he and she together could protect her son.

And if not, well. Maybe a still-better opportunity would happen along if Himadra just kept playing to strong positions.

He would be ready for it if it did.

✳   ✳   ✳

THE RIDE CONTINUED. HE HAD A DOZEN MEN WITH HIM, AND THEY HAD less than two dozen horses. The mountains were rising up around them, seeming somehow steeper and more rugged than when they had passed through on the way to Ansh-Sahal.

Himadra did not fool himself that there would be no pursuit. If Sayeh survived, or if any of her household survived and had managed to organize, riders would be following, hard and fast. Riding until they pissed blood.

So Himadra's folk would ride until they pissed blood, too.

These were battle-hardened, his personal guard. His wiliest and wisest veterans. Used to hunger, accustomed to exhaustion. Able to accomplish miracles, pushing their bodies past the limits of endurance and strength. And they would do so now.

And so he, with all his pain and frailties, must also.

His men would accept that his body was weak, that his arm could not lift a sword. They would accept that the Mother had twisted him for her own reasons, and they would follow him nonetheless, for the sake of his wit and his sense of how a battle would turn. People said the true-born sons of the Alchemical Emperor had gifts. Himadra's gift might be a seventh sense of the pulse and movement of battles, as if he were an Aezin physician, and battles were living things.

Or perhaps that was the result of all his time, and study.

Whatever it was, his men would accept that he could not lead them into a battle with a sword in hand, as was proper. They would *not* accept it if he did not bear the hardships of the road with the same amused pretense of grumpy endurance as did they, and they would not understand that it was worse for him.

Well, Himadra had not *had* to choose to be a warlord. Though nothing else would have been open to him except abdication to a beggar's cup or the priesthood. You couldn't count on the support of family, when you were heir to a kingdom. Even so rough and stone-hewn a kingdom as Chandranath.

And there were no other adults in his family to abdicate to, which would have left—he sighed—Anuraja. Or one of the rajnis, who could barely hold their own lands.

His people were hungry. Himadra himself was hungry. He was hungry in the immediate physical sense—they had abandoned food, supplies, and the pack animals to carry those supplies at their camp near Ansh-Sahal, in order to make it look occupied a little longer as they snuck away with the heir. As a result, they were without shelter and short of rations. And he was also hungry in the larger sense that Chandranath was a stony, arid place that did not widely reward farming. There was only so much market for the fired clay pottery for which his folk were so justly famed, and so his people lived largely by trading and raiding, and by taxes on the goods obliged to travel through the land to richer realms that might buy them, and also down to the sea.

That hunger was also true, Himadra admitted, in the larger metaphorical sense. He *wanted* greatness. He craved it.

Very well then. He was hungry.

The child was not.

The child was fed and cared for and as cosseted as a child could be, when carried by a war-band moving fast, and kept by one nurse as stolen as the child was. His nurse had a horse of her own—a gentle gelding far more interested in meals than in running away or bucking—and had tied Drupada to her with a sling, so he could sit on the saddle in front of her and clutch at the gelding's mane without danger of falling.

Himadra was not innocent of children. He had those two, much-younger brothers. He knew this child was a mere toddler, of no age to reason or regulate his emotions. He was no more responsible for his weeping and calling and fits of temper than a weanling colt screaming for its mother.

He was also just as likely to call the tigers down upon them all as that lost and terrified foal. But after catching a glimpse of a phoenix-like flash of color high above, out of bowshot, a cold and grumpy Himadra Raja asked his sorcerer to lay an illusion of silence around him and his nurse.

He'd never gotten a satisfactory explanation from Ravana of what the difference between an illusion of silence and a real silence was. "The sound still exists, but I render it imperceptible" sounded to Himadra like nonsense or philosophy, which were two words for the same thing. In what manner did an imperceptible sound *differ* from a silence?

In any case, Himadra hated to ask for the magic, because he did not like giving the sorcerer an excuse to work magic on the child—or on anyone—but it would be worse luck for everyone if Sayeh's people or a clan of hill bandits caught them. Or actual, rather than metaphorical, tigers. Or jaguars. Or bear-dogs. Or whatever else they had in these Mother-unloved mountains that might want to eat horses or men.

And it *was* easier to think once the child stopped wailing. The nurse wailed for a while, thinking the prince had been injured in his spirit, but when she—and he—discovered that he could still speak in a normal voice, she settled quickly. And eventually, without the stimulus of his own shrieks egging him on, so did he.

These mountains were muted shades of tan and orange, colored sediments streaking their flanks as rain ran down them. The narrow, switchbacked road through their passes was slick with the intermittent monsoon. The rain fell in squalls and sheets, soaking everything. Then a wave of heat would follow, and the sodden everything would steam into a humidity that could have cooked rice . . . until the next drenching happened.

Himadra would have retreated into a blur of misery and ridden in that daze, trusting Velvet's sense of the footing. But he could not. His men were counting on him.

And so was the child, and the child's nurse. Whose name, he realized, he ought to find out. As she was likely to be a member of his household now. He'd meant to keep her until he got the boy back to the fortress city of Chandranath and pay her passage back to Ansh-Sahal, since there was no way he could ever count on her loyalty. But now there was no Ansh-Sahal to send her back to. And while Himadra had no compunctions about having his men cut the throat of an enemy soldier, he was not so without honor as to kidnap and murder defenseless women.

At his left hand rode one of his capable sergeants, Navin—the crease-faced and wiry fellow, graying in streaks at the temples. Navin was loyal, capable, independent-minded, and perhaps a tiny bit pompous, but he made up for it with a sharp-tongued wit, and Himadra had long since accepted that surrounding himself with people who were docile would require accepting that he was also surrounding himself with people who were stupid. Being a raja had never meant being unchallenged, to him.

Perhaps if his body had been large and strong, it would have. But Himadra had learned early and well how to persuade people to allow him to use their strength as if it were his own. It was not unlike training a horse to respond to a touch on the rein. The *horse* must be kept from realizing that it was much stronger than the rider, it was true. But the horse also had to trust the rider's judgment more than its own instincts, on occasion. And that was a trickier prospect than brute force would ever be.

Himadra turned to Navin and said, "Go make friends with the nurse, would you? And find out her name and family for me?"

Navin gave him a grin and a saucy wink. "In your service, Lord Himadra."

Himadra sighed and waved the sergeant off. Navin went, but not as if he had been dismissed. As if he were whistling on his way to work.

Himadra stroked Velvet's dappled neck. Her wet hair stuck together in little tufts, and her drenched mane hung in cords. The mare was specially trained for his needs. She was a wise and gentle palfrey that he had hand-raised from a foal to trust him and see him as the source of all good things. Her dam was one of several smooth-gaited western mares he had imported, in foal to various stallions, specifically to get strong, calm horses that moved with the running walk that would not jolt his body, a necessity for his safety that others had bred into the animals for comfort. His bones were not much stronger than a cat's, and he was a good deal heavier.

Despite all that, he rode her with a strong curb bit that was far more aggressive than what so steady and willing a horse would have required of an able-bodied rider. He hadn't the strength to manage even a gentle, soft-mouthed horse without the leverage it provided.

His saddle, too, was specially designed and quite different from the simple slip-saddles preferred by his men. It was padded, and made so that his weight rested on cushions. Quilted sleeves were belted around his legs and waist to support him if Velvet shied or sidestepped. If the mare fell, he'd be trapped—but the risk of falling off was much greater.

It was dangerous for Himadra to ride. He knew that, and he acknowledged the danger. A fall would be disastrous, and he did what he could to mitigate that danger. He also allowed his sorcerer to weave spells of protection around him.

But whatever the risks, Velvet was his freedom. She was his strong legs, his stout heart. Battle was dangerous, after all, and other warriors went into it. Himadra, in point of fact, went into it. A general could not command from behind the lines.

Velvet did not come into combat with him, however. She was too valuable, too trusting, too gentle. Too beloved. No, when Himadra went to war, his men carried him on their shoulders, lifted on a shield as if it were a litter. From up there, he could see farther than a tall man, and his words could be heard by those whose voices *carried*.

He was a good leader. He knew that, though he was aware also that a raja—and a general—must always be alert against self-flattery. There was no one around him to enforce him to modesty, so he must enforce it upon himself.

That was another reason he valued men like Navin. Such men would not cosset him.

He *was* a good leader. A good general. A good raja. A good brother, in as far as he could manage to be when his brothers dwelled in the house of another king, and one whose honor Himadra did not trust in the slightest. To his widowed mother, he still strove to be a good son.

But Velvet . . . to the mare, he thought, he was a good master, and a trusted friend. And she rewarded that friendship richly, not because he was raja and she sought the advantage of his regard, but because he was fair and kind to her.

He was musing on that still, the mare walking on a slack rein at the head of their little party with his lieutenant Farkadh on his dun gelding beside them, when he became aware that what he had half-assumed was the next switch of the road, glimpsed off to the right and winding down the mountain, was in fact a different road. A second and wider road, big enough for more than the two abreast or two passing of the way they now followed.

As they crested a rise, Himadra could make out the intersection ahead through the mist. He could see, too, that after that intersection his own road widened—or perhaps it would be more accurate to say that his own road disappeared into the larger one as a tributary.

He remembered this intersection, now, from the ride into Ansh-Sahal. The larger road was a smoother but less direct path into the city, of the sort that might be preferred by wagons and caravans. What

Himadra did *not* recall was seeing the muddy surface of the road freshly and heavily churned, trampled into a slimy mire that the horses would flounder up to their fetlocks in.

"An army," Himadra said, tasting the rain on his beard as his lips parted. "Between when we last passed, and this morning."

"A day ago at least," said Junayd, who was the most accomplished tracker of Himadra's trusted band. "Headed south and west, away from Ansh-Sahal."

"Refugees?" Himadra asked, second-guessing himself. Though he could not see how refugees could have gotten ahead of them on the longer road, unless they had left after the *first* earth-tremor.

"Too many horses." Junayd didn't dismount as they came up on the intersection. "Not enough other cattle. No small tracks: no children. No small dogs. Only mastiff prints, along the shoulder. Army, almost definitely."

"Well," Himadra said certainly. "It isn't *our* army."

There was a jingle of harness close behind. Too close for the horse to have come up without being heard, and yet it had.

"Anuraja," said the sorcerer Ravana, before Himadra was finished jumping in startlement. Ravana had seemed in a trance after the anti-shrieking spell. Apparently, now he was out of it.

"Not a Rasan come to take advantage of Sahal-Sarat's disarrayed politics?" Junayd asked.

Himadra chuckled. "That king of theirs seems to be operating on the theory that it's better to marry your rivals than bury them, and by the Mother's grace he does seem to have enough offspring to go around. They marry early and often up in the hills."

The hills were mountains that scraped the sky, but Himadra trusted that Junayd would appreciate his humor. As for Ravana—well, who knew what Ravana appreciated? Whatever it was, he didn't often share it.

"Not much else to do up there," Junayd answered. "Well, we know Anuraja has fielded an army. But he's supposed to be on his way to Sarathai-tia, not anywhere near Ansh-Sahal."

Himadra smiled past the churn of his gut. "Are you always where you tell your allies you were going to be, doing exactly what you said you would?"

Ravana chuckled, and after a nervous pause, so did Junayd. They were not, in fact, where Anuraja expected them to be right now, although the main body of Himadra's army was. And they were definitely not doing what Anuraja was likely to expect.

Velvet sidestepped anxiously, crowding Junayd's bay. Her head was up, her ears seeking as if she heard or scented something. Himadra was grateful for the bolsters that protected his leg from crushing.

He strained his ears, trusting the mare's senses and instincts. A slight scraping sound, maybe, under the gentle drum of rain—the noise of a hoof on stone? The rustle of motion of a large animal?

"Ambush," Himadra murmured to his lieutenant.

Junayd twisted in the saddle, reaching for the crossbow on his gelding's rump.

A rock fell, skittering down the slope rising on their left. Himadra jerked around, the sudden movement exacting a tax in pain. His eyes came up, his body tensing as he sought the silhouettes of riflemen or archers cresting the ridge—

A bloodcurdling porcine squeal shocked Himadra into grabbing for his pistol. Big galloping shapes crested the ridge, but not riders. Rather, the hunch-shouldered, bristly forms of a half-dozen monstrous bear-boars hurtled down on Himadra and his party.

The immense animals were mottled in shades of ivory and brown. They stood horse-tall and were heavier. Their crocodilian heads hung from slablike slopes of shoulder on necks bulging with mastiff muscle. Tusks shone with drool in their long snouts. Piggy eyes squinted deep in their massive skulls, armored behind bulwarks of bone. Ludicrously tiny cloven hooves, like ballet shoes on spindly legs, splashed mud and scattered pebbles, and somehow carried the gigantic animals faster and faster down the slimy scree toward the startled men and the screaming horses.

3

MRITHURI RAJNI STARED DOWN HER NOSE AT THE INTERLOPERS. IT WAS ineffectual, because her mask (snarling leopard, today) hid her expression. But if they couldn't see her displeasure, perhaps they could sense it. And it was satisfying nonetheless to glare.

She sat on her chair of estate wearing—and surrounded by—all her regal trappings. Hnarisha and Yavashuri—advisors, spymasters, guardians, and guides—rested in chairs behind a screen to her left. On her right was the perch for a bearded vulture, her massive ivory-and-black head, breast, and wings streaked with the colors of fresh and dried blood from the ochre she had groomed into her feathers. On the steps at Mrithuri's feet curled her handmaiden, Chaeri, re-robed in gold-embroidered silks and with the rain toweled out of her freshly oiled hair. At the bottom of the dais lay Syama, the brindled bear-dog, in her golden collar that Mrithuri could have worn low on her hips as a girdle. Mrithuri's bare feet were gilded in gold dust. Her fingers clattered in golden stalls—tick, tick, tick on the carved arm of her chair as she slowly tapped with them. Her head ached with the weight of her ornaments. She was grumpy and overwrought and tired out and hungover from the strain of the royal sorceries she had relied upon over the past days, and there was no hope in sight for rest. Her very *veins* itched with craving for the venom of her Eremite serpents, but she could not afford to indulge again so soon, though Chaeri would bring them to her at a word.

The venom was a poison, though, as well as a stimulant. And Mrithuri had been using too much.

So she gathered herself, and tried to keep the acid from her voice, perhaps not very successfully, as she addressed the sodden Wizard, phoenix, and captain of the guard arrayed before her.

"Haven't I met you two already?"

The Wizard—a small plump fellow in a threadbare Rasan coat—sighed. "So I am given to understand."

Mrithuri's new man-at-arms and newer lover stood behind them on one side. *His* coat was red, and even more threadbare. The Dead Man crossed his arms, making the bullet hole at the center of the coat's chest stretch, the fabric of the coat itself ripple stiffly where fresh stains the color of the stains of the bearded vulture's feathers were. Mrithuri tried to drive from her mind the source of those stains, and the reason for the absence of another old retainer who should have been in the room with them.

On the other side, and also behind, was Mrithuri's Wizard, Ata Akhimah, who had been her childhood tutor not so long ago.

The foreign Wizard—Tsering-la—cleared his throat and continued hesitantly. "I don't suppose you saved the cadaver?"

Akhimah stepped forward and grinned toward him. "And the gun."

"Mother keep those two parted," Hnarisha murmured from behind the screen.

*Too late*, Mrithuri thought. She gathered her drapes about her with the hooked tips of her fingerstalls, and stood. Syama stood as well, coming around the chair of estate to fall in at her heels.

"You trust these two?" Mrithuri asked Akhimah, gesturing with her chin.

"Your Abundance—" Chaeri protested. Mrithuri stopped her with a gesture.

"I'm willing to work under the assumption that they are telling the truth, for now," Akhimah answered.

Mrithuri reminded herself to give the air of considering. The fact of the matter was, she had already made up her mind.

"Take my cousin's Wizard to the morgue, then. My royal cousin's familiar can be housed in the royal aviary, with my own allies." Mrithuri reached out an arm and stroked Najlii's feathery nape with a single gold-wrapped finger, wishing she could feel her plumage. "Captain Vidhya, you will come with me. Once Tsering-la and Ata Akhimah have examined the assassin, and I have spoken to my commanders about the army at our gates, we will convene again that I may hear a report of your findings. And we will discuss how best to go about rescuing your rajni then."

She turned to go, gratified with the startled surprise with which Tsering-la and Captain Vidhya swept their courtesies. Maybe she had time for a short nap and some tea before Yavashuri and Hnarisha assembled the generals.

Syama followed at her heels as she swept away.

"YOU'RE PRETTY QUICK TO TRUST THEM," THE DEAD MAN SAID TO MRITHURI softly, having caught her in the hall. Her confidants drew back a little, to give them privacy for soft speech. There were no real secrets, for a rajni. Syama head-butted him, a show of affection she usually reserved for Mrithuri and Yavashuri only.

Mrithuri's pulse quickened a little as she looked at him. *Silly girl.* She also felt a little anger, that he challenged her.

She reminded herself that he had been raised both to interrogate his liege's judgment, and to follow it unhesitatingly once the decision was made. He was doing his duty as her servant.

"You brought them to me."

"I would not presume to judge for my rajni," he said, with a courtly flourish. "I would not mind understanding the logic of her judgment, however."

She soothed herself with a deep breath.

"Guang Bao," she explained.

The lines around his eyes rearranged themselves. She was getting used to reading his expressions despite the veil.

"Daughters of the Alchemical Emperor have a special way with animals."

He nodded thoughtfully. He had, after all, seen Mrithuri with her vultures. And—her cheeks heated despite the chill in her blood—her snakes.

"If the phoenix had been sent away from Sayeh without her consent and instructions, he would not be so calm or trusting of his captors. Once I have a chance to inspect him in private, I will be able to say more. My cousin Sayeh is of the bloodline. She is a true daughter of the Alchemical Emperor, and so her familiar's willing acceptance of these men means that they are acting with her blessing."

"Oh," the Dead Man said. "It doesn't make a difference that she's third-sex?"

"That doesn't make her less of a woman," Mrithuri rebuked.

The Dead Man accepted it with a wince. "All the same," he said. "I think I'll monitor these guests."

Mrithuri laid the backs of her fingers, where the stalls left them bare, briefly against his cheek above the veil.

"Thank you," she said.

"WELL," MRITHURI SAID. SHE CROSSED HER ARMS, FINGERING THE GOLD-wrought cuffs of her blouse where they ended just above her elbows. "It's not every day one is privileged to interview a mythological creature."

The phoenix cocked his head. "Pretty bird?" he asked, experimentally.

He had been fed, bathed, and allowed to groom himself dry, and was looking significantly less bedraggled. Some of the long jewel-like feathers of his crest still flopped, broken, but Mrithuri knew that when her austringers had more time, they would be able to do a great deal to repair the plumage, as well as the less obvious but more crippling damage to the strong primary feathers of his wings and tail. The process was called "imping," and involved using sections of feather shaft glued into place to splint and reinforce the bent and broken feathers until they were molted out, in the natural course of things.

Until that happened, Mrithuri doubted that the phoenix would be able to fly well, if at all. But at least for now he looked better: clean, dry, accoutered in his rightful shades of shimmering orange, golden, black, and teal as iridescently as if he were decked in silk.

"Pretty bird," Mrithuri agreed. She stepped closer, bare feet whispering on the rug. Such a relief to be stripped of her own gaudy court plumage and dressed in only a blouse, embroidered drape, her snake torc, and a dozen or so chiming glass bracelets. Her bare arms revealed the tattoos of the sacred animals, marking her rank. Her hair was braided plainly down her back, with only a rope or two of pearls. She was alone in her chambers with her closest advisors: Chaeri, Yavashuri, and Hnarisha... and of course the omnipresent rustle of the cloistered nuns behind the pierced wall panels.

"Your Abundance," Yavashuri began. Mrithuri's belly muscles braced. Yavashuri only used her title in that particular tone when she was about to, ever-so-politely, tell her rajni off.

"Yes, my child?" It was a gentle rebuke, and a deniable one. Of course, to Mrithuri in her ceremonial role as the Good Mother, every one of her people was her child. But Yavashuri was more than twice Mrithuri's age and had more or less raised her.

Yavashuri was not cowed. "It would be wise to rest before you attempt this, Rajni."

Mrithuri pressed the knuckle of her thumb to her aching forehead. She knew, of course, that Yavashuri was right. She also felt the driving ache of duty pushing her to do more.

"How would I feel if I were in Sayeh's place?" Mrithuri asked her advisors. Hnarisha, who had seemed as if he were about to speak, looked down. "My royal cousin has entrusted me with her safety, and sent her men—and her familiar—to plead with me on behalf of her, and her heir."

"That is well, Your Abundance," Yavashuri said. "But you cannot help anyone if you exhaust yourself unto destruction. You do not have an heir of your body, and while I do not dispute that you owe your royal cousin a duty of care, you owe one to your subjects as well, that you do not leave us at the mercy of Anuraja."

Mrithuri looked at the old woman and breathed out through her nose to contain her irritation.

"We're not suggesting that you abandon Sayeh," Hnarisha hastened to add. "Only that you accept that you can do nothing to assist her at this instant, and that what you are about to attempt will be safer and more effective if first you rest."

"I see," said Mrithuri. It was, in fact, a pretty good argument. As she turned it over in her mind, inspecting it for flaws as she might inspect a jewel, she felt a certain pleasure along with her annoyance. She had chosen her favorites well.

"If I may—" Chaeri began.

Yavashuri shut her up with a look. "You need rest too. Otherwise I cannot feel confident in the judgment of either of you."

Mrithuri laughed and raised her hands. "All right!" she said. "All right, Yavashuri, you win. Send for food. I will rest until I have eaten it, and then I will talk to the bird. And once I have done that, I will sleep. Until I am rested, or until the next crisis demands my attention."

"Acceptable," Yavashuri said. "If you are willing to endure my judgment as to what constitutes a sufficient crisis to awaken you."

"Somebody had better come get me if the enemy are breaching the walls," Mrithuri grumbled.

"They have not even reached the river yet," Hnarisha assured her. "Now, please, Rajni. Won't you lie down?"

She did, and even slept a little, and felt the better for it. It nagged at her that she and her soldiers had nothing better to do than sit within walls, waiting for the enemy to surround them. They would have been better to march out, to meet the enemy in the field. To prevent the siege from happening entirely. But the enemy had appeared as if from nowhere, with unknown capabilities and—as far as Mrithuri knew—at full strength.

She could rush her own people out to try to prevent the siege . . . and perhaps see them cut to ribbons.

Also, Pranaj—abruptly elevated to general in the wake of the assassination that had been meant, instead, to claim Mrithuri—had pointed out that because Anuraja's army had bypassed their borders rather than crashing through them, Sarathai-tia's defenses remained intact at his rear. The border troops might rally, and even come to lift the siege. If they could be contacted, they could be called.

And Mrithuri had her birds. So perhaps relief could be arranged.

They would permit Anuraja to surround them, and fight his numerically superior force from within the transient safety of city walls.

The food came—delicious morsels, lovingly arranged and prepared. Mrithuri forced herself to eat. Mechanically, as an act of stoking. Who knew for how long there would be fresh food?

She did feel better after, though the light meal sat inside her like a boot on her stomach. A little energy had returned, and she could stand up without bracing herself. Yavashuri flanked her nonetheless, and

Mrithuri did not point out the ridiculousness of the older woman serving as a prop for her queen.

Guang Bao, obviously as tired out by his recent adventures as any human and less self-conscious about it, had tucked his head under his wing and was indulging himself in a nap. He woke as Mrithuri approached him. She offered him a slice of dragonfruit from her own tray, and he accepted it with delicate gentleness. It was too large to swallow whole. He shifted his weight to grasp it in one large claw and clucked happily as he turned it in place, nibbling at the edges and shedding bright red, sticky bits over the footing of his perch.

Mrithuri stroked his nape with a fingertip, careful not to touch him overmuch. The balance of his feather oils was no doubt already destroyed by unceremonious and exigent handling, not to mention the bath. But she did not want to disimprove it further. He seemed to enjoy the attention, anyway, rousing and chuckling to himself and turning to preen the side of her hand.

With her left hand, she drew a jewel-tipped straight pin from her drape and jabbed it into the back of her right hand. The blood welled slowly. Mrithuri reminded herself to drink the tea she had poured and then left untasted, cooling. She turned her hand and let the thick droplet brush Guang Bao's beak.

The phoenix preened up the blood with a beak already sticky with dragonfruit. With her other hand, Mrithuri repinned her drape.

Her fingers tickled through roused feathers, finding the softness of down and the strange, prickly warmth of feathered skin. The bird made a happy cheeping noise, and Mrithuri eased herself into his memories. She saw what he had seen; she felt his confusion, his fear. She steadied herself against the heavy polished-wood perch and closed her eyes to rid herself of the disorientation of double vision. Triple vision, really—what she saw, and what the bird saw, and what the bird remembered having seen.

With him, she flew high spirals over men and horses, among dusty hills. She felt the wind among her damp feathers, drying them after the storm. The Cauled Sun warmed her. The weight of her body upon the air stretched her wings.

But what did she see below her? What did she *remember* seeing, with Guang Bao's eyes? Not an army, no.

A band. Too many for her birdy intelligence to number, but not so many that they stretched out of sight. (Mrithuri, remembering with the shard of her human intelligence that remained, recollected that birds were not particularly good at large numbers. Even very smart birds, as the phoenix was, undeniably.) They were strangers, and they rode two by two on a red road climbing up the windward side of these sharp-ridged red mountains.

The wind annoyed Guang Bao. It came from behind and shoved him forward, reducing his lift, making it feel as if the buoyancy was being sucked from beneath his wings. He let it push him—not even a dragon could fight the air—and rose into the mist below the low-hanging clouds that had piled up against the mountaintops. It would be enough to hide him, if he was careful.

When he had passed the ridge, he turned. Banking into the rising currents, cupping them with his wings. His long neck stretched forward as the air picked him up and tossed him. He crested the wave and glided down its back slope. This was more comfortable and easier to control. The Daughter had cautioned him that the men below were not his friends, that they would harm him if they saw him. She had charged him to come back safe to her again.

His second pass over the strangers was more controlled and leisurely. They did not seem particularly special to Guang Bao, however, being humans. The juvenile was familiar. One of his People. The phoenix beat his wings into the headwind to hover for a moment, getting a better look. The child didn't seem injured. He rode ahead of a female adult that Guang Bao also recognized, he thought, though he was not so familiar with her.

The others—

Guang Bao's gaze tracked a male as if drawn to it. This one was *like* the others. The rough outline was the same. The way it sat on a tired horse and urged the animal to climb, and keep climbing. But there was a dull glitter off its equipment that was compelling. Orange-pink stones, polished so they caught the light, studded the harness and shone around the edge of the tigerskin saddle blanket. There were shiny stones set into the tiger's eye sockets, and they seemed to blaze with more light than could come from the cloud-dimmed Cauled Sun and the washed-out stars.

*That* one was a predator. *That* one was a threat.

That one's head was turning. His eyes were rising. His arm coming up as if to point toward Guang Bao, hidden though the phoenix was in mist and darkness.

Guang Bao slid sideways down the slope of the wind, rowing to hasten his flight. Curving away, at the mercy of a sudden spike of the same fear he would have felt if the shadow of an eagle had fallen over him. *That one is going to eat me.*

He fled.

MRITHURI OPENED HER EYES. EXHAUSTION, NAUSEA WARRED IN HER. She wobbled and clutched the perch for safety.

She wished only to lie down.

*He saw me.* She was certain of it. He had seen through the blowing mist and seen not just Guang Bao. But somehow, he had seen Mrithuri in Guang Bao's memories, as well. Before she had been there? In retrospect, as if she had returned to that time and been there in reality?

She didn't know. But she did not think she had imagined the recognition.

"I think I saw their sorcerer," she said to Yavashuri. "Fetch paper. I will describe him to you."

"And then you will rest," Yavashuri suggested as Hnarisha bustled across the room for writing tools.

Bedraggled Guang Bao reached down and groomed Mrithuri's hair, tugging a lock free of her braid. It hurt, but she didn't have the strength to disentangle herself. So she just let her knees fold to take her out of the way.

"Yes," Mrithuri said, sinking down to the blessedly cool flagstones, heedless that the dragonfruit might stain her clothes. "Then I will rest, for certain."

4

TECHNICALLY, THE DEAD MAN SUPPOSED THAT HE WAS MEANT TO BE with the military council. But Mrithuri had not left him specific instructions, and so the Dead Man appointed himself to accompany the Wizards. That sounded like it was going to be more interesting anyway, and he trusted Mrithuri's new commander, Pranaj, to do the job of handling siege tactics as well as anyone.

He hadn't even realized that the palace had a morgue, so this was an exciting expedition. And information that might come in handy during the siege to follow, he mused morbidly. The Wizards walked down winding stairs side by side, the tall muscular woman and the round little man, and the Dead Man swept along behind them as if caught up in the skirts of a dust devil. Witchlamps danced around Tsering's head, lending brighter illumination to a way already lit by oil lanterns hanging on chains.

The palace dead were housed between the vast mortared columns of cisterns, in a basement sunk several levels down in the artificial hill upon which the palace rested. This was an interim step, a place of pause for the dead before they went to their final and lasting repose in the ossuaries, which were in catacombs levels below.

The whole edifice—hill, palace, city, concentric walls and defenses— had been raised by the Alchemical Emperor during his reign. That explained a number of its architectural peculiarities, such as the Peacock

Throne in the throne room, like a gigantic stub of melted and slumped candle studded with pavé gemstones, rising amidst barbaric glitter to higher than eye level. And such as the cisterns being mortared and cut stone, rather than dug into bedrock.

Although, the Dead Man admitted, he wasn't certain there *was* any nonporous bedrock to be dug into, here on this broad and muddy river plain. The dais the throne sat on was basalt shod in semiprecious stones, but he was given to understand that in raising that, there had been magic involved.

In any case, it made for an admirable root cellar. And morgue, occasionally.

"How deep does this go?" the Dead Man asked Ata Akhimah.

"Down into riverine caves," she admitted. "There's limestone underneath. This time of year, they're utterly flooded."

Their lanterns flickered, casting writhing shadows about them. Somewhere, a soft drip echoed.

"We won't run out of water, then." The Dead Man placed a finger on his veil and rubbed it against his nose. Their footsteps echoed in the winding, chill spaces between the cisterns. There was food storage here, racks and bins and barrels. Mostly empty, now, at the beginning of the rainy season.

Well, that was one reason to start a war at this time of year, the Dead Man supposed, thinking of the endless lakes of flooded rice fields outside Sarathai-tia, the tender seedlings about to be trampled under sandals and hooves.

"There are fish in the caves as well," Akhimah said. "Some big ones."

She must have seen the direction of the Dead Man's gaze, and guessed the direction of his thoughts.

"If only our men could breathe water we could swim out and take Anuraja on his flank."

"Huh," Tsering-la said. "Let me think about that."

"Here we are," said Akhimah, a moment after the Dead Man's nose provided him with the same information. He was surprised by the tang of decay; the assassin had not been dead long enough for the rot to be so advanced. But as they approached the shrouded tables, the Dead Man noticed that more than one was occupied.

He had not expected the second body.

"Who is this?" he asked, having approached the more redolent and flipped the shroud back to show a middle-aged, mustached face above a stiff, embroidered collar. This body was not significantly decomposed enough to be disfigured, but it was far enough along that it had begun to smell.

"Mahadijia," Akhimah said, approaching the other corpse. "Honestly, in all the fuss, I had forgotten he was down here."

"Who was he?" Tsering-la folded down the assassin's drapes with the unsqueamish respect of someone used to approaching the dead. He sucked in his breath through his teeth when he saw the damage Syama's teeth had done to the assassin. The Dead Man, who had been in the room when it happened and who was hardened to corpses, was still a little awed to be reminded of the extent of the damage.

"Stabbed," the Dead Man said, further inspecting the body. "A professional blow. Up through the ribs. Hard and certain."

Akhimah turned her head. "Interesting."

"Oh?" Tsering winced slightly at the sight of the assassin. Yellow witchlamps floated up from his body, forming into chrysanthemum squiggles. They cast a sunny, cheerful, utterly inappropriate light over everything. "That's surprising?"

"Well, yes," Akhimah said. "He was stabbed by the rajni's handmaiden Chaeri after he attempted to enter the rajni's apartments carrying the weapon. He *had* been the court ambassador from Sarathai-lae before the assassination attempt."

"Anuraja's man," said Tsering-la.

Akhimah nodded.

"Chaeri's not known to be a fighter, then?" The Dead Man hadn't thought so, but he'd been surprised before. He checked the blow again. Yes, singular and clean.

"You've met her," Akhimah answered.

The Dead Man nodded to himself. Yes, he had.

Leaving the ambassador half-uncovered, the Dead Man walked over to the other table. The raw meat of the assassin's gnawed face and throat smelled like freshly slaughtered lamb. "What can you tell from looking at him?"

"Well," said Tsering-la. "If the illusion spell had been a talisman, it would not have ended so neatly when he died. But I see no evidence on his body that he's any wielder of magics, any weaver of spells. The illusion shielded him, and it ended when he died. But I don't think the illusion was intrinsic to the assassin."

"You can tell that from a corpse?" The Dead Man was interested despite himself. "Do Wizards have an . . . aura, or something?"

"Magic does." Ata Akhimah wrinkled her nose. "A smell, anyway. To me, at least."

She looked over at Tsering-la.

He shrugged, and looked back with blatant interest. "Really? Does a dead Wizard smell different than a corpse who, in life, had no gifts?"

"Sadly, no." Her half-smile twisted her face ruefully. "'Gifts' is a funny word for it. Your lot earn magic through self-sacrifice, and not all of you even come into ready power that way. Mine earn it through years of study."

"Shamans," Tsering said. "They're born with it, or get struck by lightning. Chosen, somehow."

"And those of you who do make those sacrifices have much more direct power over nature than the rest of us who follow other paths."

"There are sorcerers," Tsering reminded. "Usually more powerful than any Wizard."

"Yes, but they sacrifice *others* to get *their* strength. There is still, at the bottom, a sacrifice. Here, look at this. Now *that* reeks of a spell."

The Dead Man, who had somewhat drifted off into daydreams during the theoretical discussion of magic—a failing, he knew—looked down to see what Akhimah was holding up in a hand protected by her handkerchief.

It was a ring, a single coral-colored cabochon gemstone set in heavy, twisted, ruddy gold. As she turned it slowly, it caught the glare of Tsering's witchlamps and a brilliant cat's-eye shimmered across it.

"That's magic?" he asked.

"It's some kind of a talisman," Akhimah confirmed.

The Dead Man shoved his hands into his pockets. "What does it do?"

"I don't know," she admitted. "It smells like . . . a link. A connection of some kind. For communication? That's what that sort of thing usually is."

Tsering produced and donned a leather riding glove, and lifted the ring from Akhimah's hand. He squinted at it. "It's theoretically possible that one *could* cast spells across such a thing." He hefted it. "I would not recommend putting it on."

"You still haven't explained why you think he was not a Wizard— or a sorcerer—though," the Dead Man said, "if you can't tell whether somebody would work magic when they were alive. Can't smell a gift on him, did you say?"

"Again, magic is not really about gifts—" Akhimah sighed, and shook her head. "That's not the answer to your question. The actual answer is that if he *were* some form of spellworker, a Wizard—or a sorcerer even more so—I would expect him to be positively festooned with little artifacts, hung about with charms, dripping amulets and talismans."

"Are you dripping talismans?" the Dead Man asked, very interested.

She smiled secretly. "A few more than Dr. Tsering, here."

He snickered.

Akhimah continued, "But this faceless fellow has a single, fairly powerful, and I think quite simple artifact. Which suggests to me that somebody gave it to him."

"How do you know it's those things? Powerful and simple?"

"The materials are rich," Tsering said. "Power is often reflected by craftsmanship and expense, though not always. But it's easier to make a valuable thing more valuable, rather than dross valuable at all. It's just because of the assortative principles of magic."

"I see," said the Dead Man, who didn't.

"And the more complex the design, the more complex the patterns of the spells that can be woven into it."

That made a little more sense, and the Dead Man said, "Oh." He eyed the elaborate collar of fine carved jade panels and misshapen baroque pearls that clasped Tsering's throat above the round, simple neckline of his six-petaled coat.

Tsering caught him looking and winked.

"So someone sent him here, and monitored him, and used an illusion to make him look like Ümmühan and make him seem as if you— Tsering-la—and your colleague Vidhya accompanied him."

"Precisely," Tsering-la said.

"And somebody within the castle sewed one of Ümmühan's hairs into my coat," Akhimah said.

"*What?*"

The Dead Man recollected that Tsering-la had arrived after that particular revelation. It was confusing, what with him having arrived twice.

"Just so," said Akhimah. "I did not recognize the illusion for what it was because countermeasures had been enacted, and the hair was linked to a camouflaging spell."

"Ümmühan was not taken captive by the enemy until quite recently," Tsering said. "I used a dragon-gate to speed Vidhya and I on our way. There happened to be a pair conveniently aligned."

The Dead Man cleared his throat. "What, exactly, is a dragon-gate?"

Tsering-la made a face. "Well, nobody knows if the name is accurate. It's an Eremite artifact that can link two places as if there were no distance between them. A Wizard—who shared my name, as it happens—spent a good deal of time mapping them, about fifty years ago."

The Dead Man had always thought that such things as mystical connections from one part of the world to another, usable by those with the right magic skills, were fairytale nonsense. And yet, here were respectable Wizards talking about them as if they were common, practical knowledge.

He filed that information away to consider later.

The Dead Man said, "So whoever has Ümmühan must have known that Tsering-la and Vidhya had been traveling with her, and that we might have some communication with them in order to know that."

"It's never wise to assume that information is not traveling when Wizards are involved," Akhimah said.

"It's never wise to assume it *is* traveling, either," Tsering replied with a grumpy laugh.

"In any case," the Dead Man continued, "the sorcerer or whatever must also have had access to Ümmühan's hairs, and gotten some to an agent here in the castle to sew into your sleeve. So we must assume that that agent is still within the palace, because this cannot have happened long ago."

"The sorcerer must be able to cast illusions," Akhimah said. "Which narrows it down some. And must have been able to send the assassin here ahead of you, Tsering-la. Despite the fact that you used the dragon-gates."

Tsering-la made a furrowing frown. "Well. Shall we get on with the autopsy, then?"

Akhimah reached down beside the table and lifted out a satchel that chinked heavily when she shifted it. Her tools, the Dead Man supposed. He assumed that she had had a servant fetch them down, or that they were stored here for this purpose, or perhaps she had conjured them from her rooms, as he would have noticed if she had carried them. Was conjuring a thing Aezin sorcerers did?

Would it be impolite to ask?

He had not the slightest idea.

He moved a little farther away from the dead ambassador to get the smell of rot out of his nostrils. That brought him closer to the aroma of raw meat, but it was less objectionable.

That was good, for it was soon to grow stronger.

It did not seem to bother the Wizards that the assassin's face had been bitten half off. Working together, as if they had done this many times, Akhimah and Tsering wielded their shears to lay the would-be assassin's body bare. The clothes—stiff with blood and less appealing substances—they set aside and saved.

The Dead Man had seen some exceedingly sharp blades in his day. Razors. Scalpels.

These tools put all those to shame. They would have been useless for war: they seemed to have been chipped from black glass. Their knapped facets glittered with barbaric splendor. But however sharp they were, they would be brittle, and they would not survive the least contact during a parry.

He'd heard of the skills to which Rasan Wizards were trained as surgeons. And he had heard as well of their volcanic obsidian dissecting knives. Said to be imbued with the power to cut living flesh so cleanly that it barely hurt, and might heal without a scar.

These knives seemed to belong to Ata Akhimah, which was logical, as she too was a Wizard. Tsering-la had apparently left his possessions behind in Ansh-Sahal, but the Lotus Kingdoms were not far from Rasa, as the trade routes ran.

Tsering-la handled the blades both meticulously and reverentially. His hands and his witchlamps were steady as he explored the wounds in the dead man's face, arm, and throat. As he did so, he discussed what he found, and Ata Akhimah also shared her opinions. The Dead Man listened, and found himself leaning closer, fascinated. And learning a few useful things about anatomy in the deal.

The Dead Man had been impressed before by the power of the bear-dog Syama's jaws. Now he was overawed.

Her first bite seemed to have crushed the assassin's arm. The next had been enough by itself to kill, destroying his face and driving finger-sized canines through the bones of the skull before the closing leverage of the jaw cracked and pulverized it. Though she had then torn his throat out for good measure, there was no possibility that he might have felt it. He had been dead before Syama shifted her grip the second time.

Tsering-la paused then, and took off his coat. He hung it on a hook that Ata Akhimah showed him, and rolled up his sleeves. Both Wizards donned aprons. The Dead Man resolved to stand well back.

By the time Tsering-la cut into the assassin's belly, the Dead Man had forgotten any squeamishness he might have harbored in the light of a newfound intellectual curiosity. He watched, fascinated, as the sublime edge of the black glass blade parted waxy flesh, revealing the pink meat and the gelled blood beneath.

"That's so sharp," the Dead Man said, aware he sounded childish and not sure he cared.

"It cuts right through the little capsules that make up the flesh," Tsering-la said, with satisfaction. "No crushing or bruising."

The Dead Man wanted to ask about the capsules. He guessed that now was not the time.

Tsering-la opened the abdominal cavity with the same care the Dead Man would use in gutting a deer. He parted muscle and membrane cleanly, then reached in and scooped the slippery gray mass of intestines aside, piling them into a basket held by Ata Akhimah. Intact, to the Dead Man's relief. He knew from personal experience how profoundly terrible the contents smelled.

"Are you looking for something in particular?"

"I try not to," Tsering-la said. "Preconceptions influence the outcomes."

That struck the Dead Man as a reasonable point. He was starting to think he could get used to being around the sort of Wizards who applied some recognizable logic to their behavior, novel though they were in his experience.

Next, Tsering reached into the abdominal cavity and groped out the liver, which was enormous and wet. The Dead Man had not previously realized the size of a human liver, or quite appreciated its resilient floppy slipperiness and the intricate lacework of blood vessels that cauled it.

"What next?" Ata Akhimah asked, as she held out another tight-woven basket to receive the organ. The meat had a soft gloss in the glow of the witchlamps.

*Still fresh,* the Dead Man thought.

"I'll go up through the diaphragm," said Tsering, and suited actions to intent. The lungs, deflated, looked exactly as the Dead Man had expected them to—frothy pink bits of sponge. The heart . . .

Something cracked loudly when Tsering-la moved his knife for the heart. It sounded like a stone whacked on stone, and Tsering-la jerked his hand back with a yelp.

There was bright blood among the wine-dark, and Tsering-la clutched his hand with a gesture that the Dead Man too well remembered. Ata Akhimah leapt forward even before the Dead Man. She grabbed Tsering-la's wrist and dragged him around until he was facing his own witchlamps. The Dead Man handed her a clean cloth from the toolkit as she peeled Tsering's clutching fingers apart.

The blood, at least, dribbled and did not gush.

Ata Akhimah clucked her tongue. "Well, it could be worse," she said. "What happened?"

"The knife broke."

"The knife—did you strike a rib?"

He looked at her with lips pursed, as offended as a cat. "Really. Did it sound like a rib?"

"I'm sorry." She pressed the small cloth to his wound. Blood that had been spattering the floor was absorbed. "Well, the cut doesn't look too deep."

The Dead Man's attention was drawn away from the tableau by a sound. A rustle, behind him.

"What's that?"

He turned.

Impossibly, the corpse was sitting up on the table, one arm pressed across its empty cavity as its sightless, faceless skull turned around. It lifted its chin, and the Dead Man could not shake the sensation that it was staring directly at them.

He shook his head, suddenly exhausted. "I wish the Gage were here."

# 5

RAVANI HAD BEEN CORRECT. THE RAJA DID WISH TO SPEAK TO SAYEH that morning.

He sent for her as the army made camp and the sky began dimming at the rim with sunrise. His nervous young messenger arrived as Anuraja's cowed personal physician was changing Sayeh's dressings. The messenger was just as obviously overawed, despite her bloodstained clothing and the unwashed hair that lay oily on her shoulders, itchy and lank with the dust of the road. The young man kept glancing behind himself as if expecting to be corrected by an invisible sergeant, but he managed to stammer out that Anuraja wished to receive his royal cousin at his pavilion for the morning meal, and that he would send bearers to lift up her litter.

Then he excused himself. His going provoked the static silence of waiting women into a flurry of activity as Nazia and Ümmühan rushed to make Sayeh regal. Or as regal as could be expected, under the circumstances.

Anuraja had gone out of his way to make Sayeh comfortable, providing her with an airy pavilion, mats she couldn't currently walk on—though they did keep the dust down—and bedding that still smelled faintly of the cologne of the junior officer who had no doubt been turned out of his quarters to make room for her. Sayeh hoped he wouldn't hold a grudge.

Sayeh also wondered if she should be worried about the concern for her comfort. She didn't think it was charity, or religious concern for her as a priestess and avatar of the Good Mother. Possibly—probably—Anuraja was smart enough to understand that protecting her royal privilege and prerogatives supported his own. Most likely he wanted something. And, of course, nothing precluded him from having multiple motives.

In any case, Ümmühan produced a comb from her traveling kit, and a flask of scented oil. She and Nazia combed as much of the dust as possible from Sayeh's dirty hair. For want of a crown or any formal symbol of rank, they dressed it as best they could and braided it through with ribbons, twisting it into an improvised diadem.

They also brushed and beat her clothes before helping her to dress in a cropped blouse from her dead gelding's saddlebags. With a great deal of cursing and a small amount of hopping, and Sayeh holding herself upright against the center pole of the pavilion, they managed to work her legs—and her splint—into a pair of Ümmühan's loose desert trousers, which were made from contrasting layers of gauzy silk and rich enough for a hard-riding queen.

Nazia cleaned Sayeh's face with oil, and Ümmühan blacked her brows and lashes and the line around her eyes with lampblack fixed with coconut oil. Sayeh herself, as a priestess as well as a queen, had a little sandalwood traveling box with two compartments. One, when the carved lid was slid aside, contained slaked turmeric, which was bright red in color. The other side held the plain turmeric spice powder mixed with sandalwood, which was fragrant and golden. With those, Sayeh dressed the part of her hair above the braids and marked her forehead as well.

She sat back down on her litter with a sigh. It had been left propped on two sawhorses with rugs thrown over them so she could get in and out more easily, making it the only elevated seat in the pavilion.

"I need a set of crutches," she said.

"You need to stay off that leg, if you want it to heal straight," Ümmühan said, no-nonsense.

"Do you talk to your own queen like that?" Sayeh asked, laughing.

"I'd talk to my *prophet* like that," Ümmühan responded tartly.

She made Sayeh miss her grandmother. Even more so, as she brought Sayeh tea, then stood protectively before her as two soldiers scratched politely at the flap for entrance. They were the same bearers as before: the ones who had ridden the horses so stolidly. They had returned to lift Sayeh up and take her away. Apparently they were detailed to her as some combination of guards and legs.

Sayeh would have to make a point of learning their names.

She worried briefly about Vidhya and Tsering-la—and her familiar, Guang Bao—and whether they would manage to win their way south and find shelter and assistance. Then she put that thought from her. She was in worse trouble than they were.

Probably.

She smiled at the soldiers in a regal fashion.

"Your Abundance, your attendance is requested," said the older of the two. They were much alike, as career soldiers can seem. Both wore their hair twisted up into a military topknot, and both wore elegant mustaches. But this one was a little shorter, broader, and grayer than the other.

"I am ready," Sayeh said. "Nazia, attend me."

Nazia stepped forward.

The bearers glanced dubiously at one another. Apparently, the older one was nominated to do the talking again. "The raja has requested only you, Rajni."

Sayeh offered him a gentle smile. "What is your name, soldier?"

"Sergeant Sanjay," he said. "This is Sergeant Pren."

"I am flattered to have two experienced men such as yourselves as guardians." She gazed up through her blacked eyelashes. "Your raja did not instruct *me* to come alone. And I certainly cannot expect him to wait on me with his own hands." Sayeh thumped her silk-concealed splint for emphasis, then regretted the careless gesture, especially as her leg was already disgruntled by her previous calisthenics. She kept her face placid despite the flutter of pain.

Sayeh needed to win this confrontation, subtly though it must be played. She needed to establish her authority at once—to carve out a little space and, with luck, to keep expanding it. A plan was forming in her mind. She didn't look at the idea too closely, lest she startle it away. Instead, she followed her hunches.

Sayeh did not look down.

Confronted with the implacable regard of a rajni, the soldiers held on to their resolve for only a few moments before they quailed. They sorted themselves to the appropriate stations and lifted Sayeh as smoothly as any of her own litter-bearers at home.

Nazia fell into step beside. Ümmühan caught Sayeh's eye as she stood aside to let them past. Sayeh could have sworn the old poetess winked above her veil.

THE JOURNEY ACROSS THE ENCAMPMENT MIGHT HAVE BEEN A TRIAL TO one less used to being on display than Sayeh Rajni. Anuraja's men were too well-disciplined to point or stare ostentatiously. But they did openly observe the litter's progress. And in observing, they freed Sayeh to observe openly in her turn.

She could have wished that Anuraja's soldiers were a little *less* disciplined. But she watched them boldly, and noticed gear in good repair and men in decent health, much to her disappointment. There were tidy ranks of tents well-pitched: no rough bivouac, this. Latrines, a cook tent, busy ostlers caring for the horses.

She kept the disappointment off her face, however. Equally, kept her curiosity as to why they had not yet crossed the river to Sarathai-tia to begin the siege, but camped on the farther shore. Kept her expression queenly and serene.

The city rose across the milk-white river. It looked prosperous and wealthy, and Sayeh felt stabbed by envy as she regarded it. Behind its many tiled rooftops in all their brilliant colors was the palace, like a golden crown atop its conical hill. Flowering vines and trees festooned the tops of its high walls.

It was no mystery to Sayeh why Anuraja would covet this place. She half-coveted it herself. But why had they not crossed the river?

Once again, she wished Vidhya were with her. She wished she had studied combat and warcraft rather than leaving such things to men. She wished she knew better how to estimate troop strength and get an idea of what terrain and forms of combat an enemy was specialized for.

Well, if she didn't have those skills, she would just have to try to live long enough to acquire them. And based on the look on Nazia's face, Sayeh was not the only person feeling slightly overwhelmed.

Perhaps they both needed a distraction.

"Look, Nazia," she said. She raised her eyes again to the golden stone walls ringing the hill beyond the river, and pointed. "It is Sarathai-tia. The Peacock Throne is there."

"Does it matter?" The girl's question, for once, seemed not sharp but open, girlish, genuinely curious.

"Does what matter?"

Nazia waved generally in the direction of the golden city. "The Peacock Throne. Who sits on it. Empires. Is one king really better than another?"

"One king might be worse than another," Sayeh answered mildly, trying not to show her amusement.

"I mean—" Nazia seemed to remember abruptly who she was speaking to. "Begging your pardon, Rajni."

"Pardon granted. Please speak on."

"But they're all kings. What are kings good for, from the perspective of the common people, except dragging your folk off to fight in other kings' wars?"

It was, indeed, an excellent question, once Sayeh closed her gaping mouth and thought about it. "We do a little to keep the roads open. Feed a few poor. Appease the gods and keep the brigands down."

"When the brigands aren't your own soldiers bored between battles," Nazia muttered bitterly.

Sayeh pressed her lips together, contemplating her own rebellious army. She'd been certain of the palace guard. Certain of Vidhya. Not so her army, from common soldier to general, it was true. They had been loyal to her late husband, for all she was Gurunath Raja's daughter.

She wondered just how much of her army had survived the catastrophe.

"Does that happen at home, Nazia?" she asked carefully.

Sayeh was conscious of the listening ears of the guards, but there wasn't much she could do about it now except keep the conversation fast and idiomatic. The odds were that one or both of these men would have been assigned to her because he spoke fluent Sahali. It's what she would have done, after all, if her role and Anuraja's were reversed. But maybe she would get lucky.

And Anuraja already knew her city was a shambles. There was no point to pretending otherwise. Let him think her a pretty idiot who could not keep a secret.

Nazia, obviously, did not yet have the political awareness to consider the consequences. She really had been raised in a box with a litter of puppies, hadn't she? The girl just shook her head and said, "Well, it doesn't matter now, does it?"

Sayeh bit her rouged lip, tasting slaked turmeric. It *did* matter. It *would* matter, if Sayeh had anything to say about it.

THE WALK TO ANURAJA'S QUARTERS WAS NOT A LONG ONE, WHICH SAYEH supposed was fortunate for the bearers. Sayeh wished she had a better idea of what percentage of the camp it took her through. If she'd thought the space seconded to her was luxurious for a war camp, a glimpse of Anuraja's pavilion disabused her.

True, it was technically a tent. But as tents went, it was a palace.

The walls were pale silk, dyed with Anuraja's colors of saffron and sapphire in patterns that reminded Sayeh of the marbled endpapers between which the leaves of some books were sewn. They approached, and someone drew a drape aside. Sayeh was carried seamlessly within. Nazia padded after, her footfalls silent by comparison with the soldiers'.

The interior was as sumptuous as anything out of an illuminated painting in one of those selfsame books. The pavilion had double walls, to keep out the heat and dust. The interior panels were brightly illustrated, but they were not tapestries, which would have been heavy. They were painted canvas, she thought, and the dead air space between the outer wall and inner made the space within surprisingly cool. Some of them had been drawn aside to let the fading light filter in through the translucent outer panels. Its glow, and the glow of the lamps hung by chains from the stays of the ceiling, was caught in several framed looking glasses. Those *were* heavy. And fragile. And Sayeh wondered at the waste of effort and resources to bring them along, though they did make the space quite merry.

In that excellent light, it would be possible to read the books and maps stacked on the low table surrounded by cushions without eyestrain. And it was equally easy to see the bright colors on the embroidered cushions, the stacked rugs, the long velvet divan on which reclined the raja.

He wore a silk robe in moiré saffron, and his bad leg—she remembered that he had a bad leg—was propped up on a pillow. Well, that was something they had in common, then. Perhaps she could build in the connection.

The bearers set Sayeh's litter down upon a set of stands not too far from Anuraja's chair. Nazia stopped beside her as they withdrew. The girl kept Sayeh—and the litter with its long poles—between herself and Anuraja, and Sayeh could not fault her instincts.

It didn't stop Anuraja from eyeing her speculatively, stroking his beard the while. He turned his gaze back to Sayeh, his eyes bright and clever. "My darling cousin," he said. "It is so very good to make your more familiar acquaintance. You will forgive me if I do not rise."

He had a good voice. Resonant. And his face might have been hand-some in a distinguished fashion behind the luxuriant whiskers. It was hard for her to tell.

She let herself laugh—tinkling and pleasant. He would never know how practiced. Men like that, so full of themselves, never knew how much women must rein themselves in, present themselves as a work of art. A performance, as much as any dance. "I hope Your Competence will also forgive me for a seated greeting."

"And this pretty child? Is she another cousin? Or some relative on your husband's side?"

"She is of no family," Sayeh said dismissively. She felt stiffness rise through Nazia, even though she did not look at the girl. "An orphan. Under my care."

"Ah," Anuraja said knowingly. "A little young for you, isn't she?"

Sayeh turned her gaze away, and studied those painted wall hang-ings. A single bright scene of the Mother separating the waters of earth and the waters of the sky. And dozens of images of red-tinged war, bared blades, the spiked wheels of chariots. A tiger being wrestled by a man. A rampaging elephant.

The divan creaked softly as Anuraja shifted himself upon the cush-ions. "Very well. Your girl may wait on us, then."

Nazia kept her face as blank as fresh paper. If Sayeh could not see her offense, she felt as if she could smell it. The girl kept her control, however, bowing her head as if in acquiescence. Not for the first time, Sayeh wondered at the life that had taught her such an iron will at such a young age.

The exchange was useful to Sayeh in another way. Almost as soon as Anuraja had spoken—and what idiot royalty would name their child and heir Anuraja Raja?—draped walls were swept aside, and slim officious mustached men in tidy burnt-orange uniforms and sky-colored turbans came in bearing golden trays and racks on which to set them. The men moved with such precision, and seemed so uniform in their appearance, that even Sayeh's trained eye had difficulty distinguishing them enough to arrive at an accurate count.

The trays were set up off to the side, not directly between Sayeh and Anuraja. Sayeh could see that they bore covered dishes, glasses, bottles, and gleaming serving implements.

The men disappeared through the curtain wall once more. When they came back, one held the drape aside, and two were carrying long, low tables. One of these was set beside Sayeh; the other beside Anuraja. They whisked themselves away without Anuraja appearing to take any more notice of them than if they had been summoned spirits.

Sayeh pressed the tip of her tongue between her teeth. No, she decided. She would not let him dictate how she treated her own people.

She looked at Nazia, speaking before Anuraja could say something else arrogant. "Thank you, Nazia," she said. "You may serve."

Nazia glanced at her. Sayeh met her gaze. The girl was quick. Sayeh hoped she had spent enough time in the castle to remember how the servers there operated. It would not do for Anuraja to suspect that Nazia was anything more than a servant girl. And definitely not that she was Sayeh's Wizard's apprentice.

Sayeh pointed her chin at the trays, and then at Anuraja. Nazia nodded faintly, and dropped a clumsy little curtsy before hurrying toward the trays.

Sayeh considered the drilled perfection of Anuraja's servers. *Well. We are supposed to be the country cousins, after all.*

Sayeh turned back to Anuraja, smiling to distract him. "So, Your Competence," she said politely. "It is an unusual choice, going to war in the rainy season. Have you some plan in place to deal with illness and hunger?"

"It won't rain forever," he said, obviously delighting in his crypticness.

He watched as, wordlessly, Nazia uncovered the dishes, releasing an array of tempting aromas into the enclosed space of the pavilion. She should have walked around behind the trays to do so, rather than presenting her back to the room, but—

*Country cousins,* Sayeh reminded herself.

As Sayeh had hinted, Nazia served Anuraja first. As she walked away, he pinched her bottom, and Sayeh saw her lips compress.

*Don't cut his hand off,* she thought. It seemed probable, anyway, that the soldiers who had captured them had relieved Nazia of her knife. They had certainly disarmed Sayeh in all things.

She glanced down to hide her smile.

In *almost* all things.

Nazia did not cut their jailer's hand off. She constructed a serving for Sayeh, and set the gilded plate on the table. Then she brought tea to each.

The design of the plate was unfamiliar. With its individual compartments of colorful dry dishes and gravied dishes, and its pile of warmed flatbread in the middle, Sayeh was reminded of a jeweled wheel. She watched out of the corner of her eye to see how Anuraja ate.

With gusto, apparently. Perhaps she had worried too much about table manners, because he balanced his plate in his lap, tore the bread into morsels, and folded each one around dainty bits of his dinner. Sayeh was not hungry, but under the circumstances she could not afford to pass up a chance to fuel herself. She copied him, and found the food more pleasant than she had anticipated in her anxiety, though she could not identify even half of it. There was garlic and ginger, for certain. But also other flavors, subtle and sweet, that she could not place.

And no meat, she realized, when she had eaten lentils, and chickpeas, and sweet peas, and she wasn't sure what else.

She was still eating when Anuraja set his empty plate aside, wiped his hands on the scented napkin Nazia brought him, and folded those hands over his belly.

He watched Sayeh eat for a few moments, and just as she put a morsel of bread dripping with sauce in her mouth, he said, "I need an heir."

She chewed and swallowed hastily, trying to remain dainty. A napkin was waiting for her as well. By the time she had dabbed her mouth, she'd thought of what to say.

"Alas. I am not equipped to assist you with that."

"You managed it once," Anuraja said dismissively. "Or so you had put about."

"Put about?" Her shock and fury must have shown.

Anuraja snapped his fingers with slow, precise sarcasm. "You are as good a politician as they say, dear cousin. Tell me, where did you get the brat? One of your dead husband's by-blows?"

Sayeh was so stunned she could not answer. Her hand rested on her belly.

"A miracle child, though. That's a good story. A clear story. Did you come up with it yourself, or is one of your people the inventor? If it's you, I could use someone like you telling stories on my behalf."

"I can show you . . . the scar," Sayeh said between her teeth.

"Oh, I have no doubt. You'd never overlook such an obvious detail. Lovely Sayeh, beloved of the Mother." He grunted. "Churches are made by men. They serve the purposes of men."

"I can see why the Mother wants little to do with you," Sayeh spat, and regretted it. It was unwise to castigate anyone who held the power of life and death over one. And yet . . . she was Sayeh, and her tongue, while often sweet, was not used to being restrained.

She took a breath. Her lovely son. She thought his interest in Drupada was a ploy. So, play it out. See where it winds up.

"If he's not mine," she said, collecting herself, "why would I work so hard to get him back?"

"Appearances, of course." He chortled, a jolly, avuncular figure. "If you want to keep your throne—"

*What throne?* she thought listlessly.

"—You must remain the devoted mother of the miracle child. Regardless of where he came from. Where is he now, your heir?"

"Himadra stole him."

"Himadra is my ally, and beholden to me to supply his army. If he is wise, he will continue to cooperate with me. What if you spoke on my behalf to young Mrithuri, and won her hand for me? That would be worth the return of your son."

"I have not met our cousin in Sarathai-tia," Sayeh said. "We have no special relationship. What is it that you think I can accomplish on your behalf, Your Competence? And even if I did woo and win her— forgive me for being indelicate—why do you think you will have better luck getting a living heir this time, who have so often suffered such disappointment?"

Anuraja smiled. He was a big man, towering and broad. He would have made half again Sayeh even if she could stand. She had to look up past the armor specially made for his enormous frame to see his face, framed in the collar of his cloak.

"Are you not women together?" he asked. "Is she not likely to heed your sisterly counsel?" His grin widened. "And what are her realistic options? It's me, or Himadra."

"Himadra has brothers."

"Has he." The raja chortled, and cocked his eyebrows in perfect derision. "Maybe he does. But is he likely to have brothers tomorrow?"

"Only the gods can say."

"The gods do what men decide," Anuraja said. "Do you think your cousin would ransom you?"

"What is the point in being ransomed into a city under siege? How would such a message reach her?"

"Messages are easily sent. And are not your men within? Would they not advocate for you?"

In spite of all her practiced serenity, Sayeh struggled to keep her face smooth. Were they within? Had they made it this far?

"Are they?" She tried for quiet doubt. It might have slid into disdain. If it did, Anuraja did not respond to the insult.

"Think you that I have no eyes within our cousin's walls? You thought highly enough of her to send to her for help."

He had given something away there, and he did not seem to realize it. A silence dragged, in which Sayeh kept the recognition off her face by reaching for her cup. She could use the clarifying reassurance of tea. The spices and milk settled her stomach, and the sweetness was just enough to be pleasant. So some of her men *had* made it to Sarathai-tia.

"I have no way to reach any refugees of Ansh-Sahal who may be within the Tian walls, my lord."

Anuraja chortled, as if his thoughts had amused him. "Do not count too much upon your young cousin for relief, Rajni. She is, as you mentioned, under siege herself—and reliant on Eremite poisons for her strength. And that is not the only serpent in her bosom."

He *did* like to gloat about his spies. Really, he was very bad at this game.

Pity he had the armies.

She set the fragile cup down again—and who, she wondered, brought the good porcelain on the war trail? She was glad that she was not the liveried footman or overworked quartermaster tasked with packing and protecting it. A commotion outside startled her so that she almost knocked it over. She had been proud of herself, that her hands only shook with rage a little and that she had succeeded in eating neatly, and controlling them.

Apparently she was nevertheless on edge.

She would have expected one of the footmen to step in and murmur in the raja's ear. Or perhaps a polite and subtle scratching at the post or hangings to announce a visitor coming in.

Instead, the drape covering the entrance was swept aside, and in strode the woman Ravani.

She was mannishly magnificent, tall and broad-shouldered, with her long stride and her mane of unrestrained mahogany-black curls. She wore boots, and the heels clopped on the rugs unrepentant as horse's hooves.

She cast a glance at Sayeh that raked Sayeh like a tiger's claws and sketched a plausible courtesy before Anuraja. It was not *much* of a courtesy. Especially from a lackey who has just charged uninvited into the presence of her lord: a lord who gave every appearance of standing on ceremony.

Anuraja's expression soured from its former smug self-possession, but he did not reprimand her. He drank his tea and frowned.

When he had gathered himself, and without looking at any of the women in the room, he said, "Serve the sweets, girl."

Nazia jumped forward as if pleased to be given a task that relieved her of the need to stand staring vaguely into space, pretending not to notice the politics in the room and the uncomfortable tableau.

"And fetch me a stool and a teacup," Ravani said blandly. "There's a good girl."

Nazia glanced at Sayeh. Sayeh looked at Anuraja, and Nazia's gaze followed. Anuraja, however, gave no sign of having heard, so Sayeh responded with a little shrug of permission. She wasn't going to get in between these two.

Nazia brought the stool from against the wall and foraged a clean bowl from among the trays of utensils. She filled the bowl from Sayeh's teapot—loath, Sayeh thought, to draw Anuraja's attention, and who could blame her?—before bearing the sweetmeats around. She took the tray first to Anuraja, who indicated that she should serve him more than half the contents. Sayeh took two of the remainder, and sent the rest on to Ravani.

Anuraja looked amused. Sayeh would have found his pettiness ridiculous, if he hadn't had an army at his back. She tasted one of the sweets. It was made with boiled milk, and like many southern confections, to Sayeh's taste it was very sugary.

"Did you ever meet the last emperor?" Sayeh asked, as an overture to further conversation.

*That* stopped Anuraja mid-chew. "Many times," he said, with a faraway expression. "He said I reminded him of his father. He said I should have been his heir."

*Did he, now?* "I met him once," Sayeh said. "I was very little and he was very old. He seemed doddering and kind."

"Ah then," said Anuraja. "You never met the real man. I knew him intimately. More tea, child!"

That last came out in a tone of such unwarranted irritation that Sayeh was certain her cousin was changing the subject. So if he had been such an intimate of their illustrious relative ... Well, if she had been in Anuraja's place—and as much a tiresome, self-involved boor as Anuraja—she never would have shut up about being so anointed.

He was ten or fifteen years older than she, if she remembered correctly. She wondered how accurate his memories on the subject were. Men frequently fooled themselves, as if comforting self-delusion were a prerogative of their social power.

Nazia set the tray of sweets down hastily and brought the tea back. She seemed to pick up on Anuraja's mood, because she poured with exquisite, self-effacing care. Anuraja seemed almost frozen while she did it.

Nazia traded pot for tray again, and brought the sweets to the sorcerer.

Ravani, who had regarded Anuraja intently through all of this, waved the sweets away, reminding Sayeh of the cat that will not be tempted by tidbits away from a mouse's den.

When her hand moved, and abruptly as if released from amber, Anuraja shook himself. He blinked, then spoke. "Think about my offer. You may go."

Sayeh would have given a great deal for a canvas bag of ice, chipped from an enormous block such as carters packed in straw and sawdust and trundled down from the glaciers to cool drinks in the dry season. She would not have cooled a drink with it, however. She would have laid it across her eyes until her head stopped pounding. Then she would have taken it off, and laid it across her aching thigh.

She also would have given a great deal just to be left alone for the rest of the day, and allowed to sleep in peace through its heat, but that was not to be. Ümmühan was just arranging the mosquito nets to protect Sayeh's couch when a scratching came upon the door of the pavilion. Unusual: the guards, if they were feeling polite, usually simply scratched and entered.

Ümmühan straightened and pulled up her veil, moving with a gliding grace that made her seem as weightless as a ghost. She drew the door aside, revealing the heroic outline of the sorcerer.

"I wanted to have that talk I promised you," Ravani said. *"Without His Competence in attendance."*

"Cross and double-cross," said Sayeh. "Is that what this is?"

"Oh." Ravani produced a flask from inside her wolf-trimmed coat and brandished it. "You tell me. May I come in?"

With a glance at Sayeh for permission, Ümmühan stood aside.

Ravani strode in. There was only one dim lamp still lit; Nazia was already on her pallet under her own sheath of netting, and did not stir or even breathe out loud.

"You may approach," Sayeh said, as Ümmühan came to prop her up on the pillows they had just removed.

"Thank you, my rajni," the sorcerer said, with a mocking bow. She really *was* a splendid figure. Sayeh found herself envying the sweep of the woman's arm, the breadth of her shoulder, her magnificent command of any space she entered. She dropped onto a cushion without being asked to sit, bringing her face well below Sayeh's. She gestured to Nazia's pallet. "Does your girl drink?"

Nazia held herself very still.

"I think she'd rather rest," Sayeh said. "Waiting on His Competence is a trying role."

Ravani snorted. "You're telling me. And will the rest of you drink with me?"

"If we incur no obligation in doing so," Sayeh said carefully.

"Then may we have three glasses, Grandmother?" she said to Ümmühan respectfully.

Ümmühan slid her eyes to Sayeh again, and again Sayeh tilted her head. Ümmühan returned with a silver tray, and on it three tiny glasses patterned in ruby cut through to clear. They were probably imported from far Messaline, and intended for minted tea in the desert style. It was not tea that Ravani poured into them now, but a fluid clear as water and strangely thicker. It left faint legs up the walls of the glasses where it sloshed as she handed it around, lifting the edge of the mosquito net to give Sayeh hers.

"A toast," she said. "To something other than our host."

Sayeh said, "I'd not attempt to direct the Mother's attention to any goodwill toward that one. Neither would appreciate it. He seems to be a creature of obligations and barter."

"May God grant long life and posterity," Ümmühan offered, as if without thinking.

Ravani looked at the poetess sidelong. "Sure," she said. "I'll drink to that."

Sayeh dipped her fingertip into her glass, and flicked aside her libation. Then she swigged. It was blood-warm from the flask, and at first seemed to have no more flavor than it did tint. Then the heat hit her, a long burn down her throat, and only after she swallowed was her mouth filled with the elusive sweetness and flavor of exotic fruit.

She gasped.

Ravani smiled at her with a blissful, slightly watery-eyed expression. "Good, isn't it?"

"What under all the suns there are is *that*?"

"They make it from a local fruit called *plums*, I think. Up near Kyiv. A worthy, warrior's fate for any produce, I would say."

Sayeh breathed out long and slow in answer. The lingering aroma followed.

"Obligations and barter, you say?" Ravani eyed her half-full glass and touched it lightly to lips that reddened at the contact rather than blanched.

"So what are you offering him?" Sayeh asked.

"I'm going to give him an heir," Ravani said.

Sayeh managed to keep the firewater she had just swigged in her mouth, but barely. She gulped it down, feeling her sinuses burn, and glanced at the woman's muscular midsection.

Ravani laughed—an honest guffaw, not a courtier's tinkle. Sayeh envied her that laugh as well. What was it like, to be a woman and to be so free of pretense for the sake of men?

"Oh, not like that," Ravani said. "Gods, can you imagine? But as you are no doubt aware, he has had some difficulties getting one in the traditional fashion."

"I've heard he blames the women," Sayeh said dryly. Liquor burned her tongue.

Ümmühan added, "All five of them."

"Hah," said Ravani. "Five is only the filet. Only the number he married. No, the problem most definitely lies with the raja. But I can do as I have said." She waved a glittering hand. "It might cost the mother's life. That life force has to come from somewhere, and Anuraja can't provide it."

"Is he sick?" Nazia asked. "Can't you just cure him?"

Ravani smiled at the girl kindly. "Oh, probably. But that's not what he bargained for, and anyway the damage is done. So that's why——"

"He lets you walk all over him," Sayeh finished.

Ravani toasted her with the glass. "That's one way to put it."

"How are you going to find him a wife?"

Ravani tossed back the last of her drink. "Oh, that's where you come in. Because I can offer you a bargain, too. And a better one than——" She jerked her thumb.

Sayeh had no place to set her glass aside, inside the confines of her couch. So she cradled it in her hands, breathing deeply away from the fumes in order to clear her head.

Ravani was pouring for herself again.

"I'm listening," Sayeh said.

"Well," said Ravani. "I am a sorcerer."

"And still looking for consent."

"Or obligation," Ravani admitted. "I am not picky. But here. I'll sweeten Anuraja's admittedly awful deal. Go represent him to Mrithuri, win her hand—and I will bring your people back together in a place where you can lead them. And I will get you back your son."

NOT TOO MUCH LATER, RAVANI TOOK THE HINT OF SAYEH'S YAWNS. After she had left, taking her little bottle of fiery cordial with her, Nazia and Ümmühan moved to help Sayeh undress.

Sayeh needed the assistance. Between the stress of the day and the liquor and her unhealed injury, exhaustion weighed on her like the chains used to break elephants. The pounding in her head was likely to be with her into tomorrow, and possibly beyond. But she still noticed that Nazia seemed troubled.

When she asked, the cloud deepened. But after some coaxing, Nazia said, "You're not going to do what she asked."

Sayeh bit her lip. "I am a queen, Nazia."

"And what does that mean, Your Abundance?" The girl managed to keep her tone pleasant, but her words came out too quickly.

"Come here," Sayeh said from under her covers. "Sit by me."

The girl was skittish and reluctant, but also not ready to disobey a direct order. She came and sat down on a cushion by Sayeh's good knee.

"There," Sayeh said. "Lean your head."

Nazia gazed at Sayeh with wide, untrusting eyes like a half-feral cat who knew her mistress was up to something.

"Indulge me."

With a sigh of protest, Nazia did.

Ümmühan busied herself cleaning up after their visitor. Sayeh smiled after her, wondering how she had survived without the poetess as a friend.

"What it means," Sayeh said calmly, picking up a comb, "is that I need to think of my son and my people, and make their well-being my priority."

The comb slid easily through the barely grown-out scruff of Nazia's hair. It was coming in lighter than Sayeh would have expected: a rich coffee brown with brighter highlights.

"But it's *wrong*." Nazia's voice was small, but courageous.

"So it is," Sayeh agreed.

Her calm tone made Nazia flinch. It couldn't have been the comb, because Nazia had not enough hair to snag it.

"Then why do it?"

Sayeh was quiet for a moment. When she spoke, it was with care. "It seems to me that the difference between a good ruler and a bad ruler is not always what they choose to do. Sometimes it is how—and why— they choose to do it, and whether they justify it to themselves."

"You are avoiding my question!"

Sayeh almost laughed. The girl was so utterly unimpressed with royalty. But Nazia only would have thought that Sayeh was laughing at her. So Sayeh kept her voice soft and said, "I have not decided that I *will* do this thing."

"Murder your cousin so that Anuraja can get an heir even though his jewels are rotting?"

"As you say." The comb moved gently, making a scratching sound. "If I do decide to go ahead with it, however, I will not lie to myself. I will not say to myself that it serves a good cause, or that Mrithuri, too, gets an heir out of it—for what is an heir of one's body whom one has no raising of?—and I will make no pretense that I have chosen to do the *right* thing. Such a deed can *never* be the right thing. Do you understand?"

Nazia did not shake her head, for she was settling under Sayeh's petting. "No. If it's not the right thing, then why do it?"

Sayeh suddenly felt even more exhausted, as if the last of the food, the spirits, the sweets, the tea, and her own tension and fear had all simultaneously abandoned her system.

"Because sometimes the wrong thing can be a necessary thing," she said. "For *my* kingdom. For my *own* child. For you, and all my subjects. But being necessary can never make a wrong thing right."

Nazia seemed to think that over for a little, as Sayeh hid a yawn. Finally, she ventured, "For me?"

"Among others."

"You dismiss me as of no family," Nazia said, her voice going flat to slip between her teeth. "Of no consequence."

Sayeh eyed her calmly, and as Ümmühan brought up the crutch she had somehow obtained while Sayeh and Nazia were at dinner, gently took Nazia by the upper arm, stood her up, turned her around, and set her back a few steps in order to look at her better. Her heart broke, a little.

She *had* wished for a daughter. A daughter as well as a son. Nazia was not a daughter, but if Sayeh had had one, well, she wouldn't have *wished* for a girl like Nazia—sulky, daring, headstrong, too smart for her own safety by half—but she wouldn't have been surprised to get one.

"Why do you suppose that is?" Sayeh said.

That drew Nazia up as sharply as a hand on the rein.

Sayeh leaned on the crutch and shook her head into Nazia's silence. "Do you suppose it would benefit you, if Anuraja thought you of good-enough family to trade on your worth as a broodmare? If not for him, for one of his noblemen made officers, perhaps? His courtiers?"

Nazia bit her lip and shook her head.

Sayeh dropped her voice to a murmur. Not a whisper. Whispers carried. "Worse yet, what if he knew you were an apprentice Wizard?"

Nazia's hand covered her mouth. "Oh."

Sayeh nodded gently. "Oh, indeed."

"I'm not much of a Wizard. I have no power, and Tsering-la had only time to teach me a *little* theory."

Sayeh accepted the crutch from Ümmühan, and with the old woman's assistance, stood. "Anuraja will let us go, if I will work for him."

"'Us'?" Nazia asked deliberately.

For a moment, Sayeh wondered if she *would* leave the girl, if that was the only way forward, or the only way to freedom. She was a queen, and queens were meant to be ruthless. Especially where their own safety and the well-being of their people was concerned.

But Nazia *was* her people. Her own frustrating, rebellious people.

Sayeh dismissed the thought of a solo escape as unworthy of herself, and tried to quell her self-doubt. *Picture yourself as a warrior,* her late husband would have said, *and you can find the path to become one.*

She missed him so.

But she was the only one who could get his son back.

Sayeh distracted herself from dwelling on her own potential inadequacies by becoming angry, briefly, at everyone who had let Nazia down. Whoever they were. Whenever it had happened. She determined she would not be one of them.

Nor would she forgive. Forgiveness was for people who acknowledged wrongdoing and sought to make amends.

"Us," Sayeh said.

Nazia looked down. "I should tell you a thing, Your Abundance."

As Ümmühan led Sayeh toward her cot, Sayeh said, "I am listening."

She swayed on her feet. Nazia sprang quickly to balance her with a hand on her arm. "The sorceress."

Her words seemed to stick. Sayeh stayed quiet, giving Nazia space to finish.

"I met someone like Ravani before," Nazia said softly.

"Someone?" Ümmühan prompted, after a little while. "Nazia, what's wrong?"

Sayeh waited, busying herself with trying to keep her sagging eyelids open. Nazia obviously wanted to tell her, so tell Sayeh Nazia would. In her own due time, if Sayeh did nothing to startle her.

"The man who told me about the bitter water. To bring an ill omen upon your reign," Nazia said at last, reluctantly. "He had eyes like hers."

Sayeh thought of her son, of the story about the elephant and the tiger prince he had made up and told her, his childish morality play.

Ümmühan turned her face aside. "There are beasts that feed on war."

"Ah," Sayeh said. She leaned on Nazia's arm, and handed Ümmühan the crutch. "Well. I do know one thing."

"And what is that?" asked Ümmühan, returning.

"I know what I mean to do," Sayeh said, in a tone intended to carry no farther than the ears of her women as they lowered her into bed. She ached with tiredness. She wasn't sure she could have managed more than an exhausted whisper if she had needed to.

"Tell us, Rajni?" Nazia asked, her lips parted but barely moving.

"It's going to be dangerous," Sayeh said. "For me, and for all of us. Anuraja will see what I mean to do as treachery, if he finds us out. And that's without considering his sorcerer."

She shivered a little, and told herself it was exhaustion.

Nazia regarded her with wide eyes. Ümmühan, long accustomed to intrigue, was oiling a pad of cloth with which to wipe Sayeh's makeup away. The touch of it upon Sayeh's temples, scented and soft, helped a little bit—though perhaps not as much as the ice would.

"I will need both of you to accomplish this," Sayeh said. "Nazia, you must be my legs for now. Ümmühan." She smiled. "You must be my words."

They nodded, each in turn.

In her bones, Sayeh felt the thrill of fear. Fear, and yes—excitement. She drew her lips back tight against her teeth. "Let my cousin think I am cooperative. But—sorceress or no sorceress—I am going to take this army away from *him*, before too long."

6

MRITHURI RAJNI FOLDED HER HANDS IN HER LAP AND CONTEMPLATED A bouquet of monsoon flowers set on the low table before her.

Critically appreciated, the arrangement was . . . unharmonious. An amateur effort at best, and one that did not reflect much natural talent or vision on the part of the person who had stuffed it into the ornate water pitcher it now resided in.

Taken on a personal level, it was an affront. For the focal point of the arrangement was a towering if slightly bedraggled bough of fragrant white almond blossoms, wrenched from a tree in Mrithuri's own sacred gardens. It had been shoved in among a huge bundle of campanula, marigolds, and other violently conflicting colored blossoms that did no favors to its delicate architecture and pale bloom. They were already wilting, as well, because the arranger had not been careful in collecting them, and many of the stems and petals were crushed.

But politically . . . oh, politically, it was useful.

Mrithuri did not delude herself for a moment that Mi Ren, the arrogant Song princeling, had wet his scented head in the chill rain or sweated in her hothouses to uproot her gardens with his own hands. But she was meant to think he had, and to be flattered by it.

She *did* wonder for a few instants if the largely—but by no means exclusively—azure-and-saffron color scheme had been a calculated affront. Probably not, she decided. Mi Ren was not subtle, and beyond a certain animal cunning he probably didn't pay enough attention to anything outside his own immediate needs to realize that those were Anuraja's colors, and that Anuraja was the person laying siege to all of them.

Mrithuri gave the folds of her costume a flick to smooth them on the cushions around her, reminding herself at the last moment to make it a ladylike gesture rather than one that was irritated. Not that it mattered too much, when the only people in the room with her were her ladies of the bedchamber and Hnarisha. And of course the nuns in their cloister within her walls.

Mrithuri was no fool. She knew perfectly well that the builders of empires, such as her great-grandfather's father, had a vested interest in convincing onlookers—and perhaps even themselves—that their empires had precedent. A lineage, a history.

Mrithuri could be that, for the right prince. Or rather, it was a honeyed fig she could tempt them with.

She stood and went to her window. The city lay below, rooftops stretching to the walls that encircled it. If she were to turn and cross the room, look out another window, she would see the gardens down to the river, and the high walls bounding them. And the dust of the army beyond, or the smoke of their camp. But from here, she could see flocks of birds rising into the brilliance of evening, and the darting gray shapes of long-tailed monkeys running across the rooftops. Their shrieks rose up with the smoke of cooking fires as they contested territory between two troops.

*That's us,* Mrithuri thought. *That's all this nonsense amounts to.*

Bitter tiredness swamped her.

She turned back to Hnarisha, Yavashuri, and Chaeri, who were all studiously engaged in appearing absorbed at such small hand tasks as embroidery and letter-writing. They were already looking up before she cleared her throat.

"I need a list," she said. "Other than Mi Ren, what nobles can I string along into competition for my hand in marriage?"

Chaeri said, "We're under siege. Won't it seem a little obvious?"

Mrithuri laughed bitterly. "Men think a grateful woman will overlook their flaws."

"Do you plan to marry one of them?" Yavashuri asked.

"Will that be necessary in order to secure my position? Or will making a few of them hopeful suffice?"

"How will you get messages out?" Chaeri asked.

Mrithuri restrained herself from rolling her eyes. Just. She raised her hands, thumbs interlocked, to symbolize the bearded vultures that were among the sacred beasts tattooed on her arms.

Hnarisha chuckled. "Well, that will impress the lads." He paused, and glanced at Yavashuri.

She nodded.

Hnarisha said, "I think we should consider sending messages to all of your potential suitors, my rajni. The Rasan princelet, and maybe a Qersnyk barbarian or two."

"How bad are the barbarians?" Mrithuri asked.

"I hear the oldest princelet has some *democratic* ideas." Hnarisha shrugged. "I'll also make a list of Song princes."

"They're all mass-marriers of one sort or another, aren't they? Rasan, Qersnyk, Song?" Mrithuri said, feeling her lip curl. She didn't want one spouse, really. Never mind a couple, and whatever other spouses they might marry. She was a ruling rajni, though. Surely she could set the expectations of any such alliance.

Yavashuri said, "We should also consider who you might actually choose to marry, in the end."

Chaeri moved with nervous steps, pouring tea, as if the conversation discomfited her. Despite her ability to generate dramatic situations, Mrithuri knew that she did not care for change.

Well, they were all going to have to adapt. Assuming they survived the siege at all.

Mrithuri said, "What about Sayeh's son?"

"Well, what about him?" Chaeri said snappily.

"He's only twenty years younger than I. If he were a girl-child, they'd have him betrothed off already."

"Twenty . . . two, I think," said Hnarisha, staring into space thoughtfully.

Mrithuri shrugged, as if it were of no consequence. "I am in no hurry."

She really was not. Twelve years, perhaps, before the boy could marry. Four years longer than that before the marriage should reasonably be consummated, whatever men did with *their* young brides. But he could be betrothed right now. If his mother would permit it.

They both needed allies.

Mrithuri could find a *stronger* ally than Sayeh, to be sure. One with armies and lands. But Sayeh had already reached out to her.

And could Mrithuri find one who was less likely to try to usurp her power?

"You'd still need to get an heir somewhere," Yavashuri said tartly, which wasn't a declaration that it could not happen. She moved behind Mrithuri with a brush and a comb. Hnarisha brought the old woman an oxbow chair, and Yavashuri sank into it. She began untangling and undressing Mrithuri's hair.

Mrithuri sighed in relief as the pulling pins and baubles came out of it. "Well. Let's hope the Gage is successful, then."

THE BEAR-BOARS CAME DOWN THE SLOPE LIKE AN AVALANCHE borne on stiff, piggy legs. Loose rocks scattered before them. Himadra suddenly had his hands full as Velvet shied, spooked, and seemed to relocate herself an arm's-length to the right without ever traversing the intervening spaces. He stayed on her through equal parts skill and saddle design, coldness prickling along his neck and in the pit of his stomach at the thought of what a fall would mean.

At least it wouldn't hurt long, once the bear-boars got their tusks into him.

Velvet's bit was far harsher than such a mild and willing mare would ever have needed, had her rider been normally strong. Himadra used the mechanical advantage of its long arms now. He touched the reins, bringing her head around, forcing her into a tight circle away from the sharp dropoff on the right. This turned her in the rough direction of the charging bear-boars, doing nothing for her physical or emotional equilibrium. It did, however, get her pointed in a straight line again, with Himadra still solidly in the saddle.

Around him, his riders were likewise wrestling whirling, shying horses. With meaty thumps, several of them staggered into one another. It was a piece of luck or the Mother's blessing that none of the animals or their riders fell. Not even the Sahali nurse, who was carrying Prince Drupada on the saddle against her belly, held in place by a sling.

It was all too much for the child, anyway, who straightaway began to scream as though he were being at that very instant murdered.

*You stole the kid,* Himadra told himself. *It's your bloody job to look after him.*

He tugged the rein sharply. Velvet's head came up in protest, her eyes white-rimmed and rolling, her ears pinned with fear. But Himadra got her to steady herself and face the charging bear-boars head-on. She shivered with the need to run, her neck bowed so sharply that her jawbone must have rested against her breastbone. Slaver blew from her mouth. She pawed, but stayed steady.

Around Himadra, his men were sorting their disarray into ranks. He'd lost track of Ravana and couldn't find him now. Maybe the sorcerer's flashy mistreated horse had bolted. Maybe Ravana had just vanished silently and wordlessly, as he seemed wont to do.

"Never a sorcerer around when you want one," Himadra grumped.

Well, he'd just have to solve this little problem himself, then.

Rocks dislodged by the charging bear-boars bounced among the horses' hooves. The very earth underfoot trembled with their thunder. Himadra took a wrap in the reins around his left hand. With his right, he pulled a pistol from the saddle holster and steadied his aim.

Velvet knew what to do for shooting, and she stood like a stone statue of a horse beneath him. The pigs were less than fifty feet away. Himadra sighted between the eyes of the one in the lead and stroked the trigger.

The pistol coughed and slammed the web of his thumb. A sharp reek of smoke stung his eyes and nostrils. The lead bear-boar staggered, shook its head so violently that Himadra could see blood fly, and dropped to one knee.

The boar immediately behind the leader ran up the leader's backside, knocked itself off its own feet, and fell down. The others, squealing, kept coming on.

Himadra blew the smoke out of his nose and reached back to drop the spent pistol in an open saddlebag. He grabbed the second one. His hand was on the grip when the lead bear-boar shoved itself to its feet and shook its head again. A red gouge gleamed on its forehead below the fungoid ears, at its bottom revealing the pale shine of bone.

"Oh, fuck me in an alley," Himadra yelled. "It bounced off? It bounced off!"

Beside him, Farkhad bent a double-curved bow fitted with a short, wicked arrow. The eyes would be a useless target, Himadra saw: too small, and nested in a ridged bulwark of bone. The chest was no better. It would be like shooting into a wagonload of steaks. The neck was thick and powerful—a cantilever of muscle and tendon that projected forward of the fulcrum of the front legs, almost equal to the mass of the proportionally ridiculous body and small rump extending behind.

The tail was nothing but a tufted whip. The hind legs looked insufficient to do much except push and keep the rear end from dragging.

Himadra was willing to bet that these things could turn a corner with supernatural agility.

"Couch spears!" he bellowed. He might not be big, but he had practiced his projection until he had an authoritative voice of command.

His men proved their discipline as well as their mettle. On his right, one arrow flew: the nocked one. Then Farkhad dropped the bow over the horn of his saddle and grabbed the spear carried upright in its holder by his cantle. All around Himadra, there came a rattle as spears were lowered, braced into their rests, and readied.

"Get the kid away!" he yelled back over his shoulder. He didn't have time to see if the nurse obeyed him.

The earth itself trembled under the charging trotters of the bearboars. Himadra could not level his spear; he did not carry one. The shock of an enemy striking the point would have broken his arm bones or shoulder.

Instead, he leveled his second gun. "The big vein behind the ear!" he ordered. "Once you have them on a spear, try to get a blade in there!"

"Just like a slaughterhouse!" boasted Farkhad.

Then the charge was upon them, and there was no time for orders anymore.

Velvet squealed in rage and fear as Himadra abruptly let her have her head again. She staggered forward because she had been leaning on the reins. Around him, his men spurred their horses. The horses, hemmed in by each other, had no place to go but directly at the pigs. Himadra let them leap past him. Velvet wanted to whirl. He widened the reins so she came backward, her head held steady and straight.

The lead pig—the wounded one—opened its mouth in an answering squeal. The face opened like a crocodile's, showing a cavernous pink-and-black mottled space, a wet tongue as long as a grown man's arm, the ridged arch of its palate. Its own blood stained its slaver. Its many teeth were yellow-streaked, unevenly broken pillars.

Himadra shot it through the uvula. Blood and matter exploded out of the back of its neck. He thought, for a wild instant, that it was going to keep running. That it was going to run over him, and Velvet, and just keep going on.

It collapsed as limply and utterly as if it had fallen beneath the butcher's hammer. It skidded forward in the rocky mud, turning half over itself before the back legs, too, quit thrashing and it fell back with a thud. Himadra's heart leaped.

The next pig behind the fallen one hurdled its body and came on, landing with a thump Himadra thought should snap its forelegs. Himadra had two more pistols, but he could not have reached them in time. The charging drift of bear-boars hit the spear thicket, each hog pushed up by the hog behind. Then two or three of the pigs were among the men, and Himadra lost track of everything except the immediate need to keep himself and Velvet from being disemboweled.

The impaled boars were not dead. There had been four at the front of the pack, and each one now squealed and thrust its way up two or three spears, snapping at the hard wood, splintering shafts as they hurled their weight against them. Life was dear to these beasts, and they were churlish of releasing it.

The horses backed and jerked, trying to escape the boars, trying to escape the spurs. The remaining boars were tangled in the hindquarters of the first rank, but soon extricated themselves and began to circle, as if they knew there was easier prey at the back.

Farkhad dropped his spear and took his bow up again. Himadra saw the sense in it. And he himself might not be able to handle the shock of an enemy striking a couched spear, or withstand the draw of a heavy war bow, but that didn't make him inept with a javelin and thrower.

And those, he had.

He couldn't hurl the throwing spears as far or as hard as a man whose bones were not brittle. But he *could* hurl them, and that was better than nothing. Especially now that he and his men had found a few vulnerable points in the bear-boars' armored bodies.

He did not fumble. His hands did not shake, though the earth trembled under Velvet's feet with the thunder of the bear-boars' charge. Himadra fitted the butt of the first javelin into the cup on the thrower and laid the whole lever-arm assemblage along his arm. He wore bracers to protect his wrists from the recoil of his pistols; they also served to prevent him from overextending the joint when he released the javelin. He looked up in time to see a pig whirl, chasing Farkhad as Farkhad reined his horse around.

*Where is that useless sorcerer?*

A horse screamed. Himadra did not allow himself to look, or flinch. The pig turned, and dipped its head to disembowel Farkhad's horse with its enormous tusks. Himadra sighted down the javelin and snapped his wrist over, the lever arm of the thrower propelling the javelin faster and more accurately than he ever could have hurled it.

It sank into the hunting pig's neck behind its fungoid ear, where the massive curve of muscled neck met the curve of the jaw and skull. A gush of blood followed, pulsing. Velvet shied as the arterial spray splashed across her face, ducking in her tracks. Himadra grunted in pain as he dropped—and stopped—with her.

The bear-boar dropped also, a terrific collapsing crash as its forelegs failed and its enormous body's momentum carried it over them in a gigantic somersault. Farkhad's gelding leaped over the predator as it jerked convulsively. The horse staggered as it landed. Farkhad somehow stayed in the saddle.

Himadra fumbled for another javelin as Velvet recovered herself. He fitted it to the thrower, but when he turned his head to seek another target there was nothing. Six boars were down, including the two he had killed personally. The rest were in flight, back the way they had come, some leaving splashes of blood in their wake. He turned Velvet, feeling her trembling beneath him, and turned her again.

Of his own men, none seemed severely injured. He could see one horse limping, but not heavily. One more was down, never to rise again. A third horse was screaming, a terrible sound. One glance told Himadra that it was beyond saving.

Himadra stretched in his stirrups a moment, feeling around his body for broken things. He seemed to have escaped unscathed, for which he thanked the Mother. Farkhad reined his blowing horse up beside Velvet and looked down at his lord.

"Have someone put that poor beast out of its misery, would you?" Himadra snapped, irritated by the waste.

Farkhad gestured for it to be done.

Two men began slitting the throats of downed but still twitching pigs, and paunching the beasts to make sure the meat stayed fresh.

Farkhad waved to the dead pigs. "That solves our little food problem, anyway."

"Temporarily. We can't stop to smoke it." Himadra wiped sweat from his brow with the back of his wrist, and realized only when he saw the pinkness on his sleeve that some of it was blood.

"And we'll be leaving some meat for the bear-boars."

The screaming stopped. Himadra forced himself to watch as the gray horse went to its knees, then crumpled. "At least much of it will be that of their comrades."

"Do you think they prey on riders here often?"

"I don't think they've met such heavily armed opposition in the past."

It had been a measure of Himadra's distraction that he had walked into an ambush. If he did say so himself, that wasn't like him.

In his defense, the ambush had been set—he thought—by nothing human. And the tactical considerations of a bear-boar were doubtless somewhat different than those of a soldier. He glanced around, considering. They hadn't come out too poorly, all things considered. A sense of tactics had saved them from a rout. And from being the dinner, rather than the diners-on.

His stomach plummeted, as if Velvet had dropped out from under him again. "Where's the nurse?" he asked.

Farkhad craned his neck. "You told her to run."

"She seems to have run a little farther than I expected! We need to go after her. Especially as there are man-eating pigs around here."

"You're lightest and on the best horse," Farkhad said. "Junayd is the best tracker. Would you like my advice, Lord?"

With a wave of his hand, Himadra granted permission.

Farkhad said, "Take him and the fastest-mounted men and go after her. The rest can remain behind and butcher as much meat as they can. I can see the tracks from here: she rode back toward Ansh-Sahal."

"There *is* no Ansh-Sahal!" Himadra snarled in frustration.

"One more reason to catch up with her fast. Before something bigger eats her."

"Or she rides into a cloud of sulfuric gas," Himadra agreed. Exhaustion seemed to press his every limb. "All right. You pick the men. Let's go."

# 7

"Oh," said Ata Akhimah, in a tone of bored exasperation. "I think we can handle *this* on our own."

She left Tsering clutching his own blood-soaked rag—if it had not been a rag before, it was one now—and made a sharp, rude gesture. It was obvious from the direction of her glare that she expected the faceless, gutless, liverless object of her ire to collapse immediately back upon the table.

The corpse swung his legs around to the side. Unmentionable things oozed down them.

"Hmm," said Akhimah. She looked at Tsering as the obsidian knife dropped out of the corpse's chest cavity and shattered on the floor.

"Definitely sorcery." The cool professionalism of Tsering's tone was ruined by his hysterical giggle.

"You don't say." The Dead Man groped for his sword. "Any advice on how to put down something that's already missing most of its internal organs?"

The Dead Man closed his eyes in denial for an instant as he heard a series of plops. And a thump. And a number of wet, sticky slithers. He forced them open, and turned to look. A basket lay upturned on the floor beside the worktable next to the slab. Several shiny lumps of meat slumped on the tiles. As he watched, another organ—large, slick, mahogany in color—humped itself over the edge of a ceramic bowl and thwapped against the floor. A liver, he decided. Definitely a liver.

A glistening edge groped out from under the basket. A long streamer of intestine followed, leaving a trail of mucus behind. The Dead Man made an inarticulate noise as the various organs began to hump, crawl, and worm their way toward himself and the two Wizards.

With a grinding noise, the autopsied corpse stood up, sliding greasily off the morgue table.

The Dead Man sighed. "Why did I get out of bed this evening?"

Ata Akhimah would have stepped up beside him, but he ushered her back. From his shoulder, she remarked, "Don't you think one animate corpse in the palace is enough?"

The Dead Man heard a rustle that was probably Tsering-la snapping a horrified glance at her. "Excuse me?"

"It's a long story." The Dead Man's saber was heavy and cool in his hand. It should have been comforting. "Do you think you can fight this thing?"

"Fire," said Akhimah.

"Just the thing for the basement of a palace."

"I should be able to use the Samarkar effect to control it," Tsering said dubiously.

The corpse took an unsteady step forward. Around its feet, jellylike blobs of flesh quivered. With each movement, it sounded like something brittle within the cadaver cracked and shattered.

"Right," said the Dead Man. "I'll hold it off. You get started."

He stepped forward, snakelike, leading with his blade. The corpse batted at him clumsily and he simply flicked the blade out of the way. Unbalanced, blind-eyed, it twisted sideways under the momentum of its own swipe. Somehow its feet stayed planted as its body craned illogically to the right, leaving its flank exposed.

"Gift horse," the Dead Man muttered. He didn't usually talk to himself during a fight, but he didn't usually fight people who had already been through an autopsy. His saber whisked back, the moon-curved edge sweeping through the corpse's left arm with a meaty impact. The Dead Man followed through, swinging his shoulders and his hips into the blow, and let the momentum carry him around. He yelled without really meaning to—a wordless battle cry—and by the time he'd returned to guard position the cadaver's severed limb had thumped to the floor in a nest of bowels.

There was, unfortunately, a splash.

The arm lay there for a moment as if stunned by the fall. Then the fingers uncurled and groped forward, dragging the mutilated object along the floor with painful scratching noises.

A glitter along the edge of his saber caught the Dead Man's attention. "Nicked my blade on the bone," he said in irritation.

"I'll sharpen it for you," said Ata Akhimah.

The Dead Man took a forced step backward and resignedly lopped off the thing's other arm. "You were saying something about fire?"

He took another step back. With sucking sounds, the organs were closing in on him.

"Working on it," said Tsering, amid a rattle of chains. "In the meantime, my advice as a Wizard would be to *get the head*."

"Noted," said the Dead Man.

Banging came from behind him, and a snapping sound. Then the welcome crackle of flames.

The corpse came on, dragging the next slow, staggering foot through a squirming pile of its own offal.

"Now, that's disgusting." With his free hand, the Dead Man made the sign of the pen. The Scholar-God would forgive him for using his left hand when his right one was engaged in so holy an activity as disassembling an abomination.

He stepped back again, almost into Akhimah. Her steadying hand on his shoulder warned him. Also, she squeaked when he nearly stepped on her.

Out of room to retreat, then.

The smell of smoke filled his nostrils. The Dead Man's stomach twisted. As if what was happening weren't bad enough, everything seemed to writhe and pulse and glisten all the more, the scene being lit grotesquely by the flickering oil lanterns and the witchlamps spiraling as Tsering moved.

"The *head*."

"It's not so easy to just lop a man's head off, Tsering!"

The Wizard's tone was sharp with tension. "I wouldn't have said it was so easy to lop an arm off either, and you seem to be managing."

The Dead Man sighed. He'd need to close. Which meant stepping into the puddle of heaving organs.

Well, he couldn't retreat any farther, and they were going to be lapping at his boots anyway, soon. The Dead Man gritted his teeth behind his veil and squashed forward into the pool of bowels.

They smelled like, well. Bowels. They were slick and squishy and they *squirmed* under his soles. And that was before the foul, cold things wrapped around his ankles and began hauling their way up his calves in loops and curls like snakes climbing a tree.

"Keep the light steady!" the Dead Man barked.

"Kind of busy here," said Tsering, but the swaying spirals of his witchlamps steadied.

"Sweet God, write this down better than it happened," the Dead Man prayed. And committed himself to the blow.

He had never been a headsman, but he thought he understood the principle. He struck fierce and hard with his blade horizontal, wishing for the Gage's strength. Wishing for an axe rather than a saber. Glad of the broad false edge in the weak of his blade, which gave it extra weight and cleaving power. All these things at once, and a ferocious concentration on where the blow must land, to cut through cartilage and between vertebrae, and not to turn on bone.

Like axing a chicken. But without the advantage of stump behind it.

The blow landed, and it landed true.

The Dead Man felt flesh part. Felt bone and cartilage snap away from one another. Felt also the fresh crunch of the trachea and the tugging resistance of death-stiff muscle. And something hard and brittle, as well, like striking glass. He felt all of it, every disparate texture.

He felt also the instant when his rear foot, planted as firmly as he could manage among the slippery mess on the floor, skittered out from under him.

He fell.

And fell hard, although he held on to his sword. He would have been hard-pressed to let go of it, when his fingers were clutching for support and balance—and he managed to fall to the side, landing on his hip and shoulder rather than the blade or his wrist.

The wind came out of him with a roar as he toppled into a pile of seething organs. "Ysmat, I am defiled," he wheezed, rolling away as the walking corpse stomped at him. From this angle he had a profoundly unpleasant view up into its scooped-out, flapping abdominal cavity. As if staring up the nostril of a bloody-nosed giant.

He had not entirely succeeded. He'd severed the spine, but the head flopped messily on a thick rope of meat, one side of the skin and muscle of the neck. Something fell upon the Dead Man as he rolled, small and puttering, stinging like pebbles. Loops of bowel wound about him, tightening like ropes. Pulling him down, though he thrashed and struggled against them. They tightened around his arms, his throat, binding his hands to his sides though they were not quite strong enough to strangle him. Somehow—in rolling among the stench of fermented, released bowels, in dodging the enraged stomps of the half-disassembled cadaver—he lost his sword. The corpse clipped the side of his head with a heel, dazing him momentarily. His eyes were blinded with substances that did not bear consideration. Something heavy and slick and cold humped up his neck and shoulder to cover his mouth and nose where his veil had twisted tight against them.

He drew breath—one last full breath through a half-strangled throat, that must see him through the suffocation and keep him fighting if he was to live, though he would have liked to have expressed it in a horrified shriek. And then, suddenly, hands were on him. Hands were hauling him up out of the strangling foulness, and a small sharp knife nicked him as it sliced the loops of intestine free.

*Well, that's going to get infected.*

Ata Akhimah pulled him stumbling to his feet and yanked him into the shelter of the curve of one of the cistern retaining walls just as Tsering-la raised an oil lantern he'd broken free of its chains and had wicked with a bit of rag. The Rasan Wizard dashed the lamp hard against the corpse's midsection.

The lamp broke open in a mess of bent bronze and a welter of shattering glass. Oil rolled down the corpse's still-stamping legs, trailed by a rill of flame, as if the cadaver had pissed himself and it was burning. Flames danced, spreading across the quivering topography of flesh. Edges began to sizzle, and the corpse stamped more frantically as its legs crisped and scorched.

Wet meat doesn't burn very well, even when it's soaked in lamp oil.

"More lamps!" Tsering yelled, as Akhimah and the Dead Man panted and stared.

Akhimah grabbed the nearest one, yanked it from its chains—which seemed to part unusually easily to her touch—and hurled it. Oil splashed, and the flames flared. Their light did little to brighten the cellar with Tsering's witchlamps still burning, but it painted the columns and the walls of the cisterns with a monstrous light.

The corpse staggered. It seemed to be burning on its own right now, its legs and lower body flickering with crawling, unnatural shades of green and coral flame. The flesh on the severed arms blistered, the nails blackening. Bubbles popped in the silverskin of the heart.

Fortunately, there were a lot of lanterns. The Dead Man tore loose and threw the next one—he had been right, the chains were sturdier than Akhimah made them look—and three or four more followed. Akhimah, Tsering-la, and the Dead Man ringed the horrible, stinking, scorching thing, throwing lamps in turn as it lunged toward first one and then another. Like baiting a bear.

Curiously, though the flames licked upward, the joists of the floor above never caught or even scorched and blackened. That must have been Tsering-la's doing.

The cadaver staggered. It reeled and fell to its knees, its feet burned away to stumps. It toppled.

Having no arms, it could not crawl. But it wormed on the floor, thrashing, almost-severed head flopping like the ball on a mace alongside. The lips curled back from the teeth, the eyes poached. The teeth blackened.

They had stopped throwing lanterns by then, because Tsering said he was having a hard time controlling the flames and keeping the rest of the palace from catching. The Dead Man's sword still rested at the heart of the fire.

"Well," he said tiredly. "That's not going to do anything for the temper."

That was when the palace fire brigade arrived, the scent of smoke and burning offal having penetrated to the upper levels at last.

✳   ✳   ✳

MRITHURI WAS HORRIFIED TO LEARN OF THE DOINGS IN THE BASEMENT. But—if she admitted it to herself—not exactly *shocked*. She took herself aside, though, and interviewed each of the people who had been involved separately, with—at first—only Hnarisha as her chaperone and secretary. She met with each of the three—Tsering-la, Ata Akhimah, and the Dead Man—in her retiring room, near the throne room. It was a more formal setting than she might have liked, but there was a table to put tea on, and wine, and she thought it likely that everyone would need it.

She spoke with Ata Akhimah first, and asked the Wizard to stay when they finished. The three of them together took Tsering-la's report. Mrithuri found Sayeh's Wizard to be precise, clever, and to have a good eye for detail. And she was very pleased that Hnarisha kept the tea coming.

She would have preferred the wine, to be honest, but she needed to stay alert. Unfortunately.

When the Dead Man replaced Tsering-la, Mrithuri was already exhausted. But at least she had her questions well-rehearsed.

She tried, while she deposed him, to talk the Dead Man into letting her replace his red coat. It reeked of grease and burned flesh in the most terrible fashion. But some things are beyond the power of even the rajni of Sarathai-tia.

She did, at least, manage to browbeat him into surrendering it and the rest of his wardrobe for cleaning. Mostly by dint of threatening to drop his entire wardrobe into an oubliette with him attached if he didn't.

"I don't believe you have an oubliette, and I can do my own laundry," he grumbled.

"Try me," she said, and prevailed. Though perhaps the laundresses would have preferred it if she hadn't. She sent him away, and told him to attend her when he smelled better. Ata Akhimah laughed, which led Mrithuri to point her toward the bathing chambers also.

In any case, the Dead Man was bathed, combed, perfumed, dressed in borrowed clothes and a borrowed veil, significantly empty of scabbard, and smelling only mildly of smoke and not at all of feces when he presented himself in her war room some time later, where no one attended them except Hnarisha. He even went so far as to admit that the

Sarathai-style tunic and trousers in undyed ivory cotton he now wore were comfortable in the hot humidity.

"You look handsome in ivory," she said, arching an eyebrow at the head wrap and veil that covered his face and hair.

He laughed.

"If you won't take a coat," she said, "accept this."

She reached beneath the sand table—currently unanimated—and drew forth a long bundle wrapped in ivory silk. She relished the slippery texture on fingers for once—in this relative privacy—bare of jeweled fingerstalls.

It was heavy when she held it out to him. She forced her arm to stay steady.

He unwrapped a golden cord and the layers of ivory silk. The raw silk had a particular smell, slightly musty, reminiscent of dried leaves. He drew out a scabbarded saber, tilted his head to contemplate it, and made a curious little noise.

He grasped the hilt and looked at her for permission. "May I?"

Hnarisha looked up from his wax tablet and his stylus, but seemed unconcerned. It seemed he had accepted that the Dead Man was no threat to her. And she had recruited his assistance in procuring an appropriate blade from her storehouses, so the exchange could not be taking him by surprise.

Mrithuri nodded at the Dead Man. "You'll need it."

The blade came free with a whisking sound. It was long, curved, single-edged. Very like the one that had been ruined, but subtly different in its details of manufacture. A Sarathani sword, not an Uthman one.

He turned it in his hand, watching the light reflect along the temper patterns. "I'm afraid I will."

He gave her a look over the forte of the blade that told her he fully appreciated the honor she did him, and the privilege of holding a naked blade in her presence.

He sheathed it again.

"Thank you." He took the empty sheath from his sash, weighed it across his palm for a moment, and laid it across the edge of the sand table.

Mrithuri thought she saw him close his eyes briefly, as if he hesitated or prayed. Then he shifted the blade and scabbard from left hand to right and slid them into place without looking down. It fitted close to how the old one had, Mrithuri noticed with pleasure.

They looked at each other. "It's hard," he said. "Isn't it?"

"Giving away swords?" She made a dismissive wiggle of her hand. "So-so. When they are as pretty as that one I do want to keep them."

He laughed. It warmed her despite the itch in her veins, the craving for venom. She scratched her arm. His eyes followed the gesture.

"Facing a siege," he said.

The playfulness fell away. That deserved a considered answer. "It might be harder if I had the option to go somewhere else," she said slowly. "But this is my city."

He made a noise that was neither confirmation nor disagreement. Mrithuri heard the shuffling footsteps of the nuns in the passages behind the filigree walls, the soft rhythms of their chant.

"You," she said, "choose to stay. I imagine that's harder."

His eyes unfocused, he glanced away. "It might be worse for me because this is not my first siege. You don't know what it will be like."

A spark of irritation lit in her. "Are you trying to frighten me?"

"It's too late now for that to change anything."

Mrithuri turned around and poured herself a glass of tea, as much for something to do with her hands as because she was thirsty. "You *do* know what it's going to be like. And still you stay, as well."

"It's too late now for *that* to change anything either," he said. Casually, he reached out and lifted one of the model cavalrymen from the sand table, turning it in his hand.

He did not even pretend to place his attention on it. He gazed at her so steadfastly over it that she noticed the faint flecks of honey color in the darkness of his eyes. Whatever answer he might have been shaping in that silence, however, he never got to render, as there came an excited pounding on the door.

Mrithuri sighed. She dropped her hand and stepped back. "Enter!" she called.

Chaeri burst into the room, the ringlets of her hair in disarray. "Rajni! The enemy have us surrounded."

Mrithuri fingered the serpent torc at her throat. The scales were cool. She made her voice cool, for coolness would be expected. "That was no more than we expected. They won't stay camped long, with the rains and the river flooding. The Mother will protect us."

Disappointment shadowed Chaeri's face, quickly dismissed. Mrithuri contained a sigh. Chaeri did so enjoy being the center of attention, but the older Mrithuri got, the less she enjoyed the thrill of excitement. Life was difficult enough when everybody kept their head.

"I'd better go and make sure of the defenses, in any case," the Dead Man said. "Some of them might stray within shot. And the first offensive will come soon."

Mrithuri's face seemed to numb as her expression was replaced by a mask. "Serhan."

He paused in the act of turning. "Rajni?"

"There's something the Wizards told me." She took a breath, aware of the eyes on her. "The blood in the assassin's arteries had turned to padparadscha stones."

Chaeri pressed a hand against her mouth in distress. She turned away, going to the low window, where she busied herself laying out crumbs on the sill for the birds.

The Dead Man breathed out once, evenly, the cloth flaring over his nose. "Coral-colored sapphires again? That's getting to be a theme."

"Himadra has a sorcerer," Mrithuri said. "I think it is his signature. His horse's tack was decked with them."

"You've seen this person?"

"Guang Bao did." Mrithuri gestured to where the phoenix snoozed upon a perch, one leg tucked up into the fluff of his belly, his head tucked under one wing. "I rode his memories."

Recalling it unsettled her. She put her hand before her eyes.

Of course the Dead Man noticed. "What happened?"

"He saw me," Mrithuri said. Her pulse beat in her throat, fluttering against the skin-warmed embrace of the snake necklet. "The sorcerer. He saw me somehow. In Guang Bao's memory."

"He saw Guang Bao?"

"He saw *me*," she insisted. "Although when he saw Guang Bao, I had not yet been there."

"Him, you say?" the Dead Man asked. It was not what she had expected him to say.

"You know something I don't."

"When I was in Chandranath, I caught a glimpse of Himadra and Anuraja. And there was a sorcerer in their retinue. Whose horse wore a tigerskin blanket, decked with padparadscha stones."

Mrithuri heard the note of hesitation. "But?" she prompted.

"But it was a woman."

"A woman."

He nodded. "A person I met said Ravani was her name."

She turned to Chaeri, who had crouched by the windowsill and was chirruping softly to a finch that seemed to be ignoring her in favor of some bits of cake. Chaeri stood, smiling sheepishly, when Mrithuri said her name.

"Send a page to fetch Yavashuri, and send the Wizards to the battlements to support the men guarding them."

THE DEAD MAN WOULD HAVE LEFT THEN, BUT AS HE STEPPED TOWARD the door, Chaeri finished by the door and returned, moving closer to the queen. The Dead Man was new here; he was a retainer of little standing. But he cared about Mrithuri, and he worried about Chaeri and her influence over the queen.

It was not his place to worry. And Chaeri seemed to have set her cap for the Gage, before the Gage had gone away, and the Gage had not seemed resistant. Maybe he was misconstruing her, he thought. He had certainly gotten people wrong before.

He worried, anyway.

As he paused, he saw Chaeri lift something from the table beside the door.

"Rajni," Chaeri said. "You seem tired."

The Dead Man watched as Chaeri extended the box she had just picked up; a heavy case of aromatic wood carved into a filigree. Within, through the small gaps in the panels, he glimpsed sliding movement. The Dead Man wasn't sure exactly how many dwelt within, but he knew what the case contained: Mrithuri's Eremite serpents, who took her blood in exchange for a venom that sharpened the mind and quickened the senses.

The Dead Man had lived long enough, in enough varied places, to know that such drugs—whether they were of natural origin, sorcerous, or from the old poisonous world of Erem—never came without a cost.

With an effort, he managed not to rest a hand on the hilt of the sword Mrithuri had given him.

Chaeri's hand was on the hinged lid of the box. The Dead Man breathed a sigh of relief when Mrithuri waved her maid away. He liked the look of Mrithuri's fingers without the elaborate golden stalls on them; sinewy, articulate. Too thin, which worried him, but at least even in a siege the rajni would eat. So long as food could be had at all, anyway.

"If only you had an heir," Hnarisha muttered. He stood, holding his tablet and stylus by his side.

Mrithuri picked nervously at her cuticles. That habit, at least, the stalls would prevent. The Dead Man wished she'd unhunch her shoulders and look less frightened. It was not good for her people to see her fearing defeat. Selfishly, he also knew that it was not good for *him*.

Chaeri stepped back. She did not put the box of snakes away. "That's what we sent the Gage to ensure, isn't it? Perhaps he will return quickly."

The Dead Man set the carven cavalryman back down on the sand table. Superstitiously, he arranged the figurine among the ranks of his fellows in an orderly fashion, as if that might have some bearing on the combat to come. "Even if the Gage makes it back with some magical philter of baby-making before the city falls, how is the rajni getting with child going to lift a siege in progress?"

Chaeri said, "It will cut down on Anuraja's reasons."

The Dead Man said, "Kings don't need reasons. They need excuses. And a tactical advantage."

At that moment, Yavashuri entered in a swirl of blue-green drapes and a quick shuffle of bare, brown feet. "I have written to your potential suitors. The vultures are on their way."

The Dead Man struggled under a great and heavy weariness as he considered whether those negotiations might have any effect. They needed to lift the siege. If Mrithuri could show strength, and the ability to withstand her cousin's advances—military and otherwise—she would be in a good position to negotiate an advantageous marriage. Preferably to a younger and malleable son of a kingdom that might dower him with some significant military might.

*Mercenaries*, the Dead Man thought, watching Yavashuri settle herself.

Mrithuri's kingdom of Sarathai-tia was not wealthy in trade or resources. It was wealthy only in the sense that it was agriculturally rich,
and had a thriving and skilled population. Those were resources, and
useful resources in a war—or to a conqueror. What she needed now,
however, was more troops.

It was traditional to recruit men into one's army with the promise
of spoils. But for that to happen, Mrithuri would have to first lift the
siege, and then pursue Anuraja's army back into his own territory, laying its people to the sword if they resisted the pillaging that was sure
to follow. Mrithuri would see those people as her people—or as her
great-great-grandfather's people, in any case. She would resist the expe-
dient path to victory.

This was, the Dead Man thought, a reason to follow her. And a reason why he might wind up dying by her side.

The Dead Man suddenly realized that in thinking, he had lost track
of the conversation. And done so at a singularly bad moment, because
what brought him back to attentiveness was Yavashuri's venomous, flat
drawl. Without the slightest edge or rise to her voice, the old spymistress was saying, "Chaeri, it was you who gave Anuraja the excuse he
needed to invade when you stuck a knife into his ambassador. So perhaps you will forgive us if we treat your political counsel with a certain
skepticism now."

"It was his own knife," Chaeri replied acidly. "Would you rather I'd
stood aside and allowed him the opportunity to stick it into our rajni?"

The Dead Man was contemplating intervening, but again was
stopped by not really being a part of this society, these relationships. If
he stepped in, he would be placing himself in the position of target on
both sides, and . . . whatever he felt for Mrithuri, the politics between
her retainers were not his business.

But apparently she realized that they were hers, because she stood
abruptly, and the quarreling stopped mid-word. "Solutions," she said.
"Not arguments."

The Dead Man said the first thing that popped into his mind. "There
are a lot of diamonds paving the Peacock Throne, Rajni. And the throne
itself . . . is gold."

"And yet here I am, a woman and not an emperor or even a raja, and
forbidden to sit in it," she answered.

"It's the treasury your ancestor left you, is it not? A few of those could hire a lot of loyalty. Mercenaries, I mean. If we borrowed them . . . against future replacement."

"The Mother would likely set fire to your hand if you tried," Yavashuri said. "You don't think Her Abundance sits in a chair of estate beside the damned thing because she doesn't *want* to claim the authority that throne would give her, I hope?"

"I assume somebody in history has tried sitting in it? Somebody not entitled, I mean?"

Hnarisha folded his hands. "Actually, I don't believe so. But the Alchemical Emperor made the thing, and it was he who proclaimed that only a true raja of the Lotus Kingdoms could sit in it. Mrithuri's grandfather did, and was not destroyed, so it is not necessary to be an emperor. The kingdoms had already broken apart during his father's long illness, and his grandchildren and cousins and nieces and nephews have not felt . . . inclined to test the Alchemical Emperor's ban. Or have not had access to the throne in order to test it. For obvious reasons."

"Can you . . . explain the line of descent? And how Her Abundance's grandfather came into possession of the throne, but not the empire?"

Hnarisha looked at Yavashuri. "You grew up here."

Yavashuri shook her head. "It's a mess. Here, I need paper."

She found some, and a brush and ink, and sketched. "Here's the Alchemical Emperor. He died . . . sixty years ago or so. At a very advanced old age of something like a hundred and ten."

"One hundred and eleven," Hnarisha said helpfully.

Yavashuri rolled her eyes at him. "You do it, Yavashuri," she mocked. "I'm a wee outlander with no history."

Hnarisha ducked his head and grinned. His complexion was such that the Dead Man could not tell if he blushed.

Yavashuri's brush darted, dotting little symbols on the paper and connecting them with lines. "Anyway, he collected brides and concubines like one of those Song princes. Who can keep track of them all? And he outlived his own senior wife, and all the senior wife's sons. The grandchildren who lived were both daughters."

"These?" The Dead Man pointed at the rightmost set of squiggles.

"No, I didn't bother putting them down." Yavashuri pointed at the left edge of the paper. "They'd be over on this side. Now here's the line that did inherit. The Alchemical Emperor's son, Gurmitra, here—he became emperor after."

"But that's not Mrithuri's line."

"Nor Anuraja's," Yavashuri said. "Though this royal family has an annoying tendency to refer to all their older generations as 'grandfather' and 'grandmother,' which worsens an already confusing dynastic situation."

"The Boneless and brothers have some of that on the distaff, I think," said Hnarisha. "One of the daughters is his . . . grandmother?"

"Anyway," said Yavashuri, "Gurmitra was already very old when he inherited. This happens when your father dies at one hundred and"— she looked askance at Hnarisha—"eleven. Two of his older siblings were already gone. And he managed to hold the empire together for a few years. But his health wasn't good, and . . . well, it was a big family."

"With a lot of ambitions," Hnarisha added.

"Long before he died, the whole thing crumbled. That would have been—well, Sayeh would have been a very little girl. And I was still pretty enough to be dangerous." Yavashuri fluttered her lashes in parody.

"It's not a big family now," the Dead Man observed. "So there was a civil war."

With slashes of her brush, Yavashuri obliterated several entire lines of descent. "There were a lot more, but the family never really recovered from them all slaughtering each other. So, in the end, what was left was a bunch of cadet branches scattered around the Lotus Kingdoms in little townships and keeps—and one remaining main line of the royal family who declared truce and decided to split up the bigger cities as spoils of war and stop killing each other. Mrithuri, Sayeh, Himadra, and Anuraja are all descended of that line."

"But isn't Anuraja oldest? Why isn't he emperor?"

"The winners of the bloodbath, if you can call them winners, were the children of Harsha Raja, son of the Alchemical Emperor. Harsha did not survive the war himself. Anuraja is from a distaff line. His mother, Indumathi, had married a wealthy commoner, somebody with a lot of shipping, I think. Her husband declared himself raja of Sarathai-lae based on fiat, royal marriage, and a private army. He had a lot of money and a lot of mercenaries and none of his in-laws really wanted to fight about it anymore, as I understand the matter."

"'Indu,' in her name. I don't know that word."

Yavashuri looked at Hnarisha. Hnarisha said, using the Asitaneh word to translate, "It means 'moon.'"

"But your sky doesn't have a moon."

"Oh, it used to," said Yavashuri, and before the Dead Man could muster words through his surprise to ask, she continued, "Indumara was our raja in Sarathai-tia. He was the oldest surviving son of Harsha's line. He was our rajni's grandfather. His youngest brother, Jagadisha, was Sayeh's grandfather. He ruled the north, and it would probably still be unified if he hadn't split the kingdom between his sons, giving Ansh-Sahal to Sayeh's father and Chandranath to Himadra's grandfather. The argument at the time was that they had different languages and no good route between them, but I think he just wanted to avoid a family quarrel while he was on his deathbed. I think I've got that all right. I may have missed a generation somewhere."

The Dead Man pressed his fingertips to his eyes. "So nobody has a really good claim to be emperor. Which is why Anuraja wants our rajni. To consolidate his claim. Didn't anybody write this *down*?"

"Records," she said, "can vanish when they are inconvenient."

The Dead Man subsided. For all he knew, these heathen gods probably *would* strike him down for his temerity if he tried prying a few stones loose. Never mind the look on Mrithuri's face if he suggested it to her. These bans and proscriptions frustrated him, however. Surely the rajni's illustrious ancestor would not have wished his descendent to fear claiming her rightful legacy simply because she happened to be a woman, and he had shortsightedly declared that only a rightful raja could sit upon his throne?

Well, maybe he would. And serve him right if he wound up with Anuraja as his heir because of it.

"Anyway," Mrithuri said, "that throne is a symbol of the Alchemical Empire. I will not be the one who defaces it."

*Even to save the people of that empire?* The Dead Man managed to keep his lips closed over that sentiment, but he did say, "There *is* no Alchemical Empire. Except in that your cousins wish to marry you by force to resurrect it."

As the words left his mouth, he flinched, expecting outrage in response. He was not prepared when Mrithuri grinned at him, showing more and sharper teeth than the Dead Man would have expected a pretty girl to have. "Let them try."

Then her frown returned. "Leave me," she said, with a grumpy sweep of her palm.

The Dead Man was the first on his feet.

"Not you." Mrithuri dismissed the rest of her entourage with a chopping gesture, more abrupt than the last one. "The rest."

"Rajni," Chaeri protested, the box of Eremite serpents in her hands, just as Hnarisha said, "The propriety—"

"Are you going to mutter about me in corners?" Mrithuri snapped. "No? Then go."

Chaeri set the box on the table, perhaps harder than was necessary. Heavy bodies slid within. Chaeri smelled of sandalwood and irritability as she brushed past the Dead Man on her way to the door.

Yavashuri was already leaving, unlocking a filigree door that the Dead Man had not previously noticed, into the filigree halls of the cloister. Hnarisha looked after her for a moment with concern, as if he might call her back. Then he followed Chaeri out with much less ostentation, closing the door behind himself with the utmost softness.

No melodrama there.

Yavashuri stopped, the door half-shut behind her. She spoke through the openwork carving. "You protect her because she is your favorite, Rajni. And because she feeds your craving for the venom and does not make you ask."

"Do not forget that you are my favorite too," Mrithuri said.

"Your Abundance . . ." Yavashuri drew herself up. "Ask yourself whose advantage is served by my counsel, and by Chaeri's."

Mrithuri closed her eyes. The Dead Man saw how delicately she avoided turning toward the box of serpents. "You may go, Yavashuri. And don't ask the sisters for any favors while you are in there. I need you back."

With a smile and a precise bow, Yavashuri closed the door behind her. It sealed seamlessly into the panels, even the hinges invisible to all but the closest inspection. She whisked away in a rustle of draperies, vanishing into the shadows of the cloister.

"Hnarisha will listen at the door, you know," the Dead Man said in a lowered tone.

"I should be disappointed in him if he did not." The tartness of Mrithuri's tone was leavened slightly by a belated smile. "But I am a queen. I can endure having only the illusion of privacy. So long as I at least get that occasionally."

She shook her head. "I wanted to ask you in private. Do you know what has become of Nizhvashiti?"

The Dead Man felt his face tighten. He thought back, picturing the gods-gifted priest who had accompanied him and the Gage to this besieged little city from a place in the mountains. "I do not know. I have not seen them . . . it . . . since . . . since right after the assassination attempt."

"Well." Mrithuri sighed. "It is freshly dead. Freshly revenant? I imagine some aspects of that might require privacy. And priests are known to meditate. Still, I will send pages to seek it, when we are done here."

"I wonder why Anuraja is holding his attack."

"He seeks some advantage."

"Possibly merely to make us anxious and hasty."

Mrithuri touched the back of his hand with the back of her own. "Would you show me your face?"

The Dead Man felt himself smile behind his veil. He hoped he sounded as if he were smiling. "If we were married."

She touched the veil. "I would not like for you to have to kill me."

"Let us avoid that outcome, then."

Mrithuri said, "I had hoped we might have a little uninterrupted time together."

"We have what we have, what is written with God's pen. And no man nor woman may know what the next day brings, no matter that we can convince ourselves otherwise."

"What about Wizards? What about portents and prophecies?"

"Man plans," the Dead Man teased. "God edits."

Mrithuri looked crestfallen, but he liked her too well to lie to her. She would learn. Grab what you can when you can honorably grab it, because everything would end in dust before long.

What lasted?

Honor. Reputation. What one built with one's hands.

The Gage.

The Dead Man smiled at that, the veil moving against his face. Yes, the Gage would last.

He wondered how his old friend was faring. He should ask the queen, who had sent one of her bearded vultures with him so there was some connection there.

But not now, not right this second. In a little while, when her grief had—not passed, for when did grief ever pass?—but settled. When they had dealt with the immediate crisis of . . . well, of waiting, and defending. Of determination.

Of *will*.

# 8

*I WISH THE DEAD MAN WERE ALONG ON THIS ONE*, THE GAGE THOUGHT, watching the ochre-stained wings of Mrithuri's bearded vulture familiar circle overhead. That was a foolish wish, of course: where he was walking, no flesh could follow. He was bound to a poisoned land. And no flesh could keep pace with him along the path to get there, either. The Gage had no need for rest. He could maintain his ground-eating stride day by day, night by night, year by year if need be.

He was not made to need rest. He was not made to need sustenance. He was not made to need companionship, or conversation, or a kindred spirit.

What his self had, by his nature, needed from before his making— or his remaking, if one prefers—well, those needs, no self-respecting Wizard would accept responsibility for. Those were between who the Gage had once been and ceased to be, and a more ultimate Creator. No interim god need be concerned.

In any case, it was a long walk. And the Gage was in a hurry.

By night, the bearded vulture flew slow loops overhead in the light of the Heavenly River, pausing to feed when they came upon something that had been unlucky. By the darkness of day, the bearded vulture found a place to roost, and the Gage toiled on. The bird always caught up again in the mornings.

The Gage realized that he did not know if the bird had a name. He'd neglected to ask, and Mrithuri had not volunteered the information. It seemed to him that he needed something to call the creature. Especially after a few days, when it came and rested on his shoulder, drying its huge wings between rainy-season squalls, in the lightless heat of the Cauled Sun, then tucked its head and roosted there.

After that, they were not parted.

Despite the lack of name, the Gage sometimes spoke to his feathered companion. He decided to call it Vara. It never answered, but he suspected Mrithuri could hear whatever he said to it, if she happened to be listening. So he related his progress, and sometimes, for lack of anything better to do, he offered a bit of his philosophy.

They were counting on him, back in Sarathai-tia. The Eyeless One had sent them a message. More than that, she had all but ordained this mission as necessary to their survival. And Wizard-Princes did not normally waste their strength on optional prophecies.

The Gage kept walking.

It occurred to him, not for the first time, that he could have made much better time on the way to Sarathai-tia, alone. He wondered if he could have survived walking across the bottom of the Arid Sea, or if the pressure of the water would destroy him. But the Eyeless One had sent him *and* the Dead Man, so she must have believed that the errand demanded both of them.

The Gage was lonely, but he was also comfortable being alone. Being who he was, what he was, when he was around people he must always be cautious. It was too easy for him to harm anything he touched—whether flesh, or artifice. So he could only be relaxed in solitude. That's when he didn't have to worry constantly about the fragility of people and dwellings and things.

The bearded vulture was his responsibility, it was true. But the vulture could largely take care of itself. And being winged, it could keep up. Or simply ride upon his shoulder, if it grew tired.

This freedom could have been intoxicating, the Gage thought. Addictive. He'd almost forgotten how fast he could move when no one was restraining him with their human frailty. He could get addicted to his own strength and independence, given half a chance. There was a joy in covering ground so efficiently. A joy in the straightness of his track, uninhibited by the need to rest or deviate in response to variances in the terrain as he would if he were accompanied by humans.

He just walked. And kept walking, through the rain and the rice fields and the mango plantations, their trees hung with black pepper vines. Through the villages and the places where cotton was planted, and up the slopes where the tea camellias grew.

People turned to watch him, and withdrew from the road before him, when he bothered to be on the roads. He paid them no heed. He walked.

And he walked in the lonely places too, where he passed no villages and fewer refugees from the war he was leaving behind—when he returned to the roads as was convenient. The armies had not yet been here. The Gage, when he spoke with Mrithuri's people, left them with a warning that they soon might.

He carried the rajni's symbol on his shoulder. Her people listened to him.

And the only advice he could give them was to hunker down, preserve such food as they were able to, and be ready to run.

He clanked his irritation to himself. If he could do more—

But for now, this was what he could do. This was the work before his hand.

ON THE TENTH DAY, THE GAGE WALKED OUT OF THE RAIN. HE CAME OVER a ridge in the mountains and beyond the narrow pass, found himself in a dry place. A desert, stretching out in a great bowl before him—and in the far distance, the shimmer of water, and a roil of cloud or steam.

He brushed the cowl down from the featureless mirrored oval of his head. He spoke to the vulture on his shoulder. "Well. Do you suppose that is the Bitter Sea? It certainly *looks* as if a volcano happened."

The vulture cocked its head, examining the reflection of its own crest and brilliant eyes in the Gage's metal dome.

This slope of the mountain range was obviously the drier side. It seemed that the clouds of the rainy season had broken for now, revealing the dark face of the Cauled Sun. The Gage's soaked robe steamed in the heat as he descended. Though the sky held clear overhead, storm clouds were piling up on the far horizon, striving as if held back by an invisible wall.

The Gage's path, still carved as straight as he could carve it, would take him by the shore of the inland sea he overlooked. He wouldn't risk walking through it, all musing aside. Brass might corrode, and the bottoms of bodies of water were notoriously soft and silty. He might wind up mired there for millennia if he weren't careful.

But he did wonder if it would cost him significant time to skirt the water more distantly. He probably wouldn't survive the direct impact of a volcanic eruption. *That* would melt the brass and fuse the gears of his limbs. But a cloud of steam, and perhaps of sulfuric acid?

Well, it wouldn't be healthy for him. But it probably wouldn't be fatal. And his parts were replaceable. If they happened to get acid-etched.

It might be worth going closer. Just to examine the damage.

Of course, he would have to send the vulture by a different route. But he had known all along that there would come a time when the bird and he must part ways, because nothing living could approach the Singing City of the dragons without succumbing to their flesh-rotting curse. He had known since he left Sarathai-tia that he would be traveling to places that nothing living could safely enter. This was just... a little sooner than anticipated.

*Yes,* he thought. *I will go and see what I can see. And I will trust the bird to have the sense to stay away from me while I do.*

So it was that the Gage was alone when he found the city of Ansh-Sahal. Or the ruins of it.

There was no life left within.

The city had not been flattened, obliterated, as the Gage anticipated. There was evidence of earthquake damage, certainly. Crumbled walls and collapsed ceilings, empty streets, the stinking corpses of livestock and pets, the reek of sulfur still rising from the poisoned earth.

The craning, barren, withered corpses of the trees. The blighted husks of crops and flowers.

Ansh-Sahal had been made a terrible place. A hot and empty hell.

Too empty.

Because as the Gage walked—at his unrelenting, unvarying pace, about half again as fast as a trained human soldier—he noticed something missing. There were dead horses, dead chickens. Dead dogs and monkeys. Corpses bloated and peeling in the steaming heat. They lay amongst the stones of tumbled buildings, the tiles of collapsed roofs. They had been scalded by the steam of a boiling sea and crushed beneath the arches of a falling bridge.

There were so many dead animals. So many.

And none of the corpses were those of human beings. Not a single one.

IT WAS WHILE HE MOVED THROUGH THE EMPTINESS OF THE DEAD CITY that the Gage found Nizhvashiti drifting beside him. Perhaps it was a hallucination, brought on by the fumes or the horror, if the Gage was capable of hallucinations. The Gage was not actually sure. In any case, there was Nizhvashiti, floating alongside smoothly, black robes trailing in the dust.

"Where did you come from?" the Gage asked equably.

The Godmade, gliding effortlessly a handspan above the ruined street, inflected a hooded face toward him. Nizhvashiti seemed to be gazing at the Gage, and perhaps smiling slightly with those drawn, cracked black lips. But neither eye in its dark face blinked, and neither was really an eye, anymore. One was a featureless orb of gilded stone; the other the translucent, chiming crystal that the Messaline Wizard-Prince called the Eyeless One had sent as her only weapon to help Mrithuri—along with a few lines of doggerel.

The effect of that regard was profoundly unsettling, even to one such as himself.

"What?" Nizhvashiti asked, in what would have been an utterly ordinary tone had it not been so dry and whispery.

"I'm beginning to understand why people find me so distressing," the Gage admitted, watching the featureless reflection of his own mirrored visage move across the mirrored surfaces of the Godmade's mismatched eyes. "Are you avoiding my question?"

"Of where I came from? No, I am not avoiding it. It's just that I do not exactly have a precise answer." The Godmade sighed, even more whispery. It seemed to find not having that precision at its disposal painful. "I suppose, first principles—"

"When a mommy saint and a daddy saint love each other very much—"

The laugh rasped more than whispered. "The word you are looking for is 'ansha.'"

"Ansha." The Gage felt it resonate within the empty spaces of his body.

"You say Godmade, but really what I am is . . . God-inhabited. A part of a whole thing," Nizhvashiti explained. "A fragment. As I have within me a fragment of the Good Daughter, embodied in this flesh, which hath a human mind and will of its own that nevertheless strives to be obedient to the demands of the godhead."

"That sounds terrible," the Gage said, unthinking.

"Speaks one who knows."

It was the Gage's turn to laugh, more in startled surprise than in humor. His laugh boomed across the devastated landscape, hollow and strange, and he felt at once awkward and terrible when it echoed back to him. What monster laughed in an apocalypse?

As the sound trailed off, Nizhvashiti gave him what might have been a sympathetic look through its drawn and wasted face. "We laugh when the pain and fear would otherwise be too much."

"And our laughter sounds like pain."

"Mine certainly does," the Godmade admitted. "I suppose my lungs will one day dry up entirely, and I shall have no voice. But . . . no, to answer your question of so many steps ago, I do not know how I came to be here. Things are . . . perhaps things are a little as if they were in a dream. If I travel, it does not seem to be entirely by will. Or my own will, under my own direction. And it does not always seem connected, one place to another, by the places in between. I was . . . elsewhere. And then I was here."

"Elsewhere?"

Nizhvashiti shrugged, robes rising and falling along with the emaciated shoulders as if there were nothing but bones within.

Honestly, that seemed likely. If not now, then soon.

"Do you think that has to do with being dead? Or with—" The Gage tapped the mirrored egg of his facelessness where an eye might have been.

Watching as Nizhvashiti's concealed feet never touched the street, the Gage realized what else was missing, besides the human cadavers.

Though this was a city destroyed by a volcano, there was no ashfall. And no lava. Just fallen stones from the shaking earth, and animals dead of scalds and poisoned air.

"The Eye of the Eyeless One?" Nizhvashiti asked, disrupting his— well, you couldn't quite call it an epiphany. "Perhaps. Who can tell where the currents of She Who Nourishes will bear us, except that as we are obedient to them, we shall wind up borne to the sea?"

*I never get to road trip with an atheist.* The Gage sighed inwardly.

He would have said it out loud, to the Dead Man. He did not feel he knew Nizhvashiti that well.

"Are you really here?" he asked instead. "Or are you—"

"A projection? I am uncertain, though my lack of contact with the ground would seem to argue in favor of the theory. If you'd care to, you may poke me, and find out."

"Not just yet," the Gage said dubiously. What if he poked Nizhvashiti and it vanished?

He found he wanted the company.

As they had been walking—or as the Gage had been walking, and the Godmade had been gliding—they had made their way closer to what must have been the palace precincts before the city fell. The stench was growing worse, the Gage noticed. That he had no more nose than he had eyes did not any more stop him from smelling than it did from seeing.

He wondered if the Godmade could see, with two mineral orbs for eyes.

He didn't feel he knew it well enough to ask that, either.

And then Nizhvashiti said, "Fascinating, is it not, that we are both after a fashion manufactured?"

"How so?"

"You by a Wizard. I by my God."

Perhaps they did know each other well enough for awkward questions, after all. "They call you Godmade, and yet so much of what I see before me is your own design. It seems to me that you have made yourself more by your own will than been formed by your god's."

The dead priest chuckled. "Would anyone do such a thing if not driven to it by an immanence?"

"Isn't that what the Cho-tse call their deity? The Immanence?"

"I don't think they would call it a deity, precisely."

It was the Gage's turn to shrug, which he did with a certain grinding and a hollow rattle. He needed sealant. Well, that was easily remedied.

"They say the self-blinded have the power of far-sight."

"So they do say," the Godmade answered agreeably.

Since they knew each other so well now, the Gage asked, "Where do you suppose all the human bodies are?"

Nizhvashiti drifted along for a moment, hands folded inside its sleeves. "It's possible survivors came and claimed them."

"Through this?" The Gage waved a brassy gauntlet through a tendril of yellowish, suffocating miasma.

"'Possible' and 'likely' are not such close cousins they must avoid marriage," Nizhvashiti said, and whatever that meant it had the tone of an admission.

THE PALACE OF ANSH-SAHAL SEEMED VERY DIFFERENT FROM THAT OF Sarathai-tia, to the Gage's perceptions. The city was not, for one thing, built up and carved out of a constructed, conical mountain, rising in a terraced spiral to the crowning fortress. Nor did it project into the broad flood of a sacred river on a slender, sweeping peninsula. This city, from its position among the hills, atop a cliff overlook, commanded the approaches across the Bitter Sea. But the palace was not raised above the city it had until so recently ruled and defended, but rather surrounded by it.

This was all poisoned, too. The Gage missed Vara. He was glad it had gone on to wait for him.

It was past sunset by the time the Gage and his possibly spectral companion at last reached the square outside the palace gates. Those weirdly piled clouds still heaped up along the horizon, like smoke swirling behind glass but somehow weightier. As if there were a pressure behind them—the heaviness that presages a storm, but constrained until it built up intolerably in the hollow spaces of the Gage's constructed body.

There was no Cauled Sun in the sky, no Heavenly River spooling its brightness across the firmament. There was blackness, and the blackness was picked out in little stars that shone with a cold silver light that cast no shadows but made everything seem as flat and foreign as cut paper shapes layered on a canvas. The Godmade's dragonglass eye shimmered with its weird green light. It was bright enough for the Gage to see. It would have been dark, for a human.

"What is this?" the Gage asked.

Nizhvashiti let its head fall back on its emaciated neck, staring blindly upward. "This is a dead sky."

Those palace gates had been immense constructions of relief-carved sandalwood once, hung on iron hinges as thick as the Gage's forearms. The Gage and the Godmade discovered them blasted off their hinges. Now, the thick dovetailed boards lay shattered into splinter-edged shards, and their sweetness could not cover the miasma that rolled with nearly visible thickness from within.

The Gage turned one hand up, cupping a puddle of reflected starlight in its hollow. He extended it toward the shattered gates. *Should we check it out?* the gesture offered.

Nizhvashiti gave one of its tattered sighs. "I think we're obligated."

"Only because we elect to be decent people."

The Godmade placed bony hands on hips that were no more than a suggestion under the flowing robes. "Honorable Gage. Do you suppose that at this point either of us really, entirely qualifies as a *people?*"

"I have a broad definition," the Gage responded. He started forward, feet ringing on the cobbles with distinction.

Nizhvashiti followed, rustling. Together, they swept within.

# 9

Himadra, Farkhad, and two other men rode hard but not incautiously. Himadra tried to keep his thoughts from circling back to the dead horses.

Nothing was without risk, of course. Especially not travel. But the waste and the delay both griped him. They would be slower now, sharing horses.

The road ahead was muddy and slick, rutted with much passage. Still, the tracks of the nurse's horse were by far the freshest, and stood out like fresh ink on the palimpsest of a scraped hide.

Himadra wondered where the rains were. They should be far from over.

He also wondered where his damned sorcerer was.

Drupada's nurse was not much of a horsewoman. As far as Himadra knew, she'd never ridden at all before he and his men kidnapped her in order to keep the heir of Ansh-Sahal alive. So it was doubly impressive that she'd managed to rein her horse away from the others in the thick of the fight, stay clear of the bear-boars, and try to run for home. Maybe not the best thinking, but Himadra had to admire her for doing any thinking, under the circumstances. Himadra's vivid imagination was one of the things that made him a good tactician, and he could hardly have kept himself from visualizing the harried, terrified woman with too tight a grip on the reins, the snapping jaws and skewering tusks, the thrusting spears at every turn. He could see the mud-stained gray horse eye-rolling, head-tossing, slopping lather as it yanked against the bit, slipping in mud that could kill it with a misstep.

Perhaps desperation had given the nurse an edge, howling babe and all. Perhaps the horse had merely bolted, and she had had the presence of mind to somehow stay on. Or even to direct it.

Velvet's gait was not so fast as a gallop, but it was much smoother. Bearable for Himadra, if he gritted his teeth, even at her top speed. She could maintain that running walk for a long while. The other three horses kept up at an easy canter.

They could have galloped pell-mell after the runaway, but the nurse in her lack of horsewomanship had let her steed stretch to his fullest length and race away unrestricted. If Himadra's men tried to follow the same way, they ran the same risks—of their horses sliding in the mud, breaking legs, throwing riders. And the nurse's gray would have bolted himself to exhaustion. He'd be staggering along at a heaving walk by now. The other horses had been in a fight, but they had also had a breather. If Himadra could restrain himself from the temptation to chase after the nurse at top speed, he and his men would run her mount down in short order.

Fortunately, if there was anything Himadra had learned from a lifetime of physical frailty, it was restraint. Caution. Consideration of the likely outcomes.

He was impressed with the nurse, that she had managed to stay in the saddle. She might be naturally gifted. Maybe they'd make a rider of her by the time the party reached Chandranath.

If she didn't die first in the poisoned remains of Ansh-Sahal. Or while running blindly toward it, Himadra thought, as they passed the point where a half-dozen other sets of racing hoofprints swung out from behind an outcrop and churned the nurse's tracks into oblivion.

Farkhad rose in his stirrups and glanced over. "What do you think?"

"Brigands!" Himadra had to shout to be heard over the horses. "Go on without me!"

It would be dangerous, running in the mud. But the consequences of being too slow had just redoubled. Leaving Drupada and the nurse at the mercy of brigands—because who else would be lying in wait behind a rock on a road lately frequented by refugees—would be far worse.

"Farkhad!" he yelled, before the other could kick his mount away. "We need their horses!"

Farkhad raised a fist, and gave his horse its head. The tired gelding accelerated, the other two pounding past Himadra in its wake. Velvet snorted in frustration: just because she was a gaited horse did not mean she *couldn't* run, and the herd was leaving her. But she remained obedient to her reins and training, and the other horses swept away.

They vanished around a switchback in the muddy, descending road. Velvet didn't love the sloppy going, but she was sure-footed. Himadra's men, meanwhile, might be riding into an ambush as well as at unsafe speeds. He had nothing left to him except to follow as safely and swiftly as possible, and trust in his men.

HIMADRA COULD STILL HEAR THE HORSES LONG AFTER HE LOST SIGHT OF them, and as he rode after them as hard as his body would bear, the sounds did not vanish entirely. He performed the mathematics of engagement in his head. The brigands' horses were fresh. Those of his people, including Drupada and the nurse, were not. But confronted with a lone woman, well-dressed and riding a quality horse, and a baby, bandits were unlikely to resort to bullets and arrows when they would see an opportunity to ride down their unarmed target alive.

The horse was worth something. The woman was worth something, ransomed or to the slavers who infested these hills. The baby was worth something likewise.

Himadra's men, however, would have no use for the brigands. Only their horses and gear. That, in itself, constituted an advantage.

And Himadra had another advantage. He himself had no need to get close to the fight.

THE ROAD VANISHED DOWN INTO A NARROW, STEEP-SIDED EROSION VAL-ley, and the churned path of hooves followed it. Himadra, though, spotted a side trail that veered off to the right. It was much narrower and rocky, climbing steeply along the valley's rim.

Elevation, too, could be a tactical advantage, and even a stone could make an effective weapon when dropped from a height.

Himadra turned Velvet off the road, despite her desire to follow her companions. She lurched and struggled up the steep trail head down and snorting, haunches bunching. Every surge jarred Himadra painfully, but he was not much weight for her to bear.

They came to the ridgeline, and Himadra could hear the hoofbeats more clearly now. They rose up from below, no longer baffled by the twists of the road, layered and complicated by echoes.

He would be silhouetted on the rim, but he took a reasoned chance that only his own men would have the presence of mind and the discipline to check along the rises while their blood was up from the pursuit. And a shot from below would have a poor chance of hitting him.

A calculated risk, but he took it.

From Velvet's back, he could see half the valley floor. The wrong half, currently. But if his reckoning was solid, once he came around the bend ahead and cleared the outcrop, he should have a view of the road.

He laughed out loud when he came around that turn in the trail and caught sight of one of his own men, Guarav—his best archer— dismounted from his mare and standing with arrow knocked just in the spot where Himadra had meant to stop and peer down.

Guarav turned, bow drawn and arrow leveled, the wind playing with the mirrored ends of his sash. He identified Himadra quickly and swung back to the sharp-cliffed valley below.

"Farkhad doesn't need me at all," Himadra said, reining Velvet in.

Guarav did not shift his attention again. But he did say, "We do try to pay attention, my lord."

The echoes of hoofbeats were growing sharper, and closer to the initial sound. A lone horse hove into view, running desperately down the road, so fast Himadra expected it to end-over-end like a tumbler. It was a gray, maybe, though so mud-spattered from the shoulders back that it might have been a chestnut.

It was flying so desperately because a few moments after it charged from obscurity, six others burst into Himadra's field of vision. Even a tired horse will run if you chase it.

That burst of speed was the gelding's last, however. Even from here, Himadra could see him struggling, the vast flare of his nostrils as he heaved.

The others were playing with his rider as they too burst down the trail, taking turns reining their animals in to rest them and surging ahead to harry the fugitive.

And if here was Guarav . . . where were the rest of Himadra's men?

Could he hear them? He held very still on Velvet, and pushed his long locks behind the rim of his ears to clear them. He let his mouth fall open, the better to hear.

Velvet, not pleased to be so close to the cliff edge, shifted, but bravely held her place.

The echoes layered one over another like the rhythms of a hammered drum, creating overtones that confused the ear and the sense of direction.

Exhausted, staggering . . . the valiant gray horse fell. Just to its knees, and somehow the rider stayed on. Clutching the saddlebow and perhaps a fistful of mane. Himadra could not see the toddler slung against her chest from this angle. He prayed Drupada was still safe, still there.

"Aim for the lead brigands when they come in range," Himadra told his man.

Guarav grunted agreement. He did not speak. His breathing slowed as he stretched himself broad and wide, within the curve of the bow. Shooting *down* a defile was not easy, either.

The brigands were whooping now, slowing, yelling incomprehensible glee at a successful hunt as they rode pell-mell down the hill, racing now to be first to their victim.

The gray horse struggled to his feet, blood streaming down his forelegs. He stumbled a step, limping but putting weight on both front feet.

Himadra let out a breath, then held it out so that the rattle of his gasp would not distract Guarav. The avalanche rumble of the riders echoed, rebounded, an earth-trembling drumbeat under their shrilling voices.

Himadra admitted to himself that he had seriously underestimated this particular gelding, but the horse was done. The nurse kicked the gray, her wrapped skirts flaring. The gray balked. She kicked him again. He put his head down, heaving. He would run no more.

Guarav's arrow sang from the string. Himadra, chest aching, gasped a breath. The second arrow was in Guarav's hand while the first took flight. On the string while the first was still climbing its arc. The third

left the bow as the first found its target. The fourth launched an instant after. Himadra saw the nurse scrambling awkwardly down from
the gray, sliding out of the saddle in a manner that would have gotten
her killed if the horse hadn't been too tired to move.

Admittedly, Himadra thought, he'd never tried to dismount while
carrying a baby.

Then Guarav, Velvet, and Himadra were all scrambling back from
the cliff edge and toward where Guarav's horse was picketed as the brigands began to return fire. A volley of arrows and balls shattered against
the cliff and sailed over the rim.

Even as he and Velvet ducked, Himadra glimpsed the effect of
Guarav's arrows. The archer had aimed at two riders. He had feathered
the first one twice, and the man, tangled in his reins and stirrup, had
slid half-from the saddle. His panicked horse whirled in circles, scattering the other brigands.

Himadra had not seen if the second rider had been hit. It was likely;
Guarav did not miss often, even from such a difficult position. Even if
he had, though, they had evened the odds a little.

Now that the headlong chase of the brigands had been broken into
milling and shouting, Himadra could hear the more rhythmic hoofbeats
of the horses of Farkhad and his other man. And so, he realized could
the brigands. Once the return shots ebbed, Guarav crept forward from
where he had intelligently picketed his horse a little back from the edge,
so he wouldn't have to worry about it getting shot. His low crouch concealed him and the nocked bow in his hands, and Himadra reined
Velvet over to the other mount.

The horses stood side by side for comfort, ears still pricked toward
the sounds of chaos from below. In a moment, when no further projectiles sizzled above the rocks, Guarav jumped up, drew his bow, and
loosed again.

He dropped as fast as he had stood. "Two fallen," he reported from
the area of Velvet's knees. "They're withdrawing into the rocks. Also, I
think the girl is climbing the cliff."

"The . . . cliff?"

"Toward our position."

Well, it was a terrible idea, but he supposed she wasn't a tactician.

"Move down the ledge that way," Himadra ordered.

"The angle of shot isn't as good."

"They've seen you here twice. I don't want to improve my ratio of men to horses by losing you."

More shouts rose from below. Himadra recognized the yelping jackal cry of his own people. Farkhad and Jeet, Himadra's second man, had arrived. Despite himself, Himadra's heart surged. The thrill of battle licked him like a heady flame.

Guarav, having scuttled down the cliff, risked another glance. And another arrow. Then one more before he ducked. "We've engaged," he reported. "Three left. They're trying to run."

"They should have picked on someone their own size," Himadra said. "We need their horses. Follow me down when it's over."

He reined Velvet around and touched her forward. She went willingly, accelerating on the slope. Ahead, Himadra could hear cries and combat, echoing as elaborately as had the running hooves. Velvet moved down the slope like a waterfall, carrying him over the steep, churned, slick road with nary a misstep. He slowed her as they approached the sounds; the last thing he wanted to do was charge into a skirmish.

Velvet shook her head at first, but accepted the contact.

The moments it took for the two of them to career down the switchbacks felt like ages. But swords were still clattering when they rounded the final curve and he got his first sight of the engagement.

Three men lay on the ground. One was still strung tangled between stirrups and reins, his terrified horse whirling ceaselessly to the right with its head sharply inflected. Himadra's men crossed swords with the last two brigands, who had managed to find shelter behind the rocks so that Guarav's continued attempts to pick them off were thwarted. Farkhad and Jeet charged forward side by side, on short, disciplined bursts, as much trying to force the brigands out of cover as to kill them. This was a sensible use of force—as long as Guarav hadn't run out of arrows—and Himadra approved.

The brigands were, understandably, on the defensive.

The nurse, as Guarav had predicted, was *somehow* halfway up the cliffside. And stuck, it looked like; she seemed to have treed herself on a ledge under an overhang, and was pressed into it, her skirts a flash of crimson against the muddy brown and ochre of the valley wall. She was high enough that Himadra winced thinking about the risks involved in getting her down again.

Even if she managed to scramble back down on her own, the nurse too would stay pinned there as long as Guarav didn't run out of arrows. And as long as she didn't realize that Guarav would not kill or harm her. Or her horse, which still stood exactly where she had left him, head down and eyes half-closed, unable to even summon the will to walk farther away from the combat.

Having assessed the larger tactical situation, the clash of swords drew his attention back to more immediate problems. The biggest of the brigands had rallied and kicked his horse, a big bay, forward against the pressure of Jeet's defense. He shouted and slashed with a heavy saber, pushing Jeet and Jeet's smaller mare back, and back again. He was going to try to escape up the road past Himadra, Himadra realized. Perhaps, locked in combat, he had not even realized that Himadra was there.

Himadra drew his third and penultimate pistol. He aimed carefully: Jeet was in his line of fire. And he discharged it into the back of the big man's head.

The other whirled to assess this new threat. Jeet kicked his horse into a charge now that his opponent was dead. The brigand backed his horse to gain a little clearance from his enemies—

—and threw his sword aside.

"I surrender!" the last brigand shouted. "I surrender!"

Farkhad checked his swing, turning it aside a moment before it would have taken the man's arm off. Jeet reined his horse into a sliding stop instants before contact. The horse looked extremely pleased at this trick.

Himadra sighed and raised his fist, knowing that Guarav on the cliff above would see him. His men reined aside to make a path for the brigand to come toward him.

If the brigand decided to pull a pistol and shoot, just then, there would be nothing anyone could do to stop him. Unless Himadra could get to his own last pistol faster.

The brigand looked at him, then at the two men-at-arms. Cautiously, he reined his horse forward. The horse blew hard and moved with tight, nervous steps down the trail.

As the man rode out from the shadow of the outcrop, the light fell across his face. Himadra saw the tiresomely familiar look of recognition on it.

"You're the one they call . . . I mean, if I knew the woman was yours, my lord—"

Himadra let drop his hand.

The brigand's expression of surprise became comical as the shaft of Guarav's arrow seemed to leap out of his right eye. As he toppled backward from the saddle, it was joined by one on the left.

His horse, like any sensible creature, bolted.

Himadra let himself relax into his painful saddle, just a little. He called out to Jeet, who was good with animals, "Catch those damned horses, would you?"

"Yes, Your Competence. And you will be . . . ?"

"Hoping I don't have to catch the girl." Himadra held out his fragile arms. "I'd be terrible at it. Farkhad, with me."

IT WAS A SHORT DISTANCE DOWN THE ROAD TO WHERE THE NURSE HAD treed herself: a ride of no more than sixty heartbeats, and they were not riding fast. It seemed more prudent to come up on the terrified woman slowly, giving her plenty of time to examine them. And it gave Himadra time to examine her, as well, which made him realize he had not paid her the attention he should before. *A man who doesn't notice servants is a man who is asking to be betrayed.*

She was older than he had assumed, and obviously—given her current position—fitter and more agile. Her clouted skirts blew in the curiously dry breeze along the valley, a flicker of red like flame against the stone. The child in his wrap was a diagonal bundle across her front, one arm protruding, one small fist knotted in the collar of her blouse. She had gotten herself high enough that her features were a thumbprint-sized smudge against the stone.

As he and Farkhad rode up, she spat down on them.

She was too high. It was a long, long way to fall.

Himadra gestured Farkhad to lean down to him. He turned his head and shielded his mouth with his hand. "Well, this is a stick in the dick and no mistake."

Farkhad's mouth quirked at the corner. Black humor kept you going through the nights of war. "A thorny problem, my lord."

Himadra dropped his hand and stared accusingly. "Just let me do the talking."

Farkhad waved him forward with a courtly gesture.

As Himadra rode Velvet forward, it was he who was snorting and shaking his head. The mare, on the other hand, was an arch-necked lady, placing each hoof with such dainty precision it seemed as if she were making a point. Possibly about the mud, and all the sprinting about in it.

They passed the gray gelding. His head was finally starting to come up, his breathing slowing. Himadra dared to hope his wind wasn't broken.

He stopped Velvet a little short of the base of the cliff. Because it was uncomfortable to crane his neck back too far, and because if the nurse jumped, he didn't want to be under her. He was sure he had her attention, so he did not bother with hailing her. He simply plunged—an unfortunate choice of metaphor—right in. "Madam, if I offer my assurance that you will come to no harm, will you climb down? We can have a rope lowered if you like. It would be less strenuous and safer."

He wasn't sure she heard the final two sentences, as she had begun laughing uproariously before he got to it. "After what you did to that man who surrendered?"

"I did not accept his surrender," Himadra said. "Right now, I am offering you my protection."

"You had that man murdered!" Her voice was crisp, and very precise.

"That man who surrendered would have sold you into slavery. And the boy too, if he hadn't decided the boy was too young to be worth selling and dashed his brains against a wall."

"I should better kill us than serve your mercies!" the nurse yelled down. She kicked a rock at his head. He couldn't tell if it was on purpose. "Humane as you are!"

The rock bounced away in the wrong direction.

*I really should have found out her name,* Himadra thought. *Names are useful when you need to talk to people.*

She made as if to step off the ledge. Himadra held up his hand. "Please, madam," he said, as reasonably as he could with his heart in his throat. "What is most humane? A merciful arrow and a painless death with relief in his heart, or to leave him here without horse or supplies amidst the curdling of the earth to starve, boil, suffocate? He attacked two princes today. And a defenseless woman. Surely the penalty for that is death, and his goods are forfeit for it. Besides. The roads are a little safer without him on them. For the next traveler. Or refugee who passes."

She didn't seem to have an immediate answer to that. She didn't kick any more rocks. At least, not right away.

Himadra turned to Farkhad and lowered his voice. "Would you go see if either of the others knows her name?"

Farkhad blinked at him with lashes like a camel's. No doubt the women loved them. "I know her name, Sire."

Himadra closed his eyes and breathed out through his nose. When his temper was stanched, he said, "Then would you very much mind telling it to me?"

"Ili, my lord."

Himadra nodded. He turned back to the cliff and the woman clinging to it.

"Ili," he began—

—and was interrupted by her barking laugh.

It also had a certain resemblance to the yelping of jackals, he noticed. "If you want to impress me," she said sardonically, "try getting my name right."

Himadra glared at Farkhad. Farkhad shrugged apologetically.

Himadra said to the woman, "Is that the respect you showed your rajni?"

"My rajni was not a kidnapper!"

"Fine," Himadra said. "What *is* your name?"

She blinked at him. It seemed to take a while for her to realize that he was still speaking to her, and what he was saying. "Iri," she answered.

"Well, I was close," Farkhad murmured.

Himadra ignored him. "That child you are holding is your prince, Iri. He is the hope of rebuilding your land and reuniting your people. And because I brought you and him away from Ansh-Sahal, he is alive."

She scoffed. "You can't tell me your motive was to protect him," she shouted back.

"Well, he's my responsibility too. And so are you. And your responsibility is to protect him, isn't it?"

Iri was clinging to some invisible outcrop on the wall behind her with one hand. Her other crept to wrap around the child in his sling.

Himadra, feeling like he was gaining ground, took a breath and called up, "I will swear to guard Prince Drupada, Iri. I am many things, but I am not an oathbreaker."

"You are so full of shit," she yelled down.

"You don't have a lot of better options that I can tell."

She closed her eyes and leaned her head back against the wall. She stayed like that for a long while, and Himadra forced himself to be quiet. So often if you just held your peace, people would give you what you wanted.

At long last, Drupada began to cry. Not a howl, as Himadra would have expected. But a low, exhausted snivel. Without opening her eyes, Iri sighed.

"Oh, fuck it. Send down the rope," she said.

"Don't move," Himadra answered. He turned Velvet back swiftly, to find that Jeet had the horses all assembled in a string, and Guarav was turning over corpses, reclaiming what arrows he could assemble.

Guarav made a noise of disgust as Himadra rode up. "Dammit, two of these shafts are broken."

"You need to practice more, so your targets always fall backward."

"Most of them . . . right. I'll get the rope, Sire."

STILL, HIMADRA DID NOT BREATHE A SIGH OF RELIEF UNTIL IRI STEPPED into the loop tied in the rope and let Guarav and Farkhad lower her and the prince to safety—or the nearest thing anyone could accomplish to it under current conditions.

Iri dusted herself off, settled her tattered skirts, and marched up to the gray gelding. He had stopped gasping, but still looked at her suspiciously as she approached.

"Not him," Jeet said. "He still needs rest. Take this mare."

The mare was one of the brigand's horses, a dark dun, and while she was tired she had not been run into the ground the way the gelding had. Iri was eyeing her dubiously when Himadra said, "You lied about not knowing how to ride."

She snorted. "Wouldn't you?"

Himadra felt the smile bending his mustache despite everything he could do to prevent it. Another failure of stern warlord demeanor.

He didn't answer, preferring to watch Iri, as she did not immediately take the reins from Jeet's hand. Instead, she crouched down and wriggled a protesting Drupada out of his sling. It was only as she did so that Himadra got his first really good look at the boy.

Drupada stood blinking, holding her hand, protesting being dislodged but not throwing a fit about it. Himadra had seen his own brothers behave much worse in their time.

He could just hear what Iri was saying to the boy. "Do you want to ride the horsie? No, not by yourself. But you can sit in the saddle with me."

It was a charming domestic scene, and Himadra could not help but feel it was being staged entirely for his benefit.

What could not have been staged, however, was the moment Drupada twisted around to look at Himadra on his horse and said, "But Auntie, he rides alone."

Iri glanced from the boy to Himadra, dawning horror disfiguring her face. But children had no malice in them, only curiosity. So he answered the boy. "I do. But I'm an adult."

"But you're only little." *Like me*, the boy didn't have to say, though Himadra flattered himself that he had a few handspans on a two-year-old.

"I am not tall," Himadra admitted.

"How old are you?" Drupada asked.

Himadra laughed honestly at that. "So old," he said. "I am nearly thirty-two. See this gray in my beard?"

Drupada stretched up on tiptoe, frowning. Himadra pushed his beard forward with the fingers that were not holding the reins. The boy stared, then made a disappointed huff and turned away, realizing that Himadra was not a potential playmate.

Iri looked at him worriedly, but Himadra just waved her aside. What under the Mother River had he gotten himself into, with kidnapping this child and this woman?

He shook his head in self-amusement and glanced to the right. And nearly jumped clean out of the saddle into a fall that would have broken bones for sure.

"Mother's milk!" Himadra spat. Ravana sat his horse to the side, as if he had always been there.

The bay was awash in nervous lather, ears flicking grumpily. But it always bore Ravana like a chore; it showed no signs of being tired—just angry. Himadra would have heard them, anyway, if they had come up at a canter.

Ravana smiled at him.

"Where did you come from?" Himadra asked.

Ravana's smirk turned into a chuckle. "I see you haven't *entirely* lost your hostages."

"No thanks to you. Were you off doing sorcery while we were fighting bear-boars and brigands?"

"As a matter of fact," Ravana said agreeably. "You seem to have managed. And I did warn you I wouldn't be responsible for women and children."

Himadra grunted because the alternative was repeating himself, with more profanity.

"I'm glad to find you here," Ravana continued. "Because our next step is tricky."

"Our next step is evacuating the neighborhood of Ansh-Sahal before the sea explodes again."

Ravana waved a dismissive hand. Himadra noticed that Iri had gotten Drupada into the saddle and mounted herself, much more competently this time.

Ravana said, "Not right now, it shouldn't. And we should have dry weather for a while."

Dry weather in the heart of the rains. But Himadra thought of the strange pile of clouds on the horizon, heaped like hungry sheep against a fence. Of the remarkable lack of rain.

Ravana probably *had* been off doing sorcery.

"No," Ravana said, kicking his horse in the ribs to stop it sidling. "What you must do now is send word to Mrithuri."

"Excuse me?"

"She's under siege by Anuraja. Tell her that Ansh-Sahal has fallen and that its surviving prince is in your care. Send out banns announcing that you are Lord Protector of Ansh-Sahal now, in the wake of a terrible disaster, and that its prince is safely your ward."

"Ansh-Sahal is a *crater*."

"It will not always be. And some of its people and lands survived."

"And the boy won't always be two."

"I'd say that's up to you," Ravana said, with a slicing gesture of his left hand.

"You counseled me not to take the child," Himadra said, not bothering to keep the frustration out of his voice. "Now you counsel me to claim him." *And murder him, maybe.*

As he made the complaint, he found himself struck by a flash of understanding that was almost an epiphany. Ravana had promised him many things, as part of their alliance. One of those things was an heir.

Himadra had not mentioned to Ravana his idea that Sayeh's son would be clean of the curse that haunted his own bloodline. He had not mentioned it to anyone. He was in the habit of keeping his own counsel.

But he wondered now if Ravana had guessed, and if Ravana worried Himadra might come to that recognition if he had not, already. He wondered now if Ravana was counseling him not in Chandranath's best interests, but in order to reassert control over him.

Himadra did not understand the relationship between Ravana and the other sorcerer, the woman, Ravani. They had come from the east, he knew. They were fairer-skinned than his own folk, but they did not have the willow-leaf eyes of the Rasan, Qersnyk, Song, or other eastern peoples. They might be siblings; they might be something else. And then there was the coincidence of names.

Maybe it was a title from their school of magic. He simply did not have enough information to understand, and Ravana was not receptive to . . . personal questions.

Things Himadra did not understand *also* worried him.

"I adapt to the circumstances," Ravana said silkily. "And you are, always, in control."

# 10

SAYEH ROUSED HERSELF FROM HER COUCH IN THE HEAT OF THE AFTERNOON. Again she could hear no rain on the pavilion roof, and she could taste the dust on her tongue. A hot stillness lay over the camp, like the stillness of the dry season but worse—oppressive—because it was humid.

She levered herself up on her elbows. Sitting upright by herself without assistance struck her as far too risky, especially as her leg twinged warning. She blinked, trying to focus in such dim daylight as filtered through the pavilion. Of late, she had noticed that her vision did not seem as sharp, especially when she was attempting to read something close to her, or work a fine embroidery.

There was old age, lurking at the roadside, lounging by the corner, whistling with crossed arms as if it had nowhere to be and no particular plans. Lying in wait for her.

The worst part, for Sayeh, was missing her own bed. Not just because the lack was visceral, compelling. But because it was so small. So personal. From it, she could not hide behind her office. By such a trivial nuisance, she was made too small to be a rajni.

Other people had lost loved ones. Children, parents, lovers, spouses, friends. Homes and livelihoods. Pets. Lives. Sayeh herself had lost her kingdom, her home, her people, and—(she devoutly hoped) temporarily—her son.

Her bed was such a small and comprehensible loss. And perhaps that was why it struck her so deeply and consistently. The other losses were so huge they were unspannable. Somehow, her own feather pillows, rugs, and bolsters—so small a thing—had come to symbolize the greater tragedy.

Perhaps it was just her broken thigh, and that she could not get up off this couch.

Perhaps it was time, wearing human life down as the Mother River's roots wore down the very Steles of the Sky. Time was a series of terrible losses and unpredictable gains.

Ümmühan and Nazia were both within the tent. Ümmühan sat by a low table, books and pens and brushes spread around her. Nazia knelt by the brazier, stirring tea. The coals only added to the oppressive atmosphere, and Sayeh wondered how the thin girl could stand it, and why she had not taken the brazier outside in the absence of rain.

If the rains kept failing, would the Mother River carry enough water down from the Steles of the Sky to see people in Sarathai-tia and Sarathai-lae and the farmlands between through the dry season? What about those who lived along the Mother's tributaries, or in places like Ansh-Sahal? (*No one lives in Ansh-Sahal anymore*, Sayeh thought, and bit her lip against a pain that had nothing to do with the injuries of her body.) Empty cisterns and catchments meant people dead of thirst. Or dead more slowly of famine when the crops failed.

It also meant armies on the move that much more easily, without mud and landslides to contend with.

From her couch, Sayeh could see the guard by the flap. At least one of them. From her current position, she could not see if the second one was present.

She cleared her throat. Ümmühan stood from her cushions, a little creakily but nimble. It took her a moment to straighten, but Sayeh—feeling the chill breath of mortality on her neck—hoped she made it so far and was still so spry when it happened.

Her leg felt so strange. No, that wasn't quite right. *She* felt so . . . strange about the leg.

It wasn't the pain. The pain was bad, but it was just pain. It was the *terror* that she struggled not to be incapacitated by. Terror of the leg never working again; terror of a permanent injury; terror of being hurt again. She was not afraid of the scar: she had scars, including a terrible puckered one sprawled across her abdomen through which Drupada had been born. What she was afraid of . . .

It was something visceral. Elemental. Profound. Self-protective, she imagined; a body's way of reminding you that you had a lot to lose. That maybe risk-taking wasn't the wisest idea, when—even if you survived—it could render you helpless. *Who built us to be so fragile? So reliant on others when we come to grief?*

She was a priestess of the Mother. She knew. And she knew why, as well. To teach people their interdependence. To teach them that they needed each other. That they could not live long alone, without relationships and pacts of mutual assistance.

She thought of Anuraja, and sighed. What a pity it was that some people could look that lesson in the face their whole lives, and learn nothing from it but the need to dominate and control.

Well, right now what she needed was the pot. And she was going to have to ask one of her women to fetch it for her.

That, she decided, would be humility enough for one day.

SHE MIGHT HAVE TRIED TO SLEEP AGAIN AFTER. SHE FELT EXHAUSTED enough. But sleep was not setting her free, except in a metaphysical sense. And there was a chance that plotting would.

So when Ümmühan helped prop her on cushions and Nazia brought her a share of the tea, she accepted it. And said to Ümmühan, who had drawn up an ox-collar chair to sit beside her, "The camp is quiet, is it not? Even for midafternoon."

She spoke in an unremarkable conversational tone, without emphasis. Men did not always heed the conversations of women. Perhaps the one by the door would be deep in his reveries of glory or promotion or plundered gold or triumphing at a roll of the bones. Whatever it was that invading soldiers thought about while they were guarding a kidnapped queen in the territory of another queen whom they were in the process of besieging.

But it would do her no good to depersonalize him. Not when he had power over her, and she needed to get him on her side.

Ümmühan was a subtle one. She gave no sign that she had noticed the layers of meaning in Sayeh's comment, except that her gaze lingered on Sayeh's face for an extra moment. "They rode out while you were sleeping, Your Abundance."

"But the camp is still here."

"There's no point in trying to bring the supply wagons and what-not across the river, I suppose." The old woman stirred her tea and sipped, making a grimace of satisfaction after. "This keeps everything out of ballista range. And if they have to retreat from the siege position, they won't be forced to leave behind their equipment and food."

Nazia said nothing, but watched the old woman intently, a furrow between her brows. Sayeh had seen her look at Tsering-la the same way.

Sayeh said, "You've quite the head for tactics."

Ümmühan laughed lightly, the practiced peal of a professional beauty. "This is not an old woman's first war."

Sayeh glanced sidelong toward the flap. The guard—there was only one—had slipped outside.

"Do you think it can work?"

"I have been captive in more dire straits than these," Ümmühan said. "And yet from that captivity I changed the world, and the people around me."

"Yes, but you are Ümmühan."

"And you are Sayeh."

That was inarguable. And perhaps being Sayeh would be enough. Sayeh took a breath, thinking to ask for advice on how to begin her campaign, but was interrupted by voices from outside the canvas wall. She couldn't make out the words, but the timbres were clear enough. One belonged to the guard . . . and the other was the contralto of the woman Ravani. Back to trouble them again.

Footsteps approached, quick and determined, boot-heeled. Sayeh put her teacup before her face, more to hide her expression than because she was thirsty for the sweet, spiced, milky brew. Reflexively, she scraped her teeth along the rim of the cup, but it was Song porcelain and not the unglazed clay of a proper teacup, meant to be nibbled along with the tea.

The flap drew aside, admitting the tall sorcerer, borne on a puff of hot air and dust. Somehow, none of the dust seemed to have settled on

Ravani, however. All her jewels, silks, embroidery, and bullion shimmered undimmed.

Sayeh contemplated whether it was worth taking up sorcery just for the reduction in laundry. It was a means of making her face expressionless as she lowered the porcelain cup at last. "You came back."

Ravani squared herself as the flap fell back into place over the doorway. "They're marching on your cousin's city, Rajni. I have no desire to be present for the boiling oil."

"Rational," Ümmühan commented.

Ravani glanced sidelong at her.

Sayeh cleared her throat. "You are a sorcerer. Why have the rains stopped coming?"

Ravani looked at Sayeh in enough surprise that it took moments for her to find her voice. "Rajni. Someone has obviously decided they should."

Sayeh said, "Can one just do that? Decide?"

"The Alchemical Emperor could."

Sayeh wondered how the sorcerer knew.

"If anyone sat on the Peacock Throne, that might be of some use."

"What is true now is not true forever." Ravani waved aside an offer of tea from Nazia. She pointed to Sayeh's leg. "How are you healing?"

Sayeh eyed the sorcerer suspiciously. "I'll walk again eventually, I suppose. Are you offering to speed the process?"

"Are you giving me consent to work magic on you?" A steady gaze, challenging. Behind Ravani, Ümmühan rose abruptly with the tea tray, ready to let it "clumsily" tumble all over the sorcerer.

Sayeh let a little smile curve her lips. "Perhaps . . . not."

"The rajni is cautious," Ravani replied. "The rajni is wise."

Ümmühan stepped back with the tray and turned aside, to set it upon a stand.

"Still," Ravani continued. "It would be convenient to be able to walk, would it not? Especially if it were not generally known that one had regained one's feet ahead of schedule."

"And the agent of one's captor is just the person one would trust to keep such a secret from him," Sayeh observed, equally as bland. Nazia retrieved the teapot from the tray Ümmühan had moved and refilled her cup. Again, Ravani refused.

"I am no one's agent." Ravani's voice held an edge. Sayeh wondered if it were honest anger, or an actor's art. "I am my own, and I act for my own reasons."

"Then what are your reasons for helping Anuraja invade?" Nazia said, forthright, what Sayeh only considered.

The sorcerer lifted her chin. "It's a mutually beneficial arrangement. A partnership."

Nazia opened her mouth again, but swallowed what she might have said at the flicker of Sayeh's lids. The girl was learning. Would learn more, if Sayeh could keep her alive long enough.

*Whatever I have to do to get my son back,* Sayeh told herself. "I shall have to consider your kind offer," however, was what she said.

"Of course," Ravani said smoothly.

"Are you sure you won't have tea?" Sayeh asked.

Ravani shook her head, her wrist-thick braid slipping over her shoulder. She pushed it back. "I am afraid duty calls."

*Three times she refuses. I wonder if it is a ritual.*

Sayeh said goodbye politely, and Ümmühan showed Ravani to the door. When the flap fell shut behind her, Nazia leaned close to Sayeh and whispered, "You cannot mean to trust her."

"I do not mean to trust anyone," Sayeh answered, with a show of placidity. "But I need a plan. And sitting here with a useless leg is *not* a plan. She says she's Anuraja's partner—"

"A partnership she's willing to betray for the possibility of a very slight advantage."

"We can perhaps use that too," Sayeh said.

Ümmühan said, "My people speak of beasts that feed on war. For whom strife itself is food."

Nazia nodded, and Sayeh felt herself inclining her head in agreement as well. "You mentioned that before. As a metaphor."

"Well, as an actuality," Ümmühan said amusedly. "But I offer it as a metaphor."

"It is a good one. And it gives me an idea of how to proceed." She looked at Ümmühan. "Do you still sing, my lady poetess?"

"Oh, yes," Ümmühan answered, with a wicked smile. "Though my voice is not what in days of old broke hearts and laid thoughts to rest . . . yes, I still sing."

Nazia cleared her throat. "And what will you do, my rajni?"

Sayeh sighed. "If I have no other choice, if my plan to steal his army does not work ... quickly enough ... I am going to tell Anuraja that I will speak to Mrithuri on his behalf. But not today."

Sayeh survived a single day longer on her couch before she ordered them bring her a second crutch.

Well, "ordered" might not be the correct word. It would be more precise, though more painful to her pride, to admit that she prevailed upon Ümmühan against Ümmühan's advice and better judgment. And Ümmühan—also against Ümmühan's better judgment, and with many dire warnings that Sayeh's leg would never be right again if she did not rest it—again went and persuaded the guards in her turn.

That turned out to be a wise choice. Ümmühan's brand of persuasion was much more delicate than the one Sayeh, in her frustration, was inclined to. Delegating to strength was fortunately one of the tools of rulership. She embraced it, and recused herself while Ümmühan employed a good deal less "because I said so" than Sayeh would have been prone to. Effective, in a situation where one was without social power to back up one's demands.

Najal, one of the guards currently on duty, brought her the crutches.

Good ones, too. Cut to her height and padded. And a sling to support and lift her lower leg, so it was not pulling on the bone within the splint. The contraption felt weird, belted around her, but it did the job. She almost wept at the lessening of pain.

It took her only moments to learn to use the crutches, though after days bedridden, Sayeh could tell it would require some time to get her strength back. And probably to summon up new strength, that she had not had before.

Najal and Sanjay would have carried her, she was sure. They would have to accompany her anyway. It's not as if she would be allowed to wander the camp on her own. But she had had enough of being treated as a parcel. She had had enough of being *regarded* as a parcel, even more so. And the key to ending that was to get up on her feet.

She had been right about the crutches hurting, after the first few minutes, even though the handholds and the crossbars that tucked under her arms were padded. Well, no matter. She touched the scar on her belly, just visible between the blouse and wrap of the southern-style drape that Nazia had managed to somehow barter or blandish from one of the camp followers. She touched the splint that held her femur straight. She touched her breast over her heart, where the ache of widowhood and the loss of her child and people remained.

This was not the first time Sayeh Rajni had encountered pain.

It was not even bad enough to make her scream this time.

"Where would you like to go, my rajni?" Nazia asked her, as if this were any outing. She carried a little basket with what might be deemed necessities by a spoiled dowager.

"Out," Sayeh intoned on a sigh. "I have been trapped within this pavilion for days. I would see the sky, and the stars, since there is no rain. Is there usually rain here in this season?" she asked Najal, all innocence.

"In this season, Your Abundance, there is indeed usually rain. It might be wise to bring an umbrella—"

"Pluck me a palm frond if it comes to it," she said with a lighthearted laugh that she did not even think sounded calculated.

And so they set out, the five of them. Toward the river, because it seemed to Sayeh that that was the swiftest way to get the lay of the land. And as a priestess of the Mother—called Fecund, called White Honey—she both desired and needed to pay her respects.

First, though. She must make her way through the rubble of the abandoned town where many of Anuraja's men had bivouacked.

The residents, in falling back to the castle or taking to the road—or the river—as refugees—had obviously done their best to leave nothing useful behind. Holes had been hacked in walls and roofs, covered now with waxed canvas sheets, and in some cases one or more legs had been hacked out from under stilted huts, leaving them off-kilter drunken storks.

Cleanup was still underway, for those given abandoned residences as shelter, though the waste and rubble was just being heaped in the street. Sayeh kept having to pick her way around it, except the pieces small enough for Najal and Sanjay to kick aside. The huts had been intentionally befouled, that much was plain, and among the trash in the streets were little piles of reeking human waste.

"What a mess for you," she said, as sympathetically as she could manage. It was too easy to imagine her own city invaded, infested, over-run with foreigners. She needed to remember that, even as these men were kind to her and she encouraged them to be kind.

Except she had no city anymore.

Quite unexpectedly, Sergeant Sanjay turned to her and said, "Would you like to see ours?"

"Excuse me?"

He hesitated, as if afraid he had overstepped. Then said, "Your Abundance. No offense is intended. I merely wondered if you would like to see the hut where Pren, Najal, Vaneer, and I are staying."

*All my guards together,* Sayeh thought. Not the best of tactics. Though it did facilitate communication. "I can't climb up," she said.

"You can shout encouragement," Sanjay said, with an unexpected flash of humor. "I think Pren is washing the floor down again. It still stinks, somehow."

They turned to the south and wound through passageways that were neither formal nor defined enough to really be considered streets. The routes left open for foot traffic wound around the huts, between and sometimes under them, and might be blocked here or there with withy hurdles laced together to make a sort of wall, or with piles of junk or ordure.

It was slow going on the crutches, especially after Sayeh stubbed the toe of her good foot on a cracked-open chest, lying shattered on its side. But they persisted.

She visited her guards' domicile—barracks, or dormitory, she was not quite sure what to call it—and did in fact shout encouragement to Pren. He was outside on a narrow catwalk, lying down and nailing a strip of wood to the inside of a cracked stilt.

"That seems like a lot of work for a house that isn't yours," Nazia said softly to Sanjay.

He grinned at her. "We're going to be here at least till the end of the rainy season, and probably longer. Might as well be comfortable. Anyway, someday it might be mine."

She looked at him, a furrow between her brows.

"Spoils of war," he said cheerily. "Somebody's going to wind up with all this land!"

Sayeh took her leave of Pren and turned away as if she had not heard.

She knew from Sanjay's accent that he was from a poor class, and his parents were probably tenant farmers on someone else's land.

It was only a few long swings between the crutches from here to the edge of the river.

Sayeh handed one of her props to Ümmühan, who—deep in her protest against Sayeh's stupidity—had not spoken a single word since the crutches were obtained and fitted. She used the other to brace herself as she leaned down over her one good leg, the broken one serving as a cantilever. It still felt . . . fragile, and disconnected, and Sayeh felt that she was taking an unbelievably careless chance.

A chance she could not avoid taking, if she stood any chance of winning a scrap of power with these people, in this place.

She lowered her free hand and at full, aching extension, just managed to dabble her fingertips in the water that kissed the sloped edge of the bank. Murmuring a prayer, she lifted her fingers to her lips and sucked.

Silt, algae. Cool sweetness. The green taste of living water. The presence of the Goddess was here with her, and Sayeh almost closed her eyes.

Until a long ripple stroked the surface of the opaque, white water. She straightened, in case it was a crocodile coming toward her. It might be one of the blind river dolphins; a long arc of those was some distance upstream, leaping and playing and squeaking as if the unusually boatless river were a special treat only for them. They moved away fast, and their pale wet skin gleamed the same clay white as the water. It was moments only before they vanished against it, or perhaps fell into it between the floating leaves and flowers of lotus.

The wake of whatever cut the water from beneath turned away from the bank and slipped upstream, leaving the papercut flowers of lotus lifting, falling, and then bobbing in its wake.

Clopping hoofbeats on mud drew Sayeh's attention. She turned with a deft-enough swing of her single crutch that she felt a little smug about it, and found Anuraja on his horse on the packed trail beside the river.

She drew her drapes around her and with the assistance of her prop, managed a fairly creditable courtesy.

Wordlessly, scowling behind her veil, Ümmühan handed her the other crutch back.

Sayeh drew herself up straight, aware of Anuraja's appraising gaze. She might as well have been a broodmare in foal. From the way he assessed her, she expected him to demand she produce a pedigree.

He knew her antecedents as well as he knew his own. They were . . . very similar.

"That is quite a scar," he admitted grudgingly. "Your Wizard does good work."

She smiled at him. "I'm alive," she said.

He did not seem to register the coldness in her voice.

She turned and pointed. "What's that, Your Competence?"

"The dolphins?"

"Whatever's chasing the dolphins."

"Oh, that." His head turned, as if he too were tracking the heavy ripple in the water.

"Something terrible," Anuraja said with an air of great self-satisfaction.

# 11

THE STORM HAD NOT BROKEN ON THAT DAY. THE DARK HEAT OF THE
Cauled Sun was unmitigated by the low, gray, rainless overcast that lid-
ded Sarathai-tia. Mrithuri slept poorly, and no artifice of servants wielding fans to make a whisper of breeze could ameliorate the heat for her
comfort, to make slumber possible.

Tsering-la had offered to settle a chill over the palace. But Mrithuri,
though tempted, had told the foreign Wizard to save his strength for
war.

The rajni's insomnia was the reason she walked the city walls just
before the end of day, more plainly garbed than usual in tunic and trousers. And so she was there to see Anuraja's army begin to move.

Anuraja commenced his attack at sunset. The troops did not cross
the Mother River—called Giver of Bread, called Milk of the Earth,
called Pearl—in the shadow of the city walls, where the defenders might
rain death on them. They formed companies, as Mrithuri watched first
with her spyglass and then with a naked eye, to get a sense of the scale
of the thing. They marched north—upstream—and men and livestock
towed confiscated barges, sculls, and whatnot along the far bank, long
out of bowshot.

Just as they began to move, the alarm sounded behind Mrithuri. She
did not shift from her position, though running feet broke around her,

and barrels of oil and siege stones for dropping on enemy heads continued to be winched into place behind the dragonglass topped battlements.

Anuraja's army did not begin ferrying themselves across the water immediately, as Mrithuri had expected. Instead, they lashed their boats stem to stern, creating a long and flexible floating finger. The current bent it down until it pointed at Sarathai-tia.

"Anuraja's boat-dick is limp, I'd say." Yavashuri's voice was acerbic and unexpectedly close to Mrithuri's elbow. Mrithuri jumped, banging herself in the eye with the spyglass. She whirled, lowering it, and gasped in surprise.

"Yavashuri!"

The old woman grinned. "I can still walk quiet when I want to."

The Dead Man stood behind her. He walked to the wall, careful not to lean against the faintly glowing shards of dragonglass. "He's got means to make it stick out enough to be useful. Watch."

He pointed.

One more boat, with four men rowing and four more seated idle between them, crossed the current. Mrithuri, through her spyglass, could see the curved rill behind it. It was towing something like a net.

The boat reached the near shore and the men jumped out, wading through shallow water and slick mud to beach it. They hauled the trailing thing out. Not a net: a rope.

The light was still dim, gloaming, though growing brighter. When Mrithuri lowered the spyglass to get a better sense of the scene, the men were squirmy dots, just discernable. They were hauling the rope, and it seemed unreasonably heavy and hard to pull. She raised her spyglass again and saw that they were struggling against the rope with all their might. And that slowly—slowly—the long trail of lashed boats across the river was bending toward them.

"I bet they wish they had an elephant," Mrithuri said.

"Anuraja thought this through better than I had hoped," the Dead Man answered. "Look, they are lashing another rank of boats alongside the first."

"What is it for?" Mrithuri asked.

Yavashuri drew her drape up tight around her. "It's a bridge. It gives them a route of attack. And a route of escape if we drive them back."

"Anuraja has a lot more men than I do."

"Aye, and his stronghold is tents pitched in the smoldering ruins of the village beyond. You have walls." The Dead Man touched her arm in reassurance.

"We can try to burn the flotilla once it gets dark again," Yavashuri suggested, gallantly keeping her eyes averted from the scandalous breach of protocol going on beside her.

"We shall," agreed Mrithuri.

Of course, Anuraja could then go upriver, or even—more inconveniently—down, and steal more of the boats Mrithuri's people relied upon to live. But those people, if they were wise, had fled already. And maybe many of them had taken their boats, though they would have to travel through the delta and the main channel of the river past Anuraja's trade city, Sarathai-lae. And perhaps be captured there.

After that, there was the Arid Sea to brave. In tiny boats meant for calm river swells.

No one would be fishing this river soon.

Mrithuri and her lieutenants watched in silence as Anuraja's men in their incongruously cheery orange-and-blue livery finished lashing together their crude bridge. By the time they finished the sun had set, and the sky behind the weirdly unfecund clouds was brightening.

The spyglass, when Mrithuri raised it again, showed her an army massed on the far bank, its first ranks making their cautious way over the bridge.

"We could sortie," said Yavashuri. "This will go better for us if we keep them on the other side."

"We *have* to sortie," the Dead Man agreed. "We have to get that bridge down. It makes it too easy for him to bring troops across the river."

"Yes." Mrithuri's face was a death mask. "Do it now, while we still have lee to open the gates."

"What about the Rasan Wizard?" the Dead Man said. "Can't he manage something?"

Mrithuri lowered her glass once more. She turned to a nervous young soldier shivering within earshot.

"Send for my general," she told the lad. He was beardless, and she wondered if he would ever grow one. "And also send for Tsering-la."

*     *     *

THE DEAD MAN DID NOT LEAD THE CHARGE WHEN THEY SORTIED. THAT was not his place in this fight. His place was to guard what the queen deemed precious, and that was more important: at least to the well-being of the queen. So he rode beside Hathi, Mrithuri's elephant, and the Wizards on her back. And he thought he knew Mrithuri well enough to appreciate what trust in him that indicated.

Even at this remove, there was a heady delight in riding toward the enemy. In having something simple and direct to *do*, after so much painful waiting.

The vanguard was well before them, moving much faster with its chariots and cavalry than the rumbling pace of an armored and elderly white elephant. Hathi wore the armor as if it were a costume, using her trunk to fiddle with the buckles, weaving her head from side to side to make the starlight that streamed through the rents in the cloud cover gleam on the facets in her brass chamfron.

Hathi was not meant to be a combatant, and it was the Dead Man's job to keep her out of the fight. She *did* serve as a mobile spellcasting platform, a vantage point for Ata Akhimah and Tsering-la to get above the fight and see what was going on.

At least the local technology in mobile siege engines did not yet run to cannon. There were a few inside the walls of Sarathai-tia—designed on imported knowledge and placed by Ata Akhimah. Anuraja's forces did not seem to be bringing any across the river.

You took your blessings where you could get them. The last siege the Dead Man had endured, during the final throes of the Uthman Caliphate, had involved more than enough cannon for a lifetime.

His borrowed horse kept up with Hathi and her passengers easily. He could not see well enough past the vanguard to have much of a sense of when Mrithuri's sally would make contact with the invaders. But the infantry were not yet running with lowered spears, chasing the whirring chariots. The rank of archers had not yet begun to let their volleys fly. So they were not yet in range for the charge.

What he could see was most of the makeshift pontoon bridge, and watch the boats that made it up dip and toss as men scrambled to reach the near shore, racing against the defenders who came to cut the bridge adrift, or burn it under them. The archers would have flame arrows.

They would do what they could. Sarathai-tia would not be easy prey.

"There they go!" Ata Akhimah yelled from her perch astride Hathi's neck, legs tucked behind the great, flapping, freckled ears. Her position offered the superior vantage. It was a moment more before the Dead Man saw what she had—the wheat-field wind-ripple of spears lowering in ranks. The thump of running feet, the chorus of shouting voices, the pounding of horses' hooves followed a moment later, delayed by distance.

The cavalry and chariots were all Mrithuri's. Anuraja's horses could not cross that pontoon bridge.

Hathi ambled forward, waving her trunk cheerily at all the fuss. She was unperturbed by the clash of arms, the shouts of warriors, the screams and groans of the injured.

It was strange, the Dead Man thought, to be far enough from the battle that it seemed . . . not unclean.

Mrithuri's archers—closest to Hathi, at the back of the sortie—loosed in rows, then ducked beneath the rectangular shields of stiffened hide carried by their aides. A moment later, a return flight feathered the earth around them. Hollow thuds, like rain on a broken drumhead, resonated from the shields. A few of the longest-ranged fell near enough to Hathi to give the Dead Man pause.

Apparently to give the Wizards pause as well, because on the rug behind Ata Akhimah, Tsering-la raised his hands and allowed a nimbus of lemon-white light to spill from them. It swirled through the air like ink in water, surrounding Hathi, extending to enclose the Dead Man as well. It painted an enormous target on them, of course. But Tsering-la and Ata Akhimah were already riding an elephant.

"How did I get to be Speaker to Wizards?" the Dead Man muttered to himself grumpily. But he followed as Ata Akhimah turned Hathi to the right, paralleling the course of the combat away from the river.

"What do you see?" the Dead Man yelled up to them.

"A lot more men than I expected," Tsering yelled back. "I've no idea how they've gotten so many soldiers across that joke of a bridge this quickly!"

"Maybe some swam along it on the upriver side?" the Dead Man suggested.

"Maybe they're not all there," Ata Akhimah replied. "He has got a sorcerer, remember. It wouldn't be his first time using illusion against us."

"Kithara Raja," the Dead Man said, remembering a conversation with Mrithuri where she has explained just such a stratagem. "That will waste some arrows."

"But if we can tell our men to charge," said Akhimah, "there will be gaps in the enemy's shield and spear wall."

"Aye, but they won't know where they are until they're on them." Their shielding light flickered with the intensity of Tsering's emotion.

"Well," the Dead Man said ruthlessly, "the weight of the charge should push them through regardless."

Akhimah nodded. She whispered into her hands, then pointed. There was a ripple in the air as her words flew to Pranaj, Mrithuri's new general, promoted since Madhukasa died taking an assassin's bullet for his queen. The Dead Man could not hear her words, but he saw the result. The rear rank of Mrithuri's foot soldiers, beyond the line of archers, seemed to shiver as if they were one eager animal. There was a pause, a moment of stillness. Then, like a wave cresting on the shores of the White Sea, the stillness broke. And fell forward with a renewed momentum, crashing into the banners of the army beyond.

The Dead Man could see very little. Dust rose everywhere, choking and obscuring—dust! In the rainy season! And his task was not tactics on this day, he reminded himself. It was to assess any threats to the Wizards, and Hathi, and keep *them* safe.

More dust from the hills to the right. He pointed to draw Akhimah's attention; he could not see the cause. The source was concealed.

Another flight of arrows sleeted around him, deflected away from the Dead Man and his horse and Hathi and her Wizards by those swirls of pale gold light. The Dead Man glanced at his charges and caught Tsering-la in the middle of a gesture like wiping a window free of steam. It seemed as well to wipe away the arrows that would have fallen among Mrithuri's archers. A moment later, the Dead Man felt a gust of wind sharp enough to make him grab the saddlebow, and understood how it was done.

He reined his horse alongside Hathi's enormous head. She reached out and poked him in the arm with a flexible, fibrous trunk-tip, nearly unseating him. It seemed like an affectionate gesture nonetheless.

He drew a pistol into his left hand, on the side away from those he guarded. Mrithuri's men seemed likely to turn Anuraja's men back at the shore, and burn the boats, as they hoped. What the Dead Man could see of the line was moving away, pushing into the invaders, pushing them back.

It seemed too easy. Until the screaming began.

"Hold fast!" Pranaj bellowed. "Hold fast, damn your eyes!" His voice carried, amplified by the Wizards' works.

A twist of wind carried a new sound of hooves to the Dead Man's ears. He understood, perhaps. He thought he did, as the defending line in front of him crumbled as if in an avalanche. Anuraja must have sent his cavalry upstream, and forded them, and brought them back down the near bank in concealing terrain.

"Fall back!" he yelled at the Wizards. His voice did not ring like Pranaj's. But then, it did not have to.

Thunderously, Hathi turned. The Dead Man had never seen an elephant whirl before. It was as earth-shaking, as ponderous as he would have imagined—and far more quickly done.

"If we run, it will be a rout!" he yelled. This might be a battlefield, but even in the chaos of war it was hard not to notice an elephant running away.

Ata Akhimah seemed to understand. She touched Hathi on the neck and the elephant responded, walking on a long diagonal toward the city gates, but not fleeing the field of combat.

The Dead Man glanced over his shoulder. Mrithuri's archers loosed again. They too were drawing back: not exactly in calm order, but not quitting the field in a frenzy, either. Not discarding weapons and armor.

The Dead Man shuddered. He'd seen such flight before. He did not care to see it ever again, though the image of that past time came to him intrusive and unbidden. Battering at his self-control like a great tree trunk swung against the gates of a keep. His borrowed horse caught his mood and spooked and shied beneath him. He stayed on her as much by luck as skill and shook himself, chastising himself for inattention. He calmed her with shaking hands, thinking *everything in this life is borrowed.*

*The life itself, most of all.*

Fatalism claimed him, familiar and soothing. He spoke the secret name of his god into his veil, and that calmed him also.

A little.

Enough, maybe. How calm did you need to be to watch what you cared for die?

Maybe he would be blessed to fall first, this time.

*Stop it.* All would be as God willed, for Her own reasons. Acceptance of—obedience to—Her will was acceptance of his own fate. He might die here. If he did, then dying would be over. And what awaited then was just an end to pain, as the priests of Kaalha in Messaline might say.

He glanced over his shoulder again at the shrieks and clamor. The line was still holding, though it was falling back almost fast enough to count as a retreat. Being driven back, step by blood-soaked step. The Dead Man could see the enemy horse now. They had tried to flank the defenders. They had succeeded, after a fashion, but Mrithuri's chariot-eers had managed to swing around and meet them force to force before they could close the crushing grip of the pincher. Some of the scream-ing was the unbearable screaming of horses.

It was Pranaj's voice alone holding the line now. Almost by force of will, as if he sustained each of his men with his own hands, pressed them forward, held them up. But if the enemy horse were willing to turn their backs on the charioteers, take the losses and ride pell-mell down on the Wizards . . .

They could reach—and probably destroy—the little contingent the Dead Man guarded.

Something shattered in the globe of light before the Dead Man's gaze. Bits flew everywhere, scattering like the sparks from struck flint. The largest portion bounced and rolled away like an enormous parody of a child's toy. It would have crushed through Mrithuri's archers and the rest of her men if Tsering-la had not reached out with both hands, and with a grunt of effort somehow . . . hefted . . . it aside. It went bound-ing over Mrithuri's line and slammed into Anuraja's, scattering real soldiers—some of them in pieces—and passing ghostlike through phan-toms.

The shield of yellow light was gone. Tsering-la leaned forward, bracing his hands against Hathi's back. "Fuck, I think I pissed myself a little."

The Dead Man watched the bounding thing go, realizing too late what he saw. It was a huge boulder, a stone chipped into a sphere. A cannonball.

A cannonball from within the defenses of Sarathai-tia. Friendly fire, and it had nearly flattened Mrithuri's Wizards all at once. Fortunes of war.

"Your shield!" the Dead Man yelled at Tsering-la, as the sky above the armies was darkened by a flitting pall like the rising of an enormous flock of starlings. The Wizard swore again, and raised his hands with the expression of a man who would like to double over around a cramp. The light shimmered up, ragged and flickering at first, barely seeming to solidify before the flight of arrows spattered from it like rain from a window. The shield was tattered and incomplete, leaving the Dead Man in mind of the torn veils of light that wavered across the night sky in the far cold northlands where he and the Gage had journeyed once.

Tsering-la tried to push it out, to stretch it over Mrithuri's men. He moved like a man with a bullet in him, or one who has torn a muscle in his groin. Jerky, clutched around his middle. But still striving.

Maybe Wizards had some toughness in them after all, and the Dead Man had been uncharitable. But there were more arrows behind the first flight, and streamers of that first flight were raining through the gaps in Tsering-la's shield like sunlight ribboning through the gaps in a cloud.

"Where the hell is he getting all these archers from?" Akhimah asked angrily.

Tsering-la's reply was right. "I'm not sure there are any. Or that many, anyway."

"They're not arrows," the Dead Man said, letting his spyglass drop upon its cord. "Or at least, they aren't arrows anymore."

He reined his horse back, watching the black, streaking blurs writhe from their arced trajectories and twist into flocks that moved with the will and volition of birds. *Even more like starlings.*

Whether they were birds, or arrows, or something else—they curved and feinted and fell with savagery, pecking and shrieking, upon Mrithuri's men.

*Carrion birds.* He raised the spyglass again. But not crows, and not ravens. Something dull black, not shining, with a more sharply hooked beak, though not much bigger.

The men shrieked in turn. Even from this far away, the Dead Man could see that the ones who were swarmed waved their arms wildly, swatted, shrieked, and either broke and ran or fountained blood and died.

The Dead Man stood in the stirrups, craning his head up to the Wizards. Tsering-la, his complexion thunder-green with strain, shook his head.

The Dead Man swallowed.

"Fall back!" he shouted. "Tell Pranaj to fall back! Fall back within range of the guns!"

It wouldn't get them to the bridge. It wouldn't get the bridge demolished. It wouldn't keep the noose of the siege from closing around Sarathai-tia. But it might keep the army alive long enough to rally and make another push.

It was a testament to Pranaj's ability that the retreat remained as orderly as it did.

Before the gates, behind the collapsing front of the army, Hathi and the Wizards made their stand. They would have time to fall back, if worst came to worst. Perhaps even time to make it within the gates, then hold the portal long enough to close them.

The Dead Man struggled to believe Mrithuri's people had another push in them. He turned his mare in a tight circle as she fought the rein. He could see the improvised bridge from where she yanked the bit and sidled. It was just a little more than a cannon shot away.

It seemed very close.

There was nothing to prevent him from just riding up to it and setting it on fire. A matter of minutes was all it would take. Except there were two warring armies and a pitched battle between here and there.

Inconvenient, that.

*There has to be a way.*

Well, no, there didn't. The Dead Man wasn't naive enough to recite soothing platitudes to himself without that moment of correction. Where there was a will, he knew from harsh experience, there was often no result but sorrow. And the good guys—in that rare circumstance where anything like an actual good guy was determinable—were by no means predestined to win.

But it also wasn't over until the last tactical miscalculation was registered and the last hilltop and tower fought for. He'd seen a lot of stunning defeats and last-minute victories in a career that spanned over forty years of active service, from the time he was a lad of ten. Most of that service, he admitted to himself, on the losing side.

But maybe not this time.

What the hell. It was worth a try. What did he have to lose except the inevitable specter of defeat, after all?

Above and behind him, the cannons thundered. It was a sound so long familiar it did not even draw a flinch.

The Dead Man stood in his stirrups to watch the war. He peered through engloving light to see that Pranaj was firming his line. The charioteers had pushed the enemy horse back, and now Anuraja's cavalry had lost the advantage of flanking. The defenders seemed to have found their stride, and recollected their will in the teeth of the realization that half or more of the enemy were phantoms.

Will alone could not win a battle. But lack of will could lose one.

Tsering had gotten his shields re-ordered. The shrieking flocks of arrow-birds passed overhead, eyes coral and glowing with hate, feathers like clotted blood. Most of them could no longer get through. The Dead Man would see, sometimes, blood on the beaks and talons of those that had succeeded.

"Fuck that sorcerer," he snarled.

Akhimah grunted a laugh. "You first."

And now the cannonballs ripped over the defenders' heads. They plunged through the enemy line, and their passage made it manifest through slaughter which men were real and which illusion. The illusionary ones did not shred apart and scream so redly.

Cannon were an unholy weapon. An arrow could pierce; a spear could paunch; a sword could sever. These were all terrible things. But none were such a red pen writing wanton destruction as a cannonball. Especially—the Dead Man winced, but for the love of his own life and the rajni's resisted averting his gaze—especially when the trajectory of the ball fell short and it crashed through the friendly line as bloodily as it might the enemy.

And they were no more unholy than the arrow-birds.

Oh, well. No war was perfect, except perhaps the war in the afterlife aspired to by the fabled warriors of the north. They believed in a heaven of endless, joyous carnage, with resurrection and feasting to end and celebrate each eternal day.

The Dead Man's current mood was that he'd gotten enough of carnage in this lifetime, and that he'd prefer to spend eternity reading.

In the meantime, however: here was a war, and it was once again coming toward him.

"Fall back!" he yelled to the Wizards, and spurred his reluctant horse toward the defending line.

THE DEFENDING LINE WAS COLLAPSING. MRITHURI, FROM HER EYRIE ON the walls, could see it all. The cannon had brought them a respite. But she had not enough men to drive a rally, and though they had managed to hold longer than she expected after that unexpected cavalry charge, and though the illusory greater numbers of the enemy no longer paralyzed her people with fear—every bowshot aimed at an enemy that did not exist was wasted. Every sword-cut and spear-jab targeting a phantasm opened the delivering warrior up for retaliation by a real man.

Her men were doing well that it wasn't a rout. But it could still become one.

"We won't get the bridge cut this way," Yavashuri said at her shoulder.

Mrithuri made an angry, inchoate noise. Her head felt fuzzy and full of distractions. She needed clarity. She needed her snakes.

"Where is Chaeri?"

"Rajni—"

Mrithuri turned over her shoulder and skewered her advisor on a glance. "Moralizing is less than useful now. Send her to me. I will be in my stellar."

MRITHURI SHOULDN'T SNAP AT THE OLD WOMAN SO, AND SHE KNEW IT. Rajni or not, cruelty did not win you loyalty, though fear could net obedience. It was an uncreative obedience, however. One that was afraid to seek solutions on its own. She stalked some of her fury off, Syama pacing at her heels.

By the time Mrithuri reached the breezy broad-windowed room at the top of her palace, she was deciding how to apologize. She still intended to do what she must, but she *wanted* her advisors to challenge her. Biting their heads off was not the means by which to ensure this.

The stellar was a women's space by design, a social center where one could write or read or sew by the bright light of the Heavenly River, without squinting under lamps as one must in the more defensible chambers of the palace. Mrithuri found Lady Golbahar there already, ensconced with her embroidery. Golbahar jumped up, needle poised, but waited to speak until the rajni indicated her wishes.

Mrithuri would have been quite pleased to see her, if she had not already sent for and been expecting Chaeri. Chaeri, and the Eremite serpents, in whose intoxicating venom perhaps a solution lay.

There was a rustle behind the pierced sandalwood partitions as nuns, too, set down their needlework and stood in courtesy to the rajni. Mrithuri could have ordered them all out. But this was the space in the palace that gave light for such delicate work.

And there was comfort to be found in the presence of Lady Golbahar, who was quick-witted and pleasant, and whose station in life constrained her in many of the same ways Mrithuri was constrained.

Still, Mrithuri turned away for a moment to collect herself. Sayeh's phoenix was in a corner of the room, looking less bedraggled but very much older. Its broken feathers had been imped to replacements. But phoenix feathers were not the sort of thing that even most royal mews had lying around, so in among Guang Bao's own iridescent red-gold-violet-green were speckled the dirty-white and black primaries of Mrithuri's bearded vultures. The long lyred tail's losses had been made up from the molted plumage of royal peacocks.

The least annoying use for which those mid-sleep screamers might have been put, Mrithuri thought, touching the outline of one inked under the skin of her arm. There was a bear-dog too, and as she touched that, she looked over at Syama, lounging by the door with her tongue lolling in the heat.

She turned back toward Golbahar and cocked her head at the foreign lady. "Sit," she said. "You're putting too much tension on your thread, standing like that."

Golbahar smiled and settled again among the cushions. Mrithuri joined her. "Working on your trousseau?"

"Thank the Scholar-God, no!" Golbahar replied, her laugh a practiced bell.

Golbahar had been traveling from her home to an arranged marriage somewhere in Song when the inconvenient fact of Mrithuri's familial squabbles had intersected her journey.

"You sound remarkably cheerful, for somebody caught in a siege not her own."

Golbahar squinted at her needle. "My whole life has been a siege."

"Meaning?"

The lady sighed. "Anything that keeps me a maiden for a few months longer is not an unrelieved trial."

"If they breach the walls—" Mrithuri bit her lip. Even if they did not breach the walls, how would the willowy girl manage when starvation stalked the streets? And Mrithuri's own men might become as much a threat as the enemy, if their discipline did not hold.

Well, she had Pranaj and the Dead Man to keep her own troops from murder and rape of their own city. And none of them had any choice about where they were now. So, Golbahar might as well be cheerful, she supposed.

And if it was a facade . . . well, it was a facade of strength. One that might comfort others, Mrithuri included. And that behooved Mrithuri to appreciate it.

She watched Golbahar's needle move, thinking that sometimes it is easier to talk to strangers. Strangers have not judged you. They do not assume they know who you are, how you think, what you have experienced. How you feel.

Friendships come with so much weight of history that sometimes one's friends cannot see one in truth for all the things they think they know about you.

So it was that Mrithuri found herself talking frankly to Golbahar without ever being quite sure that she knew how the conversation had developed.

"I think," Mrithuri said, "that I have gone through my whole life without faith."

"But aren't you a priestess?" Golbahar asked interestedly.

"The Mother—and the Good Daughter—they are easy. Besides, They don't reward faith. The Mother looks on us as chickens in the henhouse. What's one individual, more or less, now and then? So long as the flock survives? And the Good Daughter will slaughter what she needs, when she needs them. You can't make an omelet without breaking eggs, after all.

"But people. People will purport to care about you. *You.* But just let the going get tough . . . or let them want something you prove inconvenient to. And see where your faith in them gets you."

Golbahar's needle stitched the pale linen like a blind dolphin stitching the river. "It sounds like you might be thinking about this a lot."

Mrithuri looked down at her hands, strangely bare for the moment of all the ornaments that rendered her so dependent on others. Her hands were taking advantage of their nakedness to strangle one another.

"I might be having an attack of . . . of faith," she admitted.

"Faith in a person?"

Mrithuri nodded.

"It's a terrible poison," Golbahar said, amused. "It will only make you ill."

"It does not feel like a poison."

"Then it is a prison." Stitch, stitch. A pattern of poppies emerged, blood spreading beneath the surface of milky water. "It will have you in chains."

"I want to trust somebody," Mrithuri said. "I want to just . . . relax. Feel safe. A novel desire."

"Fight it," counseled Golbahar.

"What if it were you?"

"Doubly don't," the lady rebuked softly. She glanced aside, eyes abashed above her veil. "I can promise no loyalty to anyone."

A swishing sound, as the door was whisked aside. The Dead Man walked into the room, hard-stained with battle. Both women fell silent and drew gently apart. Golbahar touched her veil.

"Everyone is here but the person I have sent for," Mrithuri said with a laugh she thought sounded natural. She hooked the Dead Man toward her with a crook of bare fingertips. "How goes the war?"

He followed her gestures to settle on the cushions near her feet. "Not well," he admitted. "We need to break their bridge."

Mrithuri saw his eyes flick down. He had followed the motion of her hand, she realized, as she unconsciously stroked the outline of a blind river dolphin inked upon her skin.

His eyebrows lifted inquiringly beneath the edge of his indigo head scarf.

Apprehension stopped her breath. "Not unless I have no choice."

"The enemy are across the river," the Dead Man said. "Not quite to our gates, because they still respect our cannon. But that will last as long as our gunpowder does. There are more where these came from, and they're going to keep coming."

"There are bats in the caverns under the palace," Mrithuri said, hearing her own bland satisfaction. "And we have two Wizards here. I'm not *too* concerned about running out of gunpowder."

Somewhere within the walls, an anchorite stroked her harp in a gentle glissando.

"You've no bats among your ornaments," the Dead Man said.

"They're not especially sacred to the Mother. But they do keep the bugs down."

"Food will also be an issue."

"It will," Mrithuri agreed. "We have fish, and water—"

"Until Anuraja poisons the river—"

Mrithuri's hand fell to her lap in shock. The Dead Man paused mid-thought.

"Rajni?" said Golbahar, when the silence had stretched.

"He would not." Even speaking it, Mrithuri knew her protest was ridiculous. But she spoke it anyway. "He . . . never."

"We must anticipate the unthinkable." The gentleness in the Dead Man's voice made her feel she must appear very small and very young.

"But to poison the Mother? To *poison* the *Mother*?"

Golbahar remarked, "People do poison their parents from time to time."

The Dead Man sat very still, as one will when imparting bad news. "Especially when they are impatient to inherit."

Mrithuri knew her own naiveté rang in her voice when it burst outraged from her lips but could not hold it back, for all it shamed her. "That would be blasphemy! That is anathema!"

His voice grew gentler still. "Will religious feeling stop your enemies any more than familial duty shall?"

She laid her hands flat on her thighs, and with a supreme act of will, kept them soft there. "The dolphins would not survive that, either."

"Neither would anything else in the river." The Dead Man had a terrible manner of agreeing with her when she most wished he would argue. "But take heart, Rajni. I spoke with the Wizards. They are of the opinion that poisoning an entire river of that size would be an extreme technical challenge."

"Comforting to think that difficulty might stay a hand when ethics will not."

Golbahar clicked her needle on her porcelain thimble. "Apologies, Rajni," she said, when Mrithuri looked at her. "But they do have a sorcerer."

Mrithuri swore. "Yes."

Restlessness infused her limbs. She wanted to jump up and pace. She craved the sweet focus and strength of her venom.

She was a rajni. She would comport herself. She willed herself still, folded her hands, and composed her dignity. "We need to keep the cisterns filled, then. Especially"—she nodded to the windows—"if the rains keep failing. We . . . oh, send for Hnarisha and Yavashuri."

A patter of slippers sounded from behind the partition. The nuns would pass the message, and Yavashuri and Hnarisha would soon be with her.

She looked at the Dead Man. "We must speak with Nizhvashiti. It is possible the Godmade can work a miracle or two. Isn't multiplying bread supposed to be the sort of thing that Godmade are good for?"

"If I knew where it was, I would speak to it," the Dead Man said. "May I rise, Rajni?"

She nodded.

*He* had no compunctions about pacing. He strode back and forth, his hands folded behind his back. He again wore the torn red coat. She watched as he slid his hands into the pockets, how he smoothed his thumbs across the seams.

The bullet hole at the breast had been darned, and the worst patches of wear at hems and elbows. Laundry women had their own arts that bordered on magic, and while the borders of the bloodstain were still faintly brown against the faded fabric, the worst of it had been scrubbed and soaked and alchemized away.

"Well," he said. "That was . . . not decisive. At least we've kept them back from the walls."

"Cannon," she said. "Good for something."

He nodded in a manner that looked like shaking his head.

She put a hand on his sleeve, forgetting herself for a moment. Surprised, he looked at her.

Soothingly, she said, "Don't worry. When the Mother rises, they will learn that they have been camping underwater."

A rustle behind the pierced screens. A slip of paper. Golbahar rose to fetch it. A silent anchorite extended a folded spill through the filigree and smiled when Golbahar's fingers brushed hers.

The foreign lady bent over the spindled paper. She smoothed it between her hands. "Yavashuri and Hnarisha request that you do them the great honor of meeting them. They say they are in the rooms of Mahadijia, and they have something they need to show to you."

Mahadijia had left some Wizardry in place around his chambers that made them hard to locate; hard even to remember the existence of. Mrithuri pressed her fingertips to her eyes. "If we can manage to find our way there."

The Dead Man looked down at her, unspeaking.

"Well," she said, pressing herself to her feet, "we'd better go. It's not as if we can leave the war to cool its heels in our parlor until we get around to greeting it."

Her bhaluukutta rose and followed them.

THE DEAD MAN FOLLOWED MRITHURI AND GOLBAHAR DOWN THE PASsages of the palace, and Mrithuri and Golbahar in turn followed one of the anchorite nuns. She sang softly to herself and walked with a little shuffling step on the other side of the piecework partition, almost as if she were dancing in a straight line. She moved with direct sureness through the winding corridors. Apparently, the nuns were not confused by geomancy.

They turned a corner. The queen said, "Oh, no."

The Dead Man unsheathed his sword.

"Who is it?" Golbahar had the better view, until the Dead Man stepped in front of her.

Mrithuri touched her cheek as if wishing for one of her snarling filigree masks of estate. Behind her palm, she whispered, "That asshole, Mi Ren."

Golbahar giggled.

"What?" asked the Dead Man, as that asshole approached, preceded by a wave of perfume.

"Oh," Golbahar murmured. "I call him that, too. And so do the nuns."

The Dead Man, who had never heard the nuns speak, might have asked another question, if the person under discussion had not just then burst in among them like a small artillery shell.

He rushed up to Mrithuri so precipitously that the Dead Man interposed himself and his sword. Mi Ren, though, just hurled himself to his knees in the hall.

It looked painful, as if the Song Prince were not much practiced at self-abasement. Mrithuri drew back with a jingle of anklets.

"Your Abundance!" Mi Ren cried. "Why do you scorn me?"

Golbahar stepped against the wall quite sensibly. A nun giggled in embarrassment, her movement revealed by the pale flutters of her raiment.

The Dead Man lowered his sword. Not to remove the threat, but so the blade remained at Mi Ren's eye level as the prince groveled. Apparently he could not bring himself to prostrate himself entirely. So he simply knelt, and extended his hands beseechingly.

Though not too close to the Dead Man's naked blade. Or the glowering teeth of Syama.

Mrithuri stood looking down at him with that practiced, waxed complacence that the Dead Man was coming to recognize as fury. Mi Ren folded one hand inside the other and begged theatrically. "I have sent you gifts, my rajni, and tokens of esteem. I have sewn my heart in petals on my robe for you. And yet you are cold to me."

The Dead Man didn't think Mi Ren saw Lady Golbahar roll her eyes at him and the nun. Or hear that she muttered, "Perhaps because there is a war in our garden?"

But the Dead Man certainly did.

What was one little war to such as Mi Ren? Surely nothing that should inconvenience him.

Mrithuri seemed to have recovered herself, though she had never lost her self-possession. She rubbed her arms with her palms, a gesture the Dead Man loathed because it meant she was coveting the Eremite snake venom. It made her sleepless and gave her thoughts the speed of racing falcons. But her voice was steady and imperious as she said to Mi Ren, "Stand up, before my bodyguard and my bhaluukutta eat you."

Syama growled as if she knew the words.

Mi Ren tried to leap to his feet, as dashing young princes were no doubt meant to in his mythology. He caught a slipper on the edge of his robe sleeve and did not quite go sprawling. Which was all for the best, the Dead Man supposed, given the danger of imminent impalement. Still, as he staggered and struggled and hopped, the Dead Man could not help but mourn a plausible accident.

As soon as Mi Ren was stably on his feet again, Mrithuri softened. The Dead Man could see it for the act it was, but he doubted that Mi Ren had the self-awareness to imagine Mrithuri finding him anything but irresistible. Therefore, any distance she imposed must be mere simpering meant to inflame.

"Now, Prince," she murmured. "You know that I have duties. There is a war at my very gates." A flash of cunning inspiration lit her features, smoothing seamlessly into coyness. "You know that nothing lesser would keep me from the pleasures of your company."

She turned her face and angled her eyes at him, as she might have if she were wielding a fan. It was a pretty, calculated trick, and the Dead Man's heart warmed that she never used it on him.

"But have I not offered the assistance of my family and our armies and wealth?" Mi Ren reached out and touched her hand. She allowed him to take it, so the Dead Man resisted his immediate urge to inflict mutilation. "Have I not told you we will march to your relief?"

"You have," she purred. "Has there been a dove from your people, then?"

"I doubt they have doves trained to come to Sarathai-tia." He pouted. "The silly birds will only fly home to their own cote. I still have a few of the ones I brought with me, however. I can send another message."

Mrithuri gazed up at Mi Ren through her eyelashes. "I would be ever so grateful," she said. "You know there's no chance of a state wedding . . . until"—she sighed as if it grieved her—"until the siege is lifted."

Mi Ren's eyes ran over her possessively. The Dead Man's fingers tightened on the hilt of the sword she had given him. "I will go right now, Your Abundance." He bowed once more, with another of his elaborate flourishes, and withdrew along the hall.

"I've heard there's a language to those flourishes, in Song," the Dead Man remarked conversationally, when Mi Ren was gone.

"I bet he speaks it with a whine," Mrithuri snarled. "I need a bath."

"Pity," said Golbahar. "The water in the cisterns is for drinking."

THE NUNS BROUGHT THEM TO ANURAJA'S DEAD AMBASSADOR'S CHAMBERS without a falter, leaving the Dead Man to wonder why Mahadijia's Wizardry did not seem to maze them. Perhaps they had Wizardry of their own. Perhaps Mahadijia had not thought to extend his illusion or whatever it was to their half-hidden warrens. Perhaps he had simply forgotten that they were people he needed to account for. Or perhaps there was some quality of the warrens themselves that pierced the confusion he had laid, or had *had* laid, over his spaces.

That he had hidden his suite in Mrithuri's palace from Mrithuri herself, and magically arranged things so that nobody noticed or even remembered to go looking, seemed a subtle and powerful magic. Not the sort of thing one might wish for on a battlefield. But profoundly useful nonetheless.

The Dead Man seemed to recall that there were Aezin Wizards who had similar abilities. He wished the Gage were here, to explain exactly what was going on. But perhaps he could take the opportunity to ask Ata Akhimah.

At last they found the blond wood door in the golden stone corridor. A sweet breeze blew from the gardens. Some trace of foul smokiness rode it: burning ships, and gunpowder. But they could not hear the war.

The door stood open, and soft voices came from within.

Mrithuri looked at the Dead Man. He nodded and stepped forward, Syama at his flank. The bear-dog still kept a wary eye on him; she only had one mistress. But she seemed to have accepted him as at least a temporary ally, if not a full member of her pack.

Gently, he scratched at the doorframe. "The rajni," he announced, as he had seen others do, and waited a few moments before he pulled wide the door. It wasn't too different from how he would have served his caliph. When there were such a thing as caliphs in the world.

He checked the room before he moved out of the way. Within were only Yavashuri and Hnarisha, and they looked calm enough. As calm as did anyone in this palace, in these days. Behind them, beside the dead ambassador's desk, was a dark pipe-narrow outline that could only be Nizhvashiti in its dark robes. When he stood aside, Golbahar preceded Mrithuri into the room and Syama flanked her, leaving him to take up the rear.

"So you found the Godmade," Mrithuri said, pausing far enough within the room to allow the Dead Man to enter after her.

Hnarisha and Yavashuri looked at one another.

"After a fashion," Yavashuri said. Warily, eyeing Mrithuri as if unsure how she might react.

Mrithuri visibly gathered herself. "Please explain."

"Well. We found its body."

The Dead Man opened his mouth and almost said, "It's *dead*?" but stopped himself in time. Of course it was dead. And not in the metaphorical sense in which he himself was dead, either. Nizhvashiti was, after all, standing right there, swathed in black, obviously dead, staring sightlessly and fixedly toward some invisible horizon with two artificial eyes.

And just as obviously not falling over.

"It's entranced," the Dead Man said, who had seen this before. Albeit, while the sainted priest was alive. "I mean, I suppose. Unless its animating force has fled. How did you come to find it here?"

Yavashuri looked from the Dead Man to Golbahar, and then to Mrithuri. Her head tilted in a question under her comb-spiked hair.

"Sure," Mrithuri said. "These two came late to the war. And the Dead Man almost died for me. It can't have been either of them that bewitched Ata Akhimah's coat."

"One poison baked in a dish doesn't mean a second can't be dripped in at the table," Yavashuri said direly. But she waved to Hnarisha with the air of one abdicating responsibility.

Hnarisha rubbed his hands as if to warm chilled fingers. He brushed the gold rings rimming his ear with the backs of them, making a faint chime sound. "We came to see if there was any clue who might have burned Mahadijia's papers. I mean, it is possible he did it himself, if he was coming to kill you."

"But you don't believe that," said Mrithuri.

"He wanted so badly to speak with you that he defiled the ceremony of Rains Return."

Yavashuri looked faintly guilty. "I thought only that his master was an apostate and a heretic, and that he had no respect for your duties. In retrospect, I might have been wrong. I think I gave you poor counsel, my rajni. And I am sorry—"

Mrithuri waved her apologies away. "I thought as you did. If you were not counseling me differently now, I would not question that judgment. So there are two mysteries."

Hnarisha nodded. "There are. Who destroyed his documents, and what was his purpose in coming to you when Chaeri killed him?"

"He had a bared dagger in hand," Mrithuri said.

Yavashuri made a noise. Mrithuri looked at her, and arched a finger to summon forth her words.

Yavashuri sighed. "So Chaeri said." Her mouth quirked, as if she anticipated a reprimand.

The Dead Man tilted his head at Hnarisha.

Hnarisha shook his head and said, "All our intelligence suggests that Anuraja wants to marry the rajni—begging your pardon, Rajni—not assassinate her."

The Dead Man touched the cloth over his fresh scar. "Well, somebody does."

The rajni rubbed her arms, an echo of Hnarisha's gesture. It was not at all cold in the room. She opened and closed her mouth once or twice, swallowing whatever words filled it each time. She closed her eyes at last and said, "I had wondered how she got the knife away from him."

It had the air of a great and painful admission, and the Dead Man's heart twisted with admiration and discomfort at her courage. He wished at that moment that he could reach out and touch her arm, that there were not the glassy and invisible shield of rank between them. But there it was, as impenetrable as the Gage's mirrored brass armor.

Then she squared herself and said, "But we don't *know*."

Hnarisha and Yavashuri shared a glance as the Dead Man schooled himself not to show disappointment. He should not, he told himself, allow himself to feel possessive toward this young queen. He *must* not allow himself to feel proprietary. Her choices were her own. She was the master of her own destiny, inasmuch as anyone could be.

That she was also master of his, and that her choices could put him and all her subjects at risk as well as herself . . . well, that was only how the world worked. He had dealt with the results before, and he felt himself to be committed here now.

Still, he was starting to develop his own ideas of how to deal with Chaeri.

Sadly, he could not think of a dutiful way to conceal such an intervention from the rajni.

When Nizhvashiti moved, the tension was not so much broken as redirected. The Dead Man jumped, and realized he had never resheathed his blade after the encounter with Mi Ren. It had been by his side in low guard ever since, as natural as his own finger. It gave him pause that no one had remarked upon it. What must Mrithuri's people think of him?

Nizhvashiti had not done much—just spread its hands from its sides a span or so. Its fingers were like the knobby, twiggy sticks of a fan. Its face remained expressionless, glass and golden eyes each unblinking. Then it turned, and a strange light seemed to kindle in the depths of the glass eye—reflecting, refracting. Pooling there like the radiance that got caught in the fibers of a cat's-eye stone.

Nizhvashiti opened dry lips that cracked without bleeding, and spoke with a voice that was not its own: windy and great and strange and cold, and resonating without booming, like the music of some great-reeded, great-chambered woodwind. "And then in the world there are islands, and each island is a ghost, a palimpsest of what has been and what is wrought upon it and what it could or might or will become. Each island has boundaries, that are more or less permeable to the ocean and the wind, and that may vary by the tide. And each island has connections to other islands, whether by necessity, accident, or desire.

"In this manner do islands resemble people. In this manner do people resemble nations. In this manner do nations resemble the winds of storms."

The voice speaking through Nizhvashiti rose and fell with expression.

It never paused and hesitated for breath, the dead priest's bony chest neither rising nor falling. "Break my chain. Break my chain. Seek the mother of the Mother River. Seek the Origin of Storms."

Mrithuri started forward. One step, two. The Dead Man almost caught after her arm before he remembered his place. It was Lady Golbahar who smoothly, without touching Mrithuri, interposed her slight body between the rajni and the Godmade, so that Mrithuri would have had to push her aside to move closer.

"Nizhvashiti?" she asked.

The Godmade did not answer. It raised one hand—the left hand—and extended a single finger tipped with a curved black nail like a claw.

"Lady—" the Dead Man began. *I do not think that that is exactly Nizhvashiti.*

He did not have time to finish.

Nizhvashiti raised the long finger and tapped the dragonglass orb of its eye, which flared with that green light, kindled deep within, and sounded a single piercing chime.

Everyone stepped back: Mrithuri, Golbahar, Yavashuri, Hnarisha. And also the Dead Man.

It felt as if something in the room broke, the way laughter breaks tension, or the way humidity and stifling heat may be broken by the clean air after a storm. As if they were riding on a puzzle piece that abruptly shifted itself, turned, rocked, and seated itself in a place from which it had somehow been dislodged and was now home in.

"The spell," Hnarisha said. "The rooms are unhidden."

"How did *you* find them again?" the Dead Man said.

Hnarisha shrugged. "I have a few skills, and trusting the Immanent Sun does offer a route to knowing illusion from reality. Illusion . . . casts a different shadow."

He grinned at the Dead Man, and the Dead Man realized that his free hand had automatically made the sign of the pen.

Mrithuri said, "That's the second time the Origin of Storms has come up. The first time, it was in the message that the Godmade brought back from the other side."

Hnarisha closed his eyes and quoted from memory: "'Seek the Carbuncle. Seek the Mother of Exiles, blind and in her singing catacomb. Time is short, and more is at stake than kingdoms. Something stirs.

Something vast and cruel stirs, to the east, beneath the sea. Your destiny lies with the Origin of Storms.'"

"Storms come from the sea thereof," Yavashuri said. "Is something Anuraja or his sorcerer doing preventing the rains from reaching us?"

"Someone certainly wants us to think so." Golbahar tilted her head to one side and studied Nizhvashiti. "But are they friend or foe?"

"Oh, for the old days, when wars were simple," Mrithuri said, and threw up her hands. Her glass bangles chimed. "None of this is amounting to anything. None of this gets us closer to salvation."

Golbahar said gently, "Your Abundance seems not much concerned about the siege."

"There is food and water in the mountain. And the river shall soon enough rise."

"Soon enough," Hnarisha said, as if agreeing. "We can keep hoping it is soon enough, anyway."

"Have you given further thought to sending your vultures to the troops at the border, my rajni?" Yavashuri asked.

The Dead Man said, "The carrion birds of the enemy—"

"I will not risk them," Mrithuri interrupted.

*Not the dolphins, and not the vultures. This is not their war.*

"We can hang on until the Gage returns," Yavashuri said soothingly.

"And then what? Give them a pregnant queen to capture?" Golbahar snorted.

Mrithuri's scarf trailed as she waved them quiet. "Search this apartment. Perhaps there are more clues in it, which will be revealed now that the spells of confusion are broken. Or perhaps we missed something before. In any case, search it. Tear it apart. And see if you can't wake up the Godmade and find out what in the deeps of nightmare it was talking about. I'll be in my stellar. Yavashuri, Golbahar, with me if you please."

She turned. Syama, who of course had never left her side, pivoted with her. The Dead Man watched her fuss with the drape of her tunic for a moment to give her women time to fall in beside her.

The sound of a cleared throat drew his attention. Hnarisha was on his left. "I wanted to talk to you about the war, anyway."

The Dead Man shook his head. "What can I tell you?"

"Anuraja. He could be doing more damage," Hnarisha said.

"He wants to take the city intact," the Dead Man answered. "The city. And the queen."

"Yes, and he is confident in his ability to do those things."

The Dead Man nodded. "Too confident. Lying in wait."

Hnarisha did not say "Chaeri." Neither did the Dead Man. Not here, where Mrithuri could overhear them. But they shared a long glance, and the Dead Man was certain he knew what lay behind it.

"We'll speak more while we search," said Hnarisha as the door from the corridor slammed open, narrowly missing the rajni. Chaeri, alone and with her garments and hair in disarray, burst in.

# 12

THE GAGE AND NIZHVASHITI WENT INTO THE DESTROYED PALACE SIDE by side and without strategy, perhaps incautiously. But the Gage was nigh-invulnerable, and Nizhvashiti was already dead. And possibly not entirely real.

What was the worst that could happen?

This palace compound, while lightly fortified by gates and walls, had mostly been built long and low within them. The devastation within the palace was worse than that without. In the outer court, they found the long column-supported promenades had entirely collapsed.

The open colonnades might have seemed incautious from a defensive standpoint. But after all, war and invasion were an infrequent threat. The heat killed every summer. Building in stone at all in an area so prone to earthquakes might have been the graver mistake. But the Gage was not sure what options anyone might have, in such a bleak environment.

The reek of death was stronger within the palace walls, though there were still no bodies bloating amidst the rubble.

The bodies were beyond it.

The sight stopped even the Gage in his tracks. He set his leading foot down with a clang quite unlike his usual attempts to walk softly, and just stood. Had he eyes, he would have been staring—or perhaps covering them in horror. Nizhvashiti drifted to a stop beside him.

Because those colonnades and the apartments they connected had largely collapsed, the Gage could see over them clearly.

To the mountain of dead that lay behind.

He might have cursed. He might have blasphemed. If he had been able even slightly to recollect the gods he had sworn by when he was alive, and their slanders. But whoever those gods had been, in this moment the memory of them utterly deserted him.

Neither was the priest inclined to speak. The two of them simply watched, stopped where they were for long moments. Until enduring the silence, at last, became worse than breaking it. Then the Gage managed to say, "Is that all of them?"

"Every one?" Nizhvashiti shook its hooded skull. Even being who it was, the gesture had a bit of a tremble to it. "We know some escaped. Sayeh Rajni herself. A few of her retainers. Some refugees who left in obedience to her will or through their own common sense, though the army ordered all to stay. And tried to enforce it. Not all chose to bow their heads to the army's threats and decrees, however."

The Gage would have frowned, had he a face for doing so. "How could you know that, Godmade?"

Nizhvashiti's dead face rearranged itself in discomfort. "You know all sorts of things in dreams."

The Gage contemplated that, along with the enormity of the pile of dead before him. "You hint that the army were not acting under Sayeh Rajni's instructions."

"In contempt of them, I would say," Nizhvashiti replied with confidence.

The Gage's mountainous shoulders collapsed a little as his posture slouched. "How terrible for her."

"Yes. And how terrible for her subjects." Nizhvashiti, by comparison, seemed to straighten. "Shall we go and see what we can do for the dead?"

*They are the dead,* the Gage wanted to snap. *They are beyond my care or yours. The time for seeing what can be done for them is past.*

But the truth of the matter was that he had little idea of what Nizhvashiti might be capable. And weren't the Gage and the Godmade, not to point the thing too finely, both already dead in their own persons?

And wasn't this, after a fashion, evidence that the dead could in some cases still do for themselves?

The Gage followed Nizhvashiti over the rubble heaps, climbing the treacherous and shifting piles with his great weight, with considerably more difficulty than Nizhvashiti evidenced in gliding over them. They approached the charnel heap with an unwavering implacability that belied the horror the Gage held within.

He had seen so many horrors in his life, and in his long existence. But before this one even he quailed a little.

There were thousands of bodies in the pile. They rose in a more steeply sided tower than the Gage would have thought possible, as if they were hung on some kind of scaffolding, or threaded on wires and drawn up by a gigantic hand toward an unseen point.

Nizhvashiti said it first. "It looks like someone's building a pedestal. As if for a throne."

"Like the Peacock Throne," the Gage answered. They had stopped, and now looked up at the horror. Nizhvashiti craned its head back. The Gage just looked without eyes, as he did, which did not require any inclination or rotation of his featureless head.

"After a fashion."

"Could you build a throne—or even a pedestal—just from a pile of corpses, though?"

"That would be too squishy," Nizhvashiti agreed.

"Bodies do have some structure inside them."

"Still," Nizhvashiti said. "Something is holding them up there."

"Yes," said the Gage. "And I think we should make an effort to find out what."

"We're—"

"On a mission, yes. I don't propose to wait long."

"This was Sayeh's place," Nizhvashiti said. "What happened here is probably important."

They did not have to wait long. Or perhaps it would be more accurate to say that they did not wait for many hours, because any quantum of time must seem long in that terrible place.

The Gage watched as Nizhvashiti examined the dead. The Godmade blessed as many as it could reach with a smudge of slaked turmeric from a square cinnabar bottle that hung on its girdle. The Gage wondered at first if the turmeric was going to run out, and then began taking bets with himself on *when* it was going to run out—and finally, when Nizhvashiti began working its way up the horrible pyramid, blessing dead while floating twice its own height in the air, the Gage accepted that the bottle was of the rumored, blessed sort that would never run dry. Or perhaps it was just another miracle from the hands of the Godmade. The Godmade could not reach the bodies at the center without digging, and the Gage was grateful not to have to watch that.

The corpses were corpses, all right, the flesh bloating and sloughing after days of rain and heat. But the rotting flesh was supported from within by a scaffolding. Not just of bones, as might have been expected. But by fretworks of stone, that could be seen protruding where the flesh had rotted away. They forked, like the roots of a tree—

"Oh," the Gage said aloud, as it dawned on him. "That's the arteries."

"And the veins," Nizhvashiti agreed.

"What a terrible way to die."

The Godmade's hood had fallen back from its dark, shaven skull. "I think they were dead already when the transformation occurred."

"Well," the Gage said. "That's a small mercy."

The Gage crouched down, examining the horrible litter at the base of the pyramid. There were crumbled bits of stone there, black with parched flesh. Steeling himself, he rubbed one gently with his fingertip.

The organic matter flaked off, showing a glimmer of translucent orange-pink within. The Gage held it up to the light. "It's a crystal."

Nizhvashiti's papery voice drifted down from near the top of the monument of corpses. "A crystal?"

"Padparadscha sapphire," the Gage elaborated, with emphasis.

"An unusual stone."

"Very. And a little obvious, don't you think?"

"Obvious?" The Godmade had not yet run short of slaked turmeric. It was performing a holy office, the Gage knew. Still, he would have shuddered at the thought of what Nizhvashiti was touching, if his maker had left it within him to shudder—or to know the sensation of touch.

"The padparadscha ring on the assassin. Now a heap of bodies partially converted into stone. And don't the Qersnyk riders call their throne the Padparadscha Seat? If we're being directed to suspect the plains tribes as masterminds, the effort is not subtle."

"The Padparadscha Seat is just a fancy name for an old saddle," Nizhvashiti reminded. "I have a sense that this is a more personal symbol. Perhaps even a mage's signature."

"Signature?" the Gage asked, in the same tone in which Nizhvashiti had said, "Crystal?"

"Are not your Wizards of Messaline known for imparting specific qualities, unique to each, to objects affected by their spellcasting?"

"Hmmm," the Gage said. "I suppose they are."

Nizhvashiti settled beside him in a slow flutter of robes that trailed over the ground but did not seem to brush it. It stoppered its little vial and said, "I don't think this enemy can *help* but leave a trail of evidence in the form of orange sapphires."

The Gage stood statuelike, in silent contemplation.

Nizhvashiti tipped its head back, frowning up at the tower of dead. "Does that remind you of anything?"

The Gage had an answer. He considered it for a moment before just spitting it out. Metaphorically speaking, as he did not have lips or a tongue to spit with. "The pedestal that comprises the Peacock Throne has a similar . . . profile."

"More than similar. As identical as two artifacts can be when one is made of gold and jewels and the other is a heap of rotting corpses."

"Jeweled corpses," the Gage qualified.

"As you say."

"You know, I'd hazard a guess that there's something symbolic going on here."

"Or metaphysical."

The Gage asked, "Is there a difference?"

Nizhvashiti flared its sleeves like mantling black wings. "One affects the hearts and wills of people. The other affects the heart and will of the world. If people don't know about it, it can't really serve a symbolic purpose. But it can serve a metaphysical one. Affecting, as it were, the structure of the world."

"Setting up a throne in opposition to the Peacock Throne."

Nizhvashiti said, "That wouldn't happen if there were an emperor on the throne. Its metaphysical power over these lands—to represent these lands, and their people—would be sealed. But without one . . ."

The Gage waited a moment or two before making a throat-clearing noise. "Without one?"

Nizhvashiti made a disgusted gesture. "That power can be arrogated. Contested."

"Claimed by someone else?" a mild voice offered from behind them.

Nizhvashiti whirled. The Gage, who did not rely on organs of perception for his senses, did not put himself out so far as to turn.

The person behind them was on foot, and had appeared as precipitously as if he had stepped sideways from under the flap of a folded universe.

He was tall, and imposingly built, wearing his jet-black hair in a long tail that fell down over the rippling agouti wolf fur of his cloak trim. To the surprise of no one, he wore a heavy silver collar over the fur, each hammered link set with a square cabochon of chatoyant padparadscha sapphire that gleamed with a band of light like the pupil of a tiger's eye.

He seemed to the Gage as if he were working very hard to be impressive, from jeweled earrings to polished boots, and very nearly succeeding.

"Is this your work?" the Gage asked, having taken the time to consider his words.

He still did not turn, preferring the mental effect of keeping his back to the other while continuing to observe him. Perhaps the stranger would know little enough of Gages to mistake his position for a disadvantage.

"Oh, not all of it," said the tall man, as if humbly declining a compliment. "And I should think nearly all of them would have wound up dead before too long anyway, and hardly so usefully. Human beings are not noted for their . . . durability over time."

The man made a sweeping gesture with his gloved hand that tended to include both the Gage and Nizhvashiti. Coral-colored crystals—or faceted padparadscha sapphire beads—sparkled on the unblemished white leather. "But I see I do not have to explain mortal frailty to such as you."

Nizhvashiti had gone very still. A breeze, redolent of corpses, ruffled its robes in waterlike rills that only served to accentuate the breathless motionlessness of its hands and face and frame.

"Are you not human, then?" the Gage asked. There was utility in the obvious questions.

"Oh, no. But who would be, that had another option? They are so . . . disposable."

Now the Gage did turn, more ponderously than necessary, to provide the impression that he was offering the stranger his full attention. "And yet here you seem to have found a use for them."

The stranger smiled without teeth.

"If people are of so little account to you, why interfere in their little lives?"

"Are these people?" the stranger said.

The Gage did not step forward. He did not extend a hand. He could see the frown of concentration on Nizhvashiti's strange-eyed countenance. Whatever the Godmade was thinking about so hard, the Gage had no intention of disrupting it with an ill-considered, uncommunicated action. So it seemed as if his best course was to keep the stranger talking.

"My apologies," the Gage said. "We seem to have neglected to introduce ourselves. I am a Gage. This is Nizhvashiti, a priest of the Good Daughter."

"Of course you are. I am Ravana," the stranger replied with a smile. With a sudden, athletic sideways vault, Ravana perched himself atop a fallen column of butter-white stone. It was fluted, delicately carved at the finials. It had been a masterwork by some great artisan. Now it lay tumbled, cracked in a half-dozen pieces.

Ravana settled his haunches more comfortably on its side, flipped the wolfskin-trimmed cloak so that it flared and draped pleasingly, and kicked one foot like a petulant student. "Do you deny," he said, sounding as if he were enjoying himself, "that the evidence suggests anything but that man is a stumbling adolescent? That there's a human cultural moment of adulthood they keep avoiding, that they might achieve when they accept that nobody's hands are fucking clean and stop making up legends about how their people arose out of oppression and therefore it's totally okay if they take those other people's stuff?"

"Perhaps," Nizhvashiti said, as uninformatively as possible.

"Are your hands unclean?" the Gage prompted.

Ravana laughed. "Oh, very. No worse than anyone else's, though—whether by deed, or ancestry. Where did the Alchemical Empire come from? Its lost glory is founded in terrible things, isn't it? Conquest and genocide?"

"I hadn't really considered it much," the Gage admitted. "I'm not from around here."

Ravana's sparkling hand made another pass in air. "They make a lot of their right of kings, this family, while slaughtering each over inheritances their ancestors stole. But did you ever ask yourself how it is that everybody on this broad and divided patch of earth came to speak the same mother tongue? Where do you think emperors come from, anyway?"

"Usually, from building empires," the Gage admitted. "A messy business."

"The messiest," Ravana agreed. "And yet, these creatures like to tell stories about it as if it's a glorious endeavor, worthy of mythology. They're creatures incapable of even recognizing their own motives and obligations on an individual level, much less acting responsibly around them."

The Gage contemplated. "Is that a fancy way of saying that most people don't know who they are or what they're doing, or even why they're doing it?"

"Oh," said Ravana. "I'd say that *people* know it. But these—" He shrugged. "And when there's a lot of them, they're even more useless. They can't manage to make a basic decision for the common good in the face of overwhelming peril, without making it all about their personal power and gain, even when the alternative is a pile of corpses."

His glistening glove indicated the obscene cairn. "They had time to evacuate, you know. They had warning. They could have worked together and saved their lives. But all they did was use the overture to the catastrophe to squabble and make postures of dominance over one another. And look at them now."

Nizhvashiti folded its arms. This was its first motion in so long that the gesture rang through the Gage's awareness like the blow of a hammer. He saw no indication that it had any similar effect on Ravana, who still sat idly kicking his toe.

Nizhvashiti said, "And were these people emperors?"

Ravana cocked his head. "Pardon?"

"Were these the folk who made those decisions? To squabble? Not to cooperate?" Nizhvashiti said politely. "Or are they merely people who were confused, who did not know who to follow, and when their leaders argued, who delayed too long?"

"If they did not decide, then can they be said to be people? Or are they pets? Livestock, like most men."

"You have not answered my question."

Ravana turned his attention, if it could be called that, back to the Gage. "Haven't I?"

Again, the Gage made a ponderous show of considering. He drummed his metal fingertips on his metal cheek. "No, I do not believe you have."

Ravana shrugged again, even more elaborately, as if to say he had done his best and it was not his fault they were slow learners. Perhaps they were boring him.

"What reason have you for building that?" The Gage waved a hand over his shoulder at the pyramid. His hand, he was pleased to note, also glittered quite well. "For influencing human affairs?"

"Oh." Yes, Ravana definitely looked bored. Or, to be precise, *more* bored. "They're in the way. And what good are they to anyone? They're children. Worse, because children grow up to be people. These just breed more."

Ravana glanced at the pile of corpses and made a *tch*ing sound. "Oh, now you've gone and blessed a lot of them. I'm just going to have to unbless them again after you are gone. What a nuisance priests are."

"Right," Nizhvashiti said in some irritation.

Then it roared.

It was not a sound that the Gage would have expected to come from a human throat. Especially a dead one. Especially one so prone to shaping papery, whispery speech as that of the Godmade. It started low in the ground, as if it came up from under the Gage's feet like a geyser. The rumble rang through his metal body as if he were a bell tuned too low for human ears to hear.

And Nizhvashiti sprang.

Not, to the Gage's bemusement—and evidently that of Ravana—at *Ravana*. But at the fermenting throne-heap, in all its horribleness. It struck out, a striped hardwood staff lashing on a long arc, the elaborately knobbed head smacking into one of the corpses with a sound like an axehead sinking into a melon.

"I can't let you do that," Ravana said, in the time it took Nizhvashiti to crush two more skulls.

He raised a jeweled hand. The Gage started forward. But no flare of magic burst from the sorcerer's fingertips. Instead, a rustle—and the cracking of stone—rose from the pile of bodies. The whole thing shifted. Heaved. Hands groped and clenched. Unclenched. Clawed. The whole mass lurched, and a thin keening sound came out of it. Within the pile, some bodies lay still, limp and stiff at once, like rag dolls hung on iron wires.

The Godmade turned its head toward Ravana and frowned. "I don't believe you'd risk something you worked so hard on. And I blessed more than that, sorcerer."

It tapped its new and faintly luminescent eye. The dragonglass chimed.

The pile of corpses was as it had been: a heap, a mockery of the massive throne back in Sarathai-tia. It twitched faintly, but the sliding, festering movement of the whole mass vanished as it if had never been.

The Gage heard Ravana sigh.

"Well, sometimes I guess you have to do things yourself." He stood from his pillar, lithe in his red boots, and brushed his cloak behind his left shoulder with an idle hand. Insouciant, he reached over his shoulder and with one hand drew free a bastard sword.

It was a western style, straight and double-edged, heavy through the diamond-shaped cross-section of the blade. Its hilt was styled to be used with one hand on the grip and the other on the pommel. He held it before him in guard with an expression of utter boredom.

The blade caught fire.

"Oh," Nizhvashiti said. "I don't think you're real either."

It tapped the dragonglass orb in its socket once more. The chime rolled forth, more sonorous and clearer than ever.

Ravana . . . wavered. He said something that by its tone was fearful, though the Gage could not quite make out the words. That in and of itself was unusual, as the Gage knew most languages by virtue of how he had been made.

Nizhvashiti tapped the chime once more. The Gage felt it through his feet.

Ravana wavered again, like an image cast on smoke. This time, he blew away.

The ground heaved under them. Not from Nizhvashiti's howl this time, but seemingly on its own. A faint hiss surrounded them. A smell of rotten eggs and farts garlanded the air.

"You woke up the volcano," the Gage said.

Nizhvashiti looked longingly at the cadaver throne. "I want to bury the dead."

The earth heaved again, like a captive testing his bonds.

The Gage started walking. "You have blessed what you can. There will be more dead if we pause to bury these."

Reluctantly, the Godmade drifted beside him. The Gage sped his steps to a run that shook and cracked the stones underfoot in its own right.

The Godmade spoke without effort, keeping up. "There will, in any case, be more dead."

"That," the Gage admitted, "has always been the case. What was that language?"

"Eremite," Nizhvashiti said. "We're lucky we're not alive. It would have blistered our eyes."

They ran. Or the Gage ran. Small rocks bounced in harmony with his stride. Nizhvashiti streamed alongside like smoke.

Nizhvashiti said, "Do you think he's setting the Kingdoms up against each other?"

"I think he as much as told us he is. Of course, who knows how trustworthy his self-assessment is?"

"At least we've identified the source of the illusions and assassins."

The Gage laughed while he ran. "Let's see if we live long enough to get out of these deadly lands, to Mrithuri's bird and tell her."

"'Live.'"

"You know what I mean. I do wonder, why wouldn't he have his corpses attack?" A veil of sulfurous steam drifted across the Gage, leaving behind a dewing of caustic condensation.

"The throne mattered more to him. The earth is cracking."

It bulged like an abscess. The Gage gathered himself and leapt the long, spidering, crumbling trench. He landed, and pried his feet from the calf-deep divots to run on. Behind them, the earth ruptured, showering them with searing mud that bubbled with superheated steam after it fell.

"I can survive this," the Gage said.

"Can you survive lava?"

"Have you seen some?"

Nizhvashiti did not answer.

The Gage ran on.

# 13

CHAERI'S ENTRANCE WAS NOT AT ALL AS MRITHURI HAD ANTICIPATED. She looked as if she had come from the garden at a run, heedless of thorny borders and reaching branches. The long spirals of her hair, usually oiled so smooth, were raddled and stuck with twigs. Her sweet face was bloated by the poppy she had been taking to aid her sleep of late, and her eyes were glassy, the pupils contracted as if by bright light. The hem of her gold-spangled deep blue drape was raggedly torn. It fluttered with each jerky step, showing plump flashes of calf.

She did not have the sandalwood casket of serpents with her, Mrithuri was annoyed to note. That annoyance allowed her to realize something else. When she looked at Chaeri, what she felt was not affection and comfort, or even the flash of ephemeral anger one might expect when confronted with an inconvenient and disappointing lifelong friend.

What she felt was rather a complex swirl of anxiety, need, and dread. It did not feel to her like *herself* at all. She felt . . . like a copy. A simulacrum with something to prove.

Like a forgery of herself.

*Don't be silly, Mrithuri,* said a voice inside her head. It might have been the voice of the Mother. It might have been the voice of her own common sense. *If you were an illusion, you would have vanished when the Godmade sounded its chime.*

It was a more comforting piece of logic, somehow, than it ought to have been.

Chaeri drew up short before her and dropped a curtsy, sniffling, head bowed and one knee to the ground. She composed her torn skirt about her scratched ankles. "Rajni . . . ?"

"Where have you been?" If Mrithuri's voice trembled, it was not for lack of effort to keep it serene. She was aware of her people drawn up around her and Chaeri like a silent ring of stones.

"Rajni, in the garden."

"You've torn your dress."

"I ran into a thicket following a songbird." Chaeri's laugh was fluttery and self-dismissive. She looked from one of Mrithuri's advisors to the next. Her gaze did not linger, except perhaps on Yavashuri. And on the corpse that was Nizhvashiti, standing like a plinth. "Mother of us all, may I speak to you alone?"

The Dead Man shot her a glance. *Does he think I need his interference at every crossroads?*

"I am as alone as I need to be." Mrithuri's own words surprised her. "These friends can hear what passes between us."

And she suddenly did not want to be alone with Chaeri at all.

Chaeri would have protested, Mrithuri thought, but she snuck a glance at Mrithuri's face and whatever expression she saw there stopped her. She had begun weeping, tears speckling her hands as she bent over them.

The door to the room opened again, and Ata Akhimah walked in. "I felt a spell bre—oh."

Mrithuri was cold. A kind of fury took her, a rage at her own foggy thoughts and limited mind. At how lacking her intellect was without the venom, and how she could feel her own flawed, heavy, painful body dragging at her. Maybe this was what had driven Nizhvashiti to that ultimate mortification of the flesh, to make itself as light and powerful as possible, a husk animated by a burning mind.

"I sent for you to bring my serpents, Chaeri. A long time ago."

Chaeri sobbed.

Mrithuri's veins burned. Her thoughts were wrapped in cotton wool. *This is farcical,* she thought. *She is not even hearing me.*

She would have liked to be a husk just then.

"What?"

It was one word, and it held all the weight of the frustrated wrath inside her.

Wordlessly, Chaeri pulled a crumpled, blood-spotted, folded sheaf of paper from her blouse. Sobs fluttered its edges.

Mrithuri stooped and took it from her. It was damp with sour-scented sweat. In her own hand, it trembled slightly as well, but that was just because she was missing the steadying influence of snakebite.

"What is this?"

Chaeri shook her head, still sobbing. Sighing, Mrithuri held out her hand to her other maid.

Yavashuri unwound a shawl from her own plump shoulders and put it in Mrithuri's hand. Mrithuri draped it over Chaeri, then unfolded the thing in her hand.

The nuns began their chant within the walls. The Cauled Sun was setting.

The room brightened, the heat of the day fading. It would have been nearly time to arise, in the usual manner of things. But what was usual during war?

Chaeri's sobs slowed. It was too dark to read the letter here, though that was rapidly ameliorating. She took the letter to the window.

It was in plain text, not a cipher, and showed the marks of much abuse. But it was written in ink that would not feather in the damp, and addressed to herself: Mrithuri Rajni, with all her dignities appended. It was in the late ambassador's hand.

*Your Abundance—*

*I write to you, my lady, in pleading. I know I have not conducted myself with dignity and rationality these days. I have made myself unwelcome in your presence with my disruptions. I regret this deeply.*

*I could not send this message by another's hand. I must speak to you directly because there is a spy in your inner circle, and I know not who.*

*I have been acting out of fear, Your Abundance. In full terror for my life. Because my loyalty to Anuraja is insufficient before his demand.*

*I have been directed to die in order to provide an excuse for war between our kingdoms. I have been directed to die.*

*And I find I do not wish to.*

More followed. An offer to join her service with such intelligence as he could provide, including code books and the like. An offer to enlighten her as to the nature of Anuraja's pet sorcerer—or, as Mahadijia seemed to have thought, the sorcerer who kept Anuraja as a sort of pet.

At the bottom was Mahadijia's personal chop, impressed in wax of brilliant green.

Mrithuri finished the letter before she realized she was not breathing. The pain under her breastbone felt physical, as if she had been struck in the chest.

She read the letter again, lingering over the phrasing. She knew the hand, and it did indeed sound like Mahadijia. She left it unfolded and handed it to Ata Akhimah. She pinched the bridge of her nose between her fingertips and said, "Oh, Chaeri. Get up, would you?"

Silently, Chaeri obeyed her, still hiding behind her draggled hair.

Mrithuri looked out the window. "You have done the enemy's work for him. And then some."

Akhimah was a quick reader, and despite the letter's length she made short work of it. She sighed, in her turn, and held it out.

The Dead Man moved next to take it.

*What a pack of fools we look. Standing around taking polite turns with a document that reveals how we could have saved our lives.*

The Dead Man held the letter at arm's length, squinting at it.

Ata Akhimah grinned at him. "I will make you reading glasses."

"In time of war?"

The Wizard scoffed. "When have you more need to read your orders?"

"Do not feel so bad, Captain," said Lady Golbahar. "It is only maturity."

The Dead Man glanced over at her. "That is a kind way of putting it."

The lady, head bowed, only smiled.

Mrithuri knew what they were doing. That they were playing a game to take the edge of the tension off. To make everything seem a little less terrible and lost. She glanced over her shoulder and said, "Read it aloud."

The Dead Man handed it back to Akhimah with a look of relief.

They stood, and listened. Mrithuri watched all the faces change except Chaeri's, which was as miserable and still as if it were carved on a temple to give a face to mourning.

"You hid this," Mrithuri said to Chaeri, when Akhimah was done.

Chaeri nodded. "Yes."

"Why?"

The maid of the bedchamber sobbed once, and seemed to steel herself. "I thought you would blame me."

"I do," Mrithuri said.

It was petty but it felt good. Sometimes you take your pleasures where you can. And it was better than slapping the girl, though that, at this point, would have been even more satisfying. Mrithuri stepped away from the window. She strode past Chaeri, into the center of the room, enjoying the freedom of movement her trousers and tunic offered. Assuming they won the war, she might almost miss it when it was over. If just for the comfortable clothing.

*Maybe I was never meant to be a queen.*

Maybe. But she was good at ruling. She was good at law-giving. She was good at all the things that came with the mantle of rajni.

And they were her job. They were her duty.

She could tolerate the inconveniences of fingerstalls and coifs and masks and stiff embroidered drapes to perform them.

"He had his knife in his hand," Chaeri said tearfully. "His knife! How was I to know?"

Mrithuri jumped in surprise as the Dead Man rounded on her handmaiden. She had never seen him display temper before, or any emotion more dramatic than anxiety, or a world-weary amusement that she found strangely comforting.

Now, without warning, he roared. "How are we to believe you that this is so? Your word is worth nothing!"

Chaeri surprised her, flaring up in self-defense. "Why would I have come to tell you about this letter if I were a murderer?"

"No one said you were a murderer," the Dead Man answered silkily.

Yavashuri and Hnarisha turned their heads from side to side, watching the outrage as if it were some lawn sport. Akhimah moved to put her body between Mrithuri and the combatants. Syama growled low and confusedly in her throat. *These are pack,* her distress seemed to say. *Which do I support?*

"You certainly implied it, if you did not *exactly* speak the words." Chaeri crossed her arms.

"This man you killed thought there was a spy in your midst." The Dead Man took a step back, his heel clicking on tile. "In order to keep that information from us . . . it would be a good reason for a spy to kill him."

"Someone got into his room and burned his papers." Chaeri glared at Ata Akhimah. "That had to be somebody with magic, didn't it? No one else could have gotten through his spell."

"He might have had some talisman on his person that allowed him to find his way back," Akhimah said, in the voice of one merely making conversation. "His killer would be the one most likely to have taken such a thing away."

"By the River of the World, just *stop* it," Mrithuri snapped. They fell silent so abruptly that she realized she was half-surprised to be listened to. *Weren't you just musing on what an effectual ruler you are?*

Chaeri turned appealing eyes to Mrithuri. "Rajni, you have trusted me in every extreme. We have known each other our whole lives. When would I have found the time to betray you?"

Mrithuri would have glared, if she had not been so tired it was all she could do not to reach out and balance with her hand against the wall. She needed venom, or rest. She needed peace and calm. *"All* of you."

Chaeri took a step back.

The door . . . opened again. And this time, the person who walked in was the middle-aged matriarch of the troupe of acrobats who had arrived in the same caravan as the Dead Man and the Gage, and Golbahar. Her name, if Mrithuri recollected, was Ritu.

Mrithuri could not have said who she might have expected less, except perhaps for her own dead grandfather.

"Your Abundance," the woman said, sweeping an elegant bow. "I was looking for you."

"Is this a farce?" Mrithuri wondered. "Or now that this room is found, does it have some mystic connection to the highway?"

"Rajni?"

"Make an appointment." She pointed rudely to Hnarisha. "There is my secretary."

Mrithuri looked around her. She knew she was scowling, the regal mask of placidity slipped utterly askew. "I am going to my rooms," she said, when she had gathered herself sufficiently that her voice might not shake. "Chaeri, you will attend me."

The Dead Man made a noise. Mrithuri turned her glare on him, and he fell silent.

But she could not quite bring herself to punish him by risking herself. Even in the depths of her craving and irritation, she knew that would be foolhardy. She hooked a hand. "Ata, you too. Unless the walls are right now falling?"

The acrobat drew back against the wall next to the door and shook her head.

"Good," Mrithuri said, and swept out, trailing her ragtag entourage of three, counting a confused and unhappy Syama.

RITU STAYED PINNED BY THE WALL FOR A MOMENT AFTER MRITHURI left, for all the world as if the rajni had glued her there. Her gaze sought the Dead Man's. He wondered if she could tell just from his eyes above the veil how stricken he was.

Lady Golbahar definitely could, however. The three of them stood staring at each other until Hnarisha cleared his throat, and they all remembered he and Yavashuri were still there. They startled collectively.

It was Ritu who broke the awkwardness. "What was that all about?" she asked, looking at Golbahar.

"The queen's handmaiden is probably a murderess," Golbahar said, with her own very precise air of deadpan succinctness.

"And definitely a killer," the Dead Man added, feeling it was the sort of distinction that needed pointing up. "I'm sorry," he said aside to Hnarisha. "I know she is an old acquaintance."

The little man made a face. "What are your theories about that little drama?"

"She likes attention," said Golbahar.

"That she does," Hnarisha admitted. He leaned back against the wall beside the window with a sigh. He lowered his voice. "Would *you* recruit her as an agent?"

The Dead Man said, "She has the queen's—"

"Rajni's."

"Rajni's, sorry. She has the rajni's ear. And affection. If not entirely her trust anymore."

Hnarisha said, "She obviously meant to distract us from searching here. And that distraction was, perhaps, important enough to anger my rajni a little. More than a little."

"The confession about the letter *was* dramatic," Golbahar agreed.

Ritu bit the nail on her thumb. "This place is important, then?"

"Pardon," Hnarisha said. "I do not know you well—"

"I will give her my parole," said the Dead Man. "I know, you do not know me well either—"

Hnarisha shook his head. "That hole in your jacket says I know you well enough." He frowned at Ritu. "These are the rooms of the ambassador who was killed a little after you arrived. By the rajni's handmaiden, Chaeri. She claimed, at the time, in defense of the rajni."

Ritu said, "And you are concerned that the rajni's handmaiden's reasons are not as provided?"

Hnarisha, judiciously, moved his chin up, and down.

"So we must search all the more," Ritu said.

There were still too many people in the room, even if one of them was the unmoving corpse of Nizhvashiti. It was hot and airless. The Dead Man picked his veil away from the sweat on his face to let his skin breathe.

"She will need more ladies of the chamber," Yavashuri said suddenly. "She has done with me, and Chaeri. Chaeri cannot be alone with her. She will need women who can counsel and protect her. And she will . . . she will resist. She does not like the cosseting and the fuss. And she does not like her . . . privacy . . ."

"Interrupted?" the Dead Man said, the word freighted with meaning.

Yavashuri turned her head as if she did not hear. "You, Lady Golbahar—"

"I am not a fighter," Golbahar said.

"I am," said Ritu. "It is not the first time I have been a bodyguard."

The Dead Man looked at her muscled arms. He remembered the sword-dance he had seen her family perform. No, he would warrant not.

And he did trust her—and Lady Golbahar. They had traveled long and hard together, and both had had plenty of chances to sell the caravan, whose master was spying for Mrithuri in foreign lands, out to Himadra and her other enemies if they had wanted.

"Talk to the rajni," he told Yavashuri. "I am afraid she is angry with me."

"She is angry at anyone who comes between her and her solace," Yavashuri said. The Dead Man thought it almost as good a euphemism as "maturity." "I will suggest that she take Ritu into service. I will complain that my old hands ache too much to hold a comb." She glanced suspiciously at Ritu. "You *can* ply a comb?"

For answer, Ritu held out her oil-sleek braid.

Yavashuri's wrinkled little mouth surprised the Dead Man by smiling. She said, "Now let us search these rooms, as we have been instructed. Perhaps we can find *something* that is not burnt."

They stepped apart, moving to investigate all the apartment's furnishings and corners. This seemed likely to take some time. The Dead Man suspected he should, while it was happening, get himself back to the war.

But as he walked out, he contrived to pass close by Ritu. "We're fucked," the Dead Man said softly to the acrobat.

"I know," Ritu answered. "Don't tell the rajni, though. I like her and she might as well have what comfort she can, for now."

"Your sword is straight and mine is curved," he murmured. "So between them we have a fit for any foe."

"Actually," she whispered, turning away, "mine is as curved as yours is."

THE DEAD MAN WENT BRIEFLY TO HIS CHAMBERS. HE COULDN'T REMEMber, exactly, when he had last set foot in them. When he'd bathed after the unpleasant incident in the cellars, he thought. He shut the door and leaned against the wall, alone.

"I could have a new coat made for you," Mrithuri had said, so diffidently he might have forgotten she was a queen.

The Dead Man's first response had been horrified denial: to spurn her offered gift. His mouth was open beneath the veil to rebut when he gentled himself, took a breath, snatched the words back. She would not understand why he spurned her gift: she would take it as a rejection, if he was not careful.

But how did you explain that the blood of your family had soaked into this coat? That the ashes of your former home were ground between the fibers and into the lanolin on the wool?

How could you say such things to a young woman who was the queen of a city under siege?

And yet, protecting her from the truth did her no favors.

Oh, of course, she could surrender. She could give up her kingdom, her body, and her life to her vile cousin. It would not be good for her loyal men and women if she did, the Dead Man suspected. Anuraja would find the means to separate Mrithuri from anyone who might put her before him.

It was in the nature of conquest to subvert as many among those you would conquer as possible, and then to set the conquered against one another. To divide, segregate, exploit such chasms and divisions as there already were.

The Dead Man fingered his threadbare sleeve. The wool had faded over the decades, like slaked turmeric left in the sun. The city of his birth had burned around the time he was born; he had always imagined that that was how he had found himself orphaned in the first place, though he had been too young to recall. Orphaned, he had been adopted by the new caliph to be raised as a Dead Man, the ancient tribe of utterly loyal warriors who owed their caliph everything.

He had served. Until the city burned again, and this time the caliphate fell completely.

He had heard they were once more rebuilding; it was an advantageous location. He did not wish to go home, and see what the place of his birth had become that was not home any longer.

He went to the mirror: dragonglass, backed with silver. They had, and used, so much of the strange green mineral here. It was amazing that more of them weren't dying of the wasting illness from being cut by it or inhaling its dust.

Perhaps they knew how to handle it better than most did.

The Dead Man looked at his image. Lean still, though not as bone-skinny as when he had arrived. That might change.

He unbuckled his belt, and laid his pistols—new and old—and his new sword aside. One by one, he undid the buttons on his old red coat.

He slipped it off, and let it hang from his hand for a moment.

Then he dusted it, smoothed the fabric, and hung it from a peg by the door. It was too hot for this wet climate anyway. He'd do better in his billowing white shirt.

He belted his weapons on again and stepped toward the door. At the last moment, he stopped. He turned over his shoulder.

"I won't forget you," he said to the silently reproachful garment. "But I don't need you right now."

# 14

Most of Anuraja's troops had moved across the river. Sayeh and her women were left in an encampment like an abandoned city. The forward lines must be sleeping rough, which would be no hardship in the dry season to men accustomed to hard bunking on the earth, but in the rainy season meant mud in every crevice, wet blankets, exposure—

Except there was no rain. Again, this day and this night . . . there was no rain.

It was impossible. Inconceivable. Sayeh knew there were legends from before the Alchemical Emperor's day of the rains failing, but it had not happened in living memory and beyond. Every child in Ansh-Sahal knew that the emperor had brokered a deal with the Mother River that she would shed the richness of her heavenly body upon the land as long as the rituals and the auguries were honored by his daughters and his granddaughters, all down the line of his blood. And Sayeh had done her part. And she was sure Mrithuri had not neglected hers, in turn.

She was trapped in her couch, or on her crutches. Her litter-bearers were also her jailers. She cajoled and flattered and sweet-talked and flirted and charmed. Ümmühan flirted too, and charmed, with a dignity that became her age and a kind of coquettishness that bordered on command. Sayeh had never seen such wiles, and stood—or reclined, rather—in awe of them. The women of the Uthman Empire were justly famed for their powers of persuasion, it seemed.

Nazia flirted with no one, but with the tutelage of Ümmühan and Sayeh, she certainly charmed. She was silent and seemingly shy, keeping her face turned aside and a half-smile flickering across her lips from time to time. "It's a pity your hair is still shorn," said Ümmühan. "You can't flirt from behind it, and you don't wear a veil. But it does show the lovely line of your neck to advantage."

No more than half a day had passed since Ravani's latest visit when Sayeh first overheard the men at the pavilion entrance muttering to one another about the kindness of the foreign rajni. They took her where she wanted, within the confines of the camp. They took to bringing her little presents—sweetmeats, and cakes, which she then shared with them. If an army traveled on its stomach, Anuraja's army rolled as if on wheels. He did not believe in stinting on chefs, did the raja from Sarathai-lae.

Ravani did not come again. Sayeh assumed that Ravani had crossed the river, and gone over to the war. "I will go and spy on them," Nazia said, head high. "At the very least let us have information."

"You will find yourself strangled in a ditch," Sayeh said. "You stay here with me, child, where the tatters of my royalty can protect you."

Nazia's face crumpled. She plucked at her own sleeve, a nervous habit, her mouth scrunched up around silent fury.

Sayeh sighed. They were all restless. All feeling ineffectual and bored. "It is not that I do not trust you, or respect your skill," she said, more gently. She reached out and captured Nazia's chin. "But this is an army, and you are a young girl. These men are gentle to me because Anuraja says so, and the others are gentle to us because they see us under the raja's . . . well, 'protection' might be too gentle a word. Bit by bit I must make them love me. I cannot do that if you are harmed."

"They're just trying to suck up to you, you know." Sulkily, Nazia picked at the tassels on the cushion she sat upon. It was new; one of the men-at-arms had left it by the door while Ümmühan was singing. "Why are you accepting gifts from them?"

"A gift creates a bond of obligation that flows both ways."

"I am so bored."

"I know," Sayeh said gently. "Come, bring my crutches. Let us go and review the troops, and see if we cannot make some friends."

On the third day, in her boredom, she asked for an audience with

Anuraja again. The messenger returned to ask if she was ready to be his emissary. When she sent back that she wished to discuss it, her suit was refused.

"Right," she told Nazia. "We're going for a stroll."

NAZIA WALKED OUT WITH SAYEH AS SAYEH WENT FORTH ON HER CRUTCHES to make a few more friends. She greeted the men, remembering the names of the ones she had met before. There were not so many, and these soldiers were clerks and quartermasters, the sort of people without whom an army falls apart, but who—unless they are very unlucky indeed—never see the front lines.

She wondered where her own soldiers were. Vidhya, and Tsering-la, and Guang Bao. And all of Vidhya's men who had ridden out with them to seek Himadra and her kidnapped son.

Her chest cramped with worse pain than her fractured leg when she thought of that. And when she thought that those men, and the refugees who had fled the first earthquake, might be the only ones of her people who still survived.

Ansh-Sahal had fallen. Sayeh was rajni of nothing now. Why did she pretend otherwise, even to herself? She was not fooling anyone.

The despair threatened to suck her down like the cold waters of the Bitter Sea. She felt the whirlpool pull, and kicked upward, forcing herself to remember that there was, indeed, a reason why.

That reason was Drupada. That reason was her son.

There could be no surrender to despair while he lived, and while he needed her.

So. The first thing she needed to do, while she gritted her teeth behind a smile and exerted an iron will to seem to bear her pained, exhausted body gracefully, was assess what resources she had to work with. She charmed a teamster and a couple of stable lads exactly as if they were generals, pretending an interest in the merits of one mule over another. At least the mules' ears were long and soft, and their inquisitive noses served as a welcome distraction from the pain she could not permit herself to show. The familiar connection with animals did soothe, though it made her (all the more) miss Guang Bao.

Anuraja, she got a sense, was not the sort to get out of a morning and handle the daily business of reviewing his troops himself. As with his servants, he preferred a relationship built on fear and distance, and he did not foster the kind of personal bonds and personal loyalty that Sayeh had been raised to treat as the source of her power. Her father had been very clear to her that a raja—or rajni, when it became increasingly obvious that that would be her fate—owed a duty of service to land, to Mother, to people. That loyalty was to be earned and not demanded. That duty flowed both ways.

She was increasingly certain that Anuraja, if he had gotten the same lecture from his parents, had scoffed at it.

Sayeh might be third-sex. She might be shandha, and of a people often scorned. But she was also chosen and blessed of the Mother, and a true daughter of the Alchemical Emperor. She had not been perfectly popular with her people because of those first things, it was true. The army had never really accepted her as dowager, feeling perhaps that she had dodged a man's fate as a soldier through cowardice. As if there were no courage in the bearing of children.

But she had been popular enough to hold a throne in her son's name after her husband's passing, and that was no small thing for one such as herself. Her people had bragged upon her uniqueness, after Drupada was born.

That—that ability—was one of her resources. Her charm, her political sense.

Another resource was Anuraja's protection. She was wise enough to know that it stemmed from her status as a chosen one of the Mother, and that his interest in her was entirely cynical. He was not a religious man. He was, in fact, an utter blasphemer. So it would only help him with those who did worship faithfully to be seen with one so incontrovertibly chosen as Sayeh. It would lend the air of divine approval to what he did.

Unless a sufficient number of someones decided that the destruction of Ansh-Sahal was an expression of divine disfavor in her.

Sayeh was excruciatingly aware that she was secure only so long as Anuraja thought he could use her. She had that even less reassuring offer from the sorcerer, whose trustworthiness she doubted even more than she doubted Anuraja's.

She stroked the curious nose of a mule. They looked ragged and hungry. Poor animals, dragged to a war they had no use for or control over.

All they wanted to do was go back to their pastures and crop cool grass in the shade.

"You might as well have been wives, poor things," she said too softly for the stableboys to hear. They wouldn't understand her grief, and she didn't want to explain it. Or make herself seem strange in their eyes when what she needed was to seem calm and thoughtful and regal, most of all regal. Regal and kind.

Nazia heard, though, and looked up at Sayeh with a compressed grin. "At least they're mules. They don't have to worry about bearing themselves to death."

"No," Sayeh said sadly, turning away. "They only have to worry about bearing others."

THE RESCUE PARTY REJOINED THE REST OF HIMADRA'S SCOUTS BEFORE they had finished butchering the bear-boars, though the first joints were already turning over trenches filled with coals. Himadra could see where his men had hacked their way into a thorny jharber thicket for the wood and to collect armloads of leafy fronds as fodder for the horses. The shrubs would have offered fruit for men to eat as well, if Himadra and his troops had traveled through at the beginning of the previous winter. For now they were shedding their flowers too soon in the dryness, and it seemed likely there would be no date-sweet fruit this year.

The men who had remained behind were cheered to see the extra horses. The rescue party was cheered to see the meat.

They camped there for two days, which was far longer than he would have liked. Himadra fretted invisibly the entire time, chafing at the delay. But there was a long ride ahead of them, and the horses would do with a rest where there was forage and water available. The delay also meant they could smoke and dry some of the meat. Where they were going, food would be invaluable.

His men would travel better for a rest as well, though with the livestock to care for and the pigs to process, it wasn't exactly indolence. Still, when they left again, the steps of the horses seemed lighter and the men sat straighter in their saddles.

Ravana was again nowhere to be found when the time for breaking camp came. When Himadra remarked on this, Farkhad snorted. "Of course he's fucked off again. This part is no fun."

"I wish I knew where he went," Himadra answered.

"So you could go with him?" Farkhad asked.

Himadra laughed and nudged Velvet forward.

The nurse rode beside him, and Prince Drupada rode in front of her. She had taken the boy from his sling and now let him sit astride the saddle before her, his chubby toddler legs sticking out to either side. It turned out that *both* of them were better riders than Himadra had been led to believe.

*Next time, don't believe the self-assessment of skills offered by your kidnap victims,* he told himself wryly.

Would there be a next time? He hoped not. Kidnapping was not, precisely, to his taste.

Watching the young prince slowly come out of his shell—point to things, ask endless questions, and collapse into unpredictable sobbing fits—made Himadra homesick for his brothers. They were not toddlers now; they would not have been toddlers for a long time. But that was how he recalled them.

Drupada seemed scared. Himadra guessed the boy was missing his mother and his accustomed nurse and surroundings. That cut at Himadra, because it too made him think of his brothers. But the boy was beginning to come out of his shell. He was still unnaturally quiet and watchful whenever he noticed Himadra, to be sure. But where before he had hidden his face and huddled, as time passed he became willing to look around, point to things, and ask questions about the changing environment.

*Children are resilient,* Himadra comforted himself. Children were preternaturally strong.

They had hills to cross, along with some tricky mountains that seemed low only in comparison to the mighty Steles of the Sky, and multiple smaller rivers to ford before they reached the broad Sarathai. The deserts at least were less obstacle in this season. If the rains had failed in the Lotus Kingdoms, at least they had fallen for a while in the early season, and there was water in the mountains still.

It was a long ride, in other words, no matter how fast they journeyed. Himadra hoped—and even prayed a little—that the remainder would be uneventful.

As is ever the case, his wishes were not entirely honored by destiny.

✳    ✳    ✳

THEY MANAGED A FEW DAYS' HARD RIDE BEFORE THE FIRST INTERRUPTION
came. The additional horses made all the difference, though the bandits no-doubt stolen animals were (unsurprisingly) not as well-cared-
for as Himadra would have preferred. At least they all proved sound.
And they were as fit and hard as might be hoped, though he worried at
their thin condition and their unshod hooves on the rocky ground.

"The bandits probably ate the soft-footed ones," Farkhad commented, when Himadra expressed as much.

Not much room for sentiment in these barrens. Even less so than in
Chandranath, and Chandranath was not a place in itself to make men
soft.

Neither, for that matter, was Ansh-Sahal. The destroyed principality of which young Drupada was, technically speaking, the rightful
raja—under his mother's regency, if Sayeh Rajni was even still alive—
was a harsh place where the populace had been forced to exercise their
creativity and will to survive the dry seasons. None of these northern
regions made for easy lives or easy folk to live them.

So Himadra was understandably cautious when they overtook an
army on the road.

THE FIRST SIGN OF MEN AHEAD WAS DUST. DESPITE THE DRYNESS, THE AIR
had mostly been clear for days. There were not many outposts here
between Ansh-Sahal and Chandranath, and even fewer habitations.
On the dry side of the Razorback Mountains, and before the Sarathai
began to enrich the earth of her shoulders, there was very nearly
nothing.

The dust could have been a herd of some beast crossing the high
desert. But animals did not migrate in the rainy season, and it seemed
likely that wisdom applied even to such an atypical rainy season as this.
Their instincts would be honed to drive them to seek safety, not brave
a journey their ancestors would have learned was full of raging rivers,
flash floods, and the sort of mud that could bog an animal until it died
if it didn't just swallow the poor thing entire.

Better to travel when the earth was hard and the rivers low. Thirst
was a terrible death but a slow one, and there was and had always been—
would always be—water on the other side.

So the dust must be men.

Himadra's next thought was that it must be a caravan. Traders who had left Ansh-Sahal ahead of catastrophe, driven by the well-honed paranoia such merchants must cultivate to survive. Caravans also did not travel in the wet season, if they could avoid it . . . though those coming across the Steles of the Sky were often constrained by the terrifying weather in those mountains, and so reduced to braving floods and mudslides once they reached the Lotus Kingdoms.

An earthquake and a boiling sea were certainly impetus enough to move even the most conservative caravan master.

The pall of dust seemed to Himadra's experienced eye to be subtly wrong to have been produced by a caravan. It followed the curve of the road, which Himadra knew from having traveled it made a broad, roughly southward bend to the west of the Razorbacks. So he could estimate from each convenient height roughly how long the cloud extended.

"Admit it to yourself," Farkhad said, the third time Himadra paused to raise a spyglass. "That's an army."

"Marching on Chandranath," Himadra agreed, when he managed to make his lips stop twitching.

"They've still got time to turn south," Farkhad said unconvincingly. "Anuraja?"

"Half the Lotus Kingdoms from where he is supposed to be according to Ravana, if it is."

Farkhad grunted. He didn't need speak any words, however. Himadra already knew his lieutenant thought Anuraja would be hard-pressed to navigate his thumb out of his own asshole. After a suitable pause, Farkhad added, "Want to catch up to him, if it is?"

"Mother, no." Himadra turned his head and spat over Velvet's shoulder.

"Well, I suppose we're not exactly where we said we would be either."

"We should send up a scout once it's darker. If they are marching on Chandranath, we are going to have to get past them."

THEY MADE CAMP WHILE NAVIN, A VETERAN AMONG HIMADRA'S MEN, reconnoitered. Farkhad lifted Himadra off Velvet and set him down on a round shield in a shaded place not too far from the pickets. He *could* walk if he had to. He could manage his own necessities. But given the risk of broken bones and the pain involved, it was prudent if he avoided taking risks when it was not absolutely necessary.

He watched as Velvet grazed calmly on what scraggly stems poked up between rocks. What should have been lush and verdant with the season was yellowed and dry. It might as well have been straw to look at. Himadra hoped for the horses' sake that it was at least a little more nutritious. But—supplemented with small quantities of the grain they carried—it was all they had to offer.

Himadra dined on meager fare in his own turn. The fresh, roasted meat they had gleaned from the bear-boars had been eaten quickly, before it could rot, and now they were back to trail rations and the smoked meat—and not much of either of those. The quartermaster had a flat stone enhanced with some Wizardry that made it hot enough to boil water. He moved it carefully in its case, because it was hot enough also to burn flesh. It made it possible to cook without light. Important, because the day was slowly darkening around them as the Cauled Sun rose and the Veil covered the sky. They did not risk a fire, and anyway the day was hot and growing hotter.

Himadra sat quietly and sipped thrice-brewed tea without milk or spices. The quartermaster—who was also the cook, in so small a band—made paper-thin pancakes using the stovestone as a griddle, brushing its surface with butter-oil. In better times, those pancakes might have been stuffed with pulses, vegetables, even a little meat, and served with spiced yogurt. Today, Himadra felt fortunate to have a scoop of cold lentils flavored with dried and pounded onion. Hunger was a constant now. And he knew it did not torment him nearly so badly as it did the full-sized men around him.

Himadra was the warlord. He could not have complained even if he were worst-off. This whole thing had been his idea in the first place.

Even Drupada ate his small portion without fussing, exactly as if that were usual for boys his age. He seemed to understand that there was not more, and chewed his food with seriousness and attention, if without coordination or manners. Himadra (and the nurse and quartermaster) were all doing their best to make sure the child never went truly hungry. But it was often a near thing.

In some little time, Navin returned from the scouting mission, panting hard from a sprint across rocky terrain. Farkhad and another man lifted Himadra's shield and brought him to where Navin was resting and being given water, so he could hear the report in private.

They set Himadra down in another place that was under cover a little from the heat.

Navin had a surprise for them. The mass of people ahead were neither solely soldiers nor civilians, but a mixture of the two—and not soldiers and camp followers, in this case. And the soldiers among them wore the livery of Ansh-Sahal.

Himadra caught himself before he could glance over his shoulder at Iri, the nurse, in surprise. He was glad he had caused his shield to be carried well out of earshot before taking Navin's report.

"Where do you think they're going?" Farkhad asked.

Himadra gestured for Farkhad to lower his voice, glancing over at Iri and Drupada. "As far away as they can get from whatever's left of Ansh-Sahal."

"I think they are refuges, Your Competence," Navin agreed. "They look tattered. And more focused on taking the next step before them than watching the terrain."

"Pity we can't march up to that army and demand supplies," said Farkhad, following the direction of Himadra's gaze.

"I think we could ambush them," said Navin. "Or at least some stragglers. They have no discipline."

"They're likely as skint as we are," Himadra answered. "If not more so. *We* had time to pack."

Drupada had begun to wail, the thin cry of a tired child. Himadra looked away, to allow the nurse to deal with him. But sitting there, watching the day darken and those in his entourage eat, Himadra had the beginning of an idea.

"What was it Ravana said? About declaring myself the boy's regent?"

"That you could slit his throat after, Lord Protector."

Himadra waved that away in disgust and lowered his voice further. "That army doesn't belong to Sayeh. It belongs to Drupada."

"That army can't even live off the land or forage until we get among people again, and the first people we reach on this road are our own. Even if these soldiers accepted you as Lord Protector. Which they won't."

"Are you sure?" Himadra asked mildly.

"Do you suppose these are her loyal troops?"

"If they didn't die because they got out ahead of the explosion, it seems likely," Himadra said. "I had word from one of my people in Ansh-Sahal that she had ordered an evacuation after the first bad shake, and the leaders of her army countermanded her. But some of her folk left anyway."

"Well, those leaders are all dead now," Farkhad said, with the utter conviction of somebody who believes in the just retribution of God. Of course insubordinate soldiers would be struck down by the very waters his people held sacred, in the person of the Mother. It was just the way the world worked, and how the gods kept it orderly.

Himadra's agent was probably dead now, too.

Himadra half-wished he had the kind of faith that made Providence seem self-evident. But the truth was that even on those occasions when he managed to convince himself there was a divine presence behind the Mother River he had a hard time extending that conviction to a belief that she *cared* about humans or the outcomes of their lives.

Maybe as a category. Definitely not as individuals.

"Anyway, if we do make contact, what's to keep Iri the nurse from selling you out to them as a kidnapper?"

"Nothing," Himadra said. "Unless she figures out that following me is in her own best interests. And those of Drupada. And of Ansh-Sahal. But she's got to accept it before they can."

"I guess that means you need to talk to her."

Himadra made a disgruntled noise.

"And assuming this works. What are you going to do with a starving army and a pack of refugees commanded by a toddler in the middle of a wasteland?"

"I don't know yet," Himadra said. "Right now? Bring them home."

HIMADRA CAUSED HIMSELF TO BE CARRIED TO IRI ON HIS SHIELD, AND wondered if she would know it for the honor he intended. She rose as he approached, sweeping Drupada against the trousers she had wrapped her skirt into, but she seemed less apprehensive. And the boy mostly seemed curious. Farkhad and his other bearer set him down beside her, and Farkhad gestured for her to be seated.

"Please take the prince for a small walk?" Himadra said to the other bearer.

Farkhad grimaced at him—worried for his safety against this woman, no doubt—but Himadra brushed his concern aside. She could certainly break every bone in his body if she went for him. Or at least quite a few of them, before Farkhad could stop her. But there were only so many risks a man could avoid without feeling like his entire life was devoted to running away.

Iri, too, seemed as if she wanted to protest. He saw the muscular flinch through her body as she kept herself from rising, and thought that Anuraja would have enjoyed that flinch, and the shadow of fear that followed it. Her eyes tracked Drupada as he was led away.

"You have questions," Himadra asked her.

She startled back into focused attention. "Your Abundance . . . what do you want with my prince?"

"I want to give your charge back his royal seat. Maybe."

Her lips tightened. "I will do what I must to ensure his safety and well-being."

Himadra laughed. "Let me tell you what you see when you look at me," he said. The anger might have gotten into his voice. Must have, because her expression of concealed disgust grew an element of fear. He let it hang there. He couldn't be arsed, right now, to worry about her feelings. "You see a squashed little thing, not even a man, don't you? You find yourself wondering how you came to be trapped here with me. Dependent on me. But here you are."

He sighed heavily, because what was in him had to come out and there were no words for it. No words that would give him the result he wanted, anyway. And it was obvious that she wasn't quite grasping the conversation.

"You pity me," he said. "And you also find me disgusting."

"Yes," she said, ashamed.

It was good, he supposed, that she had the courage to admit it. "Do you despise yourself a little for needing me?"

The shock on her face told him more clearly than any denial that she did not. Had not. Had never even considered it. That interested him. He steepled his fingers to indicate that he was listening.

Even seated, she towered over him. He pretended not to notice. He waited her out.

At last, when his frustrating body ached with sitting still, she said, "It is the way the world is."

"What is the way the world is?"

Tiredly, as if to a child who had demanded "Why?" once too often, she explained. "I am a commoner and poor. You are a raja and others do your bidding. I need you because there is no other way for me to exist. Because a commoner must have a liege, and a lord must have subjects. Men and women to support him."

*Will you teach Drupada that?* Himadra wondered.

"That is the way we have built the world, yes."

She looked at him as if the words he was saying made no sense to her.

"Do you think it has to be that way?"

She frowned at him in consternation.

"Can you envision another way?" He was growing angrier, and his voice was tight. Iri dropped her eyes and cringed. Himadra reminded himself that he was not angry with her, per se. He was angry with . . . he wasn't even sure. The world. The way it crushed people until they did not even mutter to themselves, *There has to be a better way.*

There had to be. He needed to believe it. Even if he didn't know yet what it might be.

Iri abruptly threw herself down on the ground, lowering her face into her arms.

"Iri," he said.

"Raja!" she gasped.

He looked at Farkhad.

"Will you cast me out to find another protector or perish?" she asked, in a small voice that made him ashamed of himself. "I am sorry to have offended you, Your Competence. Please tell me how I may make amends."

He silenced her with a sigh, too exhausted suddenly to speak. He gathered himself and managed, "I will protect you, Iri. Inasmuch as I can. Sit up please."

She did, and sat huddled, still too shaken to dust herself off.

"I meant only that I will put Drupada back on his throne, if that is

what is best for his people. Your people. I'm certainly not turning him—
or you—over to Anuraja, if that is what you were thinking I implied."

She nodded slightly, staring at her hands.

"Look at me."

She studied him, unsmiling. Perhaps what she saw in his expression
reassured her. "I still do not understand what you want."

"A different world with different rules," he said. "I want to build that."

Her face tightened around her mouth, as if she were thinking intently.

"There is an army ahead of us. It is Sayeh's men, and refugees
from the city of Ansh-Sahal. Will you be my representative and messenger, Iri?"

"What do you want me to say?"

"Tell them I offer my protection, and a home in Chandranath."

"For the able?"

"For all." He waved at himself. "Who is to say where ability lies?
Driving a plow is not the only work for a man."

The suspicion had not left the cast of her expression. But perhaps
something else was joining it. "Some may not listen to me."

He shrugged. "Then let them go on without us. They are refugees,
and refuge is what I offer."

She glanced after Drupada. The prince was out of earshot but well
in range of sight, and obviously enjoying being lifted up to pet a soft-
nosed Velvet, who seemed equally pleased with the interaction. Himadra
let her think.

Silence, he sometimes thought, was his greatest persuader.

"I will do this thing," she said. "If you will give me your vow on the
line of the Alchemical Emperor that Drupada will come to no harm at
your hands or by your will while I am gone."

"Drupada will come to no harm by my hands or by my will under
any circumstance," Himadra swore calmly. "That oath is not limited
by time, unless he becomes an enemy of his own choice when he is a
man grown."

Iri assessed him. Then she nodded. "I will go now, with your permission."

"Get Navin to take you." Himadra jerked a hand at his legs. "You
may rise, Iri. Don't wait for me."

She rose, indeed, and went so swiftly and silently in search of Navin that if not for a smooth place in the dust, she might never have been.

"I'd suspect you of harboring anti-royal sympathies," Farkhad said, when she was gone.

Himadra snorted. "Who's to say I don't?"

"Self-defeating."

"Don't worry, Farkhad. You'll always have a job. At least until I'm murdered and deposed."

# 15

WHEN THE GAGE AND THE GODMADE CAME TO THE CLIFF ON THE EASTern edge of Ansh-Sahal, they found the Bitter Sea below them. It was boiling slowly.

No sun or suns had ever risen. The sky was still black and strewn with dim stars in streaks and swaths, as though someone had cast handfuls of salt across dark velvet. It was not the sky of the Lotus Kingdoms. It was not, as far as the Gage knew, the sky of any land at all.

Nizhvashiti clasped its cadaverous hands. "This is what a place God has abandoned looks like."

"Has She abandoned it?" the Gage asked. "Or was She driven from it?"

Below, the thick sea bubbled silkily. Liquid domes popped like blisters. Like the roil of gruel. Splattering steaming mud on the cliff wall.

"Maybe She abandoned it," Nizhvashiti said.

"You don't know?"

"She does not tell me all her plans."

Sustaining the banter required a terrible effort before the specter of that seething sea. Even black humor felt like too much levity.

The Gage went silent.

The night reeked of sulfur, charred meat, and putrescence. The Gage was glad that even his superior senses could not perceive too clearly through the gloom to the water below. Its surface was no doubt churning with live boiled seafood, and its depths as barren as the land they had passed through.

The Godmade was gliding softly away, and the Gage went to follow. "Where are we going?" he asked after a few steps had caught him up.

"There's a temple near here," Nizhvashiti said. "I choose to pay my respects."

Of course they did. Their god was the god of duty.

"Is that really something you want to see?"

"I have to assume that it was why I was brought here," Nizhvashiti said, thereby answering the Gage's question without actually answering.

THE TEMPLE WAS WORSE THAN THE GAGE HAD ANTICIPATED. HE wondered if it might be worse than Nizhvashiti had anticipated, too. No one had collected and repurposed the dead, here. Whether because falling on hallowed ground had rendered them consecrated and defended them from the sorcerer's mischief, or for some other reason, the Gage did not know.

But there were bodies in plenty. And all of them were women.

The temple's entryway had once been a vast, vaulted structure. Now it was a ruined garden, full of boiled trees and poisoned with shards of dragonglass that had tumbled from the skylights above. Some of those shards, daggerlike, had found a place impaled in the bodies of priestesses and acolytes. Not all of them—by their positions and by the black puddles of rancid blood that in this terrible place could not even draw flies—had been dead when it rained knives on them. Some, it appeared from the positions of the bodies, had been trying to help one another crawl away or administer to one another's wounds when the poisoned, boiling air had followed.

"Does this make you want to pray?" Nizhvashiti asked, bending to touch throat after throat in a fruitless quest for a pulse.

The Gage wondered how dead flesh felt to undead fingers.

"Quite the opposite, actually."

"I wish I had time to bury the dead."

"There will be more dead if you pause to bury these."

"There will, in any case, be more dead."

"That," the Gage admitted, "has always been the case."

"The Wizard—"

The Gage made a sound as if clearing a throat he did not have. "I believe you will find that that tigerish individual is, in fact, a sorcerer."

"What's the difference, other than that Wizards have a Royal College of some sort and a social club behind them? They have a diploma and a lot of friends, and sorcerers are social outcasts and self-taught?"

The Gage tipped his head. "Shouldn't you know this? Aren't you meant to be the prophet and the wielder of the powers of the metaphysical realm in this conversation?"

Nizhvashiti drifted forward, not bothering to appear as if it were walking. "Not in my own person. And all those thaumaturgical types seem pretty similar to me."

"Well," the Gage said, "your sorcerers are usually going to be the necromancers and such, though not always. They sacrifice other people to feed their power."

Nizhvashiti looked as skeptical as an emaciated cadaver could.

"And Wizards," the Gage continued, "generally sacrifice some aspect of themselves. Time; love; freedom; their ability to bear children."

"And you're going to maintain that the Wizard who made you did not sacrifice you."

"I sacrificed myself. The Wizard . . . facilitated."

"And yet you are not a Wizard."

"Well, I didn't go to college for it. And Messaline Wizards, of the sort that, for example, created me—they tend to be self-taught. Or apprenticed."

"And so there's never been an evil Wizard."

The Gage laughed, and this time kept on laughing. "Dear Nizhvashiti. There have been thousands."

"So Wizards and sorcerers in some way oppose the divine plan through their personal power."

"I wouldn't say all of them do."

They were still moving through the abbey. Within, there were more dead, but less carnage. There had been stone vaults, many of which were well-built and had withstood the shaking of the rocks under their footings. Those who had died here had died of the searing air and poisoning. They found the library; the books within were shelved and orderly. There was no sign of the librarian.

Nizhvashiti walked to the shelves. It placed a hand on a rack of scrolls, closed its inhuman eyes, and prayed.

The Gage had grown accustomed to the rising and falling chants of the followers of the Good Mother and the Good Daughter. They were not so different, in truth, from what the people of Messaline sang as they went to worship the great gods of that city. Well, three of the four, anyway. Silver-masked Kaalha was not the sort of goddess one sang to.

Hers was the house of silence. In her house was the end of pain.

*I must not be dead then,* the Gage thought, abruptly ashamed of his own moment of introspection. It felt too close to self-pity.

Nizhvashiti, he decided, was praying for the books. For the safety of the knowledge, histories, and memories contained therein. For the protection of the tomes themselves, because what they contained was sacred. It was a prayer the Dead Man would have appreciated.

He missed the Dead Man.

There was no sign whether the Godmade's goddess heard them, or if she responded in any way. If a miracle came it came silently, without a ripple of power. Without a ghostly flutter of light.

But eventually Nizhvashiti stopped praying and turned back to him. "I have done what I can here," it said. "Perhaps someone will be able to come back for them. If they survive."

"If any of us do," the Gage said. "Tell me why you said that thing about Wizards and sorcerers? That they oppose the divine plan with personal power."

"No offense," Nizhvashiti said. "But have you looked at yourself in a mirror?"

"I am a mirror."

They walked—or the Gage walked, as softly as he could out of deference to the flagstones, and Nizhvashiti drifted. Perhaps the God-made was taking them to a postern gate. Perhaps they were just wandering.

"In the normal course of events, would you not be dead by now?"

"Look who's talking."

Nizhvashiti laughed like dry leaves rustling. "I put myself in the hands of my god, and this is what She made me."

"Can you say with confidence that no god wanted me to be here, as I am?"

"You were made by the hand of man."

"I feel like we have had this argument already."

Nizhvashiti made a cutting gesture. "If we struggle against fate, fate will befall us anyway. And we and those we love may suffer more than if we bowed our heads and acquiesced. More innocents may perish than if we bent a neck upon the first demand."

"Does the gazelle lie down for the leopard because it is only staving off the inevitable if it runs? For an hour, for a year."

"Ah," Nizhvashiti said. "There you have the heart of it."

The Gage might have smiled, were he made for smiling. "And if you accept that we live in a world without destiny, you accept that you are alone with your actions and their consequences. There is no fate. There is no divine plan. There is only you, opposed, with imperfect knowledge, making a flawed series of choices that will likely turn out terribly."

"But what," said the Godmade, "if you do not accept the lack of a divine plan?"

"Then you must accept that God puts up with a lot of bullshit," the Gage replied. "And probably isn't a nice person making good choices Herself."

They turned the corner into a blasted courtyard.

And found a woman standing there, her back to them, smoke rising from the fingertips of her left hand.

SHE TURNED TO THEM. THERE WERE BODIES AROUND HER FEET, BUT THEY were not fresh. She did not seem to need any protection from the poisoned air, though the smell of sulfur was strongest here.

The Gage could see now that the smoke rose from a rolled cylinder stuffed with shreds of some dried leaf that she held in a peculiar fashion, between the fingers. She put it to her lips and inhaled through it, as if sucking through a hollow stem. Smoke billowed through her nostrils a moment later, trickled from her lips as she lowered the hand. The Gage thought of forges.

He had seen people smoke pipes, of course, loaded with a variety of intoxicating substances. But he had never seen anybody smoke what looked like rolled-up slips of age-browned paper before. The scent was heavy, aromatic, a little unpleasant. More like burning stone than smoldering plant material.

Nizhvashiti said softly, "This wasteland sure is full of mysterious loners."

The stranger breathed in her own smoke, which swirled like water. Her hair was long and coarse, without luster, the brown-black color of basalt weathered in the sun. Her moderate complexion had an unhealthy, ashy color, as if the smoke of her odd recreation had smudged her. The irises of her eyes were a transparent, unearthly shade of orange-red.

She drew on her cylinder again, and again let the smoke escape her. She smirked them up and down like a madam surveying the clientele. When she snorted laughter, a flood of smoke came with it.

The Gage might almost have stepped back. The woman wore a heavy collar of jewels—diamonds, the Gage thought, though could stones so large truly be diamonds? There was a king's ransom on her throat, if so—cut so that they sparkled and shimmered as brilliantly as stars in the sky. A real sky, not this vacant and dimmed one. Her gown was loose, diaphanous, in layered silks of all the ocean's shades of greens and blues. It fell from her shoulders with slit-topped sleeves that billowed when she smoked, and showed a long bare arm.

The Gage had an unsettling sensation that there was another shoulder and another arm behind it. That the woman he and Nizhvashiti faced was not one woman, but the foremost in a long line of identical women moving in perfect unison, stretching back to infinity, as if two mirrors had been faced to reflect and reflect and reflect her.

"Well." Her voice was as strange as her eyes, full of hisses and crackles. "I was wondering what was taking you so long."

"You were expecting us?" the Gage asked, when Nizhvashiti remained uncharacteristically silent.

Her lips curved. She winked, then turned her gaze on the Godmade. "Surely *you* know me, one such as you are, ansha."

"I do," Nizhvashiti said. "I have nothing to offer you."

The woman nudged a body with her toe. "What's this? Oh, pork roast. Very nice. You shouldn't eat pig; it will give you trichinosis."

A sort of rage that the Gage had thought he was past stirred in him at her disrespect of the dead. Perhaps he shifted or creaked, or perhaps it was all too obvious what he would think, because Nizhvashiti shot him a warning glance—and the ashy woman an amused one.

"So protective of the dead," she said. "Would you have felt so strongly for them when they were alive? Never mind, I see you would. So nurturing for a metal . . . man. A metal thing. An artifice."

She smoked again. The diamonds on her bosom flashed as it rose and fell. She reached into her gown, and this time the Gage did step back, not knowing what to expect but knowing that no one so unimpressed with something like him was to be taken trivially. But she only produced another papery brown cylinder and, puffing, lit it from the first.

Nizhvashiti's stiffness might have been nothing but death. But its wariness was nothing the Gage had seen before, in all their encounters. This was a being who, when less powerful and still mortal, had waved off an ice-drake as if it were of very little consequence indeed.

"Who is this person, then?" the Gage asked. "Since you know her, Godmade, would you be so kind as to introduce us?"

Nizhvashiti's wariness rolled from it in palpable waves. "She is not precisely a person."

"More or less a person than you . . . or than I?" The Gage made his voice relaxed, amused. A benefit of not having the traditional means of speech at his disposal. The Godmade's discomfiture was catching.

"More than a person." Nizhvashiti's eyeless gaze never varied from the stranger's face. "And other than one."

Sulfurous smoke wreathed the stranger's words. "I am relieved you do not find me less, ansha. You may call me . . . Deep. If you like that."

Nizhvashiti's steepled hands rose and fell before its breast in a manner the Gage recognized as a gesture of fearful respect. "Did this city offend you, O great one?"

Deep flicked ash negligently. Residue and sparks fell on her bare foot, on the bodies, and on the paving stones. None of these reacted to the heat.

"Not as such," Deep admitted. There were gray strands in the coils of her hair, among the faded black. "Maybe it was just in the wrong place at the wrong time. Maybe it was not worthy of attention."

She prodded the flagstones lightly with the front of her foot. To his awe, the Gage saw that they yielded. When Deep drew her foot back, she left behind the impression of five pearl-like toes and the ball of the foot.

"But here you are, O great one," Nizhvashiti said. "Manifestly."

The Gage began to experience what would have been a queer feeling in the pit of his stomach, if he had such things as queer feelings, or stom-achs for that matter. To Nizhvashiti, he said, "This is the being that destroyed Ansh-Sahal."

The Godmade nodded. "Perhaps collaterally? O great one, were you invited here? Did you come here on some purpose of your own? I am, of course, your servant, and it would help me to understand what you need if you could trouble yourself to recall."

Deep frowned at her twist of dried herbs. "I came to see."

"What the eruption had done?" the Gage asked, ignoring Nizhvashiti's hushing gesture.

Deep smoked and smoked again. Was this what agitation looked like in a goddess? "These people were true believers."

*It did not help them,* the Gage thought.

"So am I," Nizhvashiti said. "Look at me. I am your sacrifice. Not these poor people."

"That definitely took some gall," Deep agreed. "Making that of yourself."

She seemed to struggle to follow the conversation, the Gage realized. As if only the most recent thread remained to her. Like that game where people in turn wrote a line on a paper, then another, then folded it to hide all the story but the last sentence.

"Is it a sacrifice more to your taste than pork roast?"

"It was not in my name that you did that thing."

The Gage held a tongue he did not have, and settled in to watch the Godmade remonstrate with its recalcitrant deity. Or, he thought, a chipped-off piece of same.

"Are you not all part and parcel of one another, you and your sisters?"

"I am not the Good Daughter. I am ruthless in a different way." A smoky sigh of remembrance. "In days of old they would toss strong youths and maidens into the flames."

"That was a long time ago. Something woke you, great one."

"Yes."

"On purpose?"

The goddess began to pace, and did not answer. Under the Gage's feet, the earth shuddered softly as a cat dreaming.

"Do you remember what it was that woke you? Or for that matter, whom?"

Deep turned away. Another smoke lit from the stub of the second one decorated her hand. She was so thin the lines of her skeleton showed through the shoulders of her sea-colored gown. The Gage imagined he could see a thousand other women turning with her.

"I serve your sister," Nizhvashiti said, with every appearance of calm. The Gage, for no good reason except experience, was certain the God-made was dissembling. If its heart still beat, it would be racing.

Deep's head snapped back around.

"Then go bother her!" Deep's raised voice was a rumbling crack like stone shattering. The earth lurched, and the foundations of what remained of the abbey shifted.

Nizhvashiti's hand shot out and clasped the Gage's metal wrist. The Godmade bowed as if hinged at the hips. The Gage, who *was* hinged at the hips, followed suit. They backed away without another word, heads down, Nizhvashiti gliding and the Gage sliding his feet as if on ice. They did not turn their backs until they were well out of Deep's line of sight, at which point they let go of one another, turned tail, and fled.

It occurred to the Gage as they hurried from the abbey that a volcano was one of the few things that could probably put an end to him. Melting down would probably put an end to his consciousness.

Probably.

They did not further seek the postern gate, but returned the way they had come. The earth struck the soles of the Gage's feet once or twice, jumping and trembling, but the abbey did not collapse upon them. They made it to the gate alive.

The sea still seethed and bubbled far below.

THEY CONTINUED DOWN THE ROAD FOR A LONG FEW MINUTES BEFORE THE Gage deemed it appropriate to remark, "So that was the Mother."

"An aspect of her. Perhaps. Unless it was something much older." The Godmade paused. "There are still older things."

"She did not seem . . . nurturing."

"Not all mothers are good ones."

"An ansha?"

Nizhvashiti laughed shakily. "A god."

"A volcano."

"The Bitter Sea. The volcano is only part of it."

"She seemed a little vague for a divinity."

"Are you at your best when you've just awakened?"

"I've heard of smoking mountains," the Gage admitted. "But that was hardly what I would have expected."

Nizhvashiti closed pupilless eyes and slowly shook its head.

The Gage made half a laugh. Not a happy one. "So Ansh-Sahal was not destroyed by accident."

"Indeed," Nizhvashiti agreed.

"So who woke the volcano up?" The Gage's tone was not meant to conceal that he already thought that he knew.

"At a guess?" the Godmade said, with the same timbre of resignation. "The same person with a use for thousands of bodies."

"The sorcerer can't be acting alone."

"It doesn't seem likely, does it? So the question is, who is the sorcerer working for?"

"Anuraja?"

"Anuraja might be a dupe. I have a feeling that this is something larger. Something more." The Godmade shook its head again. "Well, we can do only the work our hand can reach."

THE GAGE'S STEPS CONTINUED TIRELESSLY NORTH AND WEST. Nizhvashiti had taken its leave and gone. It had offered a blessing first, which the Gage had accepted without prejudice or any real belief. Then it had returned to Sarathai-tia in order to bring Mrithuri the news that the problem they faced was much larger and less well understood than they had thought. And hardly limited to a little internecine warfare and a particularly violent family dispute.

After a day or two, he came into a place that *had* days, and that did not reek of poison. Vara rejoined him, and he told it his story in case Mrithuri was listening. In case Nizhvashiti had somehow not managed to make it home.

The Gage had time to make up now, and a mortal fear to push him.

After the first day of accelerated walking, the Gage began to pass by refugees in the road. They stared and pointed. Some fled in terror. Many were too tired to do more than edge over, away from where he went.

He kept to the edge of the road and tried not to terrify the animals. He did not stop to speak with them. They made way for him. These were not Mrithuri's people, but they lived under the same Cauled Sun.

They might have information, it was true. But it would be far too easy for him to become distracted by a thousand side errands, and for the time being, he had chosen to believe that the errand he had been sent upon would be useful in the long run. It was possible, after all, that the Eyeless One knew something. Possible, and even likely, based on the weight of experience.

The Gage was pleased to note that one of the groups he passed seemed to be comprised of priestesses in the raiment of the ruined abbey. They surrounded a woman he took for the abbess. So a few had made it out.

For a moment, the Gage thought of stopping to tell them that their goddess had dropped by and was, to the best of his knowledge, poking around the empty halls they'd left behind, searching for her memory.

But there would be no point. They couldn't go back.

So, as much as it saddened him to think of Deep alone in the abbey's library, flipping through books and looking for answers her own mind could not supply, he steeled himself and walked on.

Soon he was beyond any humans, and he parted company with their highways and began to follow the legendary series of markers men called the Dragon Road. They were flat stones, vast and smooth, like pavements set into the earth, and they were often an hour's walk or more from each other. They would have been very evident from the air, however.

And he thought of Chaeri.

They were slightly confused thoughts. It was *possible* her interest could be genuine, he supposed. She hadn't gone out of her way to dissemble or conceal her opinions, he thought, even when they challenged his. His experience was that women who intended to manipulate someone into romantic interest tended to conceal their personalities behind a mask. And she had done nothing to seem coy, which was another common plot.

But what would anyone want with *him*?

She had seemed to decide that she did. Want him, that was. And that it was a foregone conclusion that he, in turn, would want her. Her confidence that she would be desired by any object of that desire made it seem ... rude not to reciprocate.

In all the time that the Gage had spent as a man of metal ... well. Not one single person had ever made a pass at him until now. Most didn't even seem to recognize him as sentient, as anything other than an automaton.

He thought about how people related romantically. He could not really recall from his own experience how it had been. He did remember that it had seemed tremendously important once.

Would he have *noticed*, honestly, if she had been more subtle? Because she had *not* been subtle, did he now not know how to say no?

Did he *want* to say no?

He didn't even know how to determine that.

Gages were not much accustomed to thinking about what they *wanted*.

He had gotten that far along the path of contemplation when he realized: in all of the musing he had done—all of the musing he was doing—about how Chaeri felt about him, he hadn't given a scrap of thought as to how *he* felt about Chaeri. In fact, he still didn't know, as his footsteps carried him tirelessly into the east.

# 16

THE THING ABOUT SIEGES, THE DEAD MAN REMEMBERED, WAS THAT they were dull.

And so the Dead Man had decided—certainly all on his own, without any veiled looks or urging from Ata Akhimah or Yavashuri—to keep an eye on Chaeri. And it was quite possibly the most boring bodyguarding job he had ever undertaken.

It involved . . . not quite following her from place to place. That would have kept her out of trouble, but it also would have been crowningly obvious, and part of his remit was in not putting her guard up. And if her guard went up, she would not do anything treasonous.

The thing about sieges *was* that they were boring.

He did find time to check in with Hnarisha, who told him that nothing new had been discovered in Mahadijia's old quarters—"Why all the drama, then?"—and with Golbahar to make sure that Ritu was settling into her new role. But it was crammed in between chasing Chaeri around. And since the times when he was reasonably sure Chaeri could not be getting into too much mischief were when she was with Mrithuri—and therefore under the eye of Yavashuri, Golbahar, and Ritu—it meant the Dead Man himself had very little time to spend alone with his rajni. Which currently, the love affair being new, felt like a major sacrifice.

He rather hoped Chaeri wouldn't do anything openly treasonous, because it would break Mrithuri's heart if she did. For Mrithuri's sake, he wanted Chaeri to be loyal.

For the Gage's sake . . . well, the Gage would manage. Although the more time he spent around Chaeri, the less sure the Dead Man was what the Gage saw in her. If, indeed, he was just not too polite to send her on her way. Because Chaeri almost never did anything that was not utterly routine and stultifying.

Her main task was caring for Mrithuri's sacred pets, a task that carried, at best, ritual significance, as each of them had their own attendants. It wasn't as if her duties required her to haul hay to the elephant, or scavenge carcasses for the bearded vultures. Or shovel up the result of either of those. So she helped Mrithuri dress, and then she made her rounds of stables and mews. She did trouble herself to cast a little barley to the peacocks at least. And sliced fruit for Guang Bao.

Syama would take food from no hand but that of Mrithuri Rajni alone. But since she never left the queen's side, Chaeri was not necessary to care for her.

The Dead Man found himself wondering how the animals would fare, if the siege persisted. They were sacred, it was true. But sacred cow fed a hungry man as well as the profane sort. Eating one was slightly more likely to turn your gods against you, however.

After those tasks were accomplished, Chaeri mostly wandered. Morning and night, she fed the wild birds in the palace gardens. She flirted with those above her station and quarreled with those below. She gossiped, which was not so bad, and changed the tales between tellings to cast people in a worse light, which was more of a problem. She seemed to leave scowls behind her wherever she went.

Or perhaps that was because that asshole Mi Ren always seemed to be around as well, and Mrithuri's people treated *him* with the absolute barest politeness due a foreign dignitary, and a scraping obsequiousness that the Dead Man, a lifelong servant himself, knew for the disguise worn by sneering sarcasm. They certainly didn't treat Mrithuri that way.

Mi Ren would probably think it was because Mrithuri's people respected him more. Since he was a man, and since he obviously knew how to treat them.

Anyway, when he wasn't scraping up to Mrithuri, he was scraping around after Chaeri, leaving the Dead Man to wonder exactly what he thought he was accomplishing.

Meanwhile, if Mrithuri was holding court to be her people's lawgiver, Chaeri was the only one of the rajni's intimates who went out of her way to avoid it. When she could not avoid it, she drowsed decoratively on a cushion on the dais like a silk-clad pet. And then Mi Ren did not have to divide his attentions, but lurked in the gallery in Mrithuri's line of sight and sulked.

The Dead Man considered Syama more useful.

Perhaps it was just the rivalry of a new favorite for an old. Perhaps it was a new romance sparking his protective instincts, but it *was* a new romance, and he was acutely aware of how fragile his position was. Politically even more so than with the rajni. He didn't think for a moment that Pranaj the general or Ata Akhimah would hesitate to slip a knife between his ribs if they thought he was exerting undue influence on her.

It was possible, he supposed, that the problem with Chaeri was that she simply didn't have enough to do to keep her out of trouble. She *definitely* didn't have a rich enough internal life to make up the lack with interests and accomplishments.

If she had cared about anything other than being the center of attention, she might have found useful things to do, even amid the boredom of the siege, than play the other courtiers and the servants off against one another. It was her way of being important. Her way of making herself the center of activity, of surrounding herself with drama and color and a sense that she mattered. That she was the one holding the secret scrolls.

He thought of the burned papers in Mahadijia's rooms, and wondered. If it was correct that someone could have taken a talisman off Mahadijia's corpse and gone there and burned them . . . the logical person to have done that was Chaeri. But she had been in hysterics after the killing. Could she have managed to slip away from her minders in order to conceal whatever intelligence Mahadijia had wished to present to Mrithuri?

There was, the Dead Man reminded himself, at least one illusionist somewhere in the mix. If only he had a better idea what illusionists were capable of.

After the second day—another day of siege when nothing happened, and nothing changed: a day that for the Dead Man could have been more fruitfully spent doing just about anything defensive or logistical, because the problem with sieges was that they were a battle of endurance, seeing who might succumb to hunger, exposure, boredom, thirst, the need to go home and get the crops in, or disease before the other—after the second day, he started to wonder even more.

He began to wonder how anybody could endure such a pointless existence.

The Dead Man sometimes had ambitions of retiring to a little fishing boat, perhaps. A small market farm in a pleasant climate. Maybe a sword shop or a tavern. But this . . . this *existence* of Chaeri's was so profoundly dull that the most exciting way she spent her time was in feeding wild birds. And at least the songbirds found her trustworthy.

At that moment, the Dead Man—perhaps overcome with charity or an uncharacteristic fit of fairness—admitted to himself that he could see why people might like Chaeri. She did have a few good qualities.

The Dead Man was observing her from atop the garden wall, the same one that Captain Vidhya and Tsering-la had come in over. He had arranged to be there already when Chaeri arrived, gazing plausibly into the distance toward the enemy encampment, which he could not actually see from here. It helped assuage his feelings of uselessness to be checking some element of the palace and city defenses, anyway.

He'd glanced at the handmaiden once, when she appeared below. Now he imagined what he'd observed before, Chaeri scattering stale crumbs in a flurry of wings. The bolder ones would even fly to sit on her finger and trill. He could imagine it as she chirped back, a counterpart to their tiny noises, her pointed face tilting from side to side behind her hair.

It was a few hours before sunrise, and the sky was still bright, the birds still active. He did not turn again to see what she was doing. He could hear her, and that was enough. Instead, he watched Pranaj walking the wall, speaking to the troops on guard there. Mrithuri's men had been out among the refugees and the denizens in the city, recruiting new soldiers. There was room in the Alchemical Emperor's barracks for an entire army; he could wish that Mrithuri had caused the dusty rooms to be swept out and refreshed and started building such a force earlier than she had. Of course, the Alchemical Emperor had not left stores to feed an army along with the roofs to house them. And leaving an army sitting around with nothing but time on their hands was asking for a military coup.

The eternal balancing act of princes in a world with wars.

The Dead Man shoved his fists deep into the pockets of the red linen coat that Mrithuri had given him, his shoulders hunching. The rajni had been delighted with glee like a child to deliver the present, passing it to him with her own hands that very evening.

It was the wrong shade of red, the cut wasn't what he was used to, and the fabric didn't move properly. Everything about it was wrong.

Of course he wore it.

He put it on without complaint, and took care not to scowl where the rajni could see him. And the coat was, he admitted—if only in silence and only to himself—a more fit fabric for this oppressive weather. It let the breezes through and kept the sun off, and the fabric did not cling in the humid warmth.

He missed his old one. But as the Scholar-God's scriptures taught, one always mourned who one used to be.

And who one might have been, also.

Time passed dully, and Mi Ren was following Chaeri around also. And doing a much worse job of it than the Dead Man. Especially since about half the time, he was escorted by one of his justifiably nervous lackeys. He was easy to lose, however—so easy even Chaeri could do it. And did.

The Dead Man wondered if Mi Ren had been after Chaeri to press his suit with Mrithuri. There was still, the Dead Man noted, no evidence of Mi Ren's father's armies.

The Dead Man was spending an uncharacteristic amount of time in the gardens, what with following Chaeri around. The heat and dryness were having an effect. Trees that had been preparing to flower heavily shriveled, their leaves hanging dusty and limp. The water in the river was not rising.

After the third day, he noticed the silence. It was not that there were no birds. It was just that there were *fewer*.

He wandered the gardens in the lingering cool of early morning, watching the day grow dark and the strange, sculptural shadows of the Cauled Sun refracting through the crevices between wind-stirred leaves.

He didn't expect Chaeri at this time of the morning. She should usually be helping Mrithuri prepare for bed at this hour. So what was he doing out here, alone, in this strange verdant place?

The verdancy was fading. In a nearby fig tree, he could see the outlines of a troop of monkeys roosting through the heat of the day. Their silhouettes were plainly visible against the sky because the leaves that should have concealed them drooped with drought. Fig trees were among the first to suffer from the lack of water.

The Dead Man found himself crunching slowly along a path graveled with the crushed shells of river shellfish. Their whiteness seemed to glow faintly through the dusk because of reflected daylight. He let his steps carry him where they would. Perhaps his God would guide him to the destination he needed—some portent, some clarity, some revelation.

Not a portent, it turned out. But an elephant.

He found himself at Hathi's enclosure. The elderly elephant herself was nothing but a pale shadow in the dusk, but he walked up to her fence—she could have shattered it with ease if she desired—and leaned his elbows on it. She was calmly eating a pile of river reeds and lotus that was probably the last of the fresh fodder for her, unless Mrithuri started raiding the ornamental gardens.

Mrithuri would, no doubt, soon be raiding the ornamental gardens.

The Dead Man stood in the dark and breathed. Sweat seeped from his pores. It might refuse to rain, but the humidity was unrelenting. The elephant moved comfortably about her pen.

Quiet steps slipped up the path behind him with a whispered crunch, crunch.

"The coin shows the other face now," Chaeri said silkily. "I am stalking you."

He did not turn. "Maybe you are stalking that asshole, Mi Ren."

She came to lean against the fence beside him. He was not tall, but she was a good deal smaller than him. She pursed her lips and pushed a coil of hair behind her ear. "No," she decided. "My rajni already despises him. You have nothing to gain by it."

"Is that my motivation? Personal advantage?"

She smiled and glanced aside, or so he understood the ducking of her head in the darkness. "He should be along in a moment. Will you confront him for harassing me?"

"And here I understood that you were following me."

"You certainly did excellent work of making it seem so. Did Yavashuri give you my schedule?"

Hathi came over to them. She reached out with her dexterous trunk, fumbling for treats. Chaeri, who had come prepared, handed her a dried date. The elephant turned it over once or twice, sniffing, then stuffed it into her mouth.

"Did Yavashuri teach you your tradecraft?" the Dead Man asked in reply.

Chaeri shook her head self-deprecatingly. She handed the elephant another treat. "You learn a few tricks when you work with somebody."

She was better at this than the Dead Man would have expected. Good enough to nurture his suspicions.

"Then what are you doing here?"

She handed another morsel across the fence. "Feeding the elephant."

He made a noncommittal noise.

She gestured to both sides. "Do you think these trees will set fruit, Dead Man?" Her voice was mocking and chilly. "Do you think there will be dates and mangos in the fall? Do you think this fence will hold her when she is hungry?"

The Dead Man assumed that these questions were intended as rhetoric. He did not immediately answer. He was still contemplating them, and what to say about them, when both he and Chaeri reacted to the sounds of someone "sneaking" through the garden beds. It was true: the shells would have crunched underfoot if that someone had stayed on the nearest path. But there were other paths, some flagged with laid stone. And walking on any of them softly would have been more quiet than parading through the dark ripping up the shrubbery.

Chaeri blew her hair back. "Another fool betrayed by romance."

"Mi Ren," the Dead Man murmured.

"That asshole," she agreed.

As they turned to face the newcomer, the Dead Man thought sadly that he much preferred this Chaeri to the flighty, dissembling one. Pity this was the one who probably needed killing. The rustling stopped in a nearby shadow. The Dead Man waited three heartbeats—his heart was beating strongly enough to be easily counted—and called out, "Prince Mi Ren?"

A crack of a twig, and a moment of silence, as if someone in the darkness had stepped back sharply before freezing. Shuffling followed, as Mi Ren moved forward into the dim daylight.

"So!" He made a grand gesture with his sleeve. Silk fluttered where the shrubs had tattered it. "I have at last caught you two in the act of plotting treachery!"

Hathi tugged at the Dead Man's veil, annoyed that she was no longer the center of attention. The Dead Man raised one hand to hold it in place. It would be a pity to have to kill Mi Ren right now.

Well, sort of a pity.

Mrithuri still had uses for him.

"If by treachery," he drawled instead, "you mean feeding the elephant."

Chaeri snorted in laughter. He wondered if he had ever heard an uncalculated laugh from her before. It sounded very different. They were allies in the moment, though they were not allies at all.

Mi Ren drew himself up to a furious height. It was probably more impressive when he was in a petty kingdom where his petty word was law. The Dead Man did not even bother to feel for his sword. "We'll let the rajni be the judge of that. Why, when I make my report—"

Chaeri chose that moment to beat her retreat with a tattoo of quick little steps. She edged past Mi Ren with the sketch of a curtsy but no real deference, so that he scowled after her.

The Dead Man decided to distract him. Not because he cared about Chaeri, exactly. Or Mi Ren. But because Mrithuri would prefer the peace be kept. "Even if you're right, the rajni will not like you for it. Bearers of bad news rarely win the lady's heart."

Mi Ren turned back just to better aim his scoffing. "She doesn't think that much of you."

The Dead Man smiled into his veil. He nodded after Chaeri. "I wasn't talking about myself, Your Highness. Not all of us always do. And that lady who just left us is the rajni's dearest friend."

"That servant?"

"Lady-in-waiting," the Dead Man said. "Not entirely the same thing. And a person of some power and influence, I assure you."

THE UNOPENED FLOWERS WERE DROPPING FROM THE GOLMOHAR TREES. The Dead Man watched them fall, drifting through air that should have been swept with raindrops, and mused on the similarity to the name of Lady Golbahar, who stood beside him watching the Heavenly River rise. He might have remarked on the coincidence, but they were alone, waiting for Mrithuri to come forth from her chambers, and it might have seemed too forward if he did.

They were both discreet behind their veils, and he did not wish to appear overfamiliar. Or flirtatious.

So they stood, a little apart, and listened to the nuns sing behind their partitions. The lady had a bowl of tea in her slender fingers. She had allowed her palms to be painted with henna. The custom was familiar, but the designs were strange. The result was very beautiful.

Home, that was it. She felt like home. And she felt as strange as home no doubt would, after such a long absence, even if he somehow found his way back there.

The song was eerie and sweet; the sunset was beautiful. The last filmy tendrils of the Cauled Sun's corona flickered at the horizon, so flat and far away, taking the darkness down with the day. And the Dead Man looked at it and wondered. Even the sun went veiled here. Maybe that was another reason why he kept finding himself accidentally feeling at home.

*Don't get attached,* he told himself. *Don't get comfortable. Don't get used to this. Don't you dare.*

It was not permanent. It could not ever be permanent. And fantasizing that it might be—worse, believing that it could—was the fastest route to a broken heart he could think of.

The fact of the matter was that he was getting older. The fact of the matter was that he missed having a home. He was long since too old to make a living as a sell-sword, not that that had been stopping him. And yet here he was with a sword and the selling of it as the means of keeping his soul in a warm, clean, decently fed body.

What did old mercenaries do when they ran out of battles? Buy a farm and harness their old warhorse up to the plow traces? Wasn't buying a farm a common euphemism for something else?

Maybe he should take his savings—money on deposit to a stonemason's guild in Messaline—and invest in a nice mercenary company. Pay someone else to wield the swords they were selling.

Well, before he made any retirement plans, he'd probably better make it out the other side of this little war with his life intact. Maybe when the time came for them to part, Mrithuri would set him up with a sinecure.

He dismissed as infatuation the little voice that staunchly proclaimed his lack of desire to move on anytime soon, especially if that meant moving away from Mrithuri. Loyalty was an admirable quality in a man-at-arms.

So was pragmatism.

His breath caught hard as a marble in his gullet when Mrithuri emerged from her bedchamber, where he had never been. He imagined a silk-hung, incense-scented chamber, but the glimpse through the swift door was of a bright space with grand windows facing the rising stars, and Mrithuri silhouetted against them.

She did not even really look like herself—or how he was coming now to think of her. He had already grown accustomed to the battle-ready Mrithuri, and this was the rajni once again. She did not look to him particularly beautiful, though she was jeweled and draped and painted, hung with gauds he knew she chafed under. The lower half of her face was hidden behind a snarling golden mask; her eyes were winged in kohl.

She was surrounded by her people, including Chaeri and the Wizards. An austringer bearing one of her great bearded vultures followed after. Its wings, which it mantled over the man's fist in the heat, were freshly ochre-red. The singing of the nuns swelled around them.

Yavashuri and Hnarisha were not with her, though the Dead Man had expected that they would be.

He and Golbahar turned to watch the rajni's procession. Mrithuri's eyes slid sidelong as she passed him. She said nothing, but one lid drooped its burden of soot-blacked cow-hair lashes across her cheek. She smirked saucily behind the mask.

Golbahar and the Dead Man slid in among the second rank.

The Dead Man touched the butts of his guns for reassurance, just needing that reminder that he had weapons should he need them. He wore his sword as well, and a softly chink-rustling coat of chain mail that draped his body with the pressure of swimming deep.

This was not just a court. It was a progress. They were going outside, among Mrithuri's people, and the Dead Man did not put it past Anuraja—or whomever—to have primed an assassin or two amongst the folk of the city, or the recently added refugees.

Someone, after all, had already tried to kill her once. And possibly twice, if he chose to believe Chaeri's version of events surrounding the death of Mahadijia. If the Dead Man believed the intelligence, then Anuraja could have no reason to murder Mrithuri—and, in fact, a dozen reasons not to.

The worst part was that the likely presence of enemy agents among Mrithuri's people made it more essential that she go forth among them. More essential, and more dangerous, of course. But whatever the threat, it was love of their rajni and a sense of connection to her that would stir her subjects' morale and keep them resolute through the weeks and perhaps months to come.

He fingered the scar on his bosom, but he could not feel it through the coat of mail and the padded coat he wore beneath it. Was it true, he wondered, that Anuraja had no reason to assassinate the rival queen? Maybe he thought it would be easier than marrying her.

And if Anuraja did not have such a reason, who did? And why were they using sorcery?

Mrithuri, the Dead Man could tell, was nervous, though she was surrounded by her Wizard and her men-at-arms and two ladies, with Tsering-la along for good measure. She had offered Mi Ren a place to walk with her. He had discovered a pressing need to be elsewhere. But Ritu and her family would meet them at the gates, so the rajni would be preceded by jugglers and acrobats who were also capable swordspersons.

Despite all that, and despite the Dead Man's sword at her back, and despite that she stood straight and let her hands hang soft by her sides, the rigidity of her neck and her short quick steps gave her away.

He wondered again where she had sent her two most trusted advisors. Or had Chaeri managed to maneuver them away?

Surely they would not choose to skip such a dangerous errand unless prevented.

THE DEAD MAN DID NOT NEED WONDER FOR TOO LONG. BECAUSE AS THEIR slow parade was passing through the grand processional that led between the Great Hall on one end and the Grand Doors to the palace—where they were meant to meet the acrobats with their baskets of strewing petals and their spools of ribbons—on the other, he heard two pairs of footsteps coming up behind them at a run.

His hand that had been resting on the butt of his gun closed over it. But before he could whirl and level a pistol, Ata Akhimah caught his eye and shook her head ever so faintly. So, instead, he managed to turn just his head, calmly, in time to see the missing Hnarisha pelting toward them. Yavashuri huffed along in his wake, her robes lifted in her fists to enable the pursuit.

The Dead Man himself, growing too old for sprinting, felt for her valiance.

Their faces were not masks of fear, desperation, or horror, so the Dead Man assumed that neither the enemy nor another indestructible revenant were in pursuit. What their expression did reveal was profound urgency, above and beyond the tension so consistently reflected in the faces of everyone since the siege began.

Whatever drove them was obviously a matter of great importance.

The Dead Man kept a portion of his attention on Chaeri as the other two drew up. Her expression was tight. Apprehensive.

"My rajni," Hnarisha said with a little bow. He was the less out of breath of the pair. "We have news from the north."

Chaeri's demeanor shifted suddenly. The tension—call it what it was: fear—on her features passed as if a hand smoothed sand, leaving a hint of superior anticipation. She shifted her gaze to Mrithuri's face, as if the rajni's reaction interested her more than did the news.

For his part, the Dead Man wondered briefly how any information was coming into the sealed gates of the city. That was, he supposed, why one kept such . . . connected persons . . . as Yavashuri in one's employ. But that was also the moment where he lost any doubt that Chaeri was, in the very least, withholding information. And why she would do that if she was not some species of traitor, he did not know. He could construct scenarios where she was waiting, in order to aggrandize herself by being a hero at the last minute with some critical item of intelligence—and he was sure Mrithuri would make those excuses for Chaeri, if he pressed her on it—but they were not, to his critical eye, plausible excuses.

So he shifted his gaze to follow Chaeri's and also watched Mrithuri's expression as she drew a breath, visibly steeled herself, and said, "Word from Ansh-Sahal?"

"Word from Chandranath," Hnarisha said. "Concerning Ansh-Sahal."

"Well, don't roost on the news like a hen," the rajni snapped.

Hnarisha glanced at Yavashuri, who seemed now to have collected herself and recollected her breath.

"Prince Drupada lives," she said. "And Lord Himadra has taken custody of the child and declared himself the Lord Protector of Ansh-Sahal."

The things Mrithuri's face did behind her mask were indeed worth watching.

"Regent of a wasteland," Chaeri scoffed. "How . . . effectual."

But the Dead Man recollected the precision displayed by Himadra's men when he had passed through Chandranath with Druja's caravan. "He has a plan."

Yavashuri exhaled crossly. "I don't suppose you might know what it is?"

"I could guess," the Dead Man said. "But they would be guesses only. However, I wonder if there are any assets in Anuraja's camp who can tell us how that worthy is reacting to the news, if he has it yet?"

Yavashuri and Hnarisha exchanged a glance while the Dead Man wondered why it was that Chaeri wished to downplay this news to the rajni.

"There is more." It was a new voice. A whispering one. And the Dead Man nearly shot himself in the foot with his still-holstered pistol, it made him jump so hard.

The Godmade drifted out of the shadows with no more sound than the rustle of stiff fabric. At first, the Dead Man imagined wildly that the already tall and gaunt figure had somehow mysteriously grown and attenuated more. Then he realized that his instinctive reach for the word "drifting" to describe Nizhvashiti's movement was because the God-made floated a handspan above the tiles, lower limbs hanging motion-less within the column of its robes. Trailing fabric from its hems stirred runnels of gold dust that had exfiltrated the throne room into flitter-ing swirls.

"Of course there is," Mrithuri sighed. It was a sigh that would have impressed any large, tired dog that the Dead Man had chanced to know. In fact, Syama glanced up at her mistress with a rapt expression in her liquid eyes.

Mrithuri's robes swirled elegantly around her limbs as she pivoted on the balls of her feet. She gazed up into Nizhvashiti's face and said, "Do your worst, child of the Mother."

"I have journeyed to communicate with the Gage." The Godmade spoke from an impassive face. "He is well, although traveling through blighted, blasted territory."

"You have been right here," Chaeri protested. "Do not lie to my rajni."

The Godmade's stone and metal eyes each made faintly different grinding sounds when it rolled them. "I did not travel physically, but projected my spiritual self. I was not quite really there, but only my physical form remained here."

"Are you really here now?"

"But we have learned this," the Godmade continued, as if never in-terrupted. "I do not think the sorcerer—"

The Dead Man listened with increasing horror and resignation as Nizhvashiti related their adventure. He wished something in the story surprised him more, but the corpses laced and animated by stone were too familiar. As was the utterly ruined city, air and sea and land all poi-soned, for different reasons. That it should have happened in this way at this time seemed only a logical extension of what they knew already.

Nizhvashiti's description of the sorcerer they had met drew Tsering-la up short, and sent a tingle through the Dead Man's spine as well.

Tsering-la spoke first. "I've met him. In the company of Himadra. During the fall of Ansh-Sahal."

"I . . ." the Dead Man faltered as eyes turned toward him. "There was a woman very like that. In Chandranath, with both rajas. They said her name was Ravani."

"This one was named Ravana," Nizhvashiti said.

"There are two of them?" the Dead Man said.

Chaeri laughed as if it were the most ridiculous thing she had ever heard.

"There are beings that can change their appearance at will." Nizhvashiti folded its hands inside its sleeves. The Dead Man wondered if a revenant could tremble. "And we already knew we were dealing with an illusionist."

"Unwholesome beings," said Ata Akhimah.

"Mostly," Nizhvashiti agreed. "Himadra may be under this creature's influence, then. He seemed . . . nonplussed . . . that he could not easily make the Gage and me see reason. As if he expected to be found reasonable despite being so magnificently not."

"Are you resistant to such effects?"

"That is an excellent question." The Godmade gestured as if shrugging off rain and tapped its chiming eye. The illusion-shattering peal went forth, a nearly visible ripple running with it. It felt, when it passed the Dead Man, as if he stood in water in the path of a wave. It pushed and pulled him, and seemed to slurp a bit of the tile floor out from under his feet though he moved not at all. "At least to some degree, it seems."

"The Gage often is," the Dead Man said.

Hnarisha tilted his head. "I'd like to discuss it sometime."

Chaeri's expression shifted to practiced boredom with a gloss of mild superiority.

Tsering-la's restrained excitement burned in his voice. "I'd like to get in on this conversa—"

Mrithuri cleared her throat. "Returning to the matter at hand, is this sort of . . . eruption . . . something that could happen here? If Himadra has the power to call up deadly vapors from the place where earth and waters meet, to boil the seas, and use it as a weapon . . . could something like that come out of the Mother River and end us all?"

The Wizards, Hnarisha, and Nizhvashiti looked at one another. The Dead Man, watching them, remarked to himself that there were certainly many branches of metaphysics in the world. He had grown accustomed to learning what he needed to know about them from the Gage. Being confronted with the realization of how many branches of knowledge were accounted among the wielders of mysterious forces here made him feel strange, as if along with the new coat his religion were not fitting exactly as he was accustomed.

He was luckily saved from too much contemplation when Tsering-la answered. "I should not presume to answer categorically, but consider that the Bitter Sea is, in fact, bitter. And that it has a history of such events, which to me would tend to indicate that it, like the Cold Fire"—naming the great volcano that crouched over the city of Tsarapheth—"might rest over a primordial natural furnace deep in the roots of the world. Possibly the same one, if such things can extend so far. So Sarathai-tia should be safe. At least, from that."

"I tend to agree," Nizhvashiti said. "There's other evidence as well that it is a local phenomenon." And told them about the befuddled, possibly ensorcelled, chain-smoking volcano goddess.

"Nonsense," Chaeri said, into the silence that followed. "Charlatanry. You pretend to go into a trance, and you come back with . . . tales of sorcerers and corpses and summoned gods? No one can summon the Mother. That's . . . that's blasphemy."

"And yet," Nizhvashiti said in level whispers, "it is I who am the priest here."

Mrithuri raised her hand for silence. "An unsettling priest. One who many might find uncanny."

Nizhvashiti tipped its head in acknowledgment.

"Perhaps it would be best if you did not process with us through the city, Godmade."

"Perhaps not," Nizhvashiti agreed.

"My rajni," Chaeri said. "Perhaps it would be safest if we canceled the event. You can review your people another day. The council perhaps should meet, and decide what is to be done with Nizhvashiti—"

"Shut up," Mrithuri said, her voice made hollow by the mask.

Chaeri's voice stopped as if her mouth had been sealed by magic. The Dead Man felt a small thrill of pleasure at the blessed silence following.

Mrithuri rubbed her arms. "I am going to see my people, and reassure them that I have their best interests at heart. Is that plain enough for you?"

Chaeri, downcast, nodded. Her teeth were sunk in her lip. *How can you not see how she manipulates you?* the Dead Man wanted to shout.

Mrithuri snatched the mask away from her face.

"Rajni," Chaeri began.

The Dead Man had to admire her persistence.

Mrithuri's gaze swung toward her. A long silence stretched. No one else dared speak to snap it. Mrithuri chafed her upper arms as if they hurt. As if, the Dead Man thought, she was driving the venom of the Eremite vipers more swiftly through her veins, massaging it under her skin. She finally let her glare slide off Chaeri, and slapped it on each of her followers in turn. "No one?"

Apparently not.

She tossed the mask aside. It landed on sea-colored tiles with the ring of gold, and dented. "Right then. Let's get this parade underway."

THE PROCESSION WAS AN ANTICLIMAX. AT LEAST, FROM A SECURITY POINT of view. Ritu and her family of tumblers and acrobats led them, turning handsprings and waving their banners, clashing swords in the best martial style. They were, the Dead Man thought, a nice distraction. And a nice bit of softening up for the crowds. Everyone, after all, loved a good parade.

Along with the tumblers, criers went before her, announcing the rajni and priestess by all her titles, announcing that the people of Sarathai-tia and the refugees who had taken shelter in her walls would be fed at the rajni's expense, from the rajni's coffers. That there was and would be food and shelter for all.

The Dead Man hoped fervently that Mrithuri's people had a plan for that.

Mrithuri was cheered through the streets until they grew tired. And then beyond that, because the Dead Man witnessed a transformation.

Mrithuri began tight and dutiful of expression under her cosmetics. Her face seemed weirdly marked, pale and blank, where the mask had covered it. But as they wound down the slow spiral of Sarathai-tia, as he would have expected exhaustion to press her, he saw instead her head grow higher.

The Dead Man's focus must lie in taking the temper of the crowd, not the temper of his rajni.

*His,* he thought suddenly. It was a troubling thought. She could not be his. Not for long. This could not be his place. Not for long. He had made decisions that had removed that future from the realm of possibility.

Well, enjoy it while it lasted.

Or maybe he would die here. He was too old to be going to war.

Whatever the future held, he had no time to be thinking about it—or thinking about anything—right now. He had a job to do, a job he had been raised to and trained for since infancy. A job that was the entire reason for his existence.

Mrithuri's security was his responsibility, and there was no place in that responsibility for daydreaming. Only animal awareness and trust of his instincts. Thinking could only get in his way.

He knew he should have felt far more in his element. But this was a foreign land. A foreign culture. A foreign queen.

And he had never been called upon to bodyguard his lover before.

*Poor life choices, Serhan,* he told himself. But he couldn't much bring himself to regret it, even as he forced his mind back into the broad, aware, receptive state that would let him recognize a threat before he consciously became aware of it. There were few things more frustrating than trying to work while one's own mind was doing everything possible to oppose one.

He wished he had a little more attention to spare for the tumblers and acrobats, who were marvelous. He also wished he could allow himself to spend himself on sidelong glances at Mrithuri, who seemed as brittle and beautiful as a dragonmoth.

But he was here to be her guardian, and *this* day he was determined not to fail at that task. As much as he knew it was irrational to hold himself accountable for the fall of an entire caliphate, that guilt was there, pressing at him.

That guilt would also only impair his ability to do his job. It did not want to be set aside. It fought him.

Guilt was a living thing, like desire. It did not want to die. It did not care to be ignored. It had no interest in whether it was destructive in any given environment. It cared only if it could survive—even flourish—there.

He would starve it out.

He walked silently in the rajni's entourage, head swiveling like that of some wary desert bird. He comforted himself that he was not her only protector. Those tumblers were armed with real swords they knew well the use of. The Wizards flanked Mrithuri. Every so often, with the edge of his vision only, the Dead Man could glimpse the phantasmal flicker of the shield that Tsering-la had placed around her.

Chaeri was there, though not inside the shield—despite her pouting. The Dead Man was relieved by that. He no longer harbored any doubt that Chaeri was a danger. Ritu and Yavashuri were as aware of that as he was, however, and Yavashuri at least had traction with Mrithuri. That was more than he, a foreigner and a temporary favorite, could rely on.

The crowd lining the streets and hanging from windows to view their rajni surprised him by seeming almost gleeful. He would have expected far more terror, or at least apprehension, in the face of a siege. But it seemed as if Mrithuri's people were with her, at least in the face of an enemy so universally loathed as Anuraja. *There's something to be said for vilifying your rivals after all.*

That was good. That was worth remarking upon to the council of war. Morale was a thing worth sustaining and encouraging. Especially as the Dead Man suffered no doubts that Anuraja would have placed agents in the city, and that they would already be working to erode that morale.

Yavashuri probably had her people working on it. But it wouldn't hurt to mention it to her all the same. In, of course, a polite and deferential fashion.

Not for the first time, the Dead Man remarked on the defensibility of the street plan. Most of the cities in the Lotus Kingdoms, as far as he knew, were built on an ancient and invariable grid. They had their aqueducts and sewers and hypocausts, and he had heard that it was their ancestors who had, indeed, invented such things. Each would have at least one bath, such as the one he had visited in Chandranath, and depending on size at least one granary. Each would have a palace.

Sarathai-tia was a more modern place. Built from scratch by the Alchemical Emperor, raised from level plains to be his capital and the symbol of his power, it was meant to give a message to any who would think to challenge that authority.

The main road wound the perfect spire of its artificial mountain with the regularity of a snail shell, lined on either side by buildings that housed shops on the ground level and the houses of proprietors above.

The Dead Man thought again that it would be a terrible channel of death to fight up. The palace had its own high terraced walls, tiers of them, so that it sat like an elaborate crown at the peak of the mount.

The docks had spread out along the riverbanks, but they were outside the defensible walls of the city and had been burned during the retreat. In war, some things were sacrificed.

When the Dead Man turned his head again, he found that he was walking beside Ata Akhimah. She smiled with the corner of her mouth, not making eye contact. "You're wondering why this city is so different from other cities."

"For defense, I assumed. And to show off the Alchemical Emperor's power. It's not everyone who can call a mountain up out of a muddy plain."

"That's one reason," she agreed. "But there are thaumaturgical considerations as well. He had some help from Wizards, but much of the power was his own. His seat was here. Not just metaphorically. The Peacock Throne is an object of great puissance, and it derives that power by tapping into the strength of the Mother River, and the River of Heaven, and the very land. This is the place where they meet and are focused, you see."

It sounded like advertising to the Dead Man, but he held his tongue.

Ata Akhimah continued, "The energy spirals up the tiers and is focused through the dragonglass and the structure of the throne room. It charges the throne until the throne can hold no more. Any overflow cascades down the back side of the city. Down the steps. Rejoining the flow of the Mother River."

"And a rightful emperor is supposed to be able to use that power."

"Or an unrightful one will be destroyed by it," she agreed.

"Pity we haven't got an emperor handy." He waved in the direction of Anuraja's army. "Some red-hot thaumaturgy would come in pretty handy right now. I'd settle for a nice big wave of river water."

"The Alchemical Emperor was quite the student of Vastu Shastra, the science of building. It is not so different from the geomantic skills of my own tradition of Wizardry, but is much a lost art now."

"Surely that was not so long ago."

"It was eradicated."

"Do . . . the Lotus Kingdoms have no tradition of Wizardry of their own?"

"They did," said Ata Akhimah. "A very great one. The Alchemical Emperor drove the other Wizards of the Lotus Kingdoms—the Lotus Empire, in his day—into exile. Some went to Messaline. Some to Aezin. Some to Song, or Rasa. None stayed here."

"None stayed here and lived, you mean."

Her smile was tight. "That we know of."

"What about Nizhvashiti?"

"Not a Wizard. But the royal line might be said to have some Wizardry in it. Wouldn't you say?"

Her eyes cut sideways at Mrithuri, and at Syama pacing mildly beside her. The Dead Man thought of Mrithuri's way with beasts, and nodded.

He said, "Excuse me. I should speak with the rajni."

He stepped in beside Mrithuri as Ata Akhimah went a little wider, taking his former place in the buffer zone. Mrithuri smiled at him sidelong as she waved, and waved.

The Dead Man lowered his voice for her ears only, ignoring the sweet glare Chaeri leveled. He said, "Your people do not seem much concerned with the siege. Nor do you."

"They know it is no matter. The Mother will rise soon," Mrithuri murmured. "Then let them try to blockade us by land, or even with boats."

"You put a lot of faith in the river."

"You put a lot of faith in your god, too. You do not see me mocking Her."

Her voice was not cold. It held, only, the warning of coldness. It was enough.

He stepped back, feeling that he had lost more ground to Chaeri. There were unfriendly eyes in the crowd, hidden behind smiles. They had to be there; he knew they had to be there.

And his faith in his god had not saved him before.

AT THE FOOT OF THE STAIRS BACK UP TO THE PALACE, THE DEAD MAN stopped the Wizards. Tsering-la was on the plump side, but not too much taller than the Dead Man.

"Let me borrow your coat," the Dead Man said.

"Are you passing for a Wizard?" But Tsering began unbuttoning. His collar of pearl and jade plates looked odd above the simple white shirt, stained and darned in places, that he had worn beneath the coat. Wizards without their trappings looked bare as shorn cats.

The Dead Man handed his own new coat to Ata Akhimah and donned the black one, turned inside out to show the lining. It was well-made, with closed seams. It would pass.

"No." He wound a strip of cloth around his sword-hilt. "A rogue."

He did not return to the palace with the rajni and her men and women. He went out into the city on his own, in the coat that did not fit him well, with his veil wrapped in a different style than he wore it commonly. He found a tavern. Food might be growing less varied and fresh, but his coin would still buy beer. Less of it, to be sure. But real famine and lack would not stalk the city for some time yet.

The Dead Man had no doubt that if the siege was not lifted, it would come.

So he sat and drank, and listened.

The conversation was not as subdued as he might have expected. And it was interesting, though not for the reasons he'd been afraid. Mrithuri's confidence, for all it worried him—for all he wondered how much it was founded in the effect of the Eremite venom, and a ration of the comforting self-delusion of youth—Mrithuri's confidence did seem to encourage her people for the better.

Comforting, but not useful.

He left that tavern, and found another.

This one had a darker and more suspicious air, even as he entered under a sign in the backward, left-to-right local writing that proclaimed the place to be named The Blind Dolphin. Lamps flickered on wicks trimmed short and chary of oil; the low tables were gritty and their edges whittled. The Dead Man seated himself on a bolster that smelled musty, with perhaps the memory of cat urine. He was grateful for the camouflaging, herbal aroma of cannabis and bidi from two currently unused water pipes along the side wall.

He ordered wine. Safer, he thought, to choose something stronger than beer under these sanitary circumstances.

It came in a clay cup. As he linked his hands around it, he found himself thinking of the Gage, wondering where his old friend was and whether time would find them together again, sitting across from one another and drinking. The Dead Man sipped his wine in the traditional fashion, insinuating the cup under his veil. The Gage, if he were here, would have taken it in through some mysterious process of absorption.

It was just as well the Gage was not here. Monstrous brazen automata were terrible at undercover work.

It did not take long for the Dead Man to determine that this time, he had located the proper bar. A skinny, weedy fellow dressed in wrapped workman's trousers, his narrow nose once-broken and his narrow mustache suffering from undergrown gaps, was holding forth on his political opinions from a position a few cushions to the left. His comments were ostensibly directed at his drinking companion, who was a potbellied, sunken-chested little fellow with stringy hair. But they were pitched to carry throughout the establishment, and obviously meant to engage the ear of anyone who heard them.

He spoke at length of how poorly trade and fishing had fared under the young rajni; how her grandfather should have married her off and found them a proper lord before he died. What a tragedy it was that her parents had died so young and left her so unprepared for her role in life. And that she was so full of ideas that did not suit her station. "That was the old raja's failing," the man with the terrible mustache said. "He missed his son so much he spoiled the granddaughter, you ask me. And now, since she thinks she's too good to marry and get us a proper raja, reunite the southern kingdoms . . . well, we all pay the price."

The Dead Man glanced at the proprietor. A taller fellow, though also not overly well-fed, he was engaged in dusting racks of serving dishes and rolling his eyes whenever his back was turned on the first man. He didn't interrupt him, though. It was the shopkeeper's eternal quandary: which custom did you want to drive away? None of it, by preference, unless trade was so good one didn't have to care about losing a little.

Trade did not seem to be so good here that this particular landlord could afford to send people away because he did not care for their politics. The Dead Man did wonder if his business might not improve if he sent offensive little rats like this one packing . . . but then, based on the state of the men's facial capillaries and the number of wine jugs scattered around their table, these two might almost be enough to keep a business afloat—so to speak—all on their own.

The Dead Man sighed, and finished his wine. It wasn't good, and under ordinary circumstances he might not have minded discarding it. But a siege was no time to waste sustenance. As the drunk men waved for food and more wine, he wondered where men dressed as common laborers found such excess of coin.

The landlord brought a basket of flat, risen bread, made with flour that looked to be of better quality than the wine. Another client paid his reckoning and left, sharing a long glance with the landlord. The man with the mustache and his even less prepossessing friend tore the bread and dabbled it through clarified butter and herbs. It was still steaming; perhaps it would be safe to eat. The smell made the Dead Man's stomach surprise him by rumbling.

Perhaps it was still possible to feel hunger after all. Even in such a world as this.

"That looks like good bread," the Dead Man said to the landlord. He made his voice loud enough to be heard by all. "May I have a basket, too?"

"Certainly. And more wine?"

The Dead Man touched a forefinger to his veiled brow in agreement.

The weedy man turned. "Are you one of those foreign mercenaries?"

The Dead Man considered, for a moment, how to answer. "I serve the rajni."

The potbellied one turned and spat. On the floor.

No wonder these two were so endeared to the proprietor.

"Do I not see you eating, right now, wheat from the royal stores? Her largesse fills your belly."

The fellow with the mustache wiped wine out of it onto the bare back of his arm. "The river would fill it better. And that Anuraja won't do nothing to the common folk. We're beneath notice or ransom, us. And it's we who feed the city."

"Oh, so she should just turn herself over and lie down to be fucked by a poxed murderer so you can get back to fishing."

The man flushed mahogany in embarrassment or rage. "From what I hear, he wouldn't be the first foreigner to stick it in her. One of your lot, isn't her lover supposed to be?"

"I had heard she was a maiden," the Dead Man said noncommittally.

"Every wench will tell you so. But then, every wench will tell you anything to get what she wants from you."

*Or because she's afraid of what might happen if she told you the truth*, the Dead Man thought. The hot bread arrived, and the butter-oil fragrant with coriander. He noticed that *his* portion had a sprinkle of mild fresh cheese on top, and wondered if the landlord's wife or daughter were in the back, kerchiefed and red from the stove, listening through the swinging door of slatted reeds. *His* wine, he thought, probably didn't have too much spit in it. He tore off a morsel of bread, noting the faint pattern of clay swirls on its crust where it had been slapped against the chimney of a clay oven to bake. He swirled it through the butter and slipped it beneath his veil. Smoke and grain, herbs and garlic and the grit of gray sea salt. Delicious.

It made him homesick for the puffed, stone-baked bread of his youth, leavened by heat and steam.

Having swallowed, he said, "You think your rajni is disposable."

"She's a wench," the man sneered. "What's a wench good for?"

His stringy-haired friend might have been a little less drunk, or a little less well-paid. He scooted his threadbare orange cushion out from between the provocateur and the Dead Man.

"When the wench is a queen, to say such things is treason," the Dead Man answered. His voice was low and soft now, without threat in it.

The Dead Man turned to the proprietor, who had moved closer to both of them and was cleaning a bottle on the none-too-spotless sleeve of his mustard-brown robe. Two, drunk or half-drunk, and at best armed with small knives slipped inside their trousers: that, he could handle. Three, and one sober and armed with whatever he kept behind the counter to protect his establishment? That would be dicing with the will of the Scholar-God.

He met the man's eye.

The man shrugged. He shifted his grip to the neck of the bottle. "Do your mercenaries drink?"

Ritu and her people were mercenaries after a fashion, he supposed. And there was Druja and the wranglers, teamsters, and roustabouts of the stranded caravan. Those folks *definitely* drank.

The Dead Man nodded. "Maybe not as much as these two."

"Oh, well," the landlord said. "Who does, really?"

The fellow with the mustache made his mind up. Like many of his decisions, the Dead Man suspected, it was a poor one. He got to his feet and pulled a filleting knife from his trousers.

Somebody was at least marginally dedicated to maintaining his cover.

The Dead Man didn't bother lowering his veil as he stood, careful not to overset the table. He would not insult the landlord's wife (or, perhaps, daughter) by spilling the food she had roasted herself near the hot clay oven to prepare. He did not draw his guns, either the one Ata Akhimah had modified for him, or the one she had built from the model of the first. He picked up the battered orange cushion, which was wheel-shaped, with a circle at the center, and quite hard. Stuffed with sawdust, if he was not mistaken.

"Sorry about this," he said to the landlord.

The Dead Man stepped to the side. The alleged fisherman lunged with his filleting knife. The stringy-haired fellow went wide, trying to flank him.

The Dead Man parried the knife with the cushion. Sawdust showered. The Dead Man gave the deflating cushion a twist, trapping the knife in a swirl of threadbare corduroy. He yanked it to the side, catching the second man in the ribs with an elbow. A wild swing cuffed his ear, leaving his head ringing.

He went to one knee. And used the momentum of the drop to drive the same elbow into the second man's groin, resulting in a popping sensation and a gratifying cry of dismay. The second man doubled over and kept going, landing on the floor in a position resembling an overcooked shrimp.

With a mighty jerk, the first man got his knife back. He drew it up, underhand, a trained knife-fighter's grip. The Dead Man, scrabbling, stretched the rapidly deflating pillow between his hands, braced his boot toe, and lunged.

It might even have worked.

It didn't have to.

The landlord cracked the clay bottle over the ersatz fisherman's head. It didn't knock him cold; alas, such things only happened in staged plays and melodramas. But it did drive him to his knees, and he relinquished his hold on the knife hilt. The fillet knife fell to the floor with a clatter.

The Dead Man dropped the ruined cushion and dizzily scooped it up.

*Getting old.* He touched his ear in dismay, sliding his free hand under the veil. Blood came away on his fingertips.

He looked from the blood to the knife.

The ersatz fisherman crumpled forward, both hands laced over his occipital region, and pressed his forehead to the floor. He wheezed out a terrible, suffering moan.

The door to the street flew open. In rushed two men in the livery of Mrithuri's soldiers, led by a young woman with flour on her tunic and caked up to her elbows. From this, the Dead Man deduced that the kitchen had its own door. The woman's hair was raven-black, and would have been blue as a wing if it had not been so greasy with sweat.

Definitely a daughter, the Dead Man judged, unless the landlord had hidden talents.

"Take these men back to the palace," the Dead Man told the soldiers. "Careful with them. They might be enemy agents, and they are definitely willing to kill. If they can."

"Yes, my lord," said the higher-ranking of the two.

He nudged the ersatz fisherman with a toe. The ersatz fisherman moaned.

"Don't you dare throw up," the Dead Man said. "I'm still going to eat that bread, and I don't want to smell your vomit."

"I don't want to clean up his vomit!" the landlord said.

"Well, you're the one who hit him so hard."

The landlord looked at the shards of clay bottle in his hand and shrugged. "I guess I need more practice."

The Dead Man turned the fillet knife over in his hand. "It's a good tool. Do you need it?"

"Isn't it evidence?" the landlord said.

"I shan't require it. I think I just declared martial law."

"Well," the landlord said judiciously. He rubbed his bald spot. "I suppose my wife might."

By the door, the lovely young woman beamed.

# 17

THE GAGE WAS NOT WITHOUT EXPERIENCE OF DESERTS. HE HAD BEEN born in one; been forged in one; died—after a fashion—in one. He had crossed an uncounted number in his time.

Even by his refined standards, this was an impressive example of the kind. It was not a desert of wind and sand, trackless, ever-moving, the whisper of worn grain on grain. But rather a desert of contradictions: a vast and canyoned badland, blasted as if by fire, rutted as if by water. A crackling glaze of bubbled green lay over the wasted soil, snapping under his every step. He knew he must be getting close to the poisoned city of dead dragons.

He had long since sent Mrithuri's vulture away again. No flesh could sustain itself in this place.

The burned earth glowed at night.

The sky was black at first, dusted with those lonely distant stars, deep as a well and so full of echoes. He followed the Dragon Road into smoother terrain, though no less blasted.

The scars on the land here were old, however. This was earth that had been scorched, and scorched again. Picked at by wind and burned by suns of unimaginable fury.

The sky changed. Night reigned still, but the stars that speckled it were bright and close-seeming, and three enormous moons obscured them. The smallest was brilliant ivory in color, and it moved across the sky so quickly the Gage almost felt the desire to race it. The second in measure was dappled with the colors of rust, ochre, and old blood. And the third was a vast arc of blackness visible by the lack of stars that lay behind it, a shimmer of silver at its edge, the faint violet highlights of a kind of opalescence within its curve. It loomed, and made the Gage feel small: a sensation he was not used to.

A sun like a grain of millet rose white and blazing behind the moons, casting a light that was more than starlight but less than the light of the ivory moon. It moved across the sky as the Gage walked, and that small-est moon passed two more times. There was plenty of light to see by.

Deserts are not without life, and terrible though it was, this one was no different. He saw the tracks of serpents, and once or twice their heavy, calligraphied-looking bodies. He saw a frondlike web of low plants that seemed to grow out of a skeleton like coral, and whisked back inside as quickly as polyps if he moved toward them.

The sun set, and the sky began to pale. The opalescence dancing across the face of the black moon brightened, so the Gage realized it must be reflected light. That moon had not moved at all in the sky.

A second white sun crawled into the sky, followed by two others so small that the savagery of their light astounded. They washed the stars away; washed all color from the heavens. Bleak and weird—one red, one blue—they were linked by a curve or veil, like two dancers holding the ends of a filmy scarf and whirling around one another.

The blue one burned what its light fell on. So searing was that one that it heated the Gage's brass hide until the patched robes he wore smoked and charred in places.

The dimmer red companion, bloated and soft-edged, mercifully eclipsed the blue sun now and again. The white light streaked to follow or precede the primaries, like a small child or an even smaller dog.

Ancient Erem. These were the suns of the city of ghulim; the cursed and monstrous city whose ghost still lay not too far from Messaline. These were the suns of an ancient and disastrous land. He could not mistake them. But these lay a sea and two continents away from where they should have been.

He began to find the corpses then.

They were like no corpses even he had seen. Vast metallic skeletal architectures rose against the black and changing heavens: horned skulls pitted with sockets like wind-caves, rib cages grand as palaces, spines like pathways paved with boulders, long and grasping fingers that reached farther than the stretch of these bodies from nose-tip to tail . . . but constructed not of bone. They were, instead, mighty edifices of silvery metal that might have rusted, if there were any moisture here . . . latticed with the oil-green transparency of polished olivine. Tattered leathery shreds clung to a few of the fresher corpses, rustling dryly in a ceaseless wind.

The light of the terrible stars fractured through the olivine, sparking dazzling gleams that might have blinded the Gage, if the Gage had eyes. In the darker times, when the wrestling suns dipped below the horizon, sometimes the skeletal fretworks gave off a patchy glow similar to that of the poison glass crackling underfoot.

Dragonglass.

And dragonbones.

*Did they war here?* the Gage wondered. *If they did not kill each other, then how did they all come to die, and poison this land?*

He was still wondering this when he saw something along the horizon move.

The size of it was indeterminate. Vast, he thought, and that was with the judgment of somebody who for . . . days?—he could not be certain, when the suns seemed to follow no reasonable pattern—had been walking among the sprawled bodies of dragons. It scuttled, or seemed to scuttle, on uncountable legs moving with the rippling coordination of a millipede's. But if that was what it was, he was chasing after an insect the size of a city.

Unless, of course, it was chasing him.

The Gage was largely made of brass. But that was not to say that he did not have some steel in him. Literally, as well as metaphorically. There were gears and pins and shod edges within, bearings that needed to wear hard, connecting rods and contact surfaces. Metallurgy was his flesh.

And that was how he discovered that the enormous skeletons had a magnetism.

It was not a terribly *strong* magnetism. It did not bring them hurtling across the desert to thump into him, leaving ringing dents in his metal hide—or, given the size of some of the remains, drag him skidding through a broken crust of dragonglass to ring in turn against the bones.

But it did tug at him, evoking strange, subtle sensations he had thought lost to him along with the frailty of human flesh and skin. The perception was more akin to how he might once have felt a breeze rustling against skin, or a cool current of water. Or the way fine hairs might horripilate on nape and arms when encountering a static charge.

The Gage kept expecting the snap and sting of a spark to follow, for all he had not felt such a brief, bright burst of pain in decades. It made him recollect being human and fragile. He did what was in his power to pretend he did not feel that way.

Magnetic dust had weathered off the bones. Ash-fine, it drifted now in clouds on every breeze, combined with the pale green poison dust of the crushed dragonglass, and perhaps even the plain beige dust of the mundane earth that must lie somewhere below.

These three dusts dulled his mirrors until he, too, was plain and beige. Just as well: the massive insectoid object was less likely to see him glinting in the sun.

It did not, however, coat him evenly. Because of the magnetism, the dust arrayed itself in precise patterns and alliances, almost like a decoration. It clung, and made a map on his brazen skin of all his inner workings. All of those that held some trace of iron, anyway. On his arm, he could see the internal linkages outlined.

He should bring some dust back for Ata Akhimah, if only it would not poison her. She would be fascinated by its revelations.

Along the horizon, the first vast insect scuttled out of view.

The Gage bent down and picked up a fragment of skeleton. It was definitely not bone, but some alloy of iron studded with . . . well, with crystals of peridot. Studded? Veined, rather. "I wonder," he said, though there was no one around to speak aloud to. Those wonderings were not so shaped or formal as words. It was just that he noticed a pattern, a similarity between these jewel-and-iron bones . . . and the coral-colored sapphire bones and veins of the sorcerer's victims.

It was only a matter of a few hours before another leggy, walking silhouette—equally massive and equally unsettling—hove into view above the horizon. Maybe it *was* the same one, at that—though it had come from a different direction. If it was not a second—structure? revenant? animal?—then the first one had moved extraordinarily fast once it left his line of sight.

This one was moving toward him.

He missed the company of the vulture. It had joined him again for a little while after he left the ruins of Ansh-Sahal. But then he had entered this other poisonous place, and it had had to leave again.

All flesh was so frail.

Tented hide stretched over gaunt bones surrounded him.

All flesh. So frail.

IRI WAS SUCCESSFUL, AND HIMADRA FOUND HIMSELF SHEPHERDING A much larger column of people home to Chandranath than he had departed with. But at least the rest of the journey was largely uneventful.

Feeding everybody was as difficult as anticipated. More than one horse was sacrificed along the way, but they came to the river before starvation claimed any among the baggage train except the weakest. It was not ideal, and even Himadra was thinner than he should have been—but it was better than losing everyone.

The Mother River, when they reached her, was low. Long mudbanks, pale and silty, curved beside her. They showed soupy footprints of wildlife and perhaps even livestock showing up to drink, and Himadra's hunters managed to bring back a buffalo or two within hours. They camped by the river for longer than Himadra felt was tactically sound, honestly. But people needed food to get them safely back to Chandranath.

When they set out again, he rode between Navin and Farkhad. Farkhad, looking back along the column, shook his head. "We're going to have to start raiding north, to feed this many."

North was a problem. North was into the mountains, and there were bandit princelets in the hills who thought themselves, and not Himadra, ruler of their own small fiefs. There were also Rasan towns and villages, and Himadra could not afford to bring the wrath of the whole wealthy Rasan Empire down upon his poor little mountain principality. He and his men raided south, toward Mrithuri's territory, entirely because it was the softest border and the safest direction. He almost wished she had come to him for advice; she could have used a much bigger army. And her farmlands were rich enough to support more taxes, to keep such an army fed and mobile.

Armies did quarrel, though—with each other and worse, with civilians. They needed constant tending. And having a big one could induce a person to start wars, as with Anuraja. An army was an expensive, destructive pet.

Himadra looked fondly over his people, newly salvaged and long-term loyalists, and sighed. They were his responsibility. "Well, it's a good thing we've got a bigger army, now. Iri's not going to like it, though."

Farkhad glanced around, making sure the nurse was not close enough to overhear. "I'll make sure she doesn't find out until it's too late, then."

FARKHAD'S CAMPAIGN OF DISSEMBLING WAS SUCCESSFUL ENOUGH THAT Himadra didn't get confirmation until after they got home to Chandranath that he'd been right. Iri didn't like it. Iri did not like it so thoroughly that she lay in wait outside of Himadra's morning room and caught him being wheeled in his caned chair toward breakfast. She stepped in front of him, blocking the doorway.

"I could have you flogged for that," he said mildly.

"Better than the floggings of my conscience if I do not speak!"

She had a way about her, all right.

"Is there a problem with Drupada's housing or the facilities for his care?"

It interrupted the tirade that seemed to be rising in her throat. She choked for a second, then spat out one word. "What?!"

"Have we," he said, plainly and slowly, "given you what you need to do your job?"

She gaped at him. "That's not what I am here about."

"Right," Himadra said. "You are also between me and my breakfast. Have you eaten yet?"

She had not, he was pretty sure. She must have gotten up early just to beard him so. His pain left him frequently sleepless. He often rose before sunset, and ate his breakfast at the hour when the servants would usually be gulping tea and bread before their day began. He was aware that it made him a difficult master, but there were worse ones in the world.

Anuraja, for example.

"No," she said, in a small, slightly confused voice. Excellent. People were easier to manage if you had gotten the wind out of their sails.

"Well, then, come and dine with me. And we will discuss it. Whatever it may be."

He was brought to his low table, and a plate was set before him. Another was found quickly and brought for Iri. They were metal, circular, with many small caches for different sauces and small tastes of highly spiced dishes. The menu tended toward a great deal of pulses and alliums: in his heart, Himadra was the sort of person who preferred plain fare, and not too much fuss over the serving of it. He knew how to acquit himself at a banquet, of course. But sometimes, you didn't want to bother. Sometimes, you just wanted to eat, and enjoy what you were eating.

The tea was poured into small red clay cups. It was milky and strong, sweetened with sugarcane and spices. Himadra amused himself by nibbling pieces of the clay rim like a peasant as he drank. He could hear the tiny cracks and crunches as Iri did the same.

She watched him through lowered lashes to see how he handled the bread and the small portions of spicy food, and in copying him handled hers adroitly. She nibbled at first, but when he seemed to take no notice of her she relaxed and began to eat with a fair appetite.

He was kind, and waited until her mouth was empty and she had swallowed her tea before asking, "So. There is a problem about which you wished to confront me."

"Ah." She looked up, nervous again. But not cowed, he was glad to see. "I am not sure I would use the word 'confront,' Your Competence."

"Ah," he echoed. He wiped a morsel of soft, slightly charred bread through a sauce that brought tears to his eyes. "But you see, I have met you. And I choose my words with care. So what is it?"

"You are sending your men to raid. Innocent farmers, herders. Crofters. And among your men are men I talked into joining you. Old friends and acquaintances. My fellow subjects of Ansh-Sahal."

Her voice trailed off, but her expression was alight with defiance.

He waited a moment to be certain she was done. Then: "You have seen Chandranath?"

"Your Competence?"

"You have *seen* Chandranath."

"Only in that we rode through it, my lord."

"What did it look like to you, my land?"

She hesitated.

"You will not offend me. And I know you come from Ansh-Sahal, which has its own poverties. Does Chandranath seem to you a rich land?"

"There is farming near the river." She considered. "Cattle in the hills. Is there mining?"

"Some," he admitted. He tapped his nibbled cup. "And our clay is unparalleled."

She nodded, her eyes faraway as she thought of the streaked clay cliffs in all their shades of red and pink and umber. "And trade routes. And tariffs?"

"Not so much in time of war," he admitted.

"You can feed your people without raiding," she insisted.

"That," he agreed, "is true." He eyed the tea dregs in his cup, and abruptly decided it was not too early for something stronger. His whole body still ached with the riding. With a gesture, he summoned wine.

She watched what he did, but the spookiness was fading. She watched until the little crystal glasses were brought, and filled, and until they had both tasted the drink. It was fermented from oranges and the orange rinds, with the bitter pith removed, and spiced with ginger and black pepper. It was served with slices of lemon to freshen the citrus, and to cut the sweetness somewhat.

Iri looked at it respectfully. "You don't grow oranges here."

"No," Himadra said. "But we can get the wine from Sarathai-lae. By trade, or by raiding for it."

She thought about spitting the wine out. Instead, she swallowed carefully. "It's strong."

"It is." He drank, and allowed his glass to be filled again. "I can feed my people. But I cannot feed an army, and mercenaries. And refugees. And I cannot *protect* my people—or your people—without the army, and the mercenaries."

"Aren't you Anuraja's ally?" she asked.

"He is fostering my two brothers, as I believe I mentioned." Himadra shook his head. Gently, as he did everything. So as not to strain his bones. "I would like to see them home again. I would like there to be a Chandranath for them to come home to."

He poured more wine. He offered Iri some. She did not refuse. She was looking at him very intently.

"It is useful to understand what sort of person Anuraja is. It is useful to understand what sort of person any rival or ally is. That is a big element of tactics, being able to judge what the opponent will do next. But in this case, Anuraja is the sort of person who always reacts to certain things in very predictable ways."

"What sort of person is he?"

"A lousy one," Himadra said, and laughed bitterly. "He is a person who has accomplished very little and inherited a lot. When the only reason you have to feel good about yourself is your ingrained prejudices about your innate superiority over another type of person, you will violently attack anything that threatens that bias."

Iri picked at her bread. "You keep an army to defend yourself from your ally."

He tipped his head, with a little smile. "A significant portion of my mercenaries are with him now. He seems to have invaded Mrithuri's lands and is laying siege to Sarathai-tia. Some intelligence was waiting for me when I returned."

"That's terrible," Iri said. "He'll probably marry and murder that young girl, too. Just like his others."

"Yes," said Himadra. "But he has the money. He has the seaport. He has the armies and the lands. He has my heirs as hostages. There's not a great deal I can do to stop him."

She sipped her wine.

"I am kind where I can be, as you have no cause to doubt. But this is a world of hard choices and insufficient resources."

"I see," she said. "How will you protect Drupada from him?"

"Oh," Himadra said with an easy smile. He did like surprising people. "I've adopted him."

"I AM WORRIED," SAID MRITHURI, RECLINING AGAINST THE DEAD MAN's arm. She shifted cautiously, so as not to impale him on her many hairpins, or smudge her elaborate makeup. She would be back on display this afternoon, reviewing the troops, walking the wall.

"We're all worried," the Dead Man said. "I've never been in a siege this quiet."

"I suppose they are relying on us getting thirsty, eventually." The rains still had not come. "More than that, though. Vara has not had contact with the Gage in days. Since he went into the poisoned desert."

Her arm itched, then stung. Looking down, she realized that her fingerstalls had left red welts across the tattooed outline of the peacock and the blind porpoise that adorned her. She wanted her snakes. She wanted her snakes, and she did not want to see Chaeri.

She could remove them from Chaeri's custody. But nobody else among her retinue would give her what she needed, when she needed it, without judgment and without argument. Without making her feel self-conscious.

She knew she was too reliant on the venom. But surely now was not the time to tackle that particular problem. Now, when she needed all her wits around her.

"Well," the Dead Man said, "the Gage will take a while to cross the desert. And a while to explore the Singing Towers, I am sure. He is very tough."

"We are dealing with somebody who opens up volcanoes for the joy of it." She stopped herself from scratching again, just in time. She forced herself to think of the warmth of the arm around her, the lean strength in it. It should make her feel safe.

She was determined that it *would* make her feel safe. Or at least, a little safer. For a while.

He stroked her arm with the back of his fingers, because he could not stroke her hair. They might have walked in the gardens, she supposed, but there was no privacy to be had there anymore. The gardens were full of shelters now. The rajni was doing her part to help house and feed the refugees. Her granaries still held stores, but she read over the reports with Yavashuri and Hnarisha every day, and every day it became more evident that the time they could hold out was limited.

The river was not rising.

She had been too confident.

Gently, the Dead Man caught her wrist, and moved her fingers away from her arm. "Begging your pardon, my queen." She should send for

Chaeri, and not wanting to see her be damned. That would stop the damned itching. That would make her smart, and strong.

Maybe then she would come up with some kind of an answer.

"They are waiting for something," she said. "That's the only answer."

"Rajni?" He had not been paying attention, she thought. He, too, had been ruminating over their predicament, chewing the problem of the siege over as if it were cud that could be mashed into a digestible form if only they masticated it enough.

"Why it's such a boring siege. They're waiting for something, right? They tried one push, to see if they could get in the door before we got our defenses settled. We tried one push, too, to see if we could break through. Now we're just staring at each other. The logical answer is that they expect something to change."

"They expect us to run out of food and water. And you expected the river to rise."

"The river is not rising," she admitted. If anything, it was falling. "I should have used the dolphins."

"It's not too late. Have you asked Ata Akhimah if that line of boats could be some kind of a binding? Some of this . . . Vastu Shastra she told me about. Geomancy. Wizardry. That might hold the river back."

She felt her face flex under the cosmetics. That was the sort of thing she really should have thought of herself. "If I send the dolphins now they will be slaughtered. The Mother is low; and there will be no fight on land to distract Anuraja's troops from defending from the river."

"We could make the fight on land happen. Your troops, honestly, would welcome the distraction."

The Dead Man did not mention how much of his time was taken up in keeping order with those selfsame troops. Mrithuri knew. Hnarisha told her. The defenders were restless and bored and cooped up. It was a volatile situation.

She said, "I think I was too proud, Serhan."

"What on earth do you mean?"

She closed her eyes. It was easier to talk if she pretended she was speaking into darkness. "The oracle told me I would be a bride and get an heir before the year changed. I said I would not sell myself to a marriage that meant I would not rule."

His body tensed against hers. She felt all his arguments collide within him in their eagerness to escape. He made a suffering sound and swallowed every one of them.

"Say it," she commanded.

"The Scholar-God's prophet Ysmat has written of this."

"I will hear the words of your prophet. They are usually pretty." The tension in her voice was entirely the need for venom. That was the anxiety that itched at her. Underneath it, she felt languorous, and a little cruel. Not *very* cruel. She was never *very* cruel. But a little, in that way that reminded her that she had power, and could choose the exercising of it.

Possibly it was the thought of losing that power that made her feel cruel.

The Dead Man said, *"Would it be considered a becoming modesty in a prince, if he said that he would choose a wife to be lord of him?"*

Mrithuri waited, but he did not continue. "That's it?"

"Don't you think it's enough?"

Why *was* it that what was considered the rightful exercise of sovereignty for a man was considered . . . unbecoming, unnatural . . . in a woman? Thinking about it made her feel uncomfortable. Twisted inside, with fear and rejection and an . . . attractive disquiet. A need.

A desire.

Restless, she rose. The Dead Man let her go. Only when she had stepped away from him did she realize that she missed his mild scent of sandalwood and oil. She paced back and forth. They were in a little antechamber, with silk gauze over the windows and Syama snoring valiantly on a cushion by the door, so of necessity her steps were short.

"I never imagined a future I wanted before," she said. "For me, I mean. Not because I was expected to do a thing or be a thing. Not because it was my duty or I could make a difference or had a gift. Not because I was needed. That was what I had before. But now I see something I *want*, Serhan. I want you."

"But why?" he asked, in honest puzzlement.

"For me."

He stared at her. She blew across her face in annoyance. "I want you because you see me as a person. I want you because I look at you and for the first time I see a chance at a life that feels like living, not just like performing a series of chores."

"We all have to carry the trash outside." The corners of the Dead Man's eyes wrinkled up. "Well, not you. You have servants."

Her chest tightened in frustration. She wanted to stomp a foot, but he already wasn't taking her seriously and displays would not help.

So she made her voice cold and said, "Do not mock me, sirrah."

His expression smoothed, what she could see of it. "Forgive me, Rajni." He rose to face her—which he should have done when she stood, for propriety, but there was no propriety in this room—and sketched a perfectly serious little bow.

She glared, her hands uncoiling. Marks from the fingerstalls smarted in her palms.

"I could abdicate," she said impulsively.

He regarded her, his air formal and solemn now. "Could you?"

She bit her lip. Breathed out. Breathed in.

"No."

"You will not discover that I am of hidden royal birth, I am afraid."

"Are you sure?"

"Well." His head tipped playfully. "I am an orphan. That is how one becomes a Dead Man to begin with."

There was a tension in the room, a tension between them. A lack of connection, and she could not, quite, find it and get her claws into it to cut it open and inspect its guts for the portents that would tell her what was going on in this damned love affair.

Except she knew. She knew she knew.

It was the acknowledgment from both of them that it could only ever be a temporary thing. That they must hold themselves in reserve, and not give fully. And maybe it was all right for him: he had had a wife, whom Mrithuri believed he had cared for deeply. She had . . . she had this. And then she would have a marriage, possibly to Anuraja or to somebody chosen by Anuraja. She would . . .

She would never have anyone to be close to. Not in that way. Not in that circle of trust she found herself, suddenly, craving.

And maybe it was an illusion. Maybe it was a thing nobody ever found: someone they could trust implicitly, and rely on. Maybe it only existed in tales.

"I'm sure Ata Akhimah can produce some convincing documentation, given a little time." She said it jestingly, but she said it. And watched the skin around his eyes tighten. "Of course you have no wish to be raja-consort to the rajni of a beleaguered state. My city will fall, and you will move on, if you survive the falling. And I will be left here married to that slime creature, who will probably kill me and definitely kill all my children with his poisoned seed."

"That's a foolish thing to say," the Dead Man answered. He put a hand on the window ledge as if to steady himself. "This could be my home, Mrithuri. I would stay with you if I could. I would roost here until my wings molted off, and sing a praise of each morning. But you know and I know that that is not who I am. And this is not who we are. For the same reason you can't abdicate. I can't convert to your religion, which would be the bare minimum required."

She stared at him. She was, she realized, spoiling for the fight she had been trying to provoke with him. She was brittle and unmoored, and she wanted the certainty of attack and defense. She wanted to see him flare up and know he cared about her. That he would fight for her.

He would fight for her, which is to say, he would fight on her behalf. He would not, she acknowledged, fight to keep her. She would have to hold herself by him, for he would never reach out and take her, even just to hold onto her if she seemed to be drifting away.

"Ah." She stepped back and turned aside, defusing the confrontation. She waved one hand. "No one would believe you were a lost prince anyway."

He laughed, and she saw his shoulders soften. "Too many bullet holes, for one thing."

Distantly, the nuns took up their plainchant. This room was one of those with no access directly to their cloister, but their voices still echoed through hollow stone.

Mrithuri dusted her hands down her front, smoothing her drape, careful not to snag her fingerstalls. Now she was rajni again. Now it was time for her to go and do what she was born to do. Hold Sarathaitia together, and make a display of herself. "I want to see you this evening."

"My lady's request," he replied.

# 18

THE GAGE KEPT WALKING. THE WIND ROSE; A BOILING, GLOBULAR WALL of darkness towered against the sometimes-frozen, sometimes-burning stars. It looked like crystals of malachite, but it moved. It bubbled with lightning, and what light filtered through from behind it seemed to arise from within. The bit of dragonbone was slipped into a pocket of his increasingly ragged desert robe.

The dust storm encompassed him. What whispered against his carapace was more silt than sand; so powdery it seemed to have no texture. It slipped within his joints anyway, where coarser stuff would not. It made them grit, and grind.

His feet, blunt and heavy and indelicate, could not grope their way across the badlands. You must be able to *feel* to resort to groping. But he pushed on regardless, thinking, *Once I am out of this I will lubricate. I will be fine.*

The wear, though, was happening. He could feel it restraining him. It was not painful, not precisely. It just . . . slowed him down.

The wind and the dust also slowed him. They had a weight. A pressure. The dust wore his surface away. It spoke against his skin in uncounted tiny voices, myriad soft words. A million whispers told him *No.* A million whispers told him *Stop now.*

*You cannot fight this. Even you, who are invulnerable. Even you, who are immortal. Even you, who are armored in metal and who cannot feel pain.*

*Even you cannot stand against the wind, and the dust, and the ceaselessness of time.*

Gritting, he walked. Grinding, he moved forward. He did not stagger. He could not see. None of his senses availed him. Though he did not use eyes to see, there was nothing to see but the dust, its pale green glow ashen and multivalenced. Though he did not use ears to hear, there was nothing to hear but the dust, and all it spoke in was whispers.

He slowed. Grit constrained him.

*I will be a statue here in the waste, and the help for my friends will never come.*

The legs of the massive insectoid object descended through the miasma around him.

They moved with the rippling motion of a centipede, as he had suspected. But there were rank upon rank of them. Like a hundred centipedes harnessed side by side. They descended through the swirling, poisonous dust, and each one was an architecture of glittering steel and olivine dragonbones. Each one came to a chiseled point, and ascended into invisibility in latticed triangles, obviously meant to bear weight down.

The Gage, half-destroyed by the storm, moving painfully and slow, expected at any moment to find that he had been impaled. But the feet moved deliberately, and each rank that emerged from the miasma set down in the same place as the now-vanishing rank in front of it had before it lifted. The points stepped over him, and did not harm.

He strained his senses into the swirling storm that was destroying him. There was a bulk overhead; he caught glimpses through swirling gaps in the dust. Lights burned within it. He heard . . . perhaps he heard voices.

He doubtless heard the snapping and ripping of enormous canvas sails shaking in an incomprehensible wind.

A city. A *walking city*. Powered by the endless desert wind. That's what he had been seeing on the horizon: city-ships walking on wind-powered legs across vast sandy flats.

But hadn't one that he had seen—the first one—been walking against the wind? Well, ships could tack, couldn't they? Was this just a vast ship, geared and walking on feet, but in its own way a less strange feat of engineering than him?

This one, that he had thought was coming toward him. Perhaps even seeking him. Had it only been running before the storm?

*But how does it move when there is no wind? And if it is built of dragonbones, how do the people within survive the dragon-sickness?*

He might grind to a halt here in the storm before he answered these questions. He might spend eternity as a statue in a wasteland, trapped in a carapace that would not answer him, remembering friends who had died for the want of his assistance.

The city was walking in the wrong direction. Away from the Singing Towers.

*Climb up,* the voice that had given him so much advice of finality over the years whispered to him. *Climb up, or die alive.*

THE CITY WAS HUNTING HIM. HUNTING *HIM*, HE THOUGHT, AND NOT MERELY running before the storm.

Otherwise he would have missed his opportunity, because by the time he had realized he should rush—what passed with him as rushing, right now—and clutch one of its knife-tipped spider-feet, it had danced away into the storm, taking its lights and voices with it.

He would have cursed, but he was too busy forcing himself to turn.

And then the city came back, and again passed over.

It moved with dancing lightness for its size. It must be all hollow bones and cantilevered structures, all sails made of dragonwing and gears carved of dragonbone. There must be almost no substance to it, for how large it seemed. And that weight must be spread out very neatly over its endlessly cycling feet, because they did not cut deeply into the dragonglass and whatever lay beneath. They skittered, insectile. They danced.

And each one still fell into just the place the one before had left. It seemed their reach was fixed, and when the city moved faster, its legs rippled more quickly, but did not take longer strides. Limited, he thought, by the span of connecting rods, the pivot of bearings. A pace precise, and machined.

He wished he did not find the idea as soothing as he did.

*How did it move against the storm? Not just the* wind. *But the storm.*

However the city moved, the Gage did it through sheer will. His joints all grinding and complaining, his senses fogged by the whisper of the sand. He stepped, and stepped again, his metal body squealing and complaining. He forced himself by agonizing increments to the place where one of the walking city's feet came down.

The penultimate one lifted away through the nauseous green storm-light as he stepped beside it. He grabbed—too slow, with grinding arms. It whizzed over his head. He could see how the bevels, given any true light, would glitter.

The final leg was descending. Unless the city made another pass, he would have this chance, and this chance only.

The Gage positioned his hands. He reached out. He gambled. He argued with himself that the leg would be exactly where the leg had been before. He was a machine. His reckoning of the distance was precise in memory.

He was nearly wrong.

The foot came down on its needle-point, and the lattice was a half-span of his arm farther away than he had calculated. Was the architecture of the trailing edge of the city slightly attenuated? He did not have time to investigate.

Gears shrieked. Sparks flashed from his joints. He was profoundly grateful that he was not equipped to feel *physical* pain. He felt something strip inside him. Something else bind.

His arm shot out. His hand locked in a claw onto the trellised leg.

It snapped upward, and bore him into the storm and the sky.

THE GAGE SWOOPED INTO SPACE, WHIRLED LIKE THE WEIGHT ON THE END of a trebuchet. The shock of motion traveled from his gauntlet, along his arm, to the shoulder joint, down the overlapping plates of his cara-pace, to the trailing fingertips and feet. He *snapped*, and if he had still had a human spine within his metal body, the spine would have snapped as well. He had not expected the violence and speed of the motion, which looked so smooth and . . . *riffling* . . . from the ground.

It seemed to shake some of the dust from his joints, anyway. Or maybe the shock spread his lubricant around. He moved more freely, and with mechanical strength managed to wheel his free arm around against the momentum of the swing as it was slowing. The strain stretched his linkages. He wondered about metal fatigue and shearing forces.

He had wondered, more than once, what it might take to destroy a Gage. Perhaps this was it, and instead of an intact statue in an endless, poisoned waste, he would wind up a dismembered one.

His free hand clutched at the dragonbone leg of the walking city, locked through the lattice, and gripped fast. His elbows flexed, grinding like broken axles, and pulled him close. Metal rang on metal, clear through the mumble of the storm.

Whisper, mumble. He had thought he heard voices before, the babble of a crowd. Was it possible that he had heard not, as he assumed, the noise of a city-sized ship of the desert, but voices that were haunting the very wind? He hadn't too much time to think about it, as the great leg slowed at the top of its arc and he saw the massive camshaft with its right-angle bends turning into a gap in the even more massive underside. The belly of the beast-machine was a convoluted, incomprehensible architecture of pipes and plumbing and belts of braided cable or dragonhide sliding liquidly through connection points. It reeked of heated metal . . . and lubricant.

Something he was going to need.

Lights blazed in among the machinery. They had a quality he was unfamiliar with: not witchlamps, and not flames. They cast shadows stark as the worst sun of this desert of terrible suns, the blazing blue one. They lit each individual grain of dust so that it cast a streaking shadow behind it, so that the texture of the storm was visible as it never would have been in mere daylight. It was harsh, gritty. One could almost feel the texture of sandpaper, of sharkskin, to gaze on it.

As the arc of the ascending leg slowed, the Gage braced himself for the snap, the reversal of motion. The abrupt thrust down. He could see other legs through swirling dust, a long ripple of them stabbing downward like released bolts after their climactic pause. The dragonbone, for all it seemed to be metal and stone, must be extraordinarily light in its structure. This thing would crumple under its own weight, otherwise.

He had options. He could climb, hand over hand, hauling himself up the lattice of the violently moving leg while the storm ripped at him and his joints progressively froze. Or he could wait out another cycle to get the timing and then let go before the top of the arc, and hope that either the momentum was enough to throw him into the undercarriage, or that he caught a higher point on the leg as he fell, for a net gain of absolute altitude.

At least some of the voices were definitely in the wind. Lost souls crying and moaning. The ghosts of ancient words in a language he thought that he should understand.

And some, he thought, were not haunted at all. Like the clarion shout, ringing as the cry of a ship's lookout who spots land after many days becalmed, that hailed him as he rose out of the sea of etching dust and into the painful, angled light.

The motion of the leg he clung to halted so abruptly that his own momentum almost shook him loose. His clenched fingers saved him, because he was a machine. They would tear off before they would unbend, if he so willed it. He huddled against the lattice while all around him, the ripple of motion continued down the line. Only *his* perch snapped up and locked in place with a thump that reverberated through the metal to which he clung.

For a moment, he remained motionless: a limpet, a rabbit when the shadow of a raptor passes over. For a moment, which would have been the length of a held breath and then its shuddering release. If he still breathed.

Then the moment was over. A wash of milder light fell over him, and there was a change in the tone of the wind. It whined, in addition to whispering and moaning. It whistled like the wind between the lines of a ship's sails.

Something moved toward the Gage from above, from out of the light of what must be a passage that had opened in the belly of the thing. A shape. A cage, on a cable. That was what the wind whistled through.

Inside the cage was a man. He wore robes with a hood, and a mask that covered his face entirely. His hands were wound in bandages until the strips of cloth became gloves. His legs above his boots were similarly wound. His breath hissed within the mask, the way Mrithuri's hissed through the filters in the masks she wore when she held court in her throne room filled with golden dust.

*It is the same thing,* the Gage thought, though it patently wasn't at all. The dust that caked the surfaces of *this* mask was greenish, and it faintly glowed. But . . . there was the dragonglass that made up the ceiling of Mrithuri's throne room. And maybe there was some root that bound the customs together, back there in the history of cultures.

The Gage lifted his head, pushed his carapace away from the strut. The enclosure swung to beside him. It was open on one side, like a birdcage from which the bird has flown. The man within it held with one bandaged hand to a railing that ran around the inside.

"Need a ride?" he said.

THE MAN USED A TOOL TO GRAPPLE THE CAGE IN PLACE AGAINST THE FROZEN leg, extending a thing resembling a claw on a pipe with a trigger like the Dead Man's guns that made it grab and latch. The Gage traversed the gap and mounted the platform without capsizing it, though he would not later be certain how. Once in, he did not try to stand, but crouched on the riveted plates of the floor. His body ground against itself. His joints were further stiffening.

The Gage had some internal mechanisms for self-repair. What fool Wizard would build a final servant and ultimate weapon without them? But like all creatures, he needed time to heal.

And a nice soak in a warm tub of oil would not hurt his chances for repair.

The man released his claw, and they swung free. The platform swayed on its cables, which creaked under the Gage's weight as well as whining in the wind. The Gage hoped his weight would not be the death of his rescuer.

At least the dragonhide *seemed* strong.

The swing corrected itself slowly, despite the assist it was given by the wind. The cage winched upward, and the Gage found himself relaxing into the hands of fate. They were still going in the wrong direction. He would correct that in time.

For now, however, he might survive. And that was both so unexpected, and offered such an increased chance of completing his mission, that relief made him as giddy as if he could still become light-headed. If he'd been in the body he was born in . . . well, he wouldn't have made it this far. But that aside, he probably would have collapsed, prone, and pressed his face to the metal floor.

Rivets and all.

They rose out of the storm. The wind stilled as the light surrounded them, and a moment later there was a grinding sound as a hatch slid closed below. The man with the claw swung down from the cage onto a deck of gray fabric—no, stretched leather . . . no, dragonhide. It dented under his boots, stretching slightly. Other people, as wrapped and masked as he, moved around the space that the Gage found himself in. It was as big and bright as the workshop of a Wizard of Messaline.

"Bili, get a hose up here. Qi Len, the tracks on that hatch will need to be cleaned out after we're through this rotdust. I'm headed to de-contam."

The Gage stayed where he was. Now that he did not have to move, he could feel the damage the dust had done inside him, and there was no reason to aggravate it when he did not know, really, where he was, what these people's intentions were, or what happened next. The man who had rescued him from the storm was obviously in charge, at least of these operations. The Gage could harm nothing by waiting.

That had been a hard thing to learn, when he became a Gage. How often, in a situation where things were difficult, anxiety-provoking, or exciting in threatening ways—how often the best action was not to act at all, but to wait and conserve one's self, and make plans.

It was more satisfying to thrash.

But a Gage who thrashed destroyed cities entire.

Water ran over him with a hiss. It was warm, and soapy, and seemed to be pumped through a tube by two men working a handle while the third one pointed a nozzle at him. He was being cleansed, he under-stood. The poison dust washed off him, and out of as many of his crev-ices as possible. The used water drained away through a grate in the floor. He wondered how they got the poison out of it; surely in a desert such as this, no one could afford to waste water.

"Can you understand me?" a voice asked. A masked man, the same one who had worked the nozzle.

"Yes," said the Gage. "I can." As with all the other speakers here, the man spoke a dialect of his own native tongue of Messaline. The accent was strange and there were unfamiliar words embedded—what was "decontam"?—but on the whole it made good sense.

"Can you stand and walk a little? Or shall I use the cage to move you?"

The Gage considered. "I can walk. A little."

He rose from his knees, joints grating. He stepped out of the cage, which swung wildly as his weight shifted. He followed the man across the dragonskin deck, which supported his weight, but barely. With every step he thought he must punch through, but the stuff was otherworldly in its elasticity. He imagined the people who lived here down in the desert, harvesting the stuff off of the corpses of dragons, sewing it into the fabric of their home. Did they not know it was poison?

Did they not know their whole *home* was poison?

"Here we are," the man said. "Step in."

They had stopped before a sort of tub, a little longer and wider than the Gage's body, sewn from dragonhide. It was full of some viscous liquid, dark gold and reeking of plant esters.

"What is this?" the Gage asked. His robes were mostly threads now. He picked the bit of dragonbone he had collected out of his pocket, and held it in his palm. The shreds of cloth he dropped onto the floor.

"Almond and ylang-ylang oil," the man said, mask-muffled. "Your machinery sounds like you could use it. There are strong magnets underneath; if you move around enough to dislodge the dragonbone dust, it should be drawn down to the bottom of the tub and stop fouling your gears."

The Gage lowered himself cautiously into the tub without another word.

The oil was warm. The stretchy hide was like a hammock. It was—a peculiar concept to revisit after so long as a machine—sublimely *comfortable.* He did as suggested and stretched himself, opened his filters and purged them, pumped warm oil through every hollow chamber of his body. He was, though it would have seemed strange to most who observed him, mostly hollow inside. When he was filled with oil, and surrounded by oil, he did not feel *heavy*, for once.

He was still lying there, relishing the sense of lightness, when the second man returned. "If you are refreshed," he said deferentially, "the Master Mechanic will be able to see you now."

THE GAGE WAS NOT SURPRISED TO LEARN THAT THE MASTER MECHANIC was the man who had descended to rescue him. After he rose carefully from his bath and allowed himself to drain, he was scraped down and then rubbed dry with polishing cloths. His guide then led him across the decking (he left grease stains that he assumed would probably sink into the leather and renew it, so they did not concern him overmuch) to a door.

"It's a pressure lock," the guide said. "Do not be concerned."

That was another of those words the Gage had not previously encountered.

A "pressure lock" appeared to be a door that shut behind one, uncannily like that of a cell. And another one that was *already* closed in front of one before one entered, presenting no immediate means of egress. Unless one tore it off the hinges, which seemed . . . unlikely to ensure continuance of the generous hospitality he had so far been receiving.

He pushed into the cramped space and paused there. His pauldrons brushed waxed dragonskin walls. Waxed, of course, to keep contaminants from permeating the leather.

He relaxed. He thought he understood.

A sharp puff of air gusted around him. An evacuation, and then a gentler refill. Not quite as much air as had been evacuated, he thought. Little enough that he felt a lightness on his skin.

The door before him opened, as he had assumed it eventually must. When he emerged, he found behind it a man.

The man was of moderate size and a wiry, underfed build. He wore an undyed blouse and indigo trousers. He did not wear a beard, though it looked from the shadow on his cheeks as if his beard disagreed with this sartorial expression. His hair, curly and tall at the front in that manner that defied pomade, was the black of greased ebony. His skin was light olive, his cheekbones high.

Just looking at him made the Gage feel heartsick, and homesick, and a little bit lost. It was the face of home. The face of young men lost too soon, young men lost in spite of being beautiful. Young men, perhaps, lost *because* they were beautiful.

Down to the dark hazel eyes and the half-smile, it was the face of lost love. It was unmarked by grief, by privation, by sickness, by the poisons that surrounded it. It was perfect in every regard.

The Gage straightened himself, and made himself clinical. He was not now that which had loved. He was not now that which had felt the wild strength of angels in him. Which had burned with the belief that this, this one thing in all the world, was true and wild and immortal. That it would persist. That it would never be betrayed.

He was not now that thing which had believed in love.

Now, he was the thing that had avenged it.

"Hello," he said, in as level and metallic a voice as he could muster. "I am a Gage."

"My name is Khaldi," the young man said. "Hello, Gage. Be welcome to"—he dropped into Sahali—"the Many-Legged Truth."

The Gage assumed that was the name of the city.

Khaldi continued, "Thank you for consenting to join us. I would like to offer you a tour."

"You know what I am?" the Gage asked, only mildly surprised. The accent was wrong, but the language, again, was Messaline. He could have offered thanks that this man—Khaldi, the Master Mechanic (for so he had pieced together the clues)—had rescued him. But it was his experience that no one offered assistance unless they expected to benefit from it in some fashion. So the Gage was just assuming that no thanks would be necessary, because he was going to pay.

"I am surprised to find you alone," said Khaldi, which was not exactly an answer. "Where is your Wizard?"

"I am on an errand," the Gage pretended to explain. "You want to show me your amazing machine?"

Khaldi laughed and raked his flawless fingers through that luxuriant hair. He, in the very least, did not seem to be suffering from poison. "I have every intention of talking you into a love affair with it," he admitted. "But now that that's out of the way, let's go look around!"

He had changed his sand-colored bandages and masks for clothes in shades of russets and grays. He led the Gage now down a corridor so clean and well-lit it seemed like no ship's gangway, nor even any castle corridor, the Gage had ever seen. "This is the main crew-way," Khaldi explained, gesturing to the knots of men who passed them. All men, the Gage noticed, and did not remark. All wearing wimples cut close to cover their necks and jowls, and close-fitting caps on shaved heads. All wearing shades of violet, and russet.

"Are those uniforms?" the Gage asked.

"We are a crew," Khaldi said proudly.

"What does your crew do?"

"Where do you think the dragonglass that decorates palaces and temples comes from? We harvest it."

The Gage thought of the protective gear. He thought of the dust. The people of this walking city . . . no, this *harvester* . . . must have good technology.

"That's a risky business."

"It's not dangerous unless it's broken," Khaldi said with an airy wave. "It's the dust that kills. Or if it cuts, the wound will fester."

"How do you harvest a thing," the Gage wondered, "without breaking off a piece?"

Khaldi seemed to recognize that this was a rhetorical question. He said, "We did not expect to find one such as you walking the storm. Did you come here for the glass? Did your Wizard send you?"

Well, that would save on some explanations.

"I came here to get across it, mostly," the Gage admitted. "I did not expect that it would be so bad."

"Headed where?" They walked down passageways that seemed endless. The Gage was slightly disconcerted that his footsteps neither thumped nor rang. The springiness of the dragonhide underfoot reminded him of how walking had felt when he had elastic tendons, cartilage, flesh. When he was not a structure of unyielding metal. He felt uneasy, and strange.

Khaldi looked at him speculatively, considering the depth to which the decking was stretching beneath his feet. "I think it would end badly, if I put you on a ladder. Do you mind another climb on the superstructure?"

"Does it involve going out in the storm?"

The Master Mechanic laughed. "No, I think we will climb up the inside. Follow me."

They climbed up the inside. It was more dragonbone, and the Gage noticed that Khaldi pulled on a pair of heavy gloves before touching it. Maybe they did have acceptable protocols for handling the stuff.

Maybe the Gage could learn them. Not for himself, obviously. But for the people at home.

They climbed only one level, and the effort was trivial. More walking on the trampoline of dragonhide, and now they began passing people—workers—in the corridors. Those people also wore the uniforms. It occurred to the Gage that he had not seen a person out of one.

"Is this a military vessel?"

"It's a city, basically," said Khaldi. "Why?"

"I have not seen anyone who seems to be off-duty."

"Well," Khaldi said, "this is the production floor. You wouldn't."

The uniformed people in this area did not wear filter masks. The Gage assumed they were not working directly with dragon-poison. And yet, here they lived in this . . . ship, this city. Many of them, he saw, had suffered for it. He saw mottled scalps, flaking skin. Oval, purple discolorations along their hairlines looked like finger-bruises, except the color was flat and unvaried and the lesions were unnaturally smooth and slightly depressed. Festering sores appeared white-edged on lips, around eyes and nostrils. The Gage saw more than one eye blinded and milky-blue with cataract.

Some had even become deformed. Noses had collapsed, flat against faces, the bone within eaten away. Fingers clubbed, as if the victims suffered leprosy. Heavy goiters hung from throats, and strange bulges rose near collarbones. The most afflicted, the Gage noticed, wore the plainest and most worn uniforms. They did not raise their eyes when he and Khaldi passed. They ducked their heads and skirted, backs to the wall and not to the Gage and the Master Mechanic.

"Are these your folk?" the Gage asked. "Do you lead them?"

"These are not mine," Khaldi said. "These report to the Master Sorter."

"And your mechanics? They seem to have better protective gear."

"They are skilled labor," Khaldi said. "Expensive to replace."

"So these are slaves? Conscripts?"

"We are free men," said the slavemaster. "We labor for no king. It is for our own profit that we do this."

The Gage thought about the masks caked in green poison. He looked at the sores encrusting cracking hands, the goiters, the mottled scalps shedding clumps of hair. He held his speech.

Khaldi followed the arc of his gaze. "They're not slaves. They're debtors."

The Gage had seen a lot of bullshit in his time. "Debtors."

"Men who owe money to the city. Working off their debt. They might become investors in time. Like me." He slapped his chest with self-pleasure. "The trick is not to spend your whole life in the city. You can stand a little exposure." He ran a hand through his thick, dark hair. The Gage wondered if it was a nervous tic, an unconscious statement of status, or a self-soothing gesture. "You can make a fortune here in a very short time."

*Certainly*, the Gage thought. *If you do not come in already burdened.*

He turned to the nearest laborer, a man dressed in a worn blue tunic, his feet wrapped in rags through which spots of blood and lymph were seeping. All around him, the Gage smelled suppuration.

"Are you a free man?" he said, without preamble.

The laborer jumped back, nonplussed at being addressed by a faceless tower of bronze. As, the Gage supposed, anyone might be. "Free," he said, scratching at a welted hand. He looked dubiously from Khaldi to the Gage.

"It's safe," Khaldi said. He folded his arms over his chest in anticipatory amusement.

"Are you suggesting I ain't free?" the laborer asked, lifting his chin. He must be blind in one eye; he looked as if his teeth and possibly his jaw were rotting.

"I'm asking you," the Gage said. "How do *you* feel?"

"I do honest work," the laborer said. "I pay my note. I feed my family."

*You breed another generation to be consumed by this machine.*

"You work so hard," the Gage said, in pity. "Surely you must rest."

"Oh, aye," the man said. "Every tenth day is a rest day. We ain't *slaves.*"

The Gage wished he had eyes, so that he could have closed them. He wished he had a gaze, so he could have turned it away. As it was, he took his courteous leave of the laborer, and watched the man limp away along the corridor.

Whistling.

"You could take better care of your workers," the Gage said. "You could keep them healthy."

Khaldi shrugged. "There's only so many shares of profit to go around."

"That man is rotting from the inside out, and it is your profit that has poisoned him."

"True," Khaldi said.

He waited, but the Gage waited longer.

"Ah," Khaldi said. "But what if we became men like you?"

That made a peculiar amount of sense.

"You want to buy my body."

Khaldi shrugged. "Say we want to re-create it. Say we want to use your expertise to make workers who will not suffer when exposed to the dragonbone and the dust."

"If you became men like me, you would not be men."

"We'd give you fair price for the knowledge."

"Have you Wizards?"

Khaldi, by means of exposition, waved to the enormous edifice that surrounded them. If the Gage concentrated, he could feel the individual falls of each knifelike mechanical foot. He could feel the minute shudder that ran through the insect-city with each increment that bore it forward, scuttling and utterly level, across the blasted plain.

"We have Wizards," Khaldi said.

"And how is it that you would select who became like me?"

"Those who volunteered, of course," Khaldi said. "We are not monsters."

"Would you pay them to undergo the process? Forgive their debt?" Privately, the Gage wondered what mechanisms were in place to assure that the maximum possible debt was accrued. *Everything costs something.*

Perhaps that was true.

"Well," Khaldi said judiciously. "They could no doubt pay off their debt faster, if they did agree. . . ."

The Gage could not have been less pleased if he had discovered slaves on treadmills. He *had* discovered slaves on treadmills, in fact, without stretching the metaphor. He restrained a momentary desire to smash this place, to start crushing and disassembling.

He turned his head toward Khaldi, which was not necessary for the looking at him. The looking at him, very sadly, took care of itself in the Gage's case.

He let himself think, *I could ruin this place with less effort than this "Master Mechanic" puts toward self-awareness.*

"What sort of training goes into becoming a Master Mechanic, friend Khaldi?"

Khaldi cocked his head. "Well, it depends, I guess."

"Depends."

"If you are buying in, like me . . . not much training. Mostly on the job. Your seconds will usually teach you the ropes as you go."

"You might expect that," the Gage said, without actually agreeing. It was always a little bit of effort, because of the way he was made, not to just agree with people, not to just go along with whatever self-delusions they professed. "And if you are not buying in?"

"Well, if you are working your way up from the ranks—" Khaldi shrugged. "There are a series of skill tests. And of course recommendation from one's betters plays a part in promotion."

"Of course," the Gage murmured. "How did these cities come to be, Master Mechanic?"

"They were built by the Alchemical Emperor, in his day. To harvest dragonglass for his palaces and monasteries. It was a conceit of his."

"I see it was," the Gage said, contemplating dragonglass skylights and dragonglass-lined walls. "And now you have no princes?"

"We're a joint-stock company," he said cheerfully. "We're only beholden to ourselves."

It would be easier, the Gage thought, if this were just slaves on treadmills. He could . . . he could just destroy everything. Why would the Alchemical Emperor, say, build these enormous machines, and then staff them with people from as far away as Messaline?

So as not to poison his own people, obviously. Let someone else do the dangerous, murderous, messy work. Keep your own family as far away from it as possible.

Where were the women and children associated with all these men? The Gage hoped they were far away, somewhere a little safer from the poison dust. He hoped they were not kept on some high and private level of the ships, slowly rotting away.

He *could* just destroy everything. He could disable this harvester. He could tear it apart.

And then everybody who lived inside it would die even faster, in the desert with no way to escape. He could tell himself that that would be a cleaner death, but the truth of the matter was that, no, it wouldn't.

The Gage thought about the exploited, rotting laborers. He thought about their inevitable fate.

*That would be wrong,* he told himself, and tried to make the fire inside him believe it. *It would not be mercy.*

It would be mercy if it were a horse with a broken leg. A jackal fix-eyed and slavering in the initial stages of rabies. It would be mercy for any other creature whose doom had been fixed.

*Men,* he reminded himself. *Men are not like other creatures.*

The Alchemical Emperor the people of the Lotus Kingdoms so revered with nostalgia was turning out to be no better than any other emperor, after all. The Gage was not, in particular, surprised. Honestly, he was weary enough with men and the worlds of men that he didn't even manage to feel disappointed.

"Things are much better now! We work for ourselves, and are not enslaved by princes." Khaldi clapped the Gage on the shoulder with his gloved hand.

The Gage rang like a bell.

Even beyond Khaldi—who was nothing, really, except a small man with a small sinecure and the abiding desire to feel important—even beyond Khaldi, the Gage knew, there would be others. The people who were *really* making gold off this deal, and who would never place themselves in a position of even such reduced jeopardy as the one this Master Mechanic inhabited. Those were the people with real prestige, who might come and tour the harvester. Even stay overnight. But who would never deign to spend a *risky* amount of time here.

Destroying the harvester would do nothing to harm them. Except in the pocketbook, which was tempting and perhaps the blow they would feel the most. But it was not his place to make decisions for other creatures of sensibility. Beings who had come to this place somehow, and had not left it.

There was always the problem of a sweeter peach on the next bough, to keep you reaching.

Khaldi said, "Will you help us make our people safer?"

Safer. Unhumaned. Rendered tireless. Rendered unneeding of rest. Able to toil without ceasing.

"No," the Gage replied.

He turned to Khaldi, though he did not need to orient himself by rotation to enjoy the sickly greenish pallor seeping down Khaldi's olive face. He turned entirely for the drama, so he could lower his own burnished head down over Khaldi's and enjoy Khaldi's expression as he saw himself mirrored in the Gage's faceless face. The Gage had a sense that maybe his mirror finish had been softened a little by the wearing dust. Well, staring into your own eyes was still a moment of truth, even if they were a little bit blurry.

"What I will do for you," the Gage said, "is this. Once the storm is over, and your city is once again in control of its passage and its destiny, I will make you this offer. Deliver me to the Singing Towers—"

"We don't go there!"

As if he had not been interrupted, the Gage continued. "Deliver me to the Singing Towers, and I will refrain from disabling your abomination of a city, and thus killing everyone within it much faster than they are dying already."

Khaldi folded his arms across himself and rocked back.

"This city. This . . . Many-Legged Truth. This thing you have purchased a share of, without contemplating what poison you are paying for. Your Many-Legged Truth is built from the stolen bones of dragons, and it slowly poisons everyone within it. Do you doubt that one such as I can destroy it?"

"You are not a monster who would kill ten thousand innocents," Khaldi said confidently.

The Gage permitted himself a laugh. "You rely on indentured labor. Desperate men who will die for a little money. What would it harm me to kill them a little faster, and far more mercifully?" The Gage shook his mirrored head.

"I owe you a debt for the rescue, even if you performed it for your own reasons, so if you help me a little bit more, I won't hasten their end. But—" He reached out to the bulkhead and sank his fingers into it without strain. "I would shoot a cow infested with the river-worm, Master Mechanic. Out of pity. And you are far worse than the river-worm, my friend."

# 19

"Marry me," Mrithuri said in the dark.

"For a day?" the Dead Man answered dreamily.

He was warm against her back, a wiry curve fitted against the bones of her spine. Their hips bruised each other when they slid together. She liked his spareness. He made her feel, for a moment, as if she were not too thin. She was cold all the time now, even in the heat of what should have been the rainy season. Gooseflesh stood out on her clammy skin. She imagined it puckering the outlines of the sacred animals inked into her skin: Bull, tiger, peacock. Dolphin, elephant, bearded vulture.

Strength, fierceness, confidence. Speed, steadfastness, wisdom.

She was not sure she had any of these things.

She put a hand out from under the covers and laid it on Syama's back. The bhaluukutta breathed sleepily, warm and unconcerned.

There was a war outside the walls. There was a war at their very gates.

But there was no war in the room with them, and out of simple animal pragmatism, Syama and Serhan made use of the time to rest.

Mrithuri could muster nervous energy enough for all of them. The simple act of lying still, curled in the Dead Man's arms, was an act of will. Moving was an act of will as well, because fear weighed her chest like a stone. She had been telling herself—telling everyone—that the river would come to their rescue.

But the river was not rising. And Hathi had plucked for her a blood-red lotus.

Red for birth. Or red, for war.

She drew a breath. "For a day," she answered. "For an hour. For the rest of our lives. That might not be too much of a commitment. What do you say?"

"Why?" He touched her face with the back of his hand.

Tears pressed the slits in her closed eyelids. "Because that old monster is coming, and I do not know if we can keep him out much longer. And if he gets in, he will take me. And I'll be the sixth dead queen of Sarathai-lae."

"Not because you love me?" he teased.

The gentle affection in his voice only deepened her despair. And his words stopped her cold, though his hand in her hair did not grow any less gentle. The pattern of his breathing encouraged hers to soften. She let it ease her a little. She let it smooth her ruffled sensibilities.

The weight on her chest was still there. But maybe it was a weight that she could breathe around. She pressed the back of her head into the hollow under his chin.

"You might be the one who survives him," the Dead Man said, in a voice mossy with memories.

"Poxed and rotting, if he has his way with me." She drew a shaky breath. "But one can live a long time with the rot. And so I am planning on outliving him." She stopped and pressed her nails to her mouth. "Or, planning in *case* I do outlive him, anyway. I can't plan *on* such a fragile possibility."

The Dead Man nodded into her hair.

She said, "What if there are more of those things you fought by the cisterns?"

"That would be a problem," he admitted. "Though the Wizards have a better idea what to do about them now. And Nizhvashiti might be able to call up the wrath of God or a cleansing fire or who knows what, if we ask it nicely."

It hurt to laugh.

He pressed his face into her hair. In the utter darkness of the shuttered chamber where they lay, he'd unwound his veil and kissed her mouth. She'd traced the outlines of his features with her fingertips.

"So," she said, "will you marry me?"

He sat up in the dark and drew her around to face him. He was nothing but a faintly paler blur against the blackness, but she felt the warmth of his close breath when he said, "You did not answer when I asked if you loved me."

"Does it matter?"

"Yes," he said. "As rain matters, and the birds matter, and the taste of wine in autumn matters."

It was trapped in her throat like a bone. What she loved, she lost; it was not safe to love. "I do not know," she admitted. "I do not know what love is. I do not know what it is to love."

"Thank you," he said, and kissed her forehead. "You are a truthful rajni. You may need to learn to put that behind you."

She laughed. "Does that change your answer?"

"Kindle a light," he replied.

She handed him his veil and waited through a moment of rustling. The lamp by the couch was ensorcelled with one of Ata Akhimah's many useful household magics, and when Mrithuri turned the tiny gear to move the wick, it lit of itself and burned with a light as clear as a topaz gem.

She turned and gasped. He held the creased blue length of his veil in his hand. His face was bare in the lamplight. He flinched from her expression.

"That bad, is it?"

It was a very ordinary face.

More weathered about the eyes, where there were engaging lines that showed the work of sun and wind. She had, she realized, become used to reading the entire cast of his expression from just the lines around those eyes. But the face surrounding the eyes seemed years younger, the skin unwrinkled and without the pigmented spots that sun exposure brought. His nose was pronounced, his lips much thinner and more mobile than she would have expected. His beard was flattened from being under the veil.

She considered. He seemed nervous. "I like it," she said.

"My answer is yes. For an hour, for a day. I will marry you, my rajni."

"Yours," she agreed.

She reached for his hand, but he caught her by the wrist with his free hand and laced his fingers through her own. With his other hand, he slid the end of his veil between their palms, so they held it together. With the other end and quick, skilled gestures, he bound their hands together into an unwieldy package.

"In the sight of God and Her prophet, I, a Dead Man, do wed thee, Mrithuri Rajni, and with my sword I thee endow."

Something twinged in his face as he said the words. For the second time in his life, she remembered. But he said them softly, and fervently, with a holy weight behind them.

Mrithuri thought for a moment. She was rajni, and she did have the right to perform marriages. Why not her own?

She echoed his form, but did not know the scripted response, and so made it her own. "In the sight of the Mother and her Good Daughter, I, Mrithuri Rajni, do wed thee, a Dead Man called Serhan, and with my heart I thee endow."

He leaned forward over their joined hands, and she kissed him.

The door to the chamber was flung open, admitting a shaft of witch-light split by two familiar figures. Mrithuri jumped, hilariously restrained by her bound hand. The Dead Man cursed and dragged a corner of sheet across his face as Hnarisha and Ata Akhimah burst into the room.

Syama lunged to her feet with a snarl. When she saw who it was, her stub of a tail whipped like the handle on a pedal-grinder.

"Rajni," Hnarisha said, exactly as if the Dead Man were not naked on the couch beside her. "Anuraja's army is on the move. Also," he added, with a glance at their hands, "I think you need witnesses to make that official."

He glanced at Ata Akhimah, who was staring straight ahead, over the heads of everybody in the room, her brown arms folded over her white blouse. She nodded with one quick jerk of her chin.

Hnarisha slid the door shut behind him. "I guess you'd better do what you just did all over again."

The Dead Man sighed and jerked his sheet-wrapped head in the direction of a hook on the wall. "Hand me that scarf," he said.

Mrithuri dressed herself in armor, not in finery. It was her grand-father's armor, antique in decoration and design. She was surprised to find it fit her as if it had been made for her, with the exception of the skirts and sleeves being long.

The Dead Man went with her, and she was grateful. The lacquered chain mail of her armor tunic was heavy, and swung against her thighs. He helped her braid her hair and fit her helm, his touch as impersonal as if she were any raw recruit. Then he stepped back and regarded her critically.

"A very martial queen," he decided. "It needs a weapon."

"Daggers," she said. She touched the serpent torc at her neck, which rested now over the collar of the armor. "I know how to use those. There are some with jeweled hilts. Flashy enough, I suppose."

He nodded, and at his gesture the armorer fetched them for her. Mrithuri watched, impressed by how smoothly he had integrated himself into the life of the castle and made himself the de facto captain of her guard. The colored leather of the harness, with its gilt buckles, hung over the crimson-and-sapphire lacquer of the chain. Mrithuri thought, *I will be dazzling in the Riverlight.*

The Dead Man eyed her up and down. "We need to keep you out of bowshot, dressed like that. Every archer in Anuraja's army will want to take you down."

"Unless he's given orders to take me alive," she said grimly.

The Dead Man sighed. He looked over his shoulder, as if making sure they were more or less alone. Lowering his voice, he said, "The world breaks us. That is just the way of the world. The lucky ones, or perhaps the ones who are brave enough to stand the pain, might heal stronger and better in their new shapes. But they will never be the people who were not broken again. So if you wake up a different person one day because of what we now encounter, well. Remember that if you face the pain bravely, it will not make you terrible. Just different."

She rubbed her arms through the sleeves of the chain mail, making it rattle. "Let's go watch the war."

THE NIGHT WAS BREAKING AS MRITHURI AND HER ENTOURAGE RODE DOWN through the city on the back of an elephant, then dismounted in the shadow of the main gates to Sarathai-tia. The storm clouds that had been piled uselessly on the eastern horizon seemed, if anything, to have risen higher. They seemed oddly flattened, like murky water in a tank, and there was not a hint of wind or rain. The air held all the breath-lessness Mrithuri expected of the dry season.

Syama had paced alongside Hathi. Now, as Hathi offered her trunk to assist her passengers down, the bhaluukutta went and leaned against the elephant's leg. Mrithuri was not entirely sure who was comforting whom.

Hathi waited among guardsmen and soldiers as the Dead Man dismounted, followed by Hnarisha, Yavashuri, and Ata Akhimah, Tsering-la, and Lady Golbahar. Ritu was organizing her people for castle defense, and had drafted Vidhya to her cause. General Pranaj was already commanding the soldiers manning—and now reinforcing—the walls. Chaeri did not care to come so close to the war.

The chain mail was heavy on Mrithuri, making her calves strain and ache as she climbed the stair to the battlements, Syama at her heels and her people behind and before. They came to the top, which was swarming with men and war-dogs and barrels of oil to be set afire and boys running with bundles of shafts for the ballistae and even a sure-footed donkey hauling a cart of stone cannonballs down the walk as calmly as if it were on a narrow road.

"Well," said Hnarisha, huffing slightly as he came up beside her, "I guess we'll find out what they were waiting for now. How in the shine of the River do they keep that donkey cart from pushing people right over the edge?"

"Long years of practice, I assume," Mrithuri said. She looked around, about to ask where the Godmade was, until she realized that what she had taken for a pole swathed in wind-ruffled black banners was, in actuality, Nizhvashiti standing straight and narrow atop a battlement, robes fluttering around it as if it stood in a freshening breeze that no one else could feel. As the rajni came up, it turned mismatched, unseeing eyes—one gilt, one glass—upon her. Would that ever become less unsettling?

She'd be lucky to live long enough to find out.

"What do you see, Nizhvashiti?"

"More boats," Nizhvashiti answered. "And a black cloud rising. A sorcerer upon a throne of corpses, crystallized with gemstones. Lightning."

"A storm," Mrithuri said.

"The Good Daughter does not leave her Mother in chains." The Godmade stretched out its arms, letting the long sleeves stream from a bony frame in the wind rising up the city walls. For a moment, Mrithuri thought Nizhvashiti was going to try to fall into flight like a bird of prey. But the Godmade stood there, only, the wind threatening to lift it from its feet, but otherwise unmoving.

Mrithuri watched for a few long instants before deciding that nothing interesting was going to happen right then. The strange little ritual made her think, and she looked along the wall in either direction to see her royal austringers spaced out the length of the battlements, each with a red-winged bearded vulture on a glove. Her scouts were ready. Her men were ready.

She honestly was not sure what she was doing here. She felt the need to see, with her own eyes, the war. She felt that her men, who were here willing to fight and die for her, needed to see her beside them.

"Why do you suppose they are moving now?" she asked the Dead Man.

He shrugged. "Why do you suppose they waited so long?"

While she was considering her answer, a runner—a skinny lad still devoid of body hair, clad in a dirty loincloth—came from the river side of the city. He prostrated himself before General Pranaj and, after a brief interval, was waved to his feet and allowed to report that Anuraja's people were crossing the river in more boats, coming straight for the water gate.

The Dead Man, standing beside her, muttered, "I don't know why they're bothering with more boats. If the river falls much farther, there won't be much to keep them from just walking right up to the river gate."

"Mud," Yavashuri said.

"For a few days more."

"No," she said. "I mean, if the river keeps dropping as she has . . . well, there will be no water to row across. Only a mudflat."

"Oh," said the Dead Man. "Of course. A killing field."

Mrithuri imagined it: Anuraja's men in the mire, projectiles raining down on them.

Pranaj's signalers were drumming out a complicated, nigh-incomprehensible series of changes. Mrithuri had not learned the patterns, but she watched her men respond. *They* knew what the beats meant.

"Let's go around to the river wall," Mrithuri said, on a tickle of pre-monition, as the austringers, on one drumbeat, stepped to the battle-ment and lifted their bird-heavy gauntlets high. She watched them turn their birds—her birds—to the wind, so their heavy, red-stained wings could lift them with the most ease. Large raptors prefer to fall into flight, or to fly into the wind.

She should be within, on her chair, to protect the birds. To connect with their senses; to interpret what they saw and felt. To make sure they stayed out of the path of enemy arrows, enemy bullets, enemy spells. To protect them.

She was overwhelmed by the number of things requiring her pro-tection. She could not be there for all of them. She could not put her fragile body between death, and everything.

The sacred vultures fell into the wind one by one by one, a ripple of collapse like balanced *pupai* plaques arranged to fall against each other. Mrithuri walked along behind the austringers, trailing her en-tourage, briefly reaching out to caress the wild mind of each vulture as she passed. They had been fed on her blood already; they were there in her awareness now, as she was there in theirs.

She felt another mind, more distant than the others. It was the pres-ence of the bearded vulture she had sent to accompany the Gage on his long journey.

The Gage was still not with him. The vulture waited on the ther-mals spiraling out of blasted desert, within sight of an enormous storm, a terrible upwelling of pale green dust that roiled with fungal bulges and crackled with sickly lightning. The colored light and tinted shad-ows of strange suns limned the dust cloud. Mrithuri realized she was seeing past a boundary, into a land under a sky ruled by different gods. She knew other gods made other suns: she had heard of the twin suns of Song, the Lion Sun of Messaline. She had never imagined what it would be like to see past the veil from one land into another. She did not know what sky could host so many suns, so many conflicting sources of light.

Now vulture and woman contemplated the height of the storm through the same eyes, turning wingtip on the same pinions that felt the pressure of wind and gripped it like strong fingers. They were borne effortlessly aloft on the upflow. Mrithuri could have fallen forever into the vulture's experience, lost herself in the unworried animal mind. If she snapped the tether to her own body, she would be free, and that . . . complicated meat . . . would be left behind. Let somebody else sort out succession and precedence and who would be emperor of what. She could just . . . go flying.

What was one more woman's body, in a war?

It was just a fancy, she chided herself. A temptation. She was too well-trained in her duty to walk away. Or fly, for that matter. Wasn't she?

Some little part of her was still aware of the gentle pressure of Ata Akhimah's hand on her arm as the Wizard guided her, walking along the walls. Just barely.

But her will, stretched out, trembled like a stick held out by one tip. The weight of being overextended pulled at her. All the other birds were there as well, her whole clan of sacred, red-stained minor carrion gods. The threads connecting her to them were strong. The thread connecting her to her body was weak, attenuated. Nothing kept that frail flame burning except the venom that lit its veins, and it had been some time since she had taken the venom.

She was teetering. Sliding out of herself, into the wings of the strong young bird.

"*Rajni!*" Ata Akhimah's voice, sharp and sudden. Mrithuri snapped back into herself, blinking. Scrambling, backpedaling, as if she had felt the dirt crumble from beneath her toes at the edge of a cliff.

The entire battlefield projected itself into her awareness at once. A flash of vision, as if a map were held up before her: the combined gestalt of all the eyes, all the vultures. The second flotilla of boats, moving across the low and silt-opaque river. A heavy ripple under the surface, alongside. The besieging army, still blocking the causeway. Still holding back out of ballista range. A cloud of carrion birds swirled behind them. Not Mrithuri's familiars, those. Not the sacred bearded vultures.

Something ominous. Something she did not quite recognize.

*Stay clear,* she warned her birds. *Stay close to the city. Beware bowshot, and beware what follows the enemy.* It wasn't words, exactly. But she knew they understood.

"There's so many of them," she said, and came back to herself.

Ata Akhimah was looking at her. "Are you all right?"

"No," Mrithuri said. "But would you expect me to be?"

They had come along the top of the wall to the river gate by then. The massive, figured, copper-shod doors were of ancient mahogany, dense and resilient. They were sealed, barred on the inside, closed against the seamless golden stone of the gate-arch on the outside. Mrithuri leaned out to look down on them from above, feeling no fear despite Hnarisha's shocked intake of breath. The reliefs glittered, the shadows that outlined them stark in the rising light of the Heavenly River.

The new wave of boats were still beyond cannonshot. They came across the lotus-clogged water like plows cutting green sod. The milk-pale river behind them seemed milk-thick, as well, as though the white clay silt that filled it were thicker than usual. As if the Mother were a river of potter's slip.

"The dolphins," Ata Akhimah said.

"It is not safe for them," Mrithuri said, her voice rising as it squeezed through the tight throat of fear. "The river is so low—"

"It is not safe for any of us," Ata Akhimah answered. "The dolphins can break the bridge. They can overturn the boats and put those men in the water."

"I am charged with their protection. They are sacred to the Mother. Will I win Her grace by letting them come to harm?"

Nizhvashiti's papery words echoed in her memory. *The Good Daughter does not leave her Mother in chains.*

"Aw, shit," Mrithuri said. She looked around her: The Dead Man, Hnarisha, Yavashuri. Lady Golbahar. The two Wizards, Ata Akhimah and Tsering-la. Coming up behind them now, walking as silently as a husk on the wind, Nizhvashiti. "I should have my hands in the water for this."

"Wait," Tsering-la said. "Let me see what I can do." He stepped forward, holding out a flask that sloshed. He gestured to Mrithuri, and, understanding, she cupped her hands. He filled them with cool wetness.

He cupped his hands around hers. Perhaps she should have taken offense, that he touched a rajni, but this was war and he seemed to be thinking nothing of it. And then the water in her hands began, softly, to glow.

"Spit in that," he instructed, while Ata Akhimah leaned over his shoulder, using her greater height to indulge her curiosity.

Mrithuri spat into the water in her hands. She expected the saliva to float there, like a transparent worm in a puddle. But it touched the pale golden glow and the glow silvered, brightened, became opaque. The stuff in her hands became as if river water, except lit from within. "Make your wish," Tsering-la said. "Then let the water fall."

"I wish communication with the Mother's sacred river dolphins," Mrithuri said, then did as the Wizard instructed. She flung the cupped palmful out and away from the battlement. The river had fallen so much that there were mudflats and rocks below the stairs and the landing where the water gate should have debouched onto the water. The drops of water arced out and up and down, sparkling in the light of the Heavenly River, shining with their own light as they fell. They seemed to multiply, to increase in volume and number, as if Mrithuri had caused to be thrown a whole hogshead of water and not a scant hands' grasp. They also flew farther than she thought her strength could have moved them, so that some, at least, reached the low river's edge. The rest she leaned out to see, and watched as they braided themselves into rivulets and left a shining trail through the mud before running into the water.

Then the river itself began to glow, faintly, between the matted leaves and blooms of the lotus flowers. It occurred to Mrithuri that they were like an empire in their own right—each petal a kingdom, standing tall from and joined at the sturdy base.

She had no time for another thought, as she was swept from herself by a ferocious current. She fell out of her body like a stone through water. The last thing she knew of her own physical self was that it slumped over the battlements, and only the Dead Man and Hnarisha lunging to catch her saved her from slicing her breasts and belly open on the dragonglass studding the top of the wall.

She was down in the river in a world of bright blindness, where everything was white and she could see only the difference between white-that-glowed and the white-that-was-dark. *Dark white?* She thought, but there it was, beneath and behind her, and in shadowed patches denting the roof of the world. There was a weight on her back; her calf, carried above the water so it could breathe easily. The shadowed patches were in her way. They were the little islands the bad swimmers rode around on, and they were working very hard to cross the river against the current, despite the clogging lotus that she and her sisters and brothers slipped between.

She and her kin left the little islands alone, mostly, except for sometimes when they swam alongside them and begged for fish. But these islands were different. Someone—some knowledge—was telling her that these islands were a threat. Were linked in some way to the river becoming thicker, slimier. Harder to swim.

She clicked annoyance at the little islands, hearing her family click back. *Turn the islands over. Dump them in the water!*

She hung back, for her calf, along with the other nursemaids and new mothers. The young bulls and old cows charged forward, their tails lathering the water. The first of them reached the boats. There were thumps, and the sounds of the bad swimmers shouting into their hollow islands. What they could tell from the echoes in there was beyond the cow. She chased a young bull—a calf, really, of the age to think himself invulnerable and old enough to fight and to be wrong!—back away from the conflict, back among the babies. He scolded her in clicks; she spared a few choice comments for him.

An island overturned. Another. Bad swimmers kicked and thrashed, sending echoes crashing through the water. They made the dolphin cow's ears hurt when they shouted.

Then one of her folk squealed, a high-pitched noise of pain and injury. The water tasted of blood.

The water was too low, she understood. Her people could not get under the floating islands without exposing themselves. The bad swimmers had spears and tridents, that they used to spear fish. (They were bad fishers, also.) And they were spearing her family. Her family!

And something that had been lying quiescent on the bed of the river squirmed, sending pulses of shapes through the water. It was great and ponderous, alive. She understood that it had come upstream and buried itself in the muck, and now it was awakening.

*Get away*, Mrithuri told the river dolphin. *Take the calves. Take your family! Get away now!*

The dolphin turned to flee, driving the calves before her. Mrithuri found herself back in her own fatigue-trembling body so abruptly that she reeled, and if it had not been—again—for the Dead Man and Hnarisha, she would have gone to her knees.

She needed food. She needed her snakes.

She stepped to the battlement and looked down at the river, at the patches of red pumping forth to stain swaths of it like blood poured into cream. At the center of the river, alongside the boats, something bulged. Rose like a pillar of ivory. Dripped blood and weeds and river water back into the Mother River's troubled surface.

Her voice was a whisper. "I know what they were waiting for."

It was as blind as the dolphins, the head that rose from the turgid water. There was a place for eyes in the massive skull. Even the ridge of a brow bone over each eye socket. But a white lid sealed the bulge beneath, protecting the organ from the silt of the broad, slow, rich Sarathai. It could probably see light and darkness, like the dolphins.

Like the dolphins, it came from the river, and like the dolphins it had no need to see more.

The head kept coming, rising on a long snake neck, scaled and white and webbed in waterweeds. The face quivered with barbels, and long spiral-twisted horns like an oryx's swept back over the thing's neck. Another single horn, like that of a rhinoceros, hooked between nostrils that unsealed themselves on a long, hissing breath that Mrithuri could hear all the way from the top of the wall.

"Great," the Dead Man muttered behind his veil. "Another fucking dragon."

"Sarathai naga," Ata Akhimah breathed in Mrithuri's ear. "The Mother Wyrm. I had no idea it was real." She turned to the Dead Man. "Technically speaking, it's not a dragon—"

He raised a hand to quell her. "I know. I know. Technically, they never are. How big does it get?"

"Not big enough to crawl over the battlements, I hope," Tsering-la said, watching more loops of the thing slither themselves out of the water. It seemed to have very little regard for the men in the boats, who were now rowing away from it as fervidly as they had been rowing toward the river gate a minute before. "I guess that explains why they were doing something as stupid as rowing up to the city walls to attack us."

Hnarisha squinted under his hand. "You don't suppose that's an illusion, too?"

Syama growled an answer. Hnarisha turned to Nizhvashiti.

The Godmade was already raising a hand.

A flick, and the chime in its eye socket rolled forth, heartening and crystalline: a sound that seemed to hold clarity of vision and clarity of thought in its very heart. The sound went forth from the tower in a sort of wave, as if one were looking at the bottom of a perfectly clear pool while a ripple passed through the water.

It washed over the monster in the river.

The monster in the river remained.

The Mother Wyrm squirmed closer, scaled curves propelling it. Its blunt, blind nose sought from side to side, sensory tendrils stretching and quivering. The heavy body made a sucking sound as it reached the river's mud-thick verge. Its neck coiled back, ponderously, a series of heavy side-to-side curves like a questing snake. Mrithuri saw pink indentations lining the scales of its upper jaw margin, like the pits of a viper. She was unsurprised when a pallid, forked tongue flickered.

"The gates!" the Dead Man yelled suddenly, as if awakened from a trance. He whirled and leaned over the inside wall of the battlements. "Man the gates. *Brace the gates!*"

Below, men surged forward, unquestioning. The gates were barred with heavy bars; padded tree trunks had been lowered into place in massive shoes two-thirds of the way up, their bottom ends buried in the earth and braced with boulders. Now their strength was reinforced with the backs and shoulders of men.

The Mother Wyrm struck as a snake strikes, and slammed into the gates with a force that sent Mrithuri to her knees. The wall shook, dust rising from the seamless stone. Fingers bruised Mrithuri's arm, trying to steady her.

Below, men shouted. The bracing trees creaked ominously. Someone screamed in pain.

Sparks scraped from the copper sheathing on the doors. As the Wyrm's head drew back, Mrithuri could see that the horn on its nose and the lip beneath it were sheathed in some cold-colored metal: iron, or steel.

Hnarisha tugged at Mrithuri. "We need to get off the wall, my rajni!"

"Of course," she said. "But how?"

Another slam, and the gates rang like a great bronze bell. Mrithuri, clutching the interior battlement wall—the one not studded with dragonglass—saw the gates bulge for a moment, the slim gap between them. *Hold*, she prayed. *Mother, hold.*

Lady Golbahar was by her on the other side, pointing. "The birds are coming!"

Down on the river, the invading boats had withdrawn, and were waiting. Waiting for the Mother Wyrm to crush her way into the city, so they could follow. And above them—and from the landward side as well—the black, swarming cloud of carrion birds was swirling down on Sarathai-tia like a curved, clawing arm.

The wall shuddered and bucked under them again. Syama crouched, rocking with the blow. Under his breath, the Dead Man was praying. He had a pistol in his hand and with it tracked the motion of the Wyrm's head as she drew back, coiled again.

"Too far away," he said. "I'll have to wait until it strikes again. Get down the stairs! I'll be right behind you!"

Nizhvashiti stood statue-still, wind-ruffled, opaque of expression and gaze. Mrithuri wondered if it had gone away again. She turned away. The Godmade would take care of itself.

The stairs were stone, and built against the inside wall. A few steps away only, through a gap in the inner battlement. Hnarisha swung her around unceremoniously and hurried her along.

"Don't *yank* at me," she snapped. Her arm was bruises upon bruises.

Had she used to bruise so easily?

"Forgive me, my rajni." He stepped back, extended a more ceremonious hand.

She took it and stepped onto the stair.

The stair, at the first touch of her weight, fell out from under her.

Mrithuri teetered, one foot on the wall, one foot wavering over nothing. Screams and shouts of pain rose from below as the stones tumbled down on the soldiers bracing the gate. Hnarisha clutched her wrist in both hands and threw himself backward, trying to drag her away from the precipice.

The Dead Man's pistol spoke. The Wyrm struck again. The wall jumped so hard Mrithuri felt as if the sole of her shoe had been kicked. She was falling.

She barely started to shriek in surprise when the edge of the wall hit her across the midsection, knocking the wind out of her and ending her panicked cry in an ignominious gurgle. She lay across the stone, sliding slowly toward oblivion, without the strength to scrabble for a grip or kick herself upward. Hnarisha clutched at her. Syama, too, was there, teeth grating on metal as they gripped her arm, clawed feet scrabbling on the stone. Her muscles bulged; her hot breath washed Mrithuri's face. Her jaw was locked; she would be dragged off the wall herself before she would let Mrithuri fall.

Someone else was there also, grabbing her hair, pulling on her chain coat. It was so heavy. The armor was dragging her off the wall, and the armor was also slipping off her as her friends tried to rescue her.

Then, suddenly, she was lighter. She shot upward, falling on Hnarisha and the Dead Man as they heaved at her. Syama, nimbler, dodged out of the way. Beyond their heads, she could see Tsering-la, his face a squint of concentration, his left hand outstretched and pulling back as if he hauled a fishing net.

He dropped his hand and sat down hard on the stone, gasping. Mrithuri pushed herself to her feet, trying not to plant a hand or a knee in the soft parts of the men who had rescued her. By the wall, Lady Golbahar shouted "Brace!" and the monster struck again.

This time, they heard wood snapping.

They had no way down from the wall. Nizhvashiti alone still stood, impassive, windswept in a place with no wind. The rest of them were toppled like the pieces on a chaturanga board when the table is jostled. Mrithuri could feel where Syama's teeth had pressed the links of her chain mail into the padding she wore beneath, and into the flesh beyond.

Mrithuri grasped Yavashuri's ankle. The old woman had fallen, and lay facedown on the stone. She picked her head up when Mrithuri tugged at her, blood streaming across her face from a plainly broken nose. "Not dead," she announced. "Just feel like it."

"One of the braces failed," the Dead Man called. He'd rolled over and poked his head over the gap. "The men are still holding. The brace fell on some."

"Mother," Mrithuri sobbed. Her palms were scraped and bloody.

"They're bringing up the elephant," the Dead Man said.

"Hathi," Mrithuri said. "Oh, Mother, no."

She scrambled to the wall. There was her old friend, hastily outfitted in some scraps of the armor she had worn in her youth, when she carried a raja into battle, being led up to the gate through the courtyard behind. Hathi stepped gingerly among the injured and dying men while orderlies rushed to drag the ones who might live out of the way. She moved with a self-important dignity that Mrithuri recognized as humorous overacting, as if she thought herself once again the central figure in some pageantry.

*She's too old.* Helpless rage stung Mrithuri's eyes. *She cannot do this, and she cannot fight the Wyrm. Just let me surrender. Let me surrender and save who I can—*

Hathi placed her armored forehead against the city gates.

She *leaned.*

The birds were upon them. Pecking, clawing. Diving and fluttering, a beating of black wings. Mrithuri's own bearded vultures were too few to drive them away. Mobbed, blinded by buffeting pinions, they fled back to their austringers. Mrithuri threw her hands over her head, shielding her face with her forearms. Claws raked her nape. A sharp sting of pain creased her ear.

The Wyrm struck again.

The gate rang again. But this time it rang differently. More muted. Below, Hathi grunted, and Mrithuri heard the scrape of her feet on stone, the incongruous cheery jangle of her ankle bells.

"I'd bring this arch down to seal the gate if it weren't Wizard stone," Ata Akhimah said, pushing herself to her knees.

"Seal the gate," Tsering said. "Wait, it's wood."

"Under the metal."

"Wood was alive," he muttered.

He didn't get up, or even crawl to the edge, but he spoke aloud in some tongue Mrithuri did not understand and a butter-colored light began to gather around him. The birds pecked and clawed while he shielded his eyes and face with his hands. As they all did, between waving and battling. Mrithuri groped for one of her daggers.

Then the Dead Man was on his feet, standing over all of them, his sword a whirl of silver. He spun it in overlapping spirals and whirls, and then—Ritu the acrobat was there beside him, with her son, and both of them had swords as well.

The swords, Mrithuri realized, that they used in the sword-dance.

They were not fighting. Just twisting the flashing blades in whirling patterns.

Whirling patterns that rained blood and severed bird parts down all over and around her. It was an improvement. Of a sorts. Syama fought too, lunging and snapping, dropping crushed birds, whipping blood-soaked slaver from her dewlaps as her jaws swung.

Another hammerblow struck the gate beneath them, and the three who were standing staggered and hopped, but kept their feet. Who knew there were so many uses for acrobats? Again, wood splintered. Hathi grunted in effort. Mrithuri heard the elephant's feet slide. Heard the jingle of her bells as she stepped forward once again. She glanced over the edge slick with bird-bits and saw that the gates were buckling, the crossbars splintering. The elephant could only do so much.

One more blow. Perhaps two. Then Hathi would be gone under the force of the battering Wyrm.

In a moment of silence, a massive slithering warned Mrithuri that the Wyrm was coiling again. "Tsering, whatever you are doing, do it now!"

He groaned like a man suffering an arrow pushed through his body and slapped both hands against the stone. The butter-colored light ran out of him, into the rock . . . and was gone. He fell over on his back and would have rung his skull on the stones if Golbahar hadn't been sitting there.

The Wyrm struck again, with a dull thud this time, as a dull axe thuds on a living tree it cannot bite into. The walls shook only a little. The gate held as firm as a mountainside.

"Mother," Nizhvashiti said suddenly, in a voice like that of a small girl. "It is time to break your chains."

SUDDENLY, MRITHURI FELT THE WIND.

Not the hot draft of a mad crow's passage, the whisk of black-feathered wings. The filth of the birds fouled everything—feces and blood and bits—and Mrithuri was too busy to gag. But this wind was fresh and sweet and held the scent of rain.

Nizhvashiti raised its hands.

The heaped thunderheads on the eastern horizon had seemed strangely flat in the distance, as if pressed against a wall of glass that stretched unimaginably high. Now those clouds were lit from within by a spark of lightning as huge as any that Mrithuri had seen. Though distant, it seemed to cover the entire horizon, orange-white and huge, flickering on for the space of many heartbeats as it cracked and cracked again, in utter silence except for the rising wind.

Whatever held the storm back collapsed utterly, and the clouds spilled across the sky with speed she could not have imagined. It was like watching water break a dam. In the next instant, it seemed, the storm was upon them—almost at the same moment that the distant thunder finally reached her ears.

The wind *howled*, sending the attacking birds whirling and tumbling away as if they had no more will or volition than a handful of black confetti. Around Mrithuri, the others ducked behind the battlements for cover, cowering against suddenly puddled stone to keep from being swept down the length of the wall. They were all as instantly and thoroughly wet as if they had been plunged into the river entire.

Except Nizhvashiti. Well, the Godmade was *wet*—rainwater streamed from sodden, flapping clothes and ran down the blank, bony face. But it was also immovable as a thing carved itself from stone.

Mrithuri shook the blood of carrion crows from her face. Wiping at it did nothing; her hands were covered, too. It mixed with the rain and ran slick and terrible down under her armor, into her eyes and nose. She snorted to clear her nostrils. "Tsering-la, what did you do?"

"Woke the gates up," Tsering-la gasped between wheezes. He draped a hand across his mouth and nose so he did not drown in the rain. "Convinced them to grow roots, heal themselves. Grow together. I wish I were not such a weak Wizard."

One more thud resounded, even more attenuated than the last. The wall barely trembled. Perhaps the Wyrm was tiring. Perhaps the gate-trees were too strong for it.

"I thought Rasan Wizards gave up their ability to create life," Ata Akhimah said, from where she sprawled on her back on the stone. She raised a scratched, battered arm and inspected the beads of bloodstained water that dripped from it.

They were surrounded by a rustling that they could hear even over the wind. Green branches rose around them, unfurling papery gold new leaves that shredded and blew away. The limbs bowered the battlement, making it like a road through a wood for this little way.

"Oh," Tsering-la said. "The wood was already alive. The Alchemical Emperor must have put it into stasis before it had a chance to die. It was still green and full of sap. That's why it held on so long against the Wyrm." He groaned. "I don't think you'll be able to use this river gate again, however. And we still need to get off this wall."

Hunched, the Dead Man moved toward Nizhvashiti. He shouted something into the teeth of the wind. It might have been "Godmade!" but Mrithuri could not be sure. The Godmade, however, did seem to hear him, and the howl of the wind lessened a little. Or perhaps that was the wavering, watery bubble of amber light that Tsering wove around them with hands that shook in exhaustion.

Mrithuri managed to stand up, feeling every scrape and ache in her body. Her side stabbed her each time she took a breath. She guessed her rib was cracked from the fall. Syama came to stand beside her, and Mrithuri leaned on the bear-dog's broad shoulder. "Can you end the storm?"

Nizhvashiti shook its head. "It is the Mother's storm. But look, the boats are foundering."

The Dead Man looked over the edge. "And the Wyrm has withdrawn. I expect it's still under the water, however. Nizhvashiti, I thought you said you didn't do weather control."

"I control nothing. I did find a way to break . . . Well, I suppose it was the sorcerer's . . . anathema. But removing a defilement is not the same as working your own."

"Come on," Ata Akhimah said, helping Tsering-la to his feet. The Dead Man offered Mrithuri his hand, then went to assist Lady Golbahar. Yavashuri and Hnarisha were somehow already standing. The trees—still growing—shielded them somewhat from the wind. Tsering-la's tattered spell also helped, but he was sagging against her.

"Right," Mrithuri said. She gave her husband's hand a small squeeze before releasing it again. Rain fell from her fingertips. She placed them on the battlement. It would guide her even if the falling water blinded her. She would feel her way with her toes. "Nizhvashiti, are you coming?"

"I will watch the rain," said the Godmade. "I'll be in in time."

Meticulously, Mrithuri led her people over the buckled stone. The Mother Wyrm's attack had cracked the seamless rock of the wall and walkway, but had not brought it down, though stairs and such constructed against the inside of the wall had fallen away. There was an internal stair farther along, that seemed intact. Mrithuri gropingly led her people toward it.

Going down into the hole of the well gave her the shudders. What if it collapsed while they were in there? Water was running down the steps like a brook tumbling down a waterfall. It went, she knew, into the cisterns; all part of the Alchemical Emperor's grand design. Arcane filters and purification rituals would remove any taint. One of the duties of the nuns in their cloisters was renewing the prayers and enchantments and maintaining the engineering that kept Sarathai-tia's water supply pure.

As her feet splashed through swirling black feathers and unsavory fluids, she was grateful indeed.

Hathi and guardsmen awaited them at the bottom, where the stairs debouched onto a grating that let the water fall through. Mrithuri strode up to the elephant, the skirts of her armor coat swinging, forgetting any pretense of walking with the grace and control befitting a rajni. Hathi's attendants had already removed the armor from her great face, and were trying to smear salve on her abrasions while the elephant joyously danced and splashed and jangled her bells in the rain.

She quieted as Mrithuri approached her, and lowered her trunk to inspect the rajni's bloody hair.

Mrithuri stepped into the curve of the trunk, which curled companionably around her waist. Reaching high, she touched the bruise on Hathi's forehead. "Thank you, Sister."

She would have said more, but a familiar and despised voice interrupted her. "My rajni?"

It was Mi Ren, of course, with a servant beside him holding a large umbrella over his head. Mi Ren was wearing wooden pattens over his embroidered silk slippers. Mi Ren wore a smug expression.

Despite the protection of a broad conical hat, the servant was getting drenched.

The only surprise was that Mi Ren had come out into the rain and the danger at all. He must have something even more than usually self-serving to say.

She heard the rustles and splashes of her people drawing up behind her. She stroked Hathi once again and stepped away from the elephant's embrace. Reluctantly, Hathi let her go.

Mi Ren gestured beyond the wall and said, "Holy shit, what was that thing?"

"Mother Wyrm," Mrithuri said tiredly. "Was that what you came out in the rain to ask me?"

His self-absorption was so profound that even the prospect of a river serpent that could probably have swallowed Hathi in two bites didn't cause him undue concern. "I can't show you here," he said. "The rain. Come inside, my rajni?"

She looked around. The dome of protective light failed just then, and Tsering slumped into the arms of those nearest him. The rain, falling on her unprotected head, had grown very cold. "Inside," she agreed. "By a fire. And someone summon Chaeri."

Mi Ren, falling into step beside her, was significantly taller on his pattens. They limited the length of his stride so he had to take small quick steps to keep up with her. It gave her a little petty joy that she knew she should not revel in, lest it affect her character.

The servant managed to angle the umbrella so that she was mostly shielded from the rain as well.

"That last might not be wise, my rajni."

Mrithuri turned on him. "More allegations?" Her voice was as cold as the rain. Very satisfyingly, lightning cracked overhead, the stroke so close that the thunder struck the soles of her feet and half-deafened her.

"Proof," he said.

She waved him silent and resumed walking. The puddles really did splash satisfyingly. It was also satisfying that Mi Ren panted and wobbled a little as they mounted the long, tree-lined stair. Behind them, Mrithuri's people climbed in silence. Syama walked alongside. The rain, in matting her fur to her body, revealed several long scratches from the talons or beaks of the carrion birds.

Servants met them with dry robes and hot tea in the atrium. Mrithuri shed her armor where she stood, stripping with the calculated appearance of unselfconsciousness. It rang where she dropped it on the tiles, and the padding followed. The robe, thank the Mother, was warm. Her people were cared for, too, and someone kindly led Tsering-la away.

"Come," she said, when her hair had been wrapped in a towel. Mi Ren stepped out of his pattens and started to follow. The drenched and miserable servant stepped forward. Mrithuri stopped him with a palm. "Go get dried off," she said. "I'm not having you dripping all over my drawing room."

Mrithuri settled into a chair and snuggled her robe around her. She was so cold her teeth chattered against the lip of her teacup. Her thoughts were fuzzing with exhaustion. Where was Chaeri? Where were her serpents?

Syama, her brindled fur spiky from being toweled dry, lay across Mrithuri's feet. Mrithuri gestured her followers into chairs, and drank more tea. The sugar and heat helped a little. Someone refilled her cup. She looked at Mi Ren.

"You were eager to show me something."

"I found these in your lady Chaeri's possessions." He extended a cloth roll, such as might hold a woman's earrings, or the tools for letter writing.

"Her possessions?"

"Her trunk," he admitted.

"You went *into my apartments?*"

"I had to!" he protested. "For your sake, my rajni! And technically speaking, I sent one of my servants. So if there is some ritual price to be paid, he must pay it, not I."

But the hand that still held the small bright soft cylinder trembled as if what was within was very heavy.

Mrithuri put her hand out. The Dead Man stepped between her and Mi Ren. He had not changed his clothing, merely shed his sodden coat and belted his weapons into place over his shirt and trousers. The muslin shirt was mostly transparent with rain. The trousers and veil were just as wet but had fared a little better.

He took the cloth roll from Mi Ren's hand, inspected it carefully, and only when satisfied of its safety did he pass it to Mrithuri.

She accepted the thing and weighed it across her palm.

"You could have planted this there," she said.

Mi Ren laughed in exasperation. "Ask your nuns if I planted it. They spy on everyone."

"My rajni," said Lady Golbahar softly, "would you care for me to open it?"

"No," Mrithuri said. "I can face anything."

She unrolled it, feeling small objects—jewels?—within clicking on one another. There was a rustle, like paper. And a lot of something . . . round and hard and tiny, like pearls of barley.

It was pearls of barley, in a little sack. "Akhimah," she said. "If this is magic—"

Her Wizard squinted at the thing in her hand. "I would say most definitely. What else is in there?"

"A key." Mrithuri placed it on the table beside her tea. It clicked. It was bronze and elaborate, and looked like any of the palace keys. "Do you know what it opens?"

"The dead ambassador's chamber," Mi Ren said. "I had my servant try it in the door."

"Your servants are very capable," Mrithuri drawled. She reached into the packet again. Slips of paper, this time. Very small, tightly rolled. Such as you might slip into a capsule and place on the leg of a carrier bird. Such as a homing dove. Or a bearded vulture, if you were Mrithuri.

Such as the capsules of carved coral-colored sapphire Mrithuri also shook from the recesses of the roll.

She stared at them on her palm. They were beautiful. They caught the light in their depths and turned it into flamelike shimmers. She could see the tiny seam, the cunning join. The cavity at their center. They rattled softly against one another in the hollow of her hand.

"Fuck me sideways with Her pen," the Dead Man groaned. "She's been feeding the songbirds in the garden."

"And passing messages to Anuraja's sorcerer," Lady Golbahar said, pressing a palm against her cheek through her damp veil as if to contain the heat of a blush. She stood and turned toward the door. "Where is she now?"

"I sent for her," Mrithuri said. "Some time ago."

She put a hand on her own face. The heat of her skin was almost painful. Was she fevered? Wouldn't that be a nice twist, if she caught her death in the rain?

Anuraja would be so disappointed. She choked on a giggle, swallowing it when everyone in the room turned to gaze at her in worried curiosity.

"Damn it," she said, breathing shallowly because of the pain in her side. "Fine, Dead Man. Summon the guard out. Ata Akhimah, go with him, in case there is more sorcery afoot. Arrest Chaeri. And secure the Eremite serpents. She is not to have access to any of my familiars again. The rest of you—" She waved weakly. "You stay, Golbahar. Hnarisha, you too. Yavashuri, get that knee looked at. It's getting bigger than the rest of you."

They stared at her a moment longer. She sighed. "Will you make me raise my voice?"

They scattered, leaving her alone with Hnarisha and Golbahar and that one self-effacing footman who kept pouring tea. And Syama, of course. Always loyal Syama, stretched across her feet and warming her.

"Hnarisha." She set the evidence on the table too, and levered herself to her feet like an old woman, using the arms of the chair. She stripped her robe open. "Help me."

He slopped tea over his hand, and she didn't think it was from the sight of her breasts, which were bare swellings over the corrugated architecture of her rib cage. There was a larger swelling below them, on her left side, already blossoming into virulent purple and black.

"Rajni," he sighed, and placed his hand upon her skin.

The touch, so gentle, hurt. But not as much as breathing, and a coolness seemed to radiate from his fingertips, permeating her flesh, calming the bruised ache and the stabbing pain beneath it. It seemed also to ease her craving for the snakebite, allowing her to remind herself that that, at least, she would have soon. To distract herself, Mrithuri turned to Golbahar and said, "She seems to think that everyone else vanishes the instant we are not in the room with her. As if she were the director, and we were actors—no, not even actors. Characters in a play. And when we walk off stage, we cease to exist."

Golbahar sighed. "There is an epidemic of such people in the world, my rajni. Those who act as if only they are real and have sensibilities, and no one else can think, or compare experiences. They do not even bother to lie well. What is more surprising is how many of them seem to get away with it, and for how long."

Mrithuri sucked her lower lip. "I am justly rebuked."

Golbahar turned it aside with her hand.

"I trusted her," said Mrithuri.

Hnarisha pressed deeper, ducked his head, did not speak. She drew a breath at the pain.

"You needed her," Golbahar replied. "For who else around you seemed cracked enough themselves for you to be fragile with? You are fortunate not to have encountered many such people."

"Well, we have enough of them now." Mrithuri drew a patterned cashmere shawl off the back of the chair and tossed it around her shoulders, shivering despite the unrelieved heat. The motion made her wince, and Hnarisha grumbled. "Once we have her in custody, maybe we should encourage her and Mi Ren to get to know each other, thereby making two people unhappy in the place of four."

There was a silence. Hnarisha stepped back. "That is what I can do," he said, flexing his fingers as if a chill had gotten into them. "I do not think the rib is more than cracked. But mending even a cracked bone is beyond my poor skills."

Mrithuri stretched. The bruising was better. Not healed entirely, but better. The rib still stabbed.

Golbahar, undiverted, said, "You will not execute her, then?"

Mrithuri sighed. "I must, mustn't I? Never mind, Golbahar. Don't speak. I don't want to be angry with you for saying what we both know is true."

# 20

Sayeh and her ladies sat in their pavilion in the morning. The sides had been raised to let the breeze blow through—what there was of it. Sayeh drowsed in the heat, watching the daily activity of the camp wind down.

Ümmühan had gotten a little stool somewhere, and she dragged it now under the tent edge raised as an awning and strummed and sang. When she crouched with her zither upon it, wrapped in her swirls of caramel- and citrus-colored fabric, she resembled a little nougat confection more than a woman.

The songs she sang were as sweet, as honeyed. But a thread of sharpness ran through them—longing, loss. A deep grief that rang at some times, and whispered at others.

She drew an audience, a little crowd. Some of them were camp followers: women who plied a trade among the soldiers, those who cooked and sold their food from little carts near the periphery of the camp. Some were the teamsters and quartermasters and runners and scouts who came and went at all hours. Some were the men who were recovering from injuries, or whose duties were currently here, behind the lines.

This happened more mornings than not, now, and Sayeh thought it was taking on the trappings of a small community ritual. As most nights wore out and people began to seek their ease before resting, she would see men and women passing, loitering. Strolling by with elaborate casualness. Not staring into Sayeh's pavilion, and not approaching or putting pressure on her or on Ümmühan. But just waiting to see if there would be music, or waiting for the music to begin.

Which was excellent, and suited her intent to forge a small community of her own within the larger community of Anuraja's army. In addition, Sayeh still had her salons, and she had the men who looked to her as an intermediary. As somebody who could get clean water, or bandages, or decent food.

You made a pet of a man the same way you made a pet of any animal: by teaching them to trust you, to rely on you, and to see you as a source of comfort, affection, and ease.

If there was one thing the Alchemical Emperor's granddaughters and great-granddaughters and great-great granddaughters excelled at, it was making pets of animals.

Her new friends came and gossiped in her presence, which was also useful. This was how she learned that the Tian Wizards had done something to seal the gates and that the Tians were rumored to have a revenant among their defenders.

She chalked that up to a bit of legendry.

When the sun rose fully, hot behind its cauls and darkening the sky, the music ended. Ümmühan waved to her admirers and handed her zither to Nazia, who had crouched beside her and was watching what she did with her hands. *Get the girl zither lessons,* Sayeh told herself.

Well, here was Ümmühan, and it wasn't like they lacked for time.

The ladies came inside, and slowly the guards lowered the tent flaps. Sayeh heard voices and footsteps as the crowd outside slowly broke up and wandered away.

It was close inside the pavilion without the walls raised, but Sayeh could not show pain in public, and she liked to dine in what little privacy they were permitted.

Sayeh's leg was not healed, but it was better. Well, *better*. The bone was knitting. The muscle had withered away to nearly nothing, though that was to be expected. At last she had the slender thigh of a girl—

She laughed, contemplating it. Well, one of them, anyway.

Moving about the camp on crutches had made her arms and back stronger. Her arms were sleek with muscle as they had not been since she was a girl. She and her ladies dined, and then they busied themselves with small tasks. Sayeh looked to some mending. She had grown up doing fancywork and this was a light plying of a needle by comparison, but the soldiers were happy to have their socks darned by a rajni and—again—it made her friends.

So she happened to be sitting upright in a chair, with her broken leg propped against a footstool, when the guards came back in.

Nazia jumped to her feet. Ümmühan rose more slowly, setting aside a pen.

"The raja wants you, Rajni," Pren said. "Just you," he clarified, when she waved Nazia over.

Sayeh saw the tautness on the man's face and wondered whether Anuraja had found out about her slow and careful attempts to cultivate his people. But she had not *done* anything. She had not taken any actions. She had not asked for any favors. All she had been doing was entertaining others. And perhaps . . . collecting friends.

Could that be enough for Anuraja to grow angry with her? Or was there something else? Something she did not know, and so could not prepare for?

"My ladies must help me into my chair," she said reasonably.

"He said you could come on your crutches, Your Abundance," said Najal. "You should hurry. I have seen him this impatient before."

Of course they had. And wasn't that the tactic of a tyrant? To throw one off-balance, keep one on the back foot. Stage an outlandish fury over nothing at all . . .

If it *was* nothing at all.

"Then my ladies," Sayeh said, with all the regal calmness she could muster, "must help me to stand."

She set her sewing aside and extended her hands. In a moment, Ümmühan was on one side of her, Nazia on the other. They swung her between them to her feet.

Nazia steadied her and Ümmühan fetched the crutches. Then the guard was holding the flap aside for her, and they were out of convincing delays.

Sayeh's walk across the dark, dusty camp had the quality of a bad dream. Eyes skated off her. She hitched gamely along—she was getting pretty good at it—and did not ask questions. She felt that if Pren and Najal knew, they would have told her already.

Assuming they were allowed to.

They led her to Anuraja's familiar pavilion and—unsmiling—held the flap aside.

She went in.

It was dim inside, and cooler than she could have expected. The space was lit by witchlights, leading Sayeh to wonder if it was cooled, as well, by a spell. She wished Tsering-la were here, so she could ask him.

She should not think of Tsering-la. It made her sad.

The past was beyond her. She had to live through the day, and the next. And continue building power.

And get back to her son.

Something tripped her in the darkness. She staggered hard, struggling with her crutches. She could not save herself, and fell.

The little scream that came out of her was cut short in a grunt as she struck the carpet and fur-covered floor. At least it was a soft surface to tumble onto. She struck her face, but did not think she had bloodied it. Her fingers ached sharply from being banged by the crutches. Her leg . . .

Praise the river, she did not think that she had rebroken it. But the pain that pulsed from her injured thigh was as bad as if she had been struck by a hammer. She could do nothing, for a moment, but whine through clenched teeth, prone and utterly motionless on the floor.

"Not too hurt to genuflect now, I see," Anuraja's voice said, out of the darkness.

The witchlamps flared. They were an odd coral color, and as they brightened and Sayeh managed to lift her chin, she saw that the glow glittered through the facets in cut gemstones. Was it Anuraja who had tripped her? She could not imagine him risking his own gouty feet on such an escapade. . . .

No, it was Ravani. The sorcerer leaned against one of the pavilion posts, a spear balanced in her hand. The point was raised and the butt extended toward Sayeh. As Sayeh watched, Ravani drew the butt slowly, insolently across the rugs toward herself.

"You needn't have bothered," Sayeh said around the pain of her clenching diaphragm. "In the dark, I would have fallen over one of these furs or cushions momentarily."

Ravani smirked. "We could have been friends," she said. "You're clever."

*Too clever by half,* Sayeh thought. *But I'm glad I never made any promises to you.*

She pushed herself up on her elbows. Got her good knee under her. Swung the bad leg to the side and then forward, very indelicately. Groped for her crutches, found only one of them, and gently knelt back.

Now she could see Anuraja. She clutched her prop, but remained kneeling. She could probably get up. She wasn't certain she wanted to give away that ability. And her leg did hurt abominably.

"Your Competence," she said. "I did not mean to displease you."

Anuraja rested on a rug-covered form that must be one of those boxy, uncomfortable coastal chairs. She would pad it too, if she was forced to sit in it for long. He had his own bad foot propped up, and the bandages were off his ankle.

The unhealing wound on his leg had a festering smell.

He snarled, "Did you know he had plans for the brat, and did you not tell me?"

"Excuse me?" Sayeh said incredulously.

She thought Anuraja might lunge to his feet, unbandaged abscess and all, and come at her. But she honestly did not know what he was talking about. Perhaps he read that in her pain-muzzed expression, or perhaps he was just enjoying the tears that broke over her lashes and streaked down her unpainted face. She was in the next best thing to pajamas, and she suspected that did not look prepossessing at all.

She didn't bother to straighten herself or wipe her face.

She'd skinned her knee. She could feel it bleeding into the carpets.

Serve him right if the wool rotted.

Anuraja stroked his beard between forefinger and thumb. "You heard me."

"My raja," she said. The words felt slick and greasy in her mouth. "What brat? Who is this 'he' you speak of?"

Even as she said it, she had a sickening sensation that she knew. In part, at least. There was only one child she could think of. One child who was the only thing she could think of. And she knew who had had him last.

And it was true, she had not told Anuraja everything.

She drew a breath as Anuraja continued to watch her curiously. "Prince Drupada?" she asked. "Oh, tell me, my lord, that you have found my son!"

She thought he eased a little, though she was not certain. He said, "Himadra. I am speaking of Himadra. And your son. Who was not *stolen* by Himadra, but *given* to Himadra, I have to suppose?"

*He is angry because Drupada is alive, and Himadra has him. He is angry because my heir is not dead. But I told him that Himadra*— "Why would you suppose that, my lord?"

"Because," he said coldly, "Himadra has declared himself Lord Protector of Ansh-Sahal."

Sayeh gaped. There could be no other word for it. Her mouth unhinged; her eyes bulged. She clapped the hand that was not clutching her crutch across her face.

"Lord Protector," she finally said, her words a voiceless squeak. "Of Ansh-Sahal."

"And Prince Drupada," Ravani agreed, a little greasily. The sorcerer's gaze seemed to linger on her distress even more avidly than did Anuraja's. Sayeh heard Ümmühan's voice in her head: *There are beasts that feed on war.*

"But I am Drupada's protector. I am his regent." A simple statement of fact, and it fell so flatly from her own lips that she could tell it meant nothing anymore.

"Not"—Ravani glanced at her master—"anymore."

"Well, if you *really* didn't give the boy to Himadra, then Himadra must think you dead," Anuraja said, with jollity. "Do you suppose he's told your son to mourn? Oh, here, Ravani. Help the lady up. She must be in much discomfort squatting on the floor in such a manner. Fetch her her crutches, there's a good girl. . . ."

Sayeh found herself stood up, dusted off, and sat back down again on a tuffet before she could really orient herself. They brought her a smaller tuffet for her bad leg to rest on. Her crutches were laid at her side, just a little too far away to reach conveniently. Another game; another small humiliation. Another reminder that she was dependent on him.

She had been gently raised, and lucky in her marriage. She knew, however, women who had not been. The motives behind his actions were no mystery to her.

She pushed her unbound hair from her face. "My lord," she said in all sincerity, "I did not know that Himadra had declared himself my son's guardian."

She had, it was true, known a few other things. But this statement was not a lie, and she made it boldly. There was room in the cracks of the truth.

The ache in her leg told her that Anuraja was someone she needed to get away from. She pressed her lips together to keep from trying to lick the dryness from them with an equally dry tongue. Anuraja's reversals were intended to disorient. It was a tactic of war. A tactic for breaking animals if you did not much care about the nature of the partnership that resulted, but only wanted cringing, fear, and obedience. First violence, unprovoked and incomprehensibly sudden. Then kindness salted with cruelty. There would be violence again, soon, she was sure. And after that some small gift, a present intended to soften her feelings, some lavish show of admiration and solidarity. A pretense of allegiance. Something to combine with the fear of being hurt again to erode her will, make her slavish.

Make her his thing.

All the poisoned pretend kindness of before had only been an act leading up to this. This was his move. He wanted to make her his thing.

She knew it could work. She even knew it could work on her, though she wanted to deny that weakness in herself. But she was a rajni of four decades' experience. She was a woman who had seen how men could treat the people they claimed to cherish. And not just men: there were women who bound their children to them in just such ways.

She knew the truth: under the right kind of torture, everyone breaks.

She wondered if any of his wives had loved him before he had them killed, with the sick love of something owned. She was certain, watching his face, watching him—already—regard her as if she were a possession, that he took joy in his petty cruelties, in the exercise of power.

And she was equally certain, watching Ravani's face as Ravani looked at her supposed lord and master, that the sorcerer thrived on the pain that Anuraja caused. That Ravani feasted on it, as surely as a sin-eater feasted on the guilt of unrestored crimes.

"My lord," she said, as if impulsively. "Send me to our cousin Mrithuri. I will plead for you."

He had been about to speak, but he stopped with his mouth open, one finger lordly in the air. Sayeh noticed that he had tea and cakes beside him, though she had been offered none this time. He covered his hesitation by reaching for the tray, lifting a morsel, and popping it into his mouth.

"Is that all it takes to change a rajni's mind?" Ravani said, while Anuraja was—meditatively—chewing.

Sayeh turned to the lounging sorcerer slowly, using the drama of moving her hair across her shoulder as an excuse to take her time. Having formulated her words, she simpered, "His Competence had not shown himself to be so . . . masterful . . . before."

Anuraja, having dispensed with the sweet, reached for a date. He toyed with it. It was a little withered, the flesh beginning to spot, and Sayeh in her heart was rudely glad that he was afflicted by what must seem to him a great hardship.

"And women crave masters, is that so?"

She wished real hardship on him, and fervently. "Women do like strength," she allowed. She glanced at him under her sadly unglossed lashes. "And this Mrithuri is but a girl, is it not so? Surely she must be frightened in her youth and inexperience. Surely she can be swayed to consider"—she exhaled—"such a protector."

Ravani rolled her eyes amusedly. But Anuraja was leaning forward, elbows on his knees, obviously enchanted. Sayeh blinked: was that really all it took to charm the man? A few honeyed words, a little overblown and overspoken flattery? And that little tense twitch of Ravani's mouth. Was the sorcerer afraid that Sayeh had uncovered the key to her power over the raja?

He was weak, Sayeh thought. When she had met the last emperor, he had called her daughter, though the true relationship was far more distant than that. His empire had already crumbled. He had been dying. And she had been a very little girl, but he had laid his hand upon the not-yet-crimsoned part of her hair and praised her courage, and told her then that she would need all her will and all her wiles to live as she would. But that she should not let that stop her, as he had not let it stop him.

Anuraja was older than Sayeh. He claimed he had been introduced to their illustrious relative as well. She had a thought, then. A thought that at first cruelly pleased her.

She wondered if the last emperor had not been . . . too impressed with this particular nephew.

Sayeh leaned forward, forcing her expression to remain serene. She was not bad at men, it so happened. And the category of men to which she judged Anuraja to belong did not like to think of women as human people, with physical and emotional needs. They liked to think of women as conveniences, pieces of temporary art, nuisances. To betray emotion, to rage or spit, was irrational and incomprehensible; to be bland and smooth-faced was deceptive, shallow, cold.

There really was no winning such a person over, except in using their prejudices against them.

And such men, being shallow themselves, did like to be flattered.

She felt a veritable click within herself as of gears engaging, as of some telescoping mechanism locking itself into place, erect as a spine. She felt . . . as if she fell into herself, after a long time of not knowing who she was or who she had been.

"I believe Mrithuri can be induced to give you what you want," Sayeh said. "But you must offer her an honorable excuse to do so. A rajni has her pride. She likes to feel she is making her own decisions, and if they are hard decisions, she wishes to feel she is making them for reasons of duty and honor. For the best future for her people. After all, a rajni is the Mother in her person, and her people are her children."

"Women can be broken of pride," Anuraja said, with such self-satisfied pomp that Sayeh would have broken his nose with her crutch if she could have reached it or him. Fortunately—fortunately?—she was constrained by her infirmity for long enough that her legendary self-control reasserted itself. Her hands shook as she carefully folded them and laid them demurely in her lap again. "Do you think you can manage that? Or should I rid myself of the burden of you once and for all?"

*I will strangle you with these little hands someday*, she promised. *Just let me stay alive long enough and gain power enough to do so.*

"Do not anger yourself too much, my lord," Ravani soothed. "Soon, very soon, you will mount the golden stair to the Peacock Throne. And this woman is a path to that."

"Hmph," he said, and settled back in his chair.

Ravani turned her face away from Anuraja and smirked at Sayeh.

Sayeh wondered if the sorcerer could read thoughts after all, or if *murder* was just what any woman would be thinking at this time.

"I think we can offer you some advantages," Anuraja mused.

"Advantages?"

"If we decide to accept your kind offer, you will see."

Anyone could be broken. Anyone could be crushed and abused into a shell of their former self. Sayeh herself could be, she knew. But in that moment, she also knew that she had gained another goal: not just to survive, to be reunited with and protect her son. To protect such of her people as she could find and reclaim.

She wanted to *beat* Anuraja. She wanted to see the moment when he realized she had beaten him. She wanted to relish that moment of defeat.

So maybe she and he were not so different after all.

"It is as you say," Sayeh said. "Women will do what they must. Let me go to her, my lord. I am pleading with you."

RAVANI CAME IN WHILE SAYEH WAS PACKING, AND BROUGHT THE chaturanga board.

Sayeh remained surprised, quite frankly, by how much she had to pack. Hadn't she arrived here with nothing but ragged clothes on her back? And now she had a trunk full. Where had it even all come from?

Dresses bartered or given, of course. And not all of them were hers; there were also clothes belonging to Nazia and Ümmühan, who had their own admirers and friends. It was an inadequate trousseau with which to embark on a diplomatic mission. But then, this was war.

"Are you busy?" Without being invited, the sorcerer dropped onto a tuffet just out of arm's reach. Whatever the answer was, she rocked it back onto two legs and was deploying the pieces of her game.

"I'm packing," Sayeh said.

Ravani's dubious gesture took in her hands, folded in her lap, and her raised leg propped on its little stool. It extended to Ümmühan and Nazia bustling about.

"Someone has to supervise," Sayeh replied primly.

"Oh, certainly," Ravani answered. Her sideways glance seemed to imply that supervision was especially necessary when one was confronted with such *impossible* servants as Ümmühan and Nazia. "Black or white?"

Sayeh imagined Nazia's eyeroll with stunning detail, even though the girl wisely had her back to them and was pretending not to be able to overhear.

"Black." Sayeh sipped her cooling tea, and set the cup back on the little tray beside her. "Are you here to insult me again, or just my ladies this time?"

Ravani tossed her head to move her heavy braid behind her. "You know that was just for display, Sayeh. My profoundest apologies. That was just the instructions of the raja. He wanted to see you humiliated and off-balance. He thought he might get a straighter answer out of you."

"Sure," Sayeh said. "That seems likely."

It did, though. At least a little.

"Are you sure you want to move that?"

"I touched it."

They played in silence for a while while Sayeh's ladies moved around the pavilion. Sayeh thought she was holding her own for a change until Ravani took the black rajni with a quick diagonal move.

Sayeh began to lose.

She had not been accustomed to losing, before she began to play Ravani. But now her raja was pinned between an elephant and an infantryman, and she could not move without moving it into check.

She tipped the piece over with ill grace.

"I brought you something as a sort of apology." Ravani leaned far forward to set a small casket on the tea tray beside the game. It clicked as if it were heavier than it looked. Her braid fell forward over her shoulder again. "Surely you know what it is like to serve a master you despise."

Sayeh eyed it. Ravani had been wise not to try to place it into her hand.

"Are you going to pour yourself tea next?"

Ravani smiled. "Thank you for the offer."

Sayeh was certain they were both well aware that it had not been. Was Ravani seeing how far Sayeh would risk going to stand up to her?

Ravani's hands fell back into her lap, and did not move. A little later, they did move, as she broke the stillness between them to wave dismissively. "Besides, you need me to get you into the city."

"Didn't I hear from the guards that the Tian Wizard did some sort of sorcery on the city, to seal us out?"

"The Tian Wizard." That seemed to amuse Ravani, for some reason. "Yes, you have developed quite the spy network here. Well done, Rajni."

"So how are you going to get me in?"

Ravani shrugged. "Magic, of course. Your luggage might be a bigger problem."

"I will, at the very least, need some clothes."

"With a figure like that? . . . Oh, all right."

Sayeh had to restrain herself from shaking her head. "And my ladies."

"Of course," Ravani said, with a second glance over at them. They had finished the packing—only one trunk: truly there was not much. Even if "not much" turned out to be a surprising amount. "I am trying to make myself useful to you, you know. You are going to need me. Especially once you're inside."

"Oh, yes. Anuraja's agents within."

Ravani tipped her head.

Sayeh snorted, and decided to try a little vulnerability. She wished she understood better what Ravani was driving after in their conversations. They seemed so . . . meandering. Surely the woman couldn't just be looking for a friend?

Ravani did not seem like the sort of person who had *friends*.

Sayeh said, "I do better with people when I don't let myself need anything from them. Once I need something, my emotions—my desire for attention or validation—become distracting, and it makes me sad."

Perhaps it wasn't wise, sharing her vulnerabilities so. But the best way she knew to lie convincingly was and had always been to put as much truth in it as possible. And misdirection was a kind of lying. She did not want to seem too eager to go on this mission. Anuraja might be willing to believe her resistance had caved before his force of will.

Sayeh thought Ravani was cannier. And less enamored of her own supposed irresistibility. *She* might figure out that Sayeh had more of a plan—okay, a ridiculous, desperate gamble that could backfire to destroy everything she loved—than just getting away from Anuraja.

Ravani said, "And you need something from Anuraja."

The sorcerer did not, Sayeh noticed, often use her employer's honorifics, except when in his presence.

"I need his forbearance," Sayeh agreed. "Eventually, I need my son."

"Himadra has your son."

"Himadra is Anuraja's ally. And Himadra's kingdom is not much bigger or richer than was Ansh-Sahal. I don't see him ever becoming the dominant partner."

"You're probably right," Ravani agreed, too easily. "Himadra is quite the personality, though."

Sayeh almost asked about the other sorcerer. Almost. Caution stilled her tongue. She might have risked more, if she had not been leaving.

"I believe you," she said. "But personality rarely wins wars."

Ravani laughed. "You might be surprised." She stood, leaving Sayeh with a sense of envy at her strength and freedom of movement. *It will come back.* Already she was stronger. "I'll see you in a little while. Enjoy your gift."

Sayeh waited until Ravani was gone to lean forward, wrapping her arms around her uninjured knee and pulling her forehead down to her thighs. She rested her face against her own flesh, feeling the stretch of muscles. She did not weep.

"Rajni?" Nazia murmured, from beside her.

"God, I hate that woman. Hand me that box she left, wouldn't you?"

Nazia obeyed. Sayeh opened the little casket, which was ivory and intricately carved. Inside, tucked into the slit in a white velvet pillow, was a dainty ring. Gold, thick and yellow as butter. Tiny diamonds and emeralds, sparkling and trembling in the light. And at the center, one gorgeous coral sapphire, shimmering.

Sayeh stared at it, her breath caught despite herself.

She reached to touch it.

"Accepting a gift is a form of consent," Ümmühan reminded from the other side.

Sayeh startled. Dammit, who *had* taught these women to walk so softly? She looked at Ümmühan, and drew her reaching finger back. "You are very wise."

"I am a fool," the old woman answered. "That is why God made me a poet."

# 21

"I'd give a lot for a good desert hound right now," the Dead
Man muttered to Ata Akhimah and Yavashuri. The latter had inter-
preted Mrithuri's order to get her leg seen to by bullying Ata Akhimah
into winding a length of cloth around the swelling knee, and was limping about with the kind of taut non-expression that soldiers adopted to
hide their painful grimaces.

The three of them stood over the tossed disarray of Chaeri's trunk
and its contents. Either Mi Ren was not a subtle searcher, or Chaeri
had detected the intrusion, packed hastily, and fled. Possibly both.

"How well do they track in the rain?" Yavashuri reached out with a
long-handled crochet hook to select a fluttering chiffon veil from the
pile without touching it with her hand. *Of course* the old spymistress had
the means to crochet on her person somewhere.

*You're not that much younger than she,* the Dead Man mocked himself.

"Never had the occasion to learn," he admitted. "You have something similar in the kennels here?"

"Alas," Ata Akhimah said, "the best sense of smell in the palace belongs to the rajni's vultures, and I'm not sure even she could get them
to track something living with it." She extended a hand. "But I might
be able to do something with that. Wizardry is often of little use in
the moment . . . but perhaps this time."

Using the hook, Yavashuri laid the cloth across Akhimah's hand. The dye was exceptional; the color a rich and strong mauve, shading between steel blue and dusty purple depending on how the light fell on it. "I've never seen her wear that."

"It was a bequest from the late rajni, if I remember," the Wizard said. "Pity about that."

With her fingernails, she unpicked a thread. It seemed to come loose more easily than the Dead Man would have expected, and once it slithered free of the woven length, it rapidly spooled itself around Ata Akhimah's hand as the scarf unraveled. There was a lot of thread in a silk scarf, as it happened.

Ata Akhimah whispered something to the thread. It shimmered faintly blue-violet, though whether that was the Wizard's magic or the rainy light on the silk was anyone's guess. Then one end of the stuff lifted like a snake's head, and flicked forward. It kept going, unreeling itself as fast as it had reeled itself in. At a glance from Ata Akhimah, the Dead Man followed, Yavashuri limping in their wake.

As they hurried through the outer chamber of the rajni's apartment, the temporarily piebald Guang Bao lifted his head to croak at them grumpily. The Dead Man could not disagree.

The good news was that Chaeri could hardly have gotten out of the city. The bad news was that a city was a large dune in which to seek one grain of sand. And it was still pouring outside—harder now, in fact, than ever. As the thread darted toward the gardens, though, the Dead Man hoped they might be lucky. Perhaps she had not dared to try the palace gates and their guardians. Perhaps she had gone to ground somewhere within the walls.

They did not go alone to arrest the rajni's handmaiden. Between them, along the way, they commandeered Vidhya, half a dozen palace guardsmen, and Yavashuri's agent Druja, whom the Dead Man had first encountered in his role as a caravan master. That latter, they sent on to the gates to warn the guards against letting Chaeri escape—a thing they should all have thought to do first, but things *were* happening quickly. The other seven plus their three made ten, which was probably overkill.

It seemed worth going prepared.

✢    ✢    ✢

IT WAS A GOOD THING THE THREAD WAS SO LONG, BECAUSE IT UNSPOOLED faster than they could run, even with two guardsmen lifting Yavashuri by the elbows. They charged through the rainy gardens, scattering gravel. The Dead Man and Ata Akhimah were in the lead as they ran up a flight of wet stairs that wound through the terraces, slipping precariously. A figure stood on the heights, alone, wind-whipped, wound in a faint, thready blue-violet glow.

"Got her," Ata Akhimah said, leaning forward and digging in, haul-ing herself hand over hand up the thread as if it were a rope. The Dead Man drew his one still-primed pistol, having been too wet and too busy both to have reloaded the other. Something small, black, and heavily flapping swarmed just within the swirl of ashy clouds hanging so low overhead that he ran through some of their trailing streamers.

On the height overlooking the city, Chaeri turned to face them. She had climbed up atop the wall, and was balancing herself precari-ously among the shards of dragonglass. Her black-brown ringlets blew across her face; she could not restrain them. Ata Akhimah's thread had bound her arms tight to her sides. They were crossed over the fili-gree box that held Mrithuri's Eremite serpents, flesh pressed white against the corners. The Dead Man could hear the heavy bodies hissing and striking inside. Chaeri shook her head to get the rain and her hair out of her eyes.

"Surrender!" the Dead Man shouted.

"Oh, fuck you," the handmaiden said.

She hurled herself backward, suddenly and hard, over the precipice with a scream that started late and choked off abruptly. The thread link-ing her to Ata Akhimah snapped taut. The Wizard staggered forward, toward the wall studded with poisonous glass and toward the killing drop beyond it. Vidhya lunged and caught her by the waist, throwing them both to the flagstones with a doubled grunt as the air thumped out of them. They slid and stopped, so the Dead Man whirled back and raced to the parapet.

Chaeri dangled perhaps twice the length of his body below, pale-faced and gasping with the shock, blood washed down her arms from where the corners of the box had broken the skin open. She swung, directing a glare at the Dead Man that suggested she would have spat at him if she thought it would have reached. The thread lay across the dragonglass blades, unparted. Ata Akhimah's Wizardry was perhaps a little stronger than she claimed.

He leaned back and gestured the guardsmen up with the hand that did not hold his gun. "You have gloves? Good, haul her up. Careful of the glass."

Ata Akhimah and Vidhya had gotten themselves into a sort of crouch, and he was taking the strain of the thread off her hand, which was already swelling and purpling around the blue-violet spool. Her face was clenched like a fist, her breath a concentrated pattern of in and out and in again. When the guardsmen came and took the rest of the weight, she straightened and sighed slightly, stretching out her neck. She examined the hand, still wound in magical thread, and rolled her eyes and shook her head. "Well, that's a couple of broken bones."

"You held her," the Dead Man said.

Then the carrion birds fell out of the darkening sky.

Cawing, shitting, beating their wings like shaken metal and glaring about them with angry coral eyes, the birds descended. The louring clouds left them not far to dive, and they stooped in a column so thickly packed that the rain beneath them was less than the rain elsewhere. They trailed bright scraps of something from their beaks as they flew.

The Dead Man tossed his pistol into his off hand and, with a continuation of the same movement, drew his sword. He fell back, whirling, to protect Yavashuri.

The birds swept past him, close enough to touch with a bare hand. They swept past Ata Akhimah and all the other people on the parapet. They swarmed over the edge like a black cloth whipped from a table, and dropped beyond it as if they had all, at once, folded their wings. One did not make it that far but fell, sliding across the stones, a crochet hook protruding from its eye socket.

A moment later, the guardsmen who had been bearing up Chaeri's weight staggered backward. The birds flocked up, wings straining in eerie unison. The thumps as they struck the air sounded like bootheels, like soldiers drilled to march in step. A woman laughed, triumphant and a little hysterical. "Took you long enough!" Chaeri shouted, as the birds lifted her bound body on a sling of ribbons. They strained away from the parapet, but the violet thread still connected them to the men and the Wizard below. More birds dropped from the clouds, joining the team in strange harness.

More guards ran to help Vidhya and Ata Akhimah, who was struggling to get the ensorceled thread unwound from her injured hand. They slid on the wet flags, a step closer to the precipice and the dragonglass-studded wall. Ata Akhimah yanked at the thread and groaned.

The Dead Man raised his off hand, squinted through the rain running under his veil, and leveled his gun. The birds surged forward, gaining another arm-length.

He had one shot.

The guardsmen were at the wall. One turned his back, planted his boots against the bottom of the parapet, and braced his companions as they held onto the thread. Ata Akhimah seemed to have it loose now; it was unspooling bloodily from her hand, but it was dug in and she was having to pry it from the flesh. The rain beat at all their heads, pounded the cold flesh of the Dead Man's outstretched hand.

He looked past the muzzle of the gun—the gun Ata Akhimah had made for him. He looked past the rain and the black wings. He found his target, and he did not allow himself to feel her humanity, or her fragility, or the quirks and kindnesses and cruelties he had seen in her.

He looked past the sight. His finger flexed inside the trigger guard. The pistol slammed into the web of his palm.

The thread came loose from Ata Akhimah's hand, whipped through the gloves of the guardsmen, and vanished over the edge of the parapet as the birds bore Chaeri away into the rain. Staring after them, panting through the wet fabric plastered across his mouth and nose, the Dead Man lowered his smoking gun.

"Mother—" said Vidhya, in the tones of a curse. "Did you get her?"

"Fucked if I know," the Dead Man answered. "Akhimah, how bad is it?"

"I'll probably keep it," she said in strained tones. "If it doesn't get gangrene. And if it does I'll make Tsering-la handle the amputation. I won't be doing any scribing for a while, however."

The Dead Man stepped toward her. It didn't look good, but he'd seen worse. Hell, he'd suffered worse. "Hnarisha is probably still tending to the rajni—"

"Hello," a woman's voice called from the garden terrace below them. "I seem to have arrived at a bad time."

The Dead Man turned. Below him, two women stood and a third sat in the rain. One was the poetess Ümmühan, whose facsimile he had encountered before. Another was a girl with short hair and high cheekbones, accentuated by the hollows beneath. The third—

Sitting on what looked like a piece of luggage, her shoulder leaned louchely against one of the planters that had held marigolds before the rain failed, was a woman of middle years. She was clad richly in sodden drape and blouse. Her skin was a clear pale olive, her large eyes lighter than he would have expected. Her dark hair had been dressed and jeweled before the rain got to it. Her eyebrows were plucked into an elegant, expressive, mildly startled arch. Her face was bare of cosmetics, which—given the state of everything else on this parapet—was probably a wise choice.

There was something subtly unusual about her proportions, and there was a terrible scar low on the curve of her belly, just above where the pleats of her drape began. The Dead Man had just realized who this must be—the third-sexed queen, the famous beauty from the north—when Vidhya rushed past him, flew down the steps, and prostrated himself at her feet, whatever he tried to say strangled in a sob.

"Oh, get up, Vidhya," she said kindly. "After all that I'll not have you drowning in a puddle. Is it only raining on this side of the river?"

He could not seem to answer.

She reached down and stroked his hair. "I am glad to see you made it here safely. And Tsering-la and Guang Bao? The rest of my men?"

Vidhya pushed himself to his knees but didn't get much farther. "Alive," he managed. By speaking in gasps he managed the rest of his brief report. "Tsering-la and Guang Bao are here. In order to travel faster we left the rest of the men behind, to guard the refugees where they could."

"That was well-done," the foreign rajni said. "Oh, don't weep, Captain."

"I had heard you were . . . captive," he said. And silenced himself with a wave of his hand.

While he was pulling himself together, Yavashuri limped forward. "Greetings, Sayeh Rajni," she said, with a bow over her injured leg. "I am Yavashuri, my rajni's lady of the bedchamber. In her name, I greet you."

"And wonder how I got to be here, no doubt," Sayeh said, with a smile. "I will explain when we're inside. These are my attendants: Nazia, who is the apprentice of Tsering-la, and the poetess Ümmühan. I'm afraid we have come as emissaries of your enemy. No one is likely to be glad to see us for long."

The Dead Man and Ata Akhimah stepped forward. The Wizard said, "You're injured, Your Abundance."

"It's old." Sayeh, still leaning, sighed. "And somewhat healed. But I'd like to get out of this rain if I may. And . . . may I trouble you for a crutch?" She wiped the water from her eyes. "Also, is there . . . a reason why some of you are wearing bathrobes?"

MRITHURI HAD JUST TIME TO GARB HERSELF—QUITE PLAINLY, IN A SUIT comprised of a short belted jacket and loose trousers pegged at the ankles—and get Golbahar to comb out and braid her hair before the foreign rajni was shown in to see her. A drape would have shown the bandage over her ribs, and in any case she barely had the energy to stand, and her whole body shuddered with cold and the craving for her venom. She had wanted to rage when Ata Akhimah had come to tell her that Chaeri had escaped. She would have liked to hurl something. But her fingers did not want to grip, and the purpling wreck of Ata Akhimah's left hand seemed to throb in time with her own ribs, and she was too tired to get out of her chair. Too tired to walk into the throne room. Too tired to do anything except rest, slumped forward, with her elbows on her knees and her neck bent down in contravention of every convention of regal propriety.

She listened while Hnarisha sent for Tsering-la to be awakened, and listened with less than half her attention as Hnarisha clucked over Ata Akhimah's hand. He was going to exhaust himself as surely as Tsering had—but no, he said his healing strength was not his own, but a gift from an immanence. His Cho-tse religion.

*How can I do it without the venom? I haven't the strength. I haven't the intellect. I haven't the will.* Her naked fingers found and pressed the tiny scarred indentations on her arms and collarbone, as if she could somehow squeeze the drug she needed into her blood from these old wounds.

*I should surrender now, and save the lives of more of my people.*

Golbahar had effaced herself against the wall. Mrithuri wondered how haggard she must look that the vivacious young noblewoman was making a point of standing back and leaving her alone.

The scrape of feet in the corridor reached her in time for her to straighten her back and compose her face. She tried to arrange herself in a queenlike fashion on the chair, and for a moment felt self-conscious in her lack of pomp and plainness. Then she thought, *Would a raja stand on robes and cosmetics in extremis?* and shook herself, and made her expression grave and stern.

Vidhya and the Dead Man and Yavashuri preceded the rajni from the north into the room. Mrithuri gave Yavashuri a stern glance, and Yavashuri gestured to the wrap around her knee. Mrithuri's guardsmen bore Sayeh Rajni in on a litter, with two women walking behind her— one young and one old. They deployed stands and set her down across from Mrithuri, and a calculated handspan lower. She was swathed in toweling over her dripping-wet clothes.

"Forgive me, Sister," Sayeh said. "My leg is broken, or I would bow to you."

The women behind Sayeh were the poetess Ümmühan (the real one, this time, and not a counterfeit, Mrithuri presumed) and a young girl who Ata Akhimah had informed her was the apprentice of the Wizard Tsering.

"We are sisters," Mrithuri answered. A thousand pretty speeches flashed into her head. She shook it, and discarded every one. "You do not bow to me. We are equals."

Sayeh laughed bitterly. "I am a rajni without a state. And I am here to plead with you on behalf of your enemy."

"Our enemy," Mrithuri said. "Why?"

The older woman waved her hand. Her fingers were elegant, blunt-tipped, long. "I had to get away from him. And from his sorcerer."

"As simple as that?"

"As simple as that. He wishes to marry you. He offers freedom for your people, an end to war, an alliance. All you have to do is put him on the Peacock Throne."

"Such a trivial gift," Mrithuri said. "Is he as bad as they say?"

Sayeh shook her head and shuddered. "I told him that if he wished your compliance, he must give you a way to concede to him that would seem honorable to you."

"And did he agree?"

Sayeh sighed. "He listened. He did not offer any instruction. I believe I am encouraged to lie to you, Mrithuri Rajni."

"You are trusting me with a great deal, and very quickly. Without knowing me at all."

"Whom else have I to trust? I see my captain here with you, and you seem to have taken him in, and he does not seem to be under duress. I know him to be a man of honor; his service vouches for you. I have nothing. I have nowhere to turn. Lying to you gets me nothing. And I have heard my Wizard is here as well—"

Who, with his usual impeccable timing, chose that moment to bustle in, with the phoenix on his gloved hand. He looked exhausted, but at least he was dressed. Yavashuri and Akhimah, Mrithuri realized, had also procured clothes somewhere. And the Dead Man had on a dry veil and dry coat. One of the ones she had had made for him.

Sayeh turned to look at the Wizard and his burden. She smiled brilliantly at Tsering-la. "You look tired."

"War interferes with my sleep, my rajni."

"Where are your men?"

"I sent them north," he said. "To help the refugees."

She sighed in bright relief. A few less deaths to carry with her to the Mother.

Vidhya bowed low and offered her a gauntlet. Once she had accepted it, her familiar, Guang Bao, made a happy cluck and tucked his head under her chin, seeming not to care about the water still dripping from her.

"Oh, Guang Bao," she said. "What have they done to you?"

"His feathers were much damaged," Mrithuri said. "I had them imped with the molted feathers of my own. They are bearded vultures. I thought—" She shrugged. It hurt. "—he would prefer to be able to fly."

"That is tremendously kind," Sayeh whispered, with tears in her voice. She sniffed them back. "You look ridiculous, Guang Bao."

As if in answer, he preened her damp hair.

"It is well you sent the phoenix with your men," Mrithuri said to Sayeh. "We encountered your people once before, but they were only an illusion."

"What do you mean?"

Mrithuri explained about the assassin disguised as the poetess, and the illusory Vidhya and Tsering who had accompanied him. She did not mention that one of her people had been killed and another wounded. It seemed like more than her cousin could stand, because when Mrithuri told Sayeh about the padparadscha ring, and the veins converted to sapphire in the animate corpse, Sayeh pressed her hand against her mouth and turned quite green.

Tsering-la, seeming to intervene, turned to Mrithuri and said, "I'd like to examine my rajni's leg, if Your Abundance is willing."

*Too many rajnis in this room*, she thought, and nodded. "Hnarisha, if you would help him? And guardsmen, you may go. Send someone to bring fresh clothes for the rajni and her ladies. And Captain Vidhya. And send food and tea."

Vidhya smiled at her with a grateful duck of his head.

It did not take long for Tsering-la to render his verdict on Sayeh's injury. "You'll have a limp. Or we try breaking it again."

"Mmm. Not right now. Maybe after the war. My sister—" She turned to Mrithuri. "Would you believe me if I told you that I have come to believe it might not be a terrible thing for you to marry Anuraja, if you can find a way to put off bedding him until after he sits on the Peacock Throne?"

"If it comes down to it, I can fake my courses as well as any woman," Mrithuri admitted. The Dead Man looked shocked behind his veil. She stifled a laugh, and so did not manage to ask her next question before the conversation moved on.

"Rajni," said Lady Golbahar, who had not spoken.

Mrithuri was amused to note that both her head and Sayeh's snapped around.

"We have to hold out as long as possible and give the Gage a chance to get through and return. Have we a means at our disposal to delay negotiations with this Anuraja, while making him think that you would seriously consider his . . . offer?"

Mrithuri's head throbbed. Her skin itched as if with the bites of a thousand insects. "We can still hold out for a while. If the walls will hold back the Mother Wyrm—"

"Begging your pardon, Rajni," Tsering-la said, "but that is an 'if' as large as an elephant. We don't know what else he has in reserve. He, and his sorcerer."

"I feel so utterly helpless," she said. "If the river would just rise—"

She knew at once that she should not have said it. These people relied on her to be strong. To be flawless. Not to be weak and human and scared.

But there was Sayeh, looking at her with kind eyes, then putting a hand on Ümmühan's elbow to usher the old woman forward. "I believe my poetess has something to say to that."

Ümmühan chuckled. "How did you know?"

"I can see it in the way your mouth twists under the veil." Sayeh turned back to Mrithuri. "With permission?"

Mrithuri nodded.

"Helplessness, the state of accepting that one is a victim, is not learned, my rajni. It's *taught*. And the course of instruction is written in powerlessness, in kicks and blows. In dismissals. It is taught in the language of being unable to protect the things and people you value from violence. Of being unable to protect yourself from violence. It is written with the pen of denigration upon the paper of desperation. There is an older term for it."

Mrithuri raised her chin.

"They called it 'breaking the spirit,' Rajni."

"Oh, yes," said Mrithuri. "So they did."

"The agent who fled. She was a confidante."

Mrithuri, despite herself, nodded.

"She took with her things you needed. Perhaps what felt like a piece of yourself."

"You are not a poetess," Mrithuri said. "You are mind-reader."

"I cheat," Ümmühan said. "Poetry is the essence of cheating."

The Dead Man straightened the hem of his coat. Mrithuri realized that he was a little overawed to be in the presence of this straight-backed old woman. His voice was more quizzical than confrontational as he said, "Did not Ysmat of the Beads write that poetry is a means of speaking the truth?"

Golbahar stepped away from the wall to stand behind Mrithuri's chair. "Those things are not incompatible, you realize. Especially when a woman uses poetry to speak truth when the truth would go unheard if spoken plain."

Ümmühan laughed. Her laugh was youthful. It made her seem to glow. "A poem is a fact / with an angled blade."

*How does she do that?*

The door cracked open and a small face peered in. A page girl, who caught Yavashuri's eye with an urgency that sent the old woman limping rapidly out into the corridor. She was gone only a few instants, which those left in the reception room filled with tense silence. When she came back in, she shut the door firmly behind her and stood with her back against it. "My rajni," she said to Mrithuri. Her voice shook.

It was the most terrifying thing that Mrithuri had ever heard. She could not find her own voice. She held her breath and nodded.

"Perhaps best in private?"

"Oh, by the Mother. Just tell us now!"

She had surged to her feet, she realized when those around her fell back.

Yavashuri swallowed. "The water in the cisterns is fouled."

Mrithuri felt her fingertips dig into her arms. Some time passed. She was not sure how much did. She took a breath, because she felt faint and realized that she had not been breathing at all. "Our water is fouled."

"Yes, my rajni."

"All of our water."

Yavashuri shook her head. "What's in barrels in the kitchens and other reserves is fine. Pitchers. There are barrels in households in the city, and some of them might have cisterns as well."

"How did this *happen?*" Mrithuri demanded.

Ata Akhimah cleared her throat. "Feathers and blood and bird shit. Washed into the cisterns."

"But the enchantments—"

"I would guess," the Wizard continued, inexorable, "that the enemy sorcerer—"

"Ravani," Sayeh said. "Her name is Ravani. She seems to have a brother up north with Himadra whose name is Ravana."

"Twins?" asked Tsering-la.

Sayeh shrugged. "Maybe."

Ata Akhimah cleared her throat. She cradled her disaster of a hand across the crook of the other arm. She said, "It seems likely that Ravani considered that when she bespelled her fetches."

"Where is Nizhvashiti?" Mrithuri asked.

"On the battlements, still," said the Wizard Akhimah. "I will go and speak with the Godmade."

"Of course," Tsering-la said. "We can try to clean it, but not knowing the magic she used—" He sighed. "As I believe I mentioned, I am not a particularly powerful Wizard."

Yavashuri said, "With this rain, the river might rise—"

"The rain is only here," Sayeh put in. "Or at least, it has not crossed the river. It does not seem to be upstream, where it would raise the flood. And there is not enough of it anyway."

"The river is not rising," Mrithuri said. It hurt her to admit it. She had comforted herself with the lie for so long. "The river is not rising. With all Nizhvashiti could do."

Everyone in the room was looking at her. Everyone in the city was relying on her. To make a decision. To save the day. She could trust Sayeh. She might have to trust Sayeh. She was cold and in pain and alone, because whatever had to be done, there was no one to do it but her.

This was what it meant to be rajni, really. She could rely on others to be her hands, her eyes, even her intellect. But she had to be the heart and the will that synthesized and guided them.

"I am going to talk to the cloistered sisters," she said.

Of all the people in the room, perhaps it was only Yavashuri who knew what that portended. Of all the people in the room, it was only Yavashuri who raised her voice to ask, "My rajni, are you sure?"

Mrithuri shook her head. "No. But I am out of ideas. Figure out a rationing plan until I get back, would you? You and Ata Akhimah and

Hnarisha are the council in my absence. And make our new guests comfortable. I may be gone some time."

WHEN ALL WAS SAID AND DONE, SAYEH FOUND HERSELF AGAIN IN THE CARE of the healer, the little fine-boned man who reminded her somewhat of Tsering-la. Apparently some form of rationing had been worked out, because once she was settled and had dismissed Nazia and Ümmühan he came to what he said would be her rooms for as long as she stayed, with cakes and tea.

"Your ladies are not here?" he observed. "I can go away and come again."

"I am an old barren widow," she replied. "No one will care if I entertain a charming gentleman without a chaperone."

He laughed and came in and set the tray down. She asked him to be seated; he obliged.

"My lord Hnarisha—"

"Just Hnarisha." He smiled and poured.

"What the rajni is doing. It is very dangerous?"

"Sometimes," he said. Faint singing came through the walls. "You do not have similar cloisters in Ansh-Sahal?"

"We have cloisters," she thought, remembering the abbess. Mourning rose up her throat in bitterness. "Not like this."

"Ah," he said. And that was all.

"Hnarisha would seem to be a Cho-tse name," Sayeh said.

"That is so," he agreed mildly.

"Those would seem to be Cho-tse earrings," she commented.

"You are very observant." He handed her tea, and a delicate plate of Song porcelain with three tiny cakes on it, each decorated with a different candied edible flower.

She picked up the cake with the marigold petals sprinkled over it. The edges sparkled with gold dust. Did they dine like this as a matter of course, under siege or no? Or was this a special show for the foreign queen? She placed the cake on her tongue. It melted into mysterious and complicated flavors. Earthy and strong.

Perhaps she should have first tasted the one decorated in rose petals. Or orange blossom. Intricacies of experiencing fine dining had not been much on her mind of late.

"My son," she said slowly, having swallowed the tidbit, "told me a story about a tiger once."

Hnarisha cupped his tea in both hands and tilted his head at her politely. "Was it flattering to the tiger?"

"Well," Sayeh said. "It was from the point of view of the elephant."

Hnarisha laughed. "How old is your son?"

In answer, she held her hand at knee level.

He laughed. "A terrible age."

"You have children?"

"Not here," he said. "For which I am currently more grateful than I would have expected. Where is your son?"

She sighed. "An enemy has adopted him."

"Oh," he said. "I understand."

She raised her eyebrows.

"You want him back."

"Of course!"

He nodded. "Go on. Tell me about the tiger."

Sayeh drank a sip of tea to fortify herself. She ate another cake, this time the orange blossom. The tea had helped to clear her palate, but there was still a little of the funk of marigold left behind.

Oh, well.

"According to Drupada"—she cleared her throat—"the tiger is a bandit lord, and very wicked. But the elephant is the prince of the animals, and so it is his job to tell the tiger when the tiger is bad, and make him stop eating the other animals."

"I see," Hnarisha said. A little curve bent his lips. "Is the tiger prone to listening?"

"Well," Sayeh said. "According to Drupada, sometimes because the elephant is the biggest he has to sit on the tiger."

"He sits on the tiger."

"That's what I said."

"And your son, Drupada? What did he say in reply?"

She laughed. "He said, 'He does. But the elephant prince tries not to hurt the tiger too much so the tiger has a chance to behave better.' He also said that sometimes the elephant has to appeal to a higher power."

Hnarisha ate a small cake himself. Sayeh noticed that *he* started with the orange blossom. *Live and learn.*

When he had finished it, he said, "A higher power?"

"His mother." She closed her eyes briefly, trying to savor the memory, the childish belief that a parent could fix the most terrible circumstances. "He said that the elephant's mother could make the tiger listen no matter what."

"I bet she can," Hnarisha agreed. "You listen to your child."

"Good mothers do."

"My people have a different version of the story."

She thought about asking *Who are your people, exactly?* But it seemed like the sort of question that broke a fragile, budding camaraderie. "Is it more flattering to the tiger?"

"Well, he's not a bandit lord. But he does want to eat the elephant."

"Wait," Sayeh said. "You're telling me this is a real story. This story my son made up and told me."

"He probably didn't make it up," Hnarisha said. "And even if he did make it up, it's still a real story."

Sayeh felt her face blush. "Of course," she said. "That was thoughtless of me. But I mean—it's a story that exists outside of my son's imagination? I did not realize that."

"Who could have told it to him?"

Sayeh sighed. She wrapped her hands around the warm teacup and sat back in the chair, pressing her doubled fists over her heart. "A nurse. A guard. An entertainer. Someone brought in by his tutors, or perhaps even a tutor themselves. There are a lot of options."

Despite herself, she thought of Nazia saying that someone like Ravani came to her and suggested she undermine the ritual and the omen that confirmed that the land and sea welcomed Sayeh's rule. If that had not happened, Sayeh wondered, would her people have been more willing to listen to her when she begged them to evacuate?

Could someone like that have told a story to Drupada, too?

*You are being paranoid.*

"Interesting," Hnarisha said. "Do you know who my people say the elephant's mother is, Sayeh Rajni?"

*Rajni of what?* Sayeh thought. But instead of speaking, she just shook her head.

Hnarisha sipped his tea. "The river."

*     *     *

MRITHURI UNWOUND HER HUSBAND'S VEIL AND KISSED HIS MOUTH. SHE leaned her forehead against his shoulder. She put her arms around his neck and embraced him.

"What you're about to do," he said. "It's something terrible."

"Likely," she agreed.

"And no one can do it for you."

She pushed her head into the hollow under his chin, ducking a little to fit herself there. The contact eased the pain in her head and her veins a little. Nothing seemed to ease her chills. "That is what it means to rule."

"Not so different from being a soldier." He set his hands on her shoulders and moved her back a step, looking into her face. His mouth curved in a smile she wasn't used to seeing. It caught in her throat.

She *would* see it again. "I will come back," she said.

"I will be here," he answered, speaking as she had: as if she were going away a long way. He squeezed her once, hard fingers flexing painfully. Then let his hands fall and stepped away.

With a gesture so practiced it seemed unconscious, he drew the indigo cloth across his face and fastened it. She smiled. He smiled too; she could tell from his eyes.

She turned away while he was still watching. Still smiling at her. She reached up and touched the smooth outline of the silver snake that coiled around her throat.

She turned its head, and slid the flexible, silver-edged dagger concealed within it free.

"I never knew that was there," the Dead Man said.

"It will remain there," Mrithuri answered. "And if I have to marry and bed Anuraja, I will wear it to his chamber. But this is the thing I need now."

She pushed a secret catch within the sheath of the dagger, and a key popped from a slot into her hand. She set it in a lock in the filigree wall before her and without turning back over her shoulder said, "From here I go alone."

With shuffling footsteps, he withdrew.

She turned the key, which turned the lock. The filigree had no knob or visible hinges. She used the key as if it were a handle, and pushed the door away from her into the shadowy, secret, scented places beyond.

Then she retrieved it, locked the concealed door behind her, reassembled her serpent torc, and faced the dark beyond.

"Sisters?"

Out of the shadows, draped in white, veiled in white, like the legendary phantasms of the great northern steppe, they came to her.

They led her into the shadows, where they were paler shadows still. The dimness was kind to her throbbing head. The chill was not so kind to her aching bones and shivering skin. The floor under her bare feet was wood, not stone, and polished smooth as silk from the passage of so many bare feet, and quite a few slippered ones. They led her down a spiral, and by strange ways that pierced walls and skirted corridors and slipped along the edges of rooms she had not known had secret passages within them.

She caught glimpses of her own familiar palace beyond the screens, in some places. There were fragments of life carried on: cooks in the kitchens, maids spreading linens, courtiers laughing over a lute. But her own familiar palace seemed strangely disconnected from the way she knew it to be. The rooms in the wrong order; corridors connected that she knew were not; chambers she knew to be on different levels now seeming to be the same.

Perhaps it was the lack of her venom, the sickness it engendered in her that made the connection to her own world seem so tenuous. Perhaps the world swam because her head was swimming.

Everything familiar was made strange.

*That is how it will be if Anuraja rules here.* She steeled herself. She would carry this through.

As they walked, one voice hummed a prayer. It was joined by another, singing words of praise in harmony. A third rose, contralto, weaving a counterpoint under the other two. Soon all the voices rose around her, echoing through the corridors so that she could not even be sure how many there were. They sang in time to their footsteps, so that without meaning to she fell into rhythm with them. They sang and walked, and walked and sang, and Mrithuri became certain that they had walked and sung, and sung and walked, for far longer than the mere confines of her palace could have supported. They seemed to wind up and down at random, and she became utterly confused as to where they were in relation to anything of the palace she had lived in her whole life.

At last, they came out into what must be a high and empty space, though she could not see that distance. Some of the nuns carried little oil lamps, but the lamps only gave a dim light—though a strong scent—and both vanished into the blackness that stretched around. It could not be an infinite blackness, however, because the nuns' song echoed all the more here. It was as though Mrithuri stood in the heart of the sounding chamber of a vast and convoluted instrument, some lute or zither of such enormousness that an entire mountain might be needed to contain it.

One by one, the nuns ceased to sing. The echoes and reverberations made up their voices, strange and haunted and attenuated, until the last woman let her voice fall away.

When the silence had stretched a little, Mrithuri cleared her throat. That, too, lingered on dying echoes.

"How is this possible?" she said, meaning the long walk. Meaning the space they stood within. Her voice had a resonance, here, like God's.

One by one, the nuns turned toward her, stepping out until they stood in a white-robed, white-veiled, white-gloved, barefoot ring. One remained where she was. It was the woman who had been in the lead, Mrithuri thought. Now she was the woman who stood closest.

"The Building Science," the nun said. "These two places touch, you see. But they do not inhabit the same *continuity*. At least, not exactly."

"The Alchemical Emperor built this."

"He did," the nun answered. "Our cloister touches your palace in the same way that the Lotus Kingdoms touch Rasa, yet exist under a different sky."

"I do not understand."

"Your Ata Akhimah might, a little," the nun said. "But your ancestor went to great lengths to ensure that his knowledge would be scattered after his death. Even we do not know much of what he understood. Merely enough to glimpse the outlines of what is hidden from us."

Mrithuri did not shake her head, because shaking made it feel as if her brain were slapping against the inside of her skull. Maybe what the nun was saying would have made sense if she weren't so befogged.

"Sister," she said instead, in capitulation. "I have come to beg your assistance."

"There is a price."

Mrithuri swallowed, but her mouth grew no less dry. "I expected there would be."

"Do you know what it is?"

"I expected you would tell me."

The nun cocked her hip and crossed her arms low in front of her, as if standing more comfortably. The flickering lamplights behind her were doing nothing for Mrithuri's migraine.

The nun asked, "Your life?"

"If it were mine to give? In an instant." Mrithuri would regret it. She had things to live for, if she could keep them. For the first time in her life she had real things; things that were her own and not inherited or borrowed.

She hoped the nuns would not ask for that. But then, if they did, she would mind dying less, if she had to.

"It is true," the nun said. "Your life is already given to your people. Well, then. Your right hand."

She shuddered. Was it the venom-need, or was it fear? "If I must. Dismembered, can I be your rajni?"

The nun chuckled in echoes like lapping water. "Something could be arranged. How about your virginity?"

Somehow, here in this dark and vibrant space, Mrithuri was beginning to feel at home. Even, mildly, bold and humorous. She said, "I need that, unfortunately. At least, the token of it. I may be forced to marry a raja, and they expect that sort of thing. Besides," she said, self-deprecatingly. "It lets me come here."

"You are the Mother in your own person. You do not need chastity to come here."

"I'm not sure what virginity I have left counts as much of a sacrifice anymore, to be completely honest," Mrithuri admitted.

The nun laughed knowingly. The nuns knew so many things. Chaeri must have used illusions to hide her nefarious activities from them. Damn that sorcerer to at least thirteen of the numberless hells of Namhansanseong.

340 ✳ ELIZABETH BEAR

"Your hair?"

"It would serve Anuraja right to have an ugly bride."

"So," said the nun, whose voice too was becoming more humorous, "not a thing that would count as a sacrifice. Your serpents."

"Already stolen," she admitted. "Not a thing I can offer in good faith to sacrifice."

"Indeed," said the shape in white. "Your hands tremble with desire for them. But think you: your enemy is also our enemy. He is a heretic and a blasphemer."

"You've heard that in your cloisters, then."

The figure's head tilted beneath her shrouds, as if she smiled. "We live in your walls, my rajni."

Mrithuri had to shake her head, eyes closing, at her own obtuseness. "I am thinking on what you mentioned. Does that mean you will aid me for your own sake?"

"It means that if our enemy has your serpents, he could use them to control you. You think you need them. Their venom certainly has a hold on you—"

"I do need them," Mrithuri said. "I am not myself enough."

"Oh," said the nun. "But what if you must be?"

Mrithuri had no answer for that. She felt weak, old. Exhausted. She wished for a chair. She wanted to lean forward and put her hands on her knees. She stood, but she could not quite make herself stand straight. She pressed her elbow against the wrapped ache in her side. Some honesty—perhaps just the sense that the woman in white would know if she was lying—compelled her to say, "Then I will fail."

"Will you? Have you yet?"

Had she? She didn't know. She had . . . been too certain that Sarathai-tia could hold against a siege. She had been too dependent on Chaeri, even when others she should have trusted more had called on her to make better decisions.

"Yes," she said.

"Did the world end?"

That made her laugh. It sounded flat, even here. "Too soon to tell."

"Did the venom prevent your failure?"

That drew her up short. She couldn't get a breath, suddenly. As if she had been punched in those cracked ribs, or in the solar plexus. It was a question, not even a truth. Not an accusation.

And yet it unraveled the entirety of everything she had been relying on since she was . . . nine years of age. "I don't know if my body can manage without it at this point."

"You have no choice," the nun said. "You will change, or you will die."

Mrithuri closed her eyes. "I feel like I am living someone else's life," she said. "Someone who should have been carefree. At least for a little while. Someone whose mother and father should have lived, and ruled, and raised her. But she died and I lived and I stole her life. She would be better at it. She would be a fine rajni. But I stole her life and I cannot give it back to her and all I can do is make a mockery of who she would have been while trying to be worthy of her legacy."

She took a breath. It shuddered. "I broke. She would be whole. I survived and she—the Other Me—she deserved to. She deserved so much more than I do."

"She doesn't exist," the sister said.

"She gave her life for me. This broken thing," Mrithuri said, with a dismissive wipe across herself.

"Well, then," the sister said. "You owe her something."

It might have been the most terrible thing anyone had ever said to Mrithuri. But it did, in fact, pierce her despair.

"I swear," she said, thickly, with a tongue that resented her. "I will give up this thing."

"Which thing?"

"I will give up the venom."

"And what else?"

"I will give up . . . I will sacrifice . . ." She couldn't quite find the words.

"You will give up this idea that you must be perfect."

She opened her eyes again, forced her arm away from her aching side, and reached out a supplicating hand to the sister. "Will you help me?"

"What help do you have in mind?"

"I must stop Anuraja from reigning over my people. I must protect them. Unpoison our water? Lift the siege?"

"We cannot do that." Mrithuri's heart sank, but the nun stepped forward and placed a gloved hand on her arm. "We will do what we can."

THE NUNS BROUGHT HER BACK TO THE DEAD MAN. THEY LOCKED THE concealed door behind her. She felt as if her soul had been scoured.

Perhaps it had. Perhaps she was finally clean.

"Take me to Sayeh," she told him, leaning hard upon his arm.

"My rajni, you are not well."

"I am well enough," she said. "There is no time to be other than well."

SHE HAD OFFERED HERSELF INTO ANOTHER GILDED CAPTIVITY, SAYEH RE-alized. Although it was a far more comfortable one. And it was good, so good, to have Guang Bao and her people around her again. Though Guang Bao really did look ridiculous with all those black-and-white feathers patched in among his own brilliant ones. She had spent some time talking with Mrithuri's austringers, assuring herself of their skills, and ascertaining that the repaired feathers would drop out naturally with Guang Bao's next molt without any intervention on her part.

Then, with a quiet pragmatism, she sent Ümmühan and Nazia and Vidhya and even Tsering-la away, and rested. Her son was in the north. He was as far out of harm's way as anyone could be in this world. Far-ther than she was, for certain. Vidhya had left men behind to watch over the refugees from Ansh-Sahal, and to seek out Drupada, if such was possible, and protect him if they could. Sayeh had the opportunity to really rest—and to rest in a room *alone*—for the first time since the fall of Ansh-Sahal. She too was safe here, she judged, at least for the time being.

So the scratching upon her door sometime later roused her from a very deep sleep indeed. She pushed herself up on her elbows quite grog-gily, blinking sleep from crusted eyes. She had no idea how long she had been asleep, or even what time it was. It took her a moment to real-ize that she was in Sarathai-tia, and that the palace had apparently not fallen to Anuraja while she was asleep. No one would be scratching so politely at her door if it had.

*Any day without sounds of looting and pillaging is a good day.* She checked briefly to make sure her pajamas were decently arrayed—another wardrobe item brought into her possession by charity—and called a greeting. Her voice rasped through a sleep-thick throat.

Still, it surprised her when the eyes that peered around the sliding edge of her door were those of Mrithuri Rajni. Sayeh would not expect a person of her rank to run her own errands. She swung herself upright and reached for her crutch. It turned out that if she was careful, she now only needed one. This, pleasingly, left her a hand free to do other things with.

Sayeh got herself to her feet—well, foot—while Mrithuri made her way into the chamber. Mrithuri's Caliphate bodyguard (and, Sayeh guessed, much more than that) followed her a handspan behind.

The rajni looked terrible. Much worse than Sayeh had, the last time Sayeh had steeled herself for a glance in a mirror. The hollows under her eyes were a darker shade of sickly green than the rest of her skin. She looked bloodless and scraped, and her hair was dull and frayed. Sayeh thought she was probably holding herself up by sheer will.

The Dead Man slid the door closed behind him, and wandered away from the women, out onto a small covered balcony. He leaned on the railing, a thoughtful silhouette against the still-gray sky, rain falling behind him. Sayeh looked away. No wonder she had no idea what time it was. The light could hardly have been more watery and indistinct.

"Please," Sayeh said. "Sit. Excuse my dishabille."

"Excuse mine," Mrithuri answered, picking a cobweb off her shoulder. "This is rather a mess."

Mrithuri sat, and Sayeh found herself wishing she had something to offer: tea, cakes. But she was here under Mrithuri's hospitality, so—comforting though it would have been to have something to do with their hands—it would have been the rankest presumption to turn that hospitality around and offer it back to her hostess.

Mrithuri—shoulders hunched, shivering in the heat—took that pressure off of her by simply saying, "So you want me to marry Anuraja."

"Anuraja wants you to marry Anuraja."

"And the sorcerer you mentioned?"

Sayeh shook her head. "She has her own agenda. She looks for ways to get promises out of people. Ümmühan is of the opinion that those are wedges for her magic."

"Ümmühan seems very experienced."

"Well," Sayeh said judiciously. "This is not her first existential threat."

Mrithuri smiled, a little painfully, and rubbed her arms.

"Are you well, Sister?" Sayeh asked her, leaning forward. "Should one of your healers be called?"

"I'm all right," Mrithuri answered.

Whether it was a lie or wishful thinking, Sayeh wasn't quite sure. "Are you free to marry?" she asked.

"I am a maiden," Mrithuri said, which wasn't quite an answer.

Sayeh's eyes cut to the Dead Man, out of earshot on the balcony. *That's what they all say.* "What about your lover?"

With an effort, Mrithuri sparkled. "There are other ways to be together and give pleasure," she remarked blandly, adopting a worldly air.

Sayeh giggled behind her hand. She *liked* this young woman. She hoped for Mrithuri's sake, for her own sake, that her mad plan had merit.

She was a priestess of the Mother. She was the *chosen* one of the Mother. Her understanding of metaphysics was not, in point of fact, particularly poor. Her mad plan had merit. She must believe in it.

"Will you do it?"

Mrithuri's forced brightness cracked. She heaved a sigh and closed her eyes. "The sisters in the walls say they cannot clean the water. I spoke with Nizhvashiti—sorry, a Godmade, you will meet it soon, I am certain—on the way here, and Nizhvashiti does not have a means to help. Ata Akhimah says the means she has for purifying water is the same as that which the befouling spell bypassed to do its evil work. And Tsering-la says we can build a still, but cleaning enough water for the ten thousand or more of my subjects crammed within these walls . . . Well, we don't have time to build that *many* stills."

Sayeh watched the young woman dispassionately, then nodded. "All right then."

"What will he offer us for terms, if we surrender? The safety of my people—"

"He will assure that," Sayeh said. "Your guard captains, generals, and Wizard must go into exile."

"My women?" Mrithuri asked.

"He does not worry much about the capabilities of women," Sayeh said. "I do not think he will notice them. Unless they are pretty. Then I'd say get them out of sight."

The Tian rajni sighed in relief. "One is. And young. But she is friendly with the cloistered sisters. I'm sure they will hide her. Will he vow to protect my nuns?"

"I don't know," Sayeh said. "But it seems from your complexion, begging your pardon, that they must have means of protecting themselves. And you said . . . there was a Godmade."

"Indeed," said Mrithuri. "Perhaps not even Anuraja will face such wrath as that simply to indulge himself among the pretty girls." She glanced out at the balcony. "My familiars must be protected. And an honor guard. Three men. Also my personal secretary."

"Get him to take those Cho-tse earrings out and I'll see what I can do."

22

The Gage alighted from the Many-Legged Truth swinging in its access cage, and did not take it even slightly amiss when they dropped him against the drifting sand with somewhat more force than was necessary.

He probably deserved it.

He disembarked, and the cage was winched away from him hastily. It would not have mattered; the Many-Legged Truth had a thousand feet, and from where he stood, the Gage could have reached several of them.

It was an abomination. And it was an abomination in which people who did not deserve his wrath suffered and lived.

The Gage held his fury, though it cost him. He turned his back on the Many-Legged Truth. He did not turn to regard it (he did not need to turn to regard it) as its gears and pulleys cranked up before the turning of the wind, and its locked feet released, and it accelerated smoothly, step by step, away.

He let it walk away from him, and he did not smash it, for all it deserved smashing. He did not smash it, for the sake of those trapped in its spidery embrace. He did not smash it, out of pity.

He turned his back on it instead.

He faced a bleached autumnal skeleton of what had been a city, in its time.

He understood how it got its name. Because here he was, looking at it across a bleached alkali flat, everything simmering in mirages. At this distance it was white as chalk, white as lime. The tall spiraling oryx-horn towers of the thing itself were bleached and perhaps melted into unsettling shapes that made him think of the bones of coral, when the animals within are dead and scoured away.

And still it sang.

It sang the hymn of wind through worn passages. Its multiphonic flutelike notes were shrill and bright, and *sharp*. Not in the sense that you could have cut yourself, but the sense that they were a touch off-key. Perhaps that was indeed because the city was melted. Perhaps it was because the ears who were meant to hear its tones were not, and never had been, human.

The Gage squared his metal shoulders and began the long, searing march across the dusty plain.

He was coated in alkali by the time he made it to the other side. If he had thought the powdered glass of the rotdust storm was fine and penetrative, he had reckoned without this stuff. It was unto dust as silk was unto burlap, and it infiltrated and coated and clung.

It was so fine that it did not bind and grit, however. One small mercy, then.

The drifted dust and sand was slowly eating a pavement, and he went out onto it with footsteps that first shuffled and then rang. The pavement led him into the city on a stately spiral, somewhat similar to the one that wound its way up the artificial mountain of Sarathai-tia. It was, the Gage could see, a kind of processional, and not intended for regular use. There were buildings that never came close to it and there were no alleys or side roads to connect them. There were no doors leading onto it, though the Gage could see ledges far above him, leading to enormous gaps in the facade.

The city was, overwhelmingly, designed for massive beings. Massive beings with wings.

THE PROCESSIONAL ENDED IN A SQUARE. AN ENORMOUS SQUARE, SPRAWLED out in the shadow of these even-more-enormous towers. And mostly filled by what the Gage at first took to be another enormous thing, a dune of white alkali sand.

As he stared at it, more details of the shape emerged, white on white in the bleaching sunshine. It lay across the dust of the courtyard, ghostly and corrugated, and the Gage wondered if it could be the shed skin of a dragon. Then he saw the gaunt arch of rib cage, the thin skin taut and stretched between ribs, the tatters of membranes stretched likewise between the bones of sprawled wings. He saw the lids that sagged wrinkled over sunken sockets and the broken talons that splayed on the drifted cobblestones.

It was a corpse. The most enormous corpse he'd ever seen, and the Gage had seen some big ones. On this trip, in fact.

"So that's where the poison comes from." As with the green glass desert, the places where dragons died—or lived for long, for that matter—were toxic to all life, and stayed that way forever. He walked up to it, and even a Gage could feel awe at what had lived here once, and lived no more.

"So."

The voice was a papery sigh, sand slipping on sand.

The Gage, who feared nothing, scrambled back as the ghost-pale head rose, bony and cadaverous, shedding streams of dust like water falling from a mossy stone. It cast about, eager whiskers cat-quivering, but the lids still drooped, and the Gage realized it was blind. The whiskers brushed him, paused, brushed back.

He stood very still indeed.

"So," the dragon said again. The flesh on its neck had withered to piteous swags; its scales were dull and brittle-seeming as shells worn translucent by the sea. "Someone has come, finally."

Of course it was not dead.

Of course there was one dragon living.

Otherwise the sky above would not have blazed with livid suns. It would have been empty, except for distant stars, like the sky over dead Ansh-Sahal.

What it meant that the suns of Erem blasted this dragon city, he began to speculate.

The dragon didn't seem about to crush him. Indeed, it huffed air over him as it drew back, like a dog seeking an elusive scent.

"I am a Gage," the Gage said.

"I am Kyrlmyrandal," the enormous creature answered politely, in a voice like paper ashes rubbed between fingers. "Some call me Mother of Exiles."

"You are the mark that is made," the Gage answered, wondering at a useful thing a Wizard had taught him. "And the act of marking."

"I am the thing that is left behind," the dragon said, and showed toothless gums in a thing that might be a smile. "What does it mean, *Gage*?"

"I am a thing that was made for revenge against the man who killed my family, and who would have killed me."

"He did not manage?"

"He left me for dead."

"And were you?"

"Only my soul. My heart still beat. A little."

"Enough to power that machine."

"The heart's long gone," the Gage said.

"But what does the *word* mean?"

"Oh," the Gage said. "It means a pledge or a troth. A guarantee. A word-of-honor. It means the object given as security on a loan. A gage is a thing used to take a measure. It means a hand. Or a gauntlet. It means the object thrown upon the ground in challenge."

"That is a fine set of meanings for a name. Are you all of those things?"

"I am," the Gage said. "Must names have meanings?"

"Ours must," said the dragon. "*Ky* means (the being) and indicates that what follows is a name. And you are correct, *myrandal* means the thing that marks, and the act of making that mark, and also the mark left by the act of marking. I am also called the First of Dragons."

"'I am the word and the pen,'" the Gage quoted. The wind-song of the towers had a tendency to creep into his hollows and echo inside of him, as if his body were only one more sinus in its gigantic, convoluted sounding chamber. It was an uncomfortable, shivery sensation, and it blurred his vision a little. An unsettling sensation for someone without eyes.

"More or less," said the dragon. "Your poetry?"

"My best friend's religion."

"Ah," said the dragon. "I have been drowsing here a long time. I am glad the world still has such things as friends."

"And religions?"

"I have never concerned myself much with religions." The dragon pushed her nose against his carapace. The flesh looked velvety soft, like a horse's muzzle. "I am glad you are here. I do not seem to die. And I have been so very lonely."

"I have come a very long way seeking you," the Gage said. "Or at least, seeking the Singing Towers."

"Singing Towers? Is that all they call us now." Kyrlmyrandal tilted her head. From whiskers to the broken stubs of horns, the head was as long as a wagon. The creature might be twice the size of the ice-drake the Gage and the Dead Man had encountered with the caravan that brought them to the Lotus Kingdoms. Or she might be three times larger. She was so big he could not estimate.

The ice-drake had been big enough to casually carry off a shaggy mountain ox.

The dragon asked. "What is it about the Singing Towers, as you call us, that you have come such a long way to seek?"

"I think a Wizard sent me to you for help."

The dragon froze, as if crystallized. The Gage feared for a moment that he had offended her. But then, creakily, she began to laugh.

If her voice was the rumble of a speaking mountain, her laughter was the hollow boom of waves in sea caverns. Finally she stopped, and wiped her eyes one by one, carefully, with her handlike, taloned front feet, though the Gage did not see any tears. Still gasping a little, she said. "That's really funny, because—as you can probably tell by look-ing at me—I cannot help anyone."

The Gage wished he had eyes to close in frustration. "That . . . is not what I wanted to hear."

"Did you come with that walking city?" the dragon asked.

"They scooped me out of the storm."

"A rescue? I had not heard they were like that."

"They came looking for me, I think. In particular. They wanted . . ." The Gage indicated his burnished chassis with the flat of a hand, passed downward. "To be more like me. They tried to take that."

The dragon preened her broken claws with all the brittle dignity of an elderly cat. "Did it occur to you to wonder how they knew to come looking?"

"It did, actually." The Gage found himself examining the improbable specter of the ancient dragon, the wrinkled skin stretched soft and slack between scales that had lost any color or iridescence they might once have had. He remembered the ice-drake, how it had shone in the sun, how its wings had been veined in glacial colors. It had been *white*. This being was . . . bleached. "Those people. They have links to Messaline, of old."

"Your human cities are a mystery to me," the dragon admitted.

"Old Erem," the Gage said. "Messaline is built on the site of Old Erem. Not Ancient Erem, which is in the mountains not too far away."

"Hmm," Kyrlmyrandal said. "Is this where you are from?"

"I have dwelt there recently."

"And who there knew where you were going?"

Kyrlmyrandal had a rather nuanced concept of betrayal and subterfuge, not to mention circumstantial evidence, for a nonhuman monster possibly older than the very stones. It was an excellent question. And one whose implications the Gage resisted, because as far as he knew, the only person in Messaline who could have told anyone that he might be en route to the Singing Towers was the one who had prophesied the need for the journey.

"It can't have been the Eyeless One," the Gage said.

"Eyeless One?"

"A Wizard of Messaline. The Wizard of Messaline. My sponsor, occasionally. She would be a very strange betrayer, having helped us so significantly along the way. It would make no sense at all for her to turn on me when this entire expedition was undertaken in her service. She could have just had us stay home and saved herself the fee."

There were certainly stories where villains did stranger things, such as hiring an assassin to investigate and avenge their own crimes. But that would be pointless, and the Gage could not imagine the Eyeless One expending her considerable strength on anything . . . pointless.

"You're very certain."

"She has everything she could want. Except godhead."

"And what if she saw a way to get that? What if someone offered it to her?"

The Gage might have blanched, had he not been made of metal. "I am not at all certain that she would desire such a thing."

"Wise," the dragon mused in her cracked voice. "My experience of godhead is that it is not all that."

Thinking of Nizhvashiti, the Gage was inclined to concur. Then another thought occurred to him, and he said, "Interesting."

"Many things are," agreed Kyrlmyrandal. "I have lived to see the oceans shift their coastlines and the very mountains rise and fall. I am the oldest living thing I have ever met. And I have yet to find the thing that is boring, if you know how to address it."

"True," the Gage said, after pausing to consider. "But I was speaking in this case of a coincidence."

"Those are especially interesting. On those rare occasions when one finds a coincidence to be truly so."

"What do you mean?" the Gage asked, his thought process interrupted by his own curiosity.

"Well," said the complacent dragon, "there is usually something meddling."

". . . Gods?"

"Often as not."

The Gage would not have expected to find the First of Dragons to be so consistently . . . agreeable. But here she was.

"This particular coincidence concerns you. Well, your name, Kyrlmyrandal."

She stirred. She rolled onto her back, careful of her sprawl of limbs and long bleached body, and exposed her withered belly and the underside of her tattered wings to the suns. The wing membranes, spread, burned with unexpected color—streaks and striations of red and red-orange, blazed with slashes of darkness that looked charred.

The Gage was so stunned by the brilliance—here in this bone-white city, upon this bone-white beast—that he took one startled step backward.

"That makes it even more likely that someone is meddling. The godheads are surprisingly terrible at finding new pieces for their games of politics, and lazily play their familiar pieces in new patterns." She rolled again and lay like a lioness, head up and wings outstretched on the ground. "Even when those pieces are chipped and worn. So I came up in conversation?"

"It was I myself who remarked on the word that makes your name. The mark, and the thing that marks, and the art of marking."

"Well," said Kyrlmyrandal tidily, "you summoned me into your story, then."

The Gage, who had been standing at his ease and nearly motionless, froze utterly. "When I named you?"

"What else are names good for?"

"Sorting out sides for kick-bladder, I suppose," the Gage said tiredly.

"Indubitably," agreed the dragon. Deadly dust puffed as she flipped her wings in to settle them against her sides. They did not fold neatly, but hung crooked, and the tip of the right one dragged. She gathered herself and—using the wings as crutches—levered herself to her splayed feet. She stood a little creakily, but seemed the better for having basked in the warmth—the searing, sterilizing warmth—of the suns. She stepped forward, her long neck curving down toward the Gage. She was . . . enormous. Castles, temples. What else was so large?

One hind foot dragged with a hitch, so when she walked she hopped both back feet forward with the sound one a little forward of the other, like an old dog. She had, the Gage thought, an injured or arthritic spine.

He would teach this one how to build a Gage's body, if she wanted. Though he could imagine little more terrifying to contemplate than an enormous automaton dragon. Could even magic make such a creature fly? Would the very bedrock crack beneath its feet and let the red lava lifeblood run free?

The Gage gathered himself. "I am sorry, most magnificent Kyrlmyrandal. If I had my choice, I would stay and talk with you forever. But I came here seeking help, and there is a war on that I promised to go back to. I must be getting on."

She sighed, but not angrily. "What do you want? Or more to the point, what does your Wizard want?"

"I was sent to find something called the Carbuncle."

"Oh," she said. "I have that. You have to stick it where the sun don't shine for it to work, though, and—not to be invasive or rude, and begging your pardon—but I think you haven't got the parts to make that function?"

"It's not for me. I mean . . . may I have it?"

The dragon blinked sightless eyes at him. "No."

"Oh," he said, surprised to realize that he was surprised by the refusal. One could, it seemed, be entirely lulled into complacency by the agreeableness of dragons. "Well, that was a long walk for nothing."

"Hasty," she said, and advanced one wing, shifting her weight onto it. The tip dragged where the Gage feared again that it might foul her talons, but she seemed to manage. "I'm coming with you. *I* will bring the stone. And I will give you a pen."

"A pen."

"Certainly. Dragons have hoards, do we not?"

"You can walk that far?"

Kyrlmyrandal took a limping step and seemed to consider. "You know, that's an excellent question. But first, let's get the pen."

KYRLMYRANDAL DID INDEED GIVE THE GAGE A PEN. A PEN SIZED FOR HUMAN hands, even, which meant it was much too small for the Gage. It was not a quill or a brush, either, but a piece of technology he had not encountered before: it had a cap which covered a sharp pointed nib with a slit in it made of what seemed to be gold, and its cap and the body were finished in some translucent black-red lacquer with a depth of color the Gage associated with semiprecious jewels.

It was beautiful, and the light of the suns caught inside it as if were an ember.

"It's named *Heartsblood*. It is supposed to have the soul of a sword," said Kyrlmyrandal.

"Well," the Gage said carefully. "They do say the pen is mightier."

"Don't patronize me," said the pen.

The Gage nearly dropped it. But, when he paused to think about it, was a talking pen any more weird than a dragon with a hoard of pens?

"I don't know what else I'm supposed to do with you."

"Take me to somebody who is worthy of me." *Obviously.*

"Aren't you full of the dragon poison?"

"Oh, probably," said the pen. "Most pens are venomous when used correctly."

"You will poison them, too."

A sense of a shrug. "Well. That's the nature of things. Besides, they'll have a few good years in using me before their fingers rot and their eyes go white. Maybe as many as fifteen! Or ten."

Ceremoniously, the Gage opened a hidden, leather-lined compartment in his body and laid the pen within. It nestled there, and when he closed the drawer again, there was nothing to indicate its existence.

"Is there anything you need before we leave, if you are coming with me?"

"I shouldn't think so," Kyrlmyrandal said. "Are you ready to go right now?"

In answer, the Gage turned, and began to walk back the way he had come. She fell in beside him, taking one slow step each for his many quick ones.

He said, "You said you were the First of Dragons. And also the Mother."

"Of course."

"Does 'First' in this case mean 'Leader' or 'Progenitor'?"

"Some of both," she said. "Are you asking about the origin of dragons?"

Something in the phrase tickled his memory. "Is the origin of dragons anything like the Origin of Storms?"

"Well," the old dragon said, wheezing with laughter, "we're both what you get when you put energy into a system. Dragons and storms are alike in that way. And we're both an activity rather than an object. Is there some reason you ask?"

"I was told to seek the Origin of Storms," he admitted. "You used the phrase, and—well, it's an unusual phrase. So what is the origin of dragons?"

"We came from a long way away," Kyrlmyrandal said. "Across the empty sky. We fell. And some of our old sky fell with us." She tilted her head up, indicating the terrifying suns. "We have still a lot of letting go to manage. My children have all forgotten me. They have forgotten where we came from. They think we have a right to be in this place, rather than a lack of options, even when our very bodies poison it. But we have not always been here."

"Where is this place, a long way away, that you came from?"

"We fell through the divided sky," Kyrlmyrandal said. "I cannot tell you *where* the other side is. But the reason I am coming with you is that we owe this land a debt, and a stewardship. It is not ours. And we ruined a great many things when we came here. We poison what we touch. Our flesh is poison. And yet we have nowhere else to go."

"And how did you come to—well, to this? Is it just age?" Then he coughed—not a real cough, of course. But an embarrassed simulacrum. "I'm sorry. That was a very personal question."

"You have answered my similar question," she said. "And as for me—I have been blind for a long time, metal man. It no longer really troubles me. Being alone troubles me far more." She sighed, a vast and billowing noise. "I was injured long ago. And injured more when my people fought their last war. The walking city brought you through the battlefield?"

"Yes," he said.

"There are a few of us left. But as I said, the ones who remain are forgetful, and scattered. But though I am old . . . I am still Kyrlmyrandal."

"Oh," said a mocking voice from the left of them. "Is *that* what you are?"

The Gage had not seen anyone there a moment before. Now, however, he caught a glimpse of the sorcerer Ravana, hopping down off a high wall and landing easily. If the Gage never met another illusionist, it would be entirely too soon.

The sorcerer strolled over to them, leaving the Gage wondering if his wolf-lined coat was an illusion, also. He couldn't imagine any creature of flesh being comfortable in that in weather like this. But Ravana was not sweating. His perfect insouciance was no less infuriating this time than the last.

"I thought you were a pile of old bones and leather," the sorcerer said to the dragon. "Or maybe a haystack that walks."

"Ignore that," the dragon said to the Gage, who had taken one firm step toward the sorcerer.

"I'm really tired of this guy," the Gage protested.

"Hitting him won't solve anything." Kyrlmyrandal took one more of her ponderous steps, again using her massive wing as a crutch to swing herself forward. "He's not really there. Just a projection."

"A projection with a really big mouth," the Gage said, turning away again.

Ravana spat in the dust by Kyrlmyrandal's giant claw. The spittle looked real enough. "Your empire is a poison, built on poisoned land."

"Tell me something I don't know," the dragon muttered, striding on.

Ravana reached out and rapped his knuckles on the Gage's shoulder. It rang. "I wasn't talking to the dragon that time, metal man. Are you *sure* you can't hit me?"

"If I had an empire I might be concerned about that," the Gage admitted. He kept walking, too, hurrying now to keep up with the dragon. To Kyrlmyrandal, he muttered, "Are you *sure* he's an illusion?"

She reached over the Gage's head with a wing and, without breaking stride, swatted at the sorcerer. Her wing passed right through.

"The Lotus Empire does not command your loyalty at all?"

"Even if it did, the Lotus Empire does not exist. And if it existed, what would you expect me to do about it?" the Gage asked. "I'm not a Wizard, and I'm not a warlord. It is not *mine*."

"You're a thing," Ravana said, and gestured at himself. So flawless. So false. His flawlessness might have filled the Gage with fury, if the Gage hadn't long ago given up on being furious at things as likely to give him ulcers. Then he remembered that he couldn't get ulcers anymore, and conceded that he might be just the tiniest bit enraged after all.

"And you are a beast that feeds on war," said Kyrlmyrandal. "And not even a very big beast. A small one. Doing the bidding of others, I imagine. Who are your masters, little beast?"

The Gage, walking as he was beside Ravana, was surprised to see the sorcerer taken aback. Just the flash of consternation across the illusionary face. He did not answer, and Kyrlmyrandal hung her great, heavy head over the Gage and said, "I hope you are very unhappy for a very long time, Ravana. And I hope you don't even learn anything from it. That is the curse I curse you with. Also, you are in my house, and my house is my power. Go now, and do not come to this place again."

Whatever the Gage expected, it was not for Ravana to freeze where he was, mouth open, and then blow away on a swirl of windswept grains as if he were two-dimensional and painted in sand. The Gage contemplated the absence where the sorcerer's image had been for a moment.

Then he asked Kyrlmyrandal, "Did you kill him?"

"Alas," said Kyrlmyrandal. "Just sent his illusion home. Come along now, metal man. Your vulture friend is waiting for you. Have you tried feeding him a bone?"

"Dragonbones are poison," the Gage protested. "And how did you know about Vara?"

"Poison is a funny thing," the dragon said. "In another dose, we call it medicine."

"Mrithuri will not thank me if I poison her pet."

"This Mrithuri is your ruler?"

The Gage rattled a shrug. "The birds answer to her. So, for the time being, do I."

"Maybe you should try a bone, then."

"I don't eat," the Gage said. "I especially don't eat sentients."

"Oh, of course," Kyrlmyrandal responded. "Sometimes I forget that not everybody is a dragon."

THEY WALKED A WHILE LONGER DOWN THE SPIRALS, AND CAME TO A PLACE where a high arch—dragon-sized, and three times the Gage's height above the processional—that the Gage had not noticed before led aside, to something like a courtyard. There was a small door next to it, at ground level. The door was closed and had no seeming means of entry. It was all the color of bleached bone: arch, door, doorframe, and the wall it stood within.

"I will walk through this arch," Kyrlmyrandal said. "You should not. You must meet me on the other side."

"Why must I not?"

She smiled a dragonish smile. "Because you do not wish at this time to be human."

She stepped up and away from him, painfully raising and folding herself into and through the empty space above. Her wings creaked tight against her sides. She lifted one back foot into the aperture and then the other, like a cat creeping into a tunnel. Then her long, scarred tail slid within. The Gage watched until it all vanished.

He looked dubiously at the entry beside the arch, and discovered that it had opened. The featureless door that had stood within the frame was gone, and through it he could see . . . a different landscape. A dry, hilly landscape of scrub and colored clay and strange round rocks that seemed the slightest bit familiar.

The Gage shook his head and walked through.

What he found on the other side was ... a landscape of the Lotus Kingdoms. Not the fertile reaches around Sarathai-tia, but the harsh hills of the north. Among it stood a woman, all in tattered white, with her long white hair braided loosely into a trailing cloud. She leaned on a stick as tall as she was, and she was quite tall.

The door behind the Gage had vanished. He could detect no sign of the arch. But he recognized Kyrlmyrandal at once, though he found her in a different place, a different body.

She raised her face to the Cauled Sun. Eyes white with cataracts, she looked unblinking at its coronaed edge, bathing her face in the warmth. She sighed quite comfortably.

"You're joining us like *that*?" the Gage said.

The dragon snorted. It didn't sound very different in her human nose than her dragonish one. Smaller, maybe. But equally resonant. "Well, I'm not going to let *that* one have all the fun."

"Ravana is not human either, I take it?"

She did not deign to answer. She set out walking at a good pace across the uneven terrain, swinging her long stick before her. The Gage moved to keep pace.

"Sing out if I'm about to walk into something," she said. "Or off of something, for that matter."

"You seem to know where you're going."

"Of course I do. So now, Gage, you are a visitor in every land you enter," Kyrlmyrandal said. "What is the history of this world that *you* would like to write, as a foreigner everywhere?"

The Gage hesitated. How did you answer a question like that? "I was born here. In this world, I mean."

"You were made," Kyrlmyrandal said. "You chose to be made."

"I am what I wanted to be."

"That is why Ravana speaks to you with such hatred." Her stick bounced off a boulder with a clatter. She sidestepped around it, slowing as she navigated her way through a maze of scrubby bushes. "Am I getting myself in hopeless trouble here?"

"No," the Gage said. "There is a road down a little."

"Ah," said Kyrlmyrandal. "Well, a road will move a little in a thousand years or so."

"Feeling hate is safer than feeling pain," the Gage said, still thinking of her comment about Ravana.

"And not feeling anything is safest of all." Kyrlmyrandal reached out without turning her head and rapped lightly on Gage's carapace with her knuckles. He rang like a flat-toned bell.

She would take liberties, he decided. On the other hand, who was going to argue with a geriatric dragon? "Are we going to walk all the way to Sarathai-tia from here?"

"Chandranath is closer," she said.

As they walked down the hill, a wide-winged shape fell out of the sky. Lower it dropped, and lower, until the Gage threw up his fist and felt the weight of his old friend Vara stroke it. The vulture settled its red-stained wings with an irritable flip, and croaked grumpily at the Gage.

The Gage inspected it. It seemed hearty and hale, for having come such a long way. No doubt the world was full of carrion.

He wondered how it had known where to meet him, or if it had taken a shortcut too. "Sarathai-tia is where my friends are under siege. Chandranath is the enemy."

The dragon smiled her toothless smile. "Then that's where we'll find your sorcerer friend." She licked her lips. "In the flesh and in the bone."

# 23

MRITHURI HANDED A HAIRPIN TO THE DEAD MAN. HE WAS, IT TURNED out, surprisingly adept at braiding hair. Hnarisha stood beside them, assisting, because Lady Golbahar had been spirited away with the cloistered sisters.

But it was the Dead Man who smoothed her coif and said calmly to her, "Don't get too invested in your narrative of having been betrayed. It won't be kind to you in the long run."

"Look who's talking, Dead Man."

She felt him shake his head. "I could promise to punish her for you."

Mrithuri laughed bitterly. The gold pins for her hair rang on the stone countertop, single sharp pings punctuated by the scatter of several tossed at once.

"Rajni." Hnarisha reproachfully straightened the pins and laid them parallel in a shallow gilded tray. "You will shatter the opals."

With an effort that hurt the muscles of her throat, Mrithuri reined herself. She pulled another pin out of her already tumbling locks with slow deliberation and laid it beside its brothers. Her mass of hair slid free, pins sliding in its length. The Dead Man sighed and stepped up beside her. He reached for her slowly and slowly, with the tips of his fingers, lifted free another pin.

He handed it to Hnarisha, and Hnarisha put it with the others.

Mrithuri was still vibrating with outrage as he searched among her tresses for the next golden pin, and the next. His touch softened her a little. She was not sure she wanted it to. "Vengeance? Do you think me a barbarian?"

"Correction," the Dead Man said. "Consequences."

She rounded on him so quickly he was forced to snatch the hand with the latest pin in it back from her face, lest it scratch her eye. But his expression was bewildered.

"You are not jesting with me."

"Rajni." He stepped back and bowed low, dropping a knee to the floor and stretching out his hands. "I am but a foreigner. I do not know what I have done to offend."

Mrithuri looked at Hnarisha. Hnarisha raised his eyebrows and tipped his head from side to side.

"Oh, get up," she said disgustedly. "I'm being an ass. And perhaps it would behoove me to remember, as a ruler of my people—for a few more moments at least—that not everybody holds to the same standards of justice."

The Dead Man stood. He folded his arms and stepped back against the latticed wall, though she noticed he checked the space behind it for nuns before he leaned against it. She wondered if he expected a nun to slip a knife between his ribs if he turned his back on her.

Then she wondered if that was the sort of thing of which a nun would be capable.

If they were like Nizhvashiti . . . without question.

"With my rajni's forbearance," he said, "that was not a concept that I was previously acquainted with. Yes of course, the laws vary from land to land. The will of the local gods and the local magistrates must have an effect. But surely justice is justice? If you sever a man's hand, should not your hand be severed in return?"

"Is that what your Scholar-God teaches?"

He tipped his hand, then made the sign of the pen. "Not in so many words, I suppose. The scripture tells us, 'Justice lies in the redress of wrongdoing.'"

"What if it was an accident? Where is the fair redress, then?"

The Dead Man cleared his throat. "I'd say it doesn't much matter to the man."

"And how does it help that man, if you are punished?"

"It—well, he gets his own back, does he not?"

Mrithuri felt Hnarisha behind her, continuing the process of taking down her hair. He raked his fingers through the tresses, being sure that all the pins were gone, then picked up the bottle of oil and the comb. "Does his field get plowed? Are his cattle milked? Are his young plants set into the mud?"

"No," the Dead Man said, after some thought. He was looking for the trap, she thought. And that was fine, because there was not one.

Mrithuri did not nod, because the comb was in her hair. "What our justice tells us is that if you sever a man's hand, you must provide him the replacement."

"So you must . . . go and be his servant?"

She shook her head. "Perhaps you must hire him a servant. Or send one of your children to foster with him. Or simply plow and harvest his fields when you plow and harvest your own, and give him all that is his due without recompense. Or—well, yes, perhaps. You might find yourself his servant, if that is the will of the court"—she pressed the back of her ringed hand against her breast—"though really, I wouldn't want the asshole who cut my hand off making my tea. So we try to avoid that sort of thing."

He stared at her. She turned away. "Braid my hair, my husband. I must go and meet the man who wants to poison my life and take you from me. Oh, and . . ."

"Yes?"

"Make sure I have my jewelry."

SAYEH SAT ON THE DAIS BESIDE MRITHURI RAJNI'S CHAIR OF ESTATE, HER own chair a little lower than the Tian monarch's—and, to judge by the look of it, more than a little more comfortable. The hall was as wonderful as Sayeh had heard, tall and wrought as if its arches and vaults were the trunks and boughs of trees, with those panes of dragonglass making up the leaves. All of Mrithuri's court was here, except for General Pranaj and Ata Akhimah. The majority of her men-at-arms—and the Song dignitary that Mrithuri referred to as "that asshole Mi Ren," who had taken Anuraja's offered safe passage with alacrity—would have ridden out of the city gates as they opened to admit the army coming in. They would have gone, and kept going.

Sayeh hoped they would be allowed to go, and that there was no ambush awaiting them.

She heard the march of boots through the hall of the palace now. She heard doors upon doors flung wide to admit the invaders who were coming. Anuraja, and Ravani, and the rest. Tramping forward in a beat that seemed to make her heart jump and keep the same accelerated time.

Mrithuri's knuckles whitened around the sheathed sword that lay across her lap.

Sayeh leaned into Mrithuri. "Flutter a little," she whispered behind her hand. "Look scared. He'll enjoy that."

The young rajni already looked suitably green around her gilt mask, shaped like a snarling bhaluukutta. Mrithuri's actual familiar, Syama, was locked away for now for her own safety. Mrithuri's hand kept creeping down to stroke empty air. Then it would come back up, and clench around the silver snake coiled at her throat.

Honestly, Sayeh felt terrible for the girl. But not quite terrible enough to tell Mrithuri what Sayeh's plan was. Either she would get her hopes up, in which case Sayeh would feel even more terrible if it didn't work— or she would think Sayeh was clutching at straws, and be that much more terrified.

"Sister, what have you gotten me into?" Mrithuri whispered.

"I told you he was awful."

The doors at the bottom of the throne room were cast wide, and men in livery the colors of blue and orange sapphire streamed into the room. Their ranks were drilled and perfect. They parted as they entered like a fan, and they streamed into the long hall in columns, herding the courtiers away from the walls and away from the central walkway up the tiles as well. They had nearly filled the room, it seemed, by the time they stopped. The tramping of boots stirred the powder of gold the floor was strewn with until all the air sparkled and swirled. *I'll be wiping that out of the corners of my eyes for weeks.*

In the pause that followed, Sayeh's hands clutched at the arms of her own chair. She scanned the crowd, picking out Vidhya, Tsering-la, Nazia, Ümmühan. The former two were dressed as simple courtiers. It reassured her to see them.

And there had been no word in the terms of surrender dictating that *her* captain of the guard and Wizard must leave Sarathai-tia. Only the people beholden to Mrithuri.

An oversight, to be sure.

Sayeh kept her face still, very still indeed.

The soldiers still within the grand doorway parted, and a man walked toward them, up the aisle. At first, Sayeh thought she did not recognize him. His limp was gone, and he walked with the vigor and authority of someone much younger. No pain showed on his face above the long beard, and his sallow complexion seemed brighter. Behind him and to the left came Ravani in her barbaric trousers and wolf-fur, gems glittering, braid bouncing on her shoulder with each stride. Shimmering gold particles flicked up in spirals to each side of the raja and his sorcerer, like desert dust curling from a falcon's wings.

Anuraja came up the dais without stopping, leaving the sorcerer at the foot of the stairs while Sayeh struggled with her crutch to kneel. She thought he would turn to Mrithuri. Instead he paused beside her chair of estate, standing in the spot where Sayeh had watched a perch for Mrithuri's bearded vulture be disassembled mere minutes before. Anuraja put his hands on his hips and leaned his head back to admire the whole sweeping height of the Peacock Throne.

Sayeh had to admit, behind the silence of her own bitten lip, that the cascade of solid gold simulating feathers, and the glimmering gemstones that paved them, were an imposing sight.

This close to Anuraja, she could still smell the festering of his wound, no matter how much authority he moved with. Another illusion, she wondered? Or some reserve of strength—or liquid courage?

He turned violently and snatched the mask from Mrithuri's face. The ribbons binding it snapped taut. He yanked them free, sending jeweled pins scattering, their tiny pings resonating through the cowed hush that filled the room. Tears started in Mrithuri's eyes. Her hand touched the nape of her wrenched neck; the blood at the lobe of her ear. The other remained at rest on the sword across her knees.

Anuraja tilted his head, examining Mrithuri. Then he shrugged and gestured at the throne. "I'd put up with worse for that pretty thing. Are you going to give me that sword or not?"

Shaking, Mrithuri slid from her chair of estate and knelt. She raised the sword on her palms, not following the motion with her eyes. Sayeh watched sidelong from behind her hair. A bowed head did hide the direction of one's gaze.

"Accept this sword in token of our surrender, my royal cousin."

Anuraja continued to study her, lip curling. Mrithuri stared down at his boots. Sayeh wished she dared reach out and stroke Mrithuri's disarrayed hair, or her goosefleshed arm. But she could not be seen to give the young rajni comfort.

"I accept your surrender," he said, lifting the sword from her palms. "And I am glad to see you have honored its terms. You will not find me an intolerable master, little thing. You need not tremble so. And your blood and my blood will make me emperor, and you the mother of emperors to come."

"I feel unwell, my raja," she whispered, lowering her unburdened hands to press against her stomach.

"Get up," he commanded.

Mrithuri stood. Her head stayed bowed as if she were humbled. Ravani was climbing the dais now. She stopped beside Anuraja.

"You told me she could give me a healthy heir," Anuraja said to the sorcerer.

Ravani poked Mrithuri's belly with a long forefinger and smirked. "She seems sound enough."

"Sayeh," Anuraja said, "get up and deal with this. Get her presentable for a wedding. We'll be married before sunrise."

Sayeh struggled up. The crutch Ata Akhimah had provided was better than the ones she'd left behind in Anuraja's camp, and did not slip on the massy lapis of the dais. "My lord," she said, bowing her head in a show of obedience. "You should know—"

She turned her face away from those below. He took a step closer to her and leaned his head down toward hers. Hurriedly, into Anuraja's ear, Sayeh murmured, "The child is on her courses, Your Competence. Can we not delay a day or three?"

His lips made that little writhe of distaste again. "Can't be helped, I suppose. Well, wedding tonight, consummation in a day or two. Good timing, anyway; if she's fertile she'll catch quick."

He hung his new sword at his belt and rubbed his hands together. Then he turned back to his audience and spread his arms.

"My people," he said. "My people of the unified lands of Sarathai and Ansh-Sahal, from this point henceforth to be known again as the Lotus Empire! I invite you to a wedding! Tonight, here in this throne room, a little before dawn! Can somebody find me a priest? Does this palace have such a thing as a priest in it?"

*Of course,* Sayeh thought. *He wouldn't have one of his own.* She remembered, though, what had been said about the one the Tians called Nizhvashiti.

"My lord," she murmured. "There is a Godmade in residence. I will cause that sacred one's meditations to be disturbed for such an august occasion."

"Good," Anuraja said. "A Godmade, eh? Then nobody can claim the union isn't clerically blessed and all that nonsense." He turned to speak privily to Sayeh once more. "Let's see what that dwarfish shit in Chandranath says now, shall we? I'll show *him* how you seize power."

Anuraja left them there, and Mrithuri could not stand on her own. Her knees were too weak; her body betrayed her. Sayeh, crutch and all, had to bend down and take Mrithuri's cold hand in her own warm, long one and lever her to her feet. Hnarisha, looking strangely shorn with his earrings stripped out, came up the steps a moment later to assist, and between the two of them they got her down the steps and into the antechamber behind the dais. Yavashuri waited there, leaning on a cane. She and Sayeh looked at each other and both laughed.

It wasn't the sort of laugh that has much humor in it.

"Did you see the shine in his eyes?" Mrithuri was horrified to hear how small her voice sounded.

"Snakebite," Hnarisha agreed.

"Oh," said Sayeh. "Is *that* what it was? I noticed he seemed much more . . . vigorous than previously."

"Well, I guess we know for sure who Chaeri was working for," Yavashuri snarled. "I wonder if he'll have the gall to bring her in here."

Mrithuri felt herself flinch, her whole body cringing. Out of kindness, the people surrounding her did not acknowledge it.

"Come along, my sister," Sayeh said, stroking her disarrayed hair. "One more little thing, and you can rest."

*   *   *

Syama and the Dead Man were both waiting for Mrithuri in her apartment, and having the bhaluukutta come and lean against her knees when she had settled herself on the bench by her vanity was only equaled in comfort by the—chaste, in front of company—hug the Dead Man gave her as she came in. She didn't think they were fooling anyone. She knew she ought to care, and she couldn't find the caring in her.

She was observing the proprieties if not the niceties, and she was a conquered rajni of a conquered nation, now.

It would have to do.

Ritu came in a moment later, bearing an armload of silks and cosmetics. She set them down and started going through them. "Red, my rajni?"

Mrithuri looked up from her misery. "Pardon?"

"Red?" Ritu shook out a drape in an appealing shade, like blood. "Traditional for weddings."

Mrithuri thought of the red lotus. She nodded, closing her eyes.

Sayeh had brought along the poetess Ümmühan as well. Ümmühan joined Ritu and Yavashuri in undressing and painting Mrithuri, while Sayeh supervised. The Dead Man took up a guard's station beside the window, and Hnarisha made himself useful procuring tea. Mrithuri, wrapped in a thin shift that did nothing to keep her from shivering, sat stolidly through the dressing and twisting of her hair, the painting of her face, the gilding of her feet and fingers. She refused tea; she refused every sweet and savory Hnarisha tried to tempt her with. Only when Yavashuri bullied her did she manage to choke down a few mouthfuls of plain rice.

Her stomach churned. Her eyes would not focus.

"I don't even know where," Ritu was saying, "to begin to go to cover that shade of green."

When the door slid open abruptly, without even a scratch of warning, she jumped in her chair and blurred the line of her kohl, but she was too far divorced from her body and its sensations even to scream. *That's good*, she told herself. Sayeh's plan was likely wishful thinking. Being divorced from her body could only be a benefit to her.

"Your Competence!" Yavashuri protested as the raja stepped into the door.

Anuraja laughed, and shouldered the old woman aside. "I'll not be barred from my wife's chambers. Besides, who's this?" He waved at the Dead Man and at Hnarisha. "A couple of cocks among the hens!"

"My rajni's secretary," Yavashuri said, bowing low despite her limp. "And her bodyguard."

"And you let him go about with that rag on his face?" Anuraja shook his head. "That won't continue now that I rule here."

Syama did not care for his abrupt manner. She rose from her place against Mrithuri's legs with muscular ease, her eyes trained on Anuraja and her hackles rising as relentlessly as the sun. She growled, but not aloud, thank the Mother. So deep inside that Mrithuri did not hear her—just felt the vibration through the contact between them, and in her bones.

Anuraja still wore her sword at his belt. It was an elaborate thing, studded with fat blue sapphires and carnelians that she had thought would please him. It had belonged to her grandfather, but it had not been her grandfather's sword: it had been one claimed in battle by the Alchemical Emperor, left in Sarathai-tia's treasure ever since.

A sword of surrender now twice over.

He drew it. The blade slid out whispering; it flashed in the light. She had had it cleaned and oiled. But not sharpened.

He advanced on Syama, whose lip curled in a snarl. Mrithuri placed a restraining hand on the bhaluukutta, feeling the rumble under her cold fingertips.

Icy sweat covered her. She shook; her knees were water. She laid the other hand on the edge of her vanity to steady herself. "If you kill my familiar, you kill me, my lord. Then there will be no marrying."

"Keep it away from me," he answered, not taking his eyes off Syama. She, in turn, did not take her eyes off him. "Once we're wed, your death will be less of a threat . . . Your Abundance.

"You will make yourself presentable for the ceremony," he said. "I suppose your ladies can manage that?"

"My raja," she said, and somehow kept her eyes up and her chin lifted until he snorted in disgust, turned, and went, the bared blade still dangling from his hand.

It seemed long moments before anyone in the room moved, or even breathed. But the sound that broke the silence was a soft click from the windows by which the Dead Man was standing, as he gently lowered the hammer on the pistol she had not seen or heard him cock. It still rested in its holster, but she knew how fast he could get it free.

She met his eyes over his veil, and knew that he would not have let Anuraja harm her. Or Syama. And that if Anuraja had died in her chambers, there would have been no controlling his men, who occupied the palace and the city.

Mrithuri looked down. Syama's big head lay under her palm, where the bear-dog had insinuated it. Mrithuri stroked the rough-soft brindled fur.

"I should have sent you with Ata Akhimah," she whispered, meaning the Dead Man as much as Syama. But she was selfishly glad she had not.

What she had would be enough. It would have to be enough, because it was all she had.


Mrithuri endured the organization of her second wedding in as many days in a blur of pain and nausea. Someone had found Nizhvashiti. The Godmade awaited them on the dais in black robes, as usual, hung with some of the gold of its finery.

"What is this creature?" Anuraja growled. "What is this mockery?"

Mrithuri felt herself too far away to respond. But Hnarisha was there too, and he stepped in with a scraping obeisance.

"You have no priest, Raja," he said reasonably. "Nizhvashiti is a chosen of the Mother, preserved beyond life. Its good offices are therefore the fastest way for you to marry."

Mrithuri was greatly disappointed that Anuraja had not further flinched from being married by someone with the Godmade's . . . unusual . . . aspect.

Someone else had managed to procure enough dishes to pass as a feast, and Anuraja's sorcerer had removed her befoulment from Sarathaitia's water. But this was no seven days of celebrations and feasting. No flowers were picked from the drought- and storm-wasted gardens. No one played music and certainly no one danced.

Syama was locked away. All of Mrithuri's comforts had been taken from her. She wanted to seek the Dead Man with her eyes, but did not dare. He was behind her, somewhere. She told herself he would always be watching her back.

*Always.*

She wished she believed it.

She had been to many awful weddings in her role as dignitary. She didn't think this one ranked better than any. Its one saving grace was that it was over quickly. Anuraja was no more eager to string it out than she was.

The investiture followed on immediately from the wedding ceremony, almost before the wedding toast was proposed and drunk. Mrithuri's new raja turned his back on her and left her standing in her crimson draperies. They had been married atop the dais, and now he crossed to pause at the foot of the longer, narrow flight of stairs that led up the height of the Peacock Throne.

Nizhvashiti turned silently and drifted back a bit, so it was standing to the right and slightly behind Mrithuri. Mrithuri unobtrusively leaned one hand on the back of her chair of estate.

Anuraja looked up at the long, golden, gemstone-paved sweep for some time, and whether he was contemplating it in triumph or nerving himself Mrithuri could not have said. She thought bitterly that her place would not change, unless she displeased him. She would have her same chair of estate. But it would feel very different to sit in it now, and she would sit there silently.

And did she really think it would be a long time until she displeased him?

She watched her cousin, watched his profile. Watched him firm his expression into stern, determined lines.

He spoke, and Mrithuri was sure the words were intended for no one but the ghosts of the throne room. But he probably did not know yet that the Alchemical Emperor had worked his Science of Building into everything he made, and that any word said on the throne, however softly, could be heard from the consort's chair. So it was she, and she alone, who heard him whisper, "Well, Grandfather. Not what you expected. But here I am."

With his own hand, Anuraja reached out and cast aside the velvet rope that guarded the perilous throne. And then, with a firm and determined step, Anuraja mounted the stair.

It was steep, and had no railings. The risers were shallow-cut, and they were unpadded gold. He leaned forward under the weight of his royal trappings. Mrithuri was glad that her back was to the assembled witnesses and so her smile as she watched him struggle to ascend without groaning was hidden. It was petty of her, she knew. It was not kind.

The borrowed strength of snakebite, she knew from experience, would be abandoning him by now. And he would feel all the worse for having relied upon it.

She wondered why his sorcerer had not suggested he use more. Not out of concern for his health: of that she was certain.

If it were anyone else—walking up that stair on legs she knew to be aching with gout, swollen with edema, and festering with sores—she probably would have felt pity. As it was she felt a sort of cruel and silent glee.

That was when she knew that being married to Anuraja would ruin her. Not because his touch would corrupt her flesh—though it would. Not because he would make a slave of her, or try to crush her spirit.

But because being near him would make her akin to him: petty, and awful, and cruel. The loathing would poison her. Remake her in the image of a bitter and twisted thing.

*These are the beasts that feed on war.*

The voice inside her was not her own. It was a woman's voice, cracked with age. It had the accent of a Messaline.

*Great,* she thought. Her fingers curved with the desire to claw her arm. *Now I'm hallucinating.*

Something clicked, then scuffed, behind her. Once, and again. And again.

She turned, stole a quick glance. Saw Sayeh ascending the broad, shallow mount of the dais on her crutches, an unintentional counterpoint to the man struggling up the much higher stair above.

In moments, Sayeh was beside her. They exchanged silent glances. Sayeh leaned her crutch into her armpit, released the crossbar, and extended her delicate hand.

Mrithuri looked at it for a moment, then with abrupt gestures stripped the fingerstalls off her fingers and took Sayeh's hand in her own beringed, hennaed one. Sayeh leaned in and kissed Mrithuri's cheek. She was much the taller.

"Trust in the Mother," Sayeh said against her ear, so close it might not carry, words stirring her earrings. Mrithuri was surprised to feel a shiver at the breath. "Trust the Good Daughter. Be thou dutiful, and justice will be served."

Sayeh's hand closed on Mrithuri's elbow, and only then did Mrithuri realize she had begun to sway. *They will think me drunk.*

*Well, who wouldn't be?*

She turned to look Sayeh in the eyes, very close. The older woman's eyes were very beautiful, flecked hazel, outlined in a little kohl. More with the shape of her mouth than with her voice, Mrithuri said back, "Do you suppose his other wives told themselves the same?"

FAR ABOVE THEM, ANURAJA TURNED AND PAUSED FOR CEREMONY.

Mrithuri heard Sayeh take and hold a breath. She heard Sayeh murmur something that sounded like a prayer.

Anuraja sat down between the mantling wings of the Peacock Throne.

For a moment, nothing happened. His fingers were curled tight on the armrests. Slowly, he leaned back, relaxing into the throne—

Both hands flew to his chest. He jerked once, as if someone had kicked him.

A vast, collective gasp echoed into the empty arches above them, and was followed by the resounding silence of some hundreds of folk. The throne room was always filled with breath and rustling, shuffling feet, low conversations. Like the murmur of blood running through veins.

This was the first time Mrithuri had ever heard it utterly silent.

Anuraja slid from the seat of the throne and tumbled, rolling, down the long flight of stairs, past the two women standing on the lapis-tiled basalt platform, down those steps as well . . . to slump, oozing blood from somewhere, on the polished tiles of the floor.

SAYEH WIPED HER EYE WITH THE BACK OF HER FINGERS. "WELL," SHE said. "That was disappointing."

Mrithuri turned to her, rearing back like a startled cobra, with as much display of threat. "You were hoping it would *accept* him?"

"Oh, no," Sayeh said. "I was hoping he'd have a minute to appreciate that he was dying, is all. I wanted to see his face."

"You knew this would happen?"

Sayeh shrugged. "I hoped for it. I admit, I also thought highly enough of our illustrious ancestor to suspect he might actually have put a death spell on the throne, just in case somebody like Anuraja tried to sit on it. Also"—Sayeh smiled—"I had a suspicion that Anuraja's marriage to you might not be valid. For one reason or another."

Mrithuri blushed. "If he's not a true emperor, who is? We're out of male relatives, Sister."

Sayeh shrugged. "There's still that bastard Himadra and his brothers. And . . . my son." She sighed, as theatrically dejected as a child. Then plucked herself up and grinned. "Well. Can't be helped now, I suppose. How does it feel to be Dowager Empress, Mrithuri?"

Sayeh might not have gotten to see Anuraja dumbstruck, but Mrithuri suspected her own face now made up for it. "I—"

Her cousin seemed a little giddy. Perhaps she was, after all, feeling the intoxication of relief. Perhaps they both were. "I know, it was a very brief marriage. But still, here we are."

Mrithuri waved one hand, heavy with clashing bangles, at the empty seat above and the body slumped below. Ravani, she thought, was coming forward to inspect her dead raja. It was hard to be certain, though. Her eyes would not focus.

She cried—she tried to cry. It came out a whisper: "You don't expect *me* to sit on that thing!"

Then she fainted.

# 24

SAYEH WAS NOT EXACTLY SURPRISED WHEN MRITHURI COLLAPSED INTO her arms. Nor was she surprised when the Dead Man seemed to step out of nowhere to sling an arm around the rajni . . . around the Dowager Empress, rather. Sayeh let him take Mrithuri's weight, and sweep the unconscious woman off her feet. She was a starved-looking bundle of sticks swathed in a universe of embroidered incarnadine, and she seemed to weigh nothing as the wiry swordsman bore her down the steps. Sayeh followed, balancing on her crutch, considerably slower.

They were met at the bottom of the steps by a huddle of Mrithuri's and Sayeh's people. "Get her out of here," Sayeh said. She waved at the passage that led behind the throne. "Tsering-la, don't leave her."

"Rajni—"

She glared at him. "*I* will be fine. Am I not Sayeh Rajni?"

He didn't drop his eyes. But he breathed out over a pinched mouth and turned away. She turned her attention to Ravani.

The sorcerer had rolled Anuraja onto his back. Anuraja's eyes were open, staring. The blood Sayeh had noticed earlier was a thin trickle from his mouth. It stained his beard, and the stones where his face had lain. Wetness spread over the front of his tunic and trousers, sharply pungent.

Sayeh cleared her throat. Ravani glanced up, and laid the wrist she had been holding across Anuraja's chest in a mockery of decorum.

Sayeh dropped her voice. "Did you know that was going to happen?"

Ravani, in comparison, raised hers to ring across the hall. "It seemed likely. I'm sure it was his heart, though, and not the throne. Snakebite is not for everyone."

The sorcerer shrugged.

"Didn't you promise him a healthy heir?"

"I keep my promises." Ravani waved at Mrithuri. "If she survives the lack of that poison, she'll be healthy enough."

Sayeh blinked. She remembered watching Anuraja strain on his way up the steps. She remembered how sick the snakebite made Mrithuri—a woman young, and strong, and healthy. "His heart?"

"Or the throne turning on him," Ravani said. "Who can really be certain?" She stood and flipped her braid behind her shoulder. Anuraja's shocked and uncertain men were starting to organize themselves and come forward. "Well, I will be going. Pity you decided not to work with me. You might have a better chance of surviving this if I helped you."

She raised her left hand, upon which a heavy silver ring gaudy with diamonds and padparadscha sapphires flashed. With a popping sound like a cupped hand clapped to flesh, she vanished.

Sayeh put her back to the dais and stood over the dead king, propped on her crutch. Dimly, she was aware of Ümmühan and Nizhvashiti coming up to flank her. Murmuring men came toward her, their faces confused, angry.

This was the beginning of an ugly ending, she knew. But it was also an event she had prepared for. And more importantly, an event she had prepared *them* for, never quite knowing what it was she intended. By moving a piece, finding an advantage, where she could. As when feeling out an opponent in chaturanga.

She raised her voice. She raised the hand that was not bracing her. "Pren!" she called, in her clearest and most queenly tones. "Najal! Are you here? Are you here, my gentlemen?"

They were. And her calling them by name had the effect she desired. Anuraja's other men stopped. They looked around. And her guards, now her allies—though they did not know it yet—stepped forward from among the others.

"Here," she said, making her voice soft and motherly now. "Here.

My friends, we have been abandoned by the treacherous sorcerer. My friends, you must see to our emperor. You must lift him and carry him. He must be cleaned and administered to. We must protect his dignity. Let us bring him to a place of privacy, where this priest can care for him."

They stared at her. Anger, confusion. A hand on a sword. More than one. But she was calm, so calm. So certain. "Najal," she said, once more. In quiet command. "Come and help your emperor again."

He blinked. Bit his lip. She thought he would look away. She thought she had lost him.

He reached out and took the elbow of the man next to him. Stepped forward. Crouched. Placed his hands under Anuraja's shoulders. The man he had touched stepped forward too. Then the other guard she had named.

She could see her words spreading among them. Calming them. Leading them. Smoothing over them, like a balm.

She did not smile, because she dared not smile. But a silent sigh of relief lifted her shoulders just a little, as—walking behind Nizhvashiti—Anuraja's men bore him away.

HIMADRA FLOATED IN WARM WATER, BRIEFLY FREE OF PAIN, AND THOUGHT that if he were emperor, he would arrange things so that he never had to leave. He would settle himself in a bath roughly the size of Chandranath itself, and his advisors and chefs could come and see him in rowboats. He'd eventually grow gills and take up a life as an newt, and leave all worldly cares behind.

It was a beautiful dream.

It ended, as so many lovely dreams do, with the harsh reality of an echoing voice calling his name.

He sighed, and opened his eyes, and swung his feet down. They did not touch the sandy bottom. He hung, treading water, gently, and turned in place until he saw Navin standing on the edge of the pool. "I'm afraid you need to come out, Lord Himadra."

"I'll do you the courtesy of assuming this is important," Himadra said between breaths as he swam over. He eased himself into his lift and waited while the attendant raised him from the water.

It hurt, leaving the water. But all sorts of things hurt. One did them anyway.

He accepted a towel, waving to Navin with an impatient spooling motion while the attendant draped him in a soft, warm robe. He hadn't even had time to wash all the sand from his beard.

Navin cleared his throat awkwardly. "There's a man made out of metal here. And an old blind woman. They say they need to talk to you."

Himadra paused. Hadn't a metal man—a Gage, they called them—come through as a caravan guard at the beginning of the rains? The caravan had moved on quickly, because of plague. . . .

He said into the towel across his face, "Of course they do."

And so it was that the lord of Chandranath found himself seated at a table on the lowest level of his palace across from a Gage—who was crouched on the floor, not in a fragile wooden chair—and a woman he was pretty sure was a Wizard of some sort. She had the air.

The table and chairs had been carried into the entryway because the Gage had insisted it was unwise for him to climb the stairs. Watching his metal feet grit on stone and carpet, Himadra could not much disagree with the Gage's assessment.

They had, however, both accepted wine. He wondered how the Gage drank it, but it seemed to go somewhere. And the exchange of hospitality made him a little more easy about whatever they had come for.

When they were settled, and the demands of courtesy satisfied, Himadra folded his hands one inside the other behind his own goblet, and asked, "My strange friends, meaning you no discourtesy, but what is it you seek with the lord of Chandranath?"

The Gage made an uncomfortable noise. "Your Competence. I hear you keep a sorcerer."

Himadra let the rich, flavorful liquor roll over his tongue. This, too, helped the pain—but he did not dare become too reliant on it. "I would not go so far as to say *keep*. Occasionally *harbor*."

"Is it your doing that he arranged the fall of Ansh-Sahal?"

Himadra sat back so abruptly that the wine sloshed in his chalice. He found he had put his hand on his beard. He looked from the metal mirror to the silent old woman and back again. "Ravana? He's barely around enough to—well, he's barely around. He did go to Ansh-Sahal with me, and there was an earthquake. And just after we left, some kind of explosion."

"And you had nothing to do with any catastrophic dealings there?" the Gage asked, sounding far more interested than accusatory.

"Well." Himadra felt himself looking faintly embarrassed. "We did kidnap the heir. And his nursemaid. But honestly he really wasn't safe there. His mother's position was quite precarious. And I've accepted guardianship of the lad."

"A pretty piece of self-justification," the Gage said.

The old woman silently drank her tea.

"You don't think your sorcerer influenced you in these decisions?"

"He counseled me with regard to them," Himadra agreed. "But I've hardly seen him since, honestly. He comes and goes like a cat. And if I remember correctly, he was against the kidnapping of the boy."

"And you've hardly seen him since?"

"Not when it would have been useful." Himadra stroked a thumb along the cool metal of the goblet, over the inset tumbled agate stones.

"Pardon me, Lord Himadra."

The old woman had been so silent it took him a moment to realize that it was she who had spoken.

When he turned to her, she continued, "I have a question that you may find impertinent. As one sufferer to another—are you often in a great deal of pain?"

"A sufficiency," he admitted. "Enough to have a little envy of our metal friend here."

"Well, get you a Wizard," the Gage said. "And give up your freedom for a while. And then find some reason to persist, after they die. I can't imagine that enduring the pain of creation would be too much of a deterrent for one such as yourself."

"Pain is an old companion," Himadra admitted.

"So I imagined," the old woman answered.

The Gage said, "It is hard for a prince to give up his arrogance and authority."

"And obligations," Himadra said.

"What are you obligated to?"

"My people need me."

"I am sure it seems so."

"What do you mean?"

"Do you think the common folk much notice one prince replacing another? They are taxed and levied just the same."

Himadra snorted. "More wine? They would notice Anuraja."

The Gage held out his goblet. He cupped the metal as if he held the most fragile bubble of glass.

"You pour," Himadra said.

The scent of wine rose.

"They might, at that," the Gage admitted, folding his fingers around the goblet's base. "So you do not think too highly of your allies, I take it? Anuraja and Ravana?"

It was eerie, Himadra thought, how silently this mass of metal could move. It was eerie as well how the wine just . . . disappeared from his goblet.

"Ravana promised me a healthy heir." Himadra shook his head. "I have one now, though not of my body. I have three, if I can get my brothers away from Sarathai-lae."

"And you don't want Mrithuri? Everyone else seems to."

"I doubt Mrithuri wants me," Himadra said, with a self-deprecating gesture.

"Men don't often care what a woman wants."

"Even *were* I of a mind to, how could I force her?" Himadra asked the Gage, with a laugh. "She could crack my bones with her hands. Even if I could get a healthy child on her, which"—he gestured to his frustrating body again—"I can't."

"Not even with sorcery?" the old woman asked.

It occurred to Himadra that he was answering these two rather freely.

"It's still not my joy in life to force myself on the unwilling. I might be a kidnapper. But I'm no Anuraja."

"You know," said the old woman, "pain is a terrible thing. But enough of it can serve as armor against certain kinds of persuasion. Possibly your sorcerer has decided he can get more of what he wants elsewhere, and left you to your own devices. Or perhaps he will be back. In which case I would guard myself strongly against his advice."

"More of what he wants?" Himadra asked. His goblet was empty. Wine eased his pain a little but the wine carafe was too heavy for his wrists. He gestured to the Gage to pour again. This was getting interesting.

The old woman made a sniffing sound. "There are those beasts that feed on war."

"Huh," Himadra answered. "I always thought that saying was a metaphor."

THE DEAD MAN STOOD BESIDE THE WINDOW OF MRITHURI'S BEDCHAMBER, arms folded, propped against the wall. His sheathed sword was in his hand.

The rajni—the *Dowager Empress*—lay upon her mattress, composed in a posture no one in natural sleep would assume. Her arms lay beside her. Her neck was straight. Her eyelids closed.

She might have been dead, except the heat that rolled off her was palpable from a handspan away. He went to her every so often and held his hand above her face to feel the warmth, leaned close to listen to the rasp of her breathing. Hnarisha and Tsering-la flitted in, and out. Golbahar, freed from her durance in the cloisters, came too. They dripped water between the Dowager Empress's closed lips. They bathed her with cool cloths. She had been stripped of her cosmetics, her bulky jewels. He looked down now into the face of a starved and fevered child: unweathered, unaged.

Syama lay beside the bed, relaxed but unsleeping.

Riders had been sent to return the exiles, though Hnarisha had told them they didn't *necessarily* have to bring back Mi Ren.

Sayeh seemed somehow to have brought the invading army to heel, and Ümmühan was spreading her truthful lies among them already. Pretty soon nobody would be able to remember what had really happened, because the poetry would have gotten in the way.

The Dead Man stood over his secret wife, and he waited.

*If you make a home, it will hurt you.*

He must be home, then. Because the feeling under his breastbone was as if he had been gutted, then sewn up again empty except for a single great stone.

He only knew it wouldn't kill him because he had lived through this once before.

He was certain of what he was certain of, however. There was only one way into this room. He had two pistols. And the new sword had fitted itself to his hand.

# ACKNOWLEDGMENTS

Thank you to my agent and her assistant, Jenn Jackson and Michael Curry, and to my editor, Beth Meacham, without whom this book would not exist. Thank you as well to my copyeditor, Deanna Hoak, and to the entire production team at Tor Books, from production managers to proofreaders to designers and artists and everybody else involved, and to the publicity team that gets the word out. I'm sorry this manuscript was so much later than intended. I owe you all one.

Thank you to Nazia Khatun, Shveta Thakrar, Ritu Chaudry, and Asha Srinivasan Shipman, who helped provide cultural context for the world.

Thank you to my friends and colleagues of the DROWWZOO, who keep me sane through the writing process.

Additionally, thank you to my Patreon patrons, especially those contributing at a Help Feed The Dog level: Alexis Elder, Anne Lyle, Asha Hartland-Asbury, Barb Kanyak, BC Brugger, Brigid Cain-O'Connor, Christopher John Santucci, Curtis Frye, Diane Wightman, dirtytanuki, Edmund Schweppe, Fred, Glori Medina, Heather H., Heather K., Helen Housand, Jack Vickery, Jean Hontz, Jeffery Reynolds, Jodi Davis, John Appel, Kevin J. Maroney, Kim Gilligan, Krystina Colton, Lisa E. Baker, M Reppy, Martin Kotowych, Max Kaehn, Michael Gates, Nancy Enge, Nancy J. Olds Magnotta, Patrick Nielsen Hayden, Persephone, Phil Margolies, the Riedesel Family, Sarah Hiat, Sara Joiner, Sharis Ingram,

Stella Evans, Thomas Brincefield, Tiff, Graeme Wiliams, Clare Gmur, Brad Roberts, S.P., Hisham El-Far, Noah Richards, Cathy B. Lannom, Brooks Moses, Kelly Brennan, Emily Gladstone Cole, Jason Teakle, Dave Pooser, D. Franklin, Besha Grey, Jenna Kass, Jack Gulick, and Mur Lafferty.

Thank you to my family, who put up with me.

And thank you to Scott, who makes it worthwhile.

Any infelicities are (of course) my own.

*Massachusetts, September 2018*